THE CHICAGO DEFIANCE MC SERIES BOOK 3

DEVIANCE

K E OSBORN

Deviance
The Chicago Defiance MC Series Book 3

K E OSBORN

This book is a work of fiction. Any references to real events, real people, and real places are used fictitiously. Other names, characters, places and incidents are products of the Author's imagination and any resemblance to persons, living or dead, actual events, organisations or places is entirely coincidental.

Disclaimer: The material in this book contains graphic language and sexual content and is intended for mature audiences, ages 18 and older.

ISBN: 978-1070326214

Editing by Swish Design & Editing
Formatting by Swish Design & Editing
Proofreading by Swish Design & Editing
Cover design by Cover Art by Kellie Dennis at
Book Cover by Design
Cover image Copyright 2018

DEDICATION

To anyone suffering from a mental illness.
You are one hell of a fighter because nothing is more
terrifying than battling the demons in your own mind every
single damn day.

ACKNOWLEDGMENTS

First and foremost, I would like to thank my mother, Kaylene Osborn, for her work as my editor. You have worked with me to make *Deviance* the best it can be. Hours of work have gone into this manuscript, and I know you put as much effort into my work as you possibly can. Thank you for believing in me and giving me the courage to trust in myself.

To Andrea – It amazes me at how whenever a smidgen of doubt creeps into my mind, you are always there to lift me right back up. Your belief in me, your support and willingness to always help me with beta edits is such a cherished part of our friendship. I love you, mama bear, and I never want to lose you from my circle.

To Diana – I'm so glad to have you on my beta team. Your feedback is always on point and every comment you make I pay special attention to. Your thoughts and ideas always help to make my stories grow, and I couldn't go on this journey without you. Thank you so much for everything you do. This series would be lost without you. And so would my team.

To Kim B – Thank you for all your thoughts and effort in your beta process for *Deviance*. Your thoughts and edits on this story were a great help, like always. I love having you on my team, and I can't wait for many more books together.

To Carol – My book world would not be the same without you. My life would not be the same without you. You are a part of my world now, and I know that I can count on you for anything, whether it be for beta reading, or a friendly chat, or just some advice. You're simply always there for me. I can't thank you enough.

To Cindy/Thia – Thank you for always being here to help out with my beta reading. You do my books justice every. Single. Time. I can't imagine my book world without you, and I'm so happy that I finally got to meet you this year. You really are a one in a million.

To all of my awesome beta readers – Thank you for once again putting your thoughts into this book. I appreciate all of your energy and ideas, and together we make a great team. Without you beautiful ladies, this book wouldn't be at its best potential. So thank you, every single one of you.

To Nicki – Thank you for proofing my new series. You did such a fantastic job on the first two, and I'm so happy to have you working on my bikers. You're a gorgeous person, and I'm pleased to have you on my team.

To Jane – Thank you for being you. Thank you for everything you do to help make my books and me better. Thank you for believing in me, even when I don't believe in myself. Thank you for pushing me. Thank you for every single damn thing. Thank you.

To Kellie – I know I can be a pain in the ass, but I like to think that we make a good team. You make some of the most amazing covers, and I like to think mine are up there in that list. Thank you for always nailing mine.

To my beautiful, playful, and utterly adorable pup, Bella. I love you more than words can say. You're my inspiration, my motivation, and my light. You make every day better. I love you puppy dog.

Last of all, I want to thank YOU, the reader. Your continued support of my writing career is both humbling and heartwarming.

I adore my readers so much, and honestly, couldn't keep going without the love and support you all show me each day. Thank you for believing in me, and I hope I can keep you entertained for many, many years to come.

Thank you.
Much love,
K E Osborn
xoxo

NOTE FOR THE READER

Below is a list of terms used in this book, including Italian/Japanese/MC explanations for your convenience.

Any questions, please do not hesitate to contact the author.

Bastardo – Bastard.
Coglione – Sucker, fool (Italian)
Cut – Vest with club colors (MC terminology)
Fiche fottute – Fucking cunts (Italian)
Hammer Down – Accelerate quickly (MC terminology)
Hog – A motorcycle (MC terminology)
Principessa – Princess (Italian)
Scarsi Dettagli – Little Details (Italian)
Siamo una famiglia – We are family (Italian)
Six – Keeping an eye on your back (MC terminology)
Stronzo – Asshole (Italian)
Yakuza – Members of organized crime syndicates originating in Japan.

THE CHICAGO DEFIANCE MC SERIES BOOK 3

DEVIANCE

CHAPTER 1

TRAX

I opened my heart to a woman once.

Then she left.

The reasons she disappeared from my life were definitely not good enough. I could have helped her. Been there for her. *Fuck!* I would have done anything for her. Killed for her.

But, she left anyway.

It makes me think back to the time when I was just a prospect—a cocky little upstart shit—and the club was at one of those big meetups where motorcycle clubs from all over the country were in attendance. The Notorious Knights MC, our brother club—who help us out from time to time just like we do them—were in attendance too. We were all having fun, getting rowdy, me maybe a little more than the others. I'd gotten myself into shit when I went off alone. Nearly started a damn war with another club, but Crest, the President of the Notorious Knights, stepped in pulling me out of it.

My dad, Guinness, was still alive and was beyond grateful Crest was able to cool shit before it had even begun, Dad telling Crest our club 'owed him one.'

My hot-head would inevitably get me into deep shit, and they all said I was from the wrong side of the tracks. Hence, when I patched in, my road name became Trax, but I digress.

Crest from the Knights never did call in his favor, even when I started seeing his daughter, Mylee. I thought for sure Crest would intervene, tell me to stop, or rip me a new asshole. But even though I was a shithead, he thought I was good for her. She obviously didn't see it the same way, though.

Pain ripples through my chest thinking about her. We spent so long together. The good times were great. The bad times—I sigh—the bad times were eye-opening. It was hard, especially because she lived four hours away. Making time for each other was difficult, so when we did see each other, we would stay together for prolonged periods of time. Mylee here at my club, usually keeping to herself, or me at the Knights' clubhouse. Either way, we stuck it out. I thought we were something. It *felt* like we were something. Like we were heading somewhere. But she threw it all away.

I still don't fully understand why. It's not like I wouldn't have been there. Gritting my teeth as anger bubbles up inside me, I clench my fists. My knuckles turn white as I shake my head pulling myself out of my inner thoughts.

Turning around, I notice Foxy walking toward Torque, and I let out a small groan. Seeing all these loved-up couples in here is doing my head in. First Sensei and Sass in the corner, now my blood brother and his Old Lady, Foxy.

I glance behind the bar to see Cindi's already pouring me another beer. "You know, Trax, you've had a long day, what with the club defeating the yakuza and all..." She pauses and smiles. "How 'bout I help you through the long night?" Cindi waggles her eyes suggestively while leaning over, her tits almost falling out of her top.

The idea of freeing some of this tension and letting loose between the sheets is appealing. "Fuck yes, I'm in," I cheer as an alarm sounds through the compound—it's the alert of an incoming, unknown vehicle. Letting out a frustrated groan, I roll my eyes and glance back to Cindi. "Rain check? I'm going to be looking for you whenever this shit's done. You got me?" I demand, and her nose twitches in a cute way.

"I got you, Trax. I'll go wait in your room." She winks then heads off down the hall. I gulp down the remainder of my beer, slamming my personalized German stein onto the bar. We all have one, it's a club thing. I stand from my stool, looking around as I watch my brothers all beginning to move about the clubroom.

Sensei catches up to me as we both advance to where Torque and Ace are standing. Without saying a word, we all head straight for the compound gate. We've only just gotten back from one hell of a war, and we don't need anything new on our doorstep.

We stare up at Gatekeeper as he looks down on us from his high post above the gate. "It's some chick with Crest from the Notorious Knights MC," he calls out.

Sensei looks to Torque, who shrugs, while he gives the signal to open the gate.

Tension rolls over me. *Why the hell would Crest show up here with some random bitch?* Last time I saw him was over two years ago. It was also the last time I saw *her*.

Slowly the gate opens as a rundown car comes into view. I don't miss the luggage crowding the backseat as Crest steps off his ride and the woman slides out of the car. It takes me a second before it registers, but when it does all the air is knocked from me. I gasp, letting out a kind of gurgled moan as I stumble slightly on the spot. Gripping onto Sensei's shoulder, I try to stabilize myself. She's just as beautiful as I remember. Her cheeks a little rounder, her hips slightly curvier, her figure a little fuller, but she was far too skinny the last time I saw her. She looks somehow sexier now. Her curves go on for days, and while some men might find her a bit bigger than the girls we're used to here, I think she looks fucking amazing. Her cute button nose is still sporting a few tiny freckles, but her eyes haven't changed. Her emerald green eyes stand out against her pale face. My heart pounds harder just looking at the scared look in those fucking gorgeous eyes—those eyes that always make my heart pound that little bit fucking quicker. The thing about Mylee is, she doesn't need makeup to look stunning. She's flawless just as she is. A natural beauty as she stands here in front of me, looking even more perfect than the last time I saw her, with her blonde wavy hair which is longer and falls around her face so perfectly that she's practically glowing.

She looks—healthy.

Happy.

She looks fucking fantastic.

Mylee weakly smiles then takes a deep, steadying breath as she looks directly in my eyes, which immediately sends a shockwave of electricity right through my very fucking foundation.

She subtly waves. "Hey, Trax." Her voice is exactly as I remember—smooth and alluring like thick honey. My entire body sags like a fucking puppy hearing its owner after being apart for a long time.

My pulse is racing as I look at the woman who broke me. The woman who stole my heart then shattered it, swept it up and took off with pieces of it. I want to run to her, and everything in me is telling me to do just that, but my brain is unsure of how to play this out. I've missed her for two, long, damn years, but right now I'm fucking angry also. She broke a part of me which I have no idea if it can ever be fixed. A myriad of emotions is running through me.

It feels like we've been standing in this position for a lifetime when in reality it's only been a matter of moments. I take a small step forward screwing up my face as I let out a long huff. "Mylee?" I ask just to make sure I'm not seeing a fucking ghost.

Her lips slowly turn up as she hesitantly steps forward.

I tense up but don't step back, feeling all my brothers' eyes on me.

"I... I know it's been a while—"

"A while? Mylee, it's been two *fucking* years!" I can't help the venom pouring from my mouth while I glare at her.

She looks to the ground, her hands knotting together—she appears more like the innocent and nervous Mylee I'm used to—then she swallows hard.

Torque places his hand on my back trying to calm me down. *It doesn't help.*

"Trax, I know you're shocked to see us here, but it's for a reason," Crest announces, his voice deep, gravelly, and gruff.

I look to the man who I once thought would be my father-in-law, but I can't find any words.

Torque pats my back again tilting his head. "Okay. Mylee, Crest... how about you come inside." He gestures to the clubhouse. "Standing at the gate will only draw attention to us."

Mylee looks up at me while my chest heaves in anger? Frustration? Hope? I have no idea what the fuck I'm feeling right now.

Shaking my head, my nostrils flare as I groan loudly. "No! She had a choice to stay here. She chose not to. You can't come back two years later because it suits you. We don't *want* you here," I spit out only marginally believing my own words as her eyes flood with tears.

She looks to Torque, he glares directly at me, then steps forward blocking my view of her.

"I'm the President, Mylee, I have final say. You're here for a reason. Are you here for Trax?" Torque asks bluntly what I was too chicken shit to question myself.

My chest tightens as I look away not wanting to know the answer.

She clears her throat like she's hesitant. "N-Not exactly."

Clenching my eyes tightly, my stomach sinks. Even though I'm being a dick to her right now, I guess some part of me was hoping she'd made a huge mistake. That she was here for me. That she wanted me back.

"She's here because of me, Torque," Crest announces, so I look over to him. "Remember that favor your club owes me? Well, here she is," he announces without batting an eyelid.

Torque clears his throat. "You in some kind of trouble, Crest?"

"I need protection on Mylee. We've got some asshole after her. He's a big deal. Has pull in high places, and right now we have shit going down at the club. We can't have anyone putting a spotlight on us. As much as I need to have Mylee protected by my club, my brothers, right now it's going to take resources I need for other shit. I need someone to watch over her, someone who I know will protect her... like family." Crest looks my way as if his words are directed at me.

It hits me right in the guts like a sucker punch.

He brought her here so *I* could watch over her.

Because of *my* attachment to her?

Fucker's using me.

Rubbing the back of my neck, I realize she didn't come here to see me at all. She never would have if Crest didn't demand it of her. Knowing I probably never meant shit to Mylee is eating me up. I can't stand here any longer aware of the fact that this woman in front of me could do me so much harm, and she doesn't even fucking know it. She has the power to bring me to my knees, yet she stands there like she isn't even affected by me.

"This is fucking bullshit," I call out as I turn on my heels, storming back toward the clubrooms. My anger's swarming through me at such a rate of knots I'm not sure if I can control it.

"Trax," Mylee calls out, but I can't be around her right now. I can't listen to what she has to say because I'm going to be sharing my clubhouse with her for God only knows how long. I honestly don't know if I'm going to be able to stand the heat that will surely burn me alive while being around this devil in disguise.

CHAPTER 2

TRAX

My muscles are so tense I don't know whether I need a stiff drink, to stab someone, or to fuck a woman senseless. But knowing Cindi is waiting for me in my room, I think I'll go for the latter. The thought I've just walked off leaving Mylee behind with my brothers to straighten her shit out, eats at me. She had her chance, and she threw it in my face.

I'm not a punching bag.

I can't fall at her feet every time she needs me.

I'm *not* that guy.

My feet pound heavy and hard as I storm down the hall toward my room. Brothers look to me as if they're unsure of what the hell is going on outside. They're hesitant as to why I've come in and the others haven't, but I don't care right now. All I care about is getting to my room, and shoving my cock so far inside Cindi she'll be screaming for hours.

My door flies open and smashes against the wall as I enter my bedroom. Cindi's on my bed waiting for me like I knew she would be. Her long brown locks flowing over her exposed breasts as she sits up on my bed in only a pair of barely-there panties.

She looks me up and down, her mouth twitches fighting back a smile. Her dark shadowed eyes giving her a sultry look as her pouted glossy lips make her seem tempting. "Looks like you're all worked up and ready to go. Got some energy you need to expel there, Trax?" she asks circling a piece of her brunette hair around her pointer finger in a way which would usually make my cock hard. Pictures of Mylee in this very room flood through my mind, so I slam my door shut with a harsh thud. My breathing is fast as I try to rid the images of Mylee and me naked in my bed, but they keep coming like a slide show.

Uninterrupted.

Persistent.

Relentless.

"Trax, honey, you okay?" Cindi's voice breaks me from my thoughts. I walk over to her determined not to let Mylee get into my brain.

"Yeah. Don't talk," I demand as she rolls over on the bed knowing exactly what I need. Her plump ass lifts up in the air, her black lace thong showing me her perfect cheeks ready for me to punish as I see fit. I step up to her clenching my fingers in and out ready to make her pretty tanned ass a nice shade of pink when suddenly I hear gentle rapping on the door which makes both our heads swing around.

"Trax," Mylee's silky voice whispers through the door.

My chest tightens as I clench my eyes shut. My cock automatically pulsing at the thought of her being in this room, in this bed, instead of Cindi.

Fucking traitor.

"Shit!" I murmur as I take a deep breath, opening my eyes to see Cindi chewing on her bottom lip, assessing me.

"Trax, are you in there?" Mylee calls out.

My hand moves from rearing back ready to slap Cindi's ass, to rubbing my temple trying to ease out the tension as I step back taking a breath.

Cindi sits up on the bed pursing her lips. "Trax, it's okay. We can finish this another time," Cindi says, the kindness in her voice I don't deserve.

"Fuck her!" I blurt out.

Cindi stands, placing her hand on my chest in an attempt to soothe me. "Trax, I've known you a long time. Whoever the girl is on the other side of that door…" she rubs her hand up and down my chest, "… you want her more than you want me. Trust me. You can try to deny it all you want, but it's written all over your face and in your body language." Cindi leans up gently placing a chaste kiss on my cheek.

I let out a stifled laugh. "Since when are you so up on body language?"

She waggles her brows. "Acting classes," she replies with a shrug then turns grabbing her clothes, holding them to her bare chest as she reaches for the door handle. She pulls the door open to Mylee, who opens her eyes wide when she sees Cindi practically naked. Mylee gasps trying to look anywhere but at her.

Cindi walks past Mylee with a chuckle. "He's all yours gorgeous, but go easy on him. He's a little rattled," Cindi mentions casually.

Mylee looks up to me with—if I'm not mistaken—a look of hurt flashing in her eyes.

Well, fuck her! I have nothing to be sorry for. And even if I did, nothing happened with Cindi, so she can stop with the fucking sad puppy eyes. "Don't look at me like that," I snap at her.

She sniffs, swallowing hard as she straightens her shoulders. "You're right. I have no reason to expect anything of you. What you do here is of your own free will."

I scoff out a laugh. "Exactly…" I pause for effect then continue, "Is there something you wanted, Mylee? Or did you just come here to screw up my fucking life again?"

Her face contorts like she's hurt by my words, but she steps inside my room closing the door behind her, making my world feel a whole lot smaller. Suddenly, it's just her and me, back where it all began. Everything rushes through my mind, and I have to turn away from her to try to gather my balls to shove them back in place.

"I know I hurt you when I left—"

I scoff interrupting. "I was fine. I am fine."

She sniffs. "Good... I'm glad. But Trax..." she lets out a heavy breath which makes me turn to look at her, her eyes are glassy and her bottom lip trembles, "... I *wasn't* fine."

I have to look away from her to try and hold myself together. "I could have helped you. Fuck! I wanted to help you." I turn to look at her, her eyes flood with tears then overflow, running down her round pink cheeks. It's enough to make me walk forward taking her hands in mine. The spark that always ignites when I touch her flicks through my fingertips. It feels like my heart restarts when I look into her glistening eyes. "I would have done fucking anything for you, Mylee. *Any. Fucking. Thing.*"

"*I know!*" she yells through a sob. "I know," she murmurs again in a more hushed tone. "That's why I had to leave. I couldn't condemn you to this life—"

"It wasn't your choice to make, Mylee," I blurt out interrupting throwing my hands in the air as I spin around letting out a loud huff.

She sobs shaking her head. "Trax, you have to understand..." she blinks a few times, "... at that time my head was all over the place. I didn't know what to think. What to do. You *have* to know that."

I turn back to face her clenching my jaw. "And now?"

She sniffs, wiping the tears from her face. "Now? I'm better now."

Raising my brow, I scoff. "So, what? You're fixed?" I snap my fingers together. "Just like that?"

She rolls her eyes, glaring at me. "You know it's not that simple. This isn't something I can fix, Trax. This isn't something anyone can fix. It's not like you have a magic treatment, and you get better. It's for life."

Gritting my teeth, I huff. "I know that, Mylee. I did my research when you were diagnosed. But then you fucking *left* me."

She looks to the floor her hands meeting together, her thumbs playing against each other nervously. I take a breath knowing this isn't healthy for her. So, I try to tone it down a notch. "It's just... you look, good... healthy. Different from how you looked last time I saw you."

A faint curve forms on her lips as she takes a step closer, grabbing my hands making a spark shoot into the dark depths of my fucking soul again.

Fuck her, and her damn magic spark!

"I was ill, for a long time after I left you. Leaving you was the hardest decision I've ever made, Trax. But being diagnosed with bipolar disorder after seeing what my mother went through, it scared me. I know you would've helped me. I know you would have stuck by me no matter what, but I didn't want you to have to go through what my father and I had to go through with my mother. This life..." she shakes her head, "... I don't want this for you."

I flare my nostrils, our bodies only a fraction apart. Her sweet smelling perfume invades my senses. It's like an intoxicating reminder of how much I love this woman, even after two years separated, even after she broke my damn heart. Except anger seeps into my pores, and even though the reminder of love is ever present, my anger is winning out, raging through me making it hard to focus on anything but.

"It shouldn't have been your call to make, Mylee. For *fuck's sake,* I was in... I was *all* in. I didn't care if you were ill. I loved you. I saw you at your lows, I saw your highs. I fucking saw it all, and I still *fucking* loved you... but you just pushed me aside when it came down to it." I sigh. "You killed a piece of me that day, Mylee."

She lets out a small sob, her hand moving to her mouth as she stares at me. "I can't apologize enough, Trax. But you have to understand—"

"No! If you try and talk to me now, I'm gonna hurt you with words if you come at me. I'll be an asshole, and you're gonna end up hating me. So, it's better if you just walk the hell away."

She pulls back from me entirely, looking down at her thumbs knotting together. Her head bobs once in acknowledgment, and a single tear slides down her rosy cheek. "Shit, of course. You're still angry, I get that. I'm sorry I left you the way I did. You have to know I wasn't in the right frame of mind."

I let out a half-laugh half-scoff. "Of course, I know that, Mylee! I was right there. In the thick of it. With you. Dammit! I wanted to help you, remember? But you wouldn't let me. You didn't have enough faith in me. You didn't fucking trust me."

She reaches out, her eyes pleading with me as she sniffs dramatically. "No. Trax, no! That's not it at all. I trusted you. I trusted you with my life. I still do. I just didn't want you dragged into my hellhole of a life."

I scoff. "I would've never been in hell with you, Mylee, but you threw me into its depths the minute you walked out on me. You should have known that. You should've known what it would do to me."

She sniffs again, looking back to her hands. "I'm sorry I hurt you. Just know I never stopped thinking about you. I had to get my head on straight... for me. Get my mind functioning properly... without any interference."

"And is it?" I ask.

She glances back up as another tear flows down her cheek. "Everything seems crystal clear to me right now, Trax."

The words hit me right in the chest like a motherfucking sledgehammer. Gritting my teeth, I don't know how much more of this I can take.

Mylee coming back into my life right now could be so fucking good.

But I'm damaged.

I'm broken.

Mainly due to her, and because of it, I'm not even half the man I was. The man I've become doesn't deserve her anymore. Things have changed for me and not for the better. I don't know if having her by my side would do her more harm than good. She needs a stable man not someone with a volatile temper and a bad fucking attitude.

Her eyes flood with tears as she takes it all in. Mylee wipes her face as she tries to step forward toward me, but I step back shaking my head. "Trax—"

"You need to leave my room." My voice is gruff, void of emotion as I keep my eyes focused on her.

Her face falls as if she's horrified like she certainly wasn't expecting me to say that.

"Trax? Really? You're just going to throw me out before we're finished talking this through?"

Turning my back to her, I head for my door, opening it. "We're done talking, Mylee. There's nothing left to say."

I hear her breath catch in her throat as the unmistakable sound of her moving toward the door rattles me, but I stand fast, holding it open as I glance out to the hallway. Luckily no one is there to watch this mess unfold.

She steps up to me, purposely looking me in the eyes as she makes her exit. "I'm going to be here for a while, Trax…" she sighs, "… we should at least be civil to each other."

I swing the door wider. I need her to go before I cave and kiss the fuck out of those delectable lips. She looks so fucking good right now, even with her tear-stained face. I hate that I've caused those tears, but they can't be helped. I'm no good for her. "Just go, Mylee. We need some space right now."

She tilts her head but walks out of my room leaving the air feeling heavy. It always feels lighter when she's around, but now the blackness of doom filters back around me as she walks down the hall.

I can't help but wonder if I've just made the fucking worst call of my life.

CHAPTER 3

MYLEE

Walking away from Trax is so much harder than I thought it would be. I've done it once before, but I certainly wasn't in the right frame of mind at that time. Walking away from him now, while in a different context, feels painful too. I wanted to sit with him, talk through things, to tell him all about what's happened over the past two years, but he wouldn't even spare me the time to go through it with him.

I get it, though. I know I hurt him, seems more than I thought. But at the time, I left for his benefit. Certainly didn't want him going through what I was going through. I didn't want to pull him down to a level so low, I knew he'd probably never climb out of it. I wish he could see the situation how I see it, but I don't think he ever will.

Life with me isn't easy. I was a freaking mess, but I have more control over it now. While my moods are far more stable, it's still a slippery slope. While some things can make me fall over the edge into a depressive state, I generally find I'm able to come out of it easier. The mania, I hardly ever experience, which is nice because those episodes are hard work. The depression can be difficult to work your way out of, and it affects those around you, and right now I can feel the heaviness of my mood shifting.

I don't like it.

I hate the weight bearing down on me—that's what it feels like—almost like a storm is rising above my head, the lightning and thunder cracking above me with the threat of imminent downpour. If I don't do something to ease the current storm, it will be a torrential deluge, and I won't be able to stop the inevitable hurricane which will follow. I need to get a handle on this now before it takes hold.

That's the thing about these past two years, it's taught me to recognize when my moods are shifting, to take note of when to take action. Like now. So as I walk back out into the clubroom, wiping the tears from my cheeks, I glance at Dad who notices instantly. His eyes open wide as he stops everything and rushes to my side along with Torque.

"Mylee, what did the little prick do?" Dad asks, making me let out a small laugh.

"Nothing I didn't kind of expect. But Dad, I need my pills."

His hard glare softens instantly as I glance to Torque who furrows his brows like he's confused. I don't know if Trax ever told anyone about my diagnosis or why I left, but by the look on Torque's face, I'm guessing he didn't. Dad turns, racing off to my bags which have obviously been brought in during my time in Trax's room. He digs around then pulls out the little pill bottle, rushes back to me opening the cap and drops out a pill handing it to me.

Torque keeps quiet watching the whole thing unfold with his arms crossed over his chest, his brow raised like he's unimpressed. "Crest, a word," Torque grunts out as I sniff, grabbing a bottle of water from the bar and throwing back the pill quickly.

The thunder above my head cracks another loud bolt, and I shudder as my anxiety creeps in.

What if being here is the wrong thing for me?

Being around these guys, even though I know them, might set me off.

They might all be against me because I hurt Trax.

They might not welcome me with open arms like I had originally thought.

Shit! Dad and I didn't think this through at all.

My breathing becomes rapid while I lean against the bar and close my eyes trying not to let this panic overwhelm me. My fingers dig into the edge as my back leans against it heavily. Everything seems so loud as the music blares on the stereo. Everything becomes vivid, so real, my senses take over. My body shudders from the cold, my heart racing so fast I can't seem to calm it. Thoughts of everyone here looking at me, laughing at me, thinking I'm some sort of crazy lunatic all flood my mind. It's all so overwhelming as tears flow freely from my eyes. Everything around me seems to be moving at a fast pace even though I have my eyes clenched so tight I can't see anything. I feel like my world is spinning as I pant and breathe so fast the storm is invading, the thunderous clouds rolling in, the fog invading every nook of my body.

I can't breathe.

Oh God, I can't breathe.

I clench at my chest as my knees buckle from under me making me collapse to the floor. My knees pull up to my chest as I try hard to pull in the air that isn't coming as someone appears in my line of sight. I remember her, her beautiful face. She appears a little older. Grown in such a short amount of time, the sight of her is distracting momentarily. Her hands reach out touching either side of my face as she looks into my eyes and controls her breathing. I know what she's doing. I've seen it before, so I follow her breaths, slowly breathing in, then slowly I breathe out. They come out ragged and puffy, but I'm doing it while my heart continues its frantic pounding.

Suddenly, Dad's in my vision and so is Torque as they stand back, letting the girl do her thing. She's doing a good job, I'm distracted enough to let the storm pass. The thunderous clouds slowly roll away as I watch Dad's somber face crinkle while he stares at me seeming completely frazzled by my sudden turn. I haven't had a panic attack for months—probably at least six. So this is not a good sign.

"Mylee?" the girl asks finally, as I look back at her, my breathing almost back to normal. "Mylee, can you hear me?"

My head bobs twice as her smile shines like the stars in the night sky. I have to stop to admire her. She's so beautiful as she slides her hand in, moving some of my hair away from my face in a soothing gesture. "You're okay now, just keep taking deep breaths. Your room is ready for you. I'll take you there where you can sleep this off. Okay?" she asks.

I glance to Dad with a forlorn look while he rubs the back of his neck. "I'm sorry, Dad," I murmur.

He lets out a small groan dropping to his knees, reaching out, grabbing my hands. "Baby, you have nothing to be sorry for. I should have seen this coming. I know the signs well enough. I should have known coming to a new place and seeing Trax again would be too much for you. I've failed you, Mylee. You rest, then we'll find another solution to our problem."

I sniff. "We have nowhere else I can go, Dad. No one knows how to handle me when I'm like this. Trax has seen it. If he's willing to look after me, then this is the best place for me."

His calloused fingers rub over the back of my hand as he looks into my eyes. "We can talk about it after your rest. Let Neala take you to bed."

Recognition soars through me. That's who she is, Trax's kid sister. She seems so grown up.

"I'm sorry you all had to see me like this," I murmur.

"Don't be silly," Neala deflects placing her arm under mine, helping me from the floor.

I feel weak. I always feel tired after an episode, and while this wasn't a major one, I still feel drained. I need to sleep. Let the medication take hold, let it alter the chemistry in my brain. Bring me back to functioning normally again. Calm me down.

I hate I've allowed myself to get worked up, I know better than this. I detest it even more that I can't switch off my thoughts—the ones racing through my mind. I glance around the room to see everyone's watching me. Judging me. Clenching my jaw, I try not to let my irrational thoughts take over again, but it's hard.

I'm not thinking straight right now.

I need to sleep.

"Neala, can you stay with her till she falls asleep?" Dad calls out as we start to head off.

I inwardly cringe as she walks with me to the sleeping quarters. I know why he's done this. I'm on suicide watch, but he should know I'm nowhere even close to that. He's completely overreacting. But I get it. After what we went through with Mom, I understand how protective he is with me. After every episode, no matter how small, he's cautious. He doesn't want to lose me the way we lost Mom.

Neala simply takes my arm as we head down the hall. She holds onto me tightly as I struggle to get my footing right. I'm so drained I can barely function, a mixture of the panic attack flowing through my system and the medication taking hold.

"I got you, Mylee, you're okay," Neala coos.

I feel safe with her.

I wish this were Trax, though.

She leads me to my room, opening the door to escort me in, and I notice it's almost opposite Trax's room. An ache squeezes deep inside my stomach as I glance at his room, his door shut from when I left moments before.

How will he react when he hears about this? It will probably push him further away, that I can be sure of.

We walk into the beautiful room, and Neala edges me to the bed then sits me down. I'm so sleepy, my eyes feel like lead weights as I blink a few times trying to focus on something, anything, but all I can think of is sleep.

Neala grabs hold of my ballet flats, pulling them off, then slowly edges me to lie down on the bed. I follow her lead not really able to think for myself as she grabs the blanket, which was sitting at the end of the bed, and slides it up over me. My head molds to the fluffy pillow feeling like a cloud, but a nice cloud, not like the storm clouds which have been rolling through my head for the past few minutes.

I feel warm.

I feel safe.

It feels like home.

Neala sits on the side of the bed gently caressing my leg, so I close my eyes. "Go to sleep, Mylee. You'll be much better when you wake. I'm glad you're back. I've missed you..." her voice trails off. "We both have," is the last thing I hear before blackness engulfs me, and I'm out like a light.

TRAX

Cooling off in my room isn't helping, but knowing she's out there in my clubhouse isn't doing me any favors either. The fact that Mylee Bannerman is going to be in my clubhouse for shit only knows how long is doing my goddamned head in. This woman, this insatiably gorgeous woman, is going to be my undoing.

I just know it.

How the hell am I supposed to stay away from her when she's forced in my face everywhere I turn? All I know is I need to be strong. I can't let her back into my life because I want it. I need to let her know she can't get away with hurting me, but more importantly, I can't let her know *I* could be fucking bad for her. We are bad for each other, there's no denying it.

Hearing some commotion outside my door, I wonder briefly what the hell is going on, but I choose to ignore it. The dueling voices are becoming louder, so intrigue gets the better of me. I walk to my door, pull it open, and notice Crest and Neala standing there trying to talk in hushed voices, but they're in a heated debate, so their hushed voices sound more like shouting. They both turn to look at me. Crest glares while Neala winces with a single shake of her head like she's warning me.

"You!" Crest grunts as he starts heading for me.

I take a step back as I wonder what the fuck's going on. He and Neala both march inside my room as I slide out of the way. Neala quickly closes the door behind her as Crest storms up to me his finger in my face as I focus on it almost going cross-eyed.

"What did I do?" I ask.

Crest scoffs lowering his hand. "My little girl is zoned out in that room all because of *you!*"

My eyebrows pull together as I look to Neala who winces, chewing on her bottom lip. "What do you mean zoned out?"

"She had a motherfucking panic attack in front of your entire goddamn club. How the hell do you think that's gonna make her feel? Her anxiety, her inner thoughts, they're gonna go through the roof." His intense stare softens as he continues, "She was doing so well, so fucking well." Crest shakes his head. "Until she spoke to you. You. Fucking. Little. Prick! I should gut you right where you fucking stand," he grunts rushing forward, his voice booming with intensity.

I simply bob my head in agreement which forces him to halt his aggressive stance toward me. His hands grip on my cut as he shakes me violently once, but I do nothing to fight back. I feel like fucking shit. *I caused Mylee to suffer an episode.* I never ever wanted that to happen. I thought she was doing better, but I've sent her backward. I *am* a fucking prick, but we all know that.

"Fight back, damn you. I can't fucking hurt you if you don't fight back," he spits.

Shaking my head, I close my eyes. "I can't. If Mylee's got issues 'cause of me, then I deserve everything you want to throw at me, Crest."

He forcibly lets me go with a push. I fall back opening my eyes again as I flop onto the bed after a stumble.

Running my hands through my hair, I let out a loud exhale in defeat. "Is she… is she all right?" I ask.

"She is… she took her medication, and she's sleeping it off. The panic attack wasn't bad, Trax, but it was definitely enough for her mind to fog in and out," Neala murmurs.

In frustration, I yank my fingers through my hair, you can practically taste the anxiety in the room—the foul tang filling the atmosphere with the dread of the unknown—the angst of anguish. The fact Mylee has slipped into an anxiety state because of me is so sickening, so powerfully agonizing to me, the thirst for blood is seeping into my pores. The need to spill God's nectar onto the earth then watch it seep into the dust is creeping into my veins.

I'm a man doomed by demons, and my demons are right on my doorstep.

But right now I have awoken hers.

It's a vicious cycle, the devil has us in his trap.

But I need to focus—focus on Mylee, only on Mylee.

Not on the demon within me.

"Can I see her?" I ask.

The silence in the room makes me look up to see Crest assessing me. His eyebrows furrow. "You want to see her? I have no idea what the hell was said between the two of you, but it was enough to let her darkness in, and… *you* want to see *her*?" he scoffs.

"I know it looks bad, Crest, but I care about Mylee. More than you know. Fuck! I'll put it all out there if you want… I fucking love her. I've loved her every moment of the past two years, I've never stopped. But shit can't just go back to the way it was, Crest. She's different. I'm a shell of the man I was. I told her I'm an asshole, and if she came at me and we tried to talk, she'd end up hating me."

He exhales. "You told her *you* were an asshole?"

His lips begin to slightly turn upward—the fucker actually smiles. "Maybe I could be swayed around to liking you again, you fuckhead. You were always my favorite. Thing is, I need a club to look after Mylee, but after this shit, I'm not sure you can do that. Her being here is obviously going to be a problem if you two aren't going to get the fuck along. She needs someone who knows how to handle her." He shrugs. "That's why I came to you, you dumbass."

I stand up, stepping closer to him. "Crest, I got this. No one can look after Mylee like I can. I know her, I know her condition. I can read her. Don't send her away. Let me do this. Even if she doesn't want to stay, I'm still her best fit."

He lets out a small huff. "Yeah, right. I can see how fucking well you read her, by the way she's sleeping *you* off right now, you damn fuckwit."

"Crest, I'll be here, too. I'll stay in the clubhouse and watch her. Be the supportive girlfriend she'll need. Don't worry, she'll be fine. We'll keep our eyes on her all the time. If at any time things get too out of hand, we'll call you... immediately," Neala intervenes.

I nod in agreement—my little sister can come in handy sometimes.

"My promise is my word, Crest. I *will* protect her and keep her safe from whatever danger is out there, and... from herself."

He raises his brow. "And what about from you?"

My shoulders slump. "And from me? I won't hurt her. She knows where we stand. I'll be there as her friend, as her support. She can lean on me... always."

"You can't be someone's friend if you're in love with them, Trax."

I grimace. "You can if it's what's best for them."

He groans. "Fine! But I want progress reports daily."

Smiling my lopsided smirk, I tilt my head. "Done! Can I go see her now?"

He narrows his eyes, gesturing for the door. "She's across the damn hall."

I glance at Neala. She opens the door walking with me then opens Mylee's door. I instantly see her curled up on the bed under a blanket, looking... well, fuck knows.

My heart sinks.

Neala sighs rubbing my back. "She'll be fine. You need to reinforce the fact that the club doesn't think any less of her. I know that's what she'll believe. They all saw it," she tells me.

I grimace as I rub my temples feeling a headache coming on. "Fuck! Okay. Thanks, little sis. Thank you for being there for her."

Her lips turn small and thin in a tight line like she's as wary about this situation as I am. Taking a breath, I walk inside then she closes the door behind me leaving me alone in Mylee's room. Mylee's soft breathing filters through the air, the sound is comforting to me. I move over to the bed, slowly sitting down on the edge. My hand immediately moving to her leg to hold her as I glance down to see her sleeping heavily. The drugs in her system have taken hold. I know she'll sleep for a good few hours. Once she's had a panic attack, she usually has to sleep to recover from it. The only difference now is she has medication to help even her out, which is good.

Last time she was here, she didn't have medication, so this part is all new to me, but as long as she knows what to do, we should all be good. I'll have Crest do a run-down with me, just to make sure. If Mylee's mind starts to go haywire, I don't want her telling me the wrong shit.

As I sit here running through a million scenarios in my mind, I can't stop watching her face. It's so calm as she rests. No pain. No anguish. She just looks peaceful. I love that look on her. She's beautiful. I could watch her like this all day.

Dinner time has come around, and I will need to spend some time with the club tonight after the events of today. It's been a fucking crazy day that's for sure, and with the Yakuza falling, then Mylee showing up, I have to admit I need to take a moment to just breathe.

Looking over her, I move my hand from her leg to the side of her face. Her cheek is almost a little hot to the touch. I wonder briefly if she's running a temperature, but I figure her body has been through something traumatic, so I move the blanket down slightly releasing her arms. It's summer after all, so it's warmer inside. As I smooth some hair behind her ear, I caress her cheek tenderly. Touching her sends a shudder through my very soul. My arm sprinkles in goosebumps as they tingle all the way down to my cock. Each one prickling harder than the next. She has such power over me. I damn well hate it just as much as I love it.

I've missed her so fucking much. It's killed me to be away from her these past two years. I never thought I'd see her again, but now she's here, seeing her like this again, brings everything back with an almighty thump. No one here knew of her condition. No one knew she had mental health problems. No one but Neala, Surge and me. I think Mom suspected, but I never actually told her. Neala saw me with her one day when I was attempting to help her come out of a bad panic attack situation. She helped me bring Mylee around from the brink. I think that's why Neala wasn't fazed today. She'd seen this before.

Surge knows because he's the Club's wise one. So when times were rough, I went to him looking for guidance, seeking solace and support. He told me to ask the club for their assistance. But

Mylee didn't want the club to think any less of her for her issues. At the time, we didn't know what was wrong with her. I knew something wasn't right. I knew it was some kind of disorder, but I didn't care. I was going to be there with her through all of it, no matter what.

When Crest confirmed what I'd suspected—that bipolar disorder ran in her family, her mother had it, then took her own life in one of her depressive episodes, and that Mylee was the one who had found her—shit got real, super quick. I forced Mylee to have the testing done. She didn't want to, but I told her I would stand by her no matter what the outcome. But at the time, I could feel she was already pulling away.

When the official diagnosis came through, that's when she ended us. She took all her stuff from the clubhouse and left without an actual goodbye. Just a note telling me not to go after her. I did, of course, but Crest was there to stop me. Not only him, but the entire Notorious Knights MC, and unless I wanted to start a war with our brother club, I needed to step back, let Mylee get a handle on things. I needed to let her father take over. And he did.

I tried once more, two months later. She was in a mental health hospital, and I went to see her without anyone knowing—not her, Crest, or my club. No one knew, but when I got there, the receptionist at the desk told me that my name specifically was blacklisted from seeing Mylee.

I kicked up a shit, demanded to know by who, then when they said it was by Mylee herself, it killed a piece of me. So I turned to walk away, then I saw her, down the hall, laughing with a redheaded male.

Anger surged through me. How could she be straining to hold it together, but laughing so freely like that. I couldn't understand. I couldn't comprehend. So, I left and decided that if she ever wanted to be with me again, she would find her way to me. But the problem was, Mylee never came back. I thought she would. I thought once she realized how good I was for her, she'd cave and come back.

But she *never* fucking did.

Until today.

Taking a deep breath, my fingers trickle along her silky skin. Her breath catching as I run my thumb along her lips that I want more than anything to kiss right now. She looks calm. It's impressive after her brain being in overdrive that it has the power to shut down and rest like this. This is what she needs. I'm fucked off that I caused this reaction. I never thought about what was happening and how it might affect her. I detest this whole fucking idea that I have the power to hurt her, to bring her to her knees.

Not able to restrain myself any longer, I lean down and plant my lips to her forehead. Her soft skin feels like fucking heaven against my lips. I kiss her gently, so I don't wake her. She lets out a small whimper like she's delighted by my touch. I slowly pull back looking down, still caressing her cheek, while letting out a long breath.

"I love you, Mylee," I murmur even though she can't hear me.

Standing up, I regrettably let her go turning to walk toward the door. When I get there, I spin around taking one more look. She appears calm, so I leave.

The weight of today feels heavy as I close my eyes. I'm not sure what my next damn move should be. Everything in me wants to go back in with Mylee, curl up behind her while she sleeps, but I can't. Rage still burns inside me so furiously hot I'm not sure I'll be able to contain it much longer. Everything about this situation is fucked up!

Walking out into the clubroom, the music filters through the air, the party atmosphere's in full swing. I might not feel like partying, but the rest of my brothers do. We had a win today. A big fucking win. We need to celebrate. So as I look around, I can see the party's definitely underway big time.

The smell of pizza filters through the air as I turn to see the Andrettis. I raise my brow wondering how the hell it has come to this. Never thought I'd see the day when the Andrettis would be here, in our clubhouse, bringing us *their* pizza, and we'd be serving them *our* beer.

I slide into a chair at the wooden table next to Torque. He looks up at me as he chews on a slice of cheese pizza, the cheese running down his forearm. Foxy's next to him with Scratch and Neala. Sensei and Sass are noticeably missing. I'm sure she's resting after the day they've had.

"Seems the festivities are in full swing?" I ask.

Torque places his pizza on his plate as Scratch raises his brow to me. "You okay, brother? It seems you're having an... interesting night?" Scratch asks.

"Interesting doesn't begin to fucking cover it," I murmur while Foxy looks at me sympathetically.

"You got a handle on this, Trax?" Torque asks.

I glance at him, letting out a huff followed by a shrug. "I have no idea, but I'm damn well gonna try."

"I'm here, brother. I know what she means to you. So you tell us what you need..." he pauses dipping his head, "... we'll support you."

Raising my brow. "Did Crest tell you? 'Bout her condition, I mean?"

His eyes soften. "Yeah. Did you know? Back then?" he questions. Foxy's hand slides up and down his arm tenderly.

I can't lie to my president, I can't lie to my brother, he would know straight away. So, I simply sigh. "I knew something was different with her. We knew she had trouble regulating her moods. I kept telling her to get checked out, and that something wasn't right. But she wouldn't no matter how hard I tried. When we finally did get the diagnosis, she freaked. When she got the diagnosis, that's when she dumped me."

Torque understands. I see it in his eyes. "So she found out she had bipolar disorder then bolted?"

"That's not surprising, Trax," Foxy states matter-of-factly.

"What do you mean?"

She straightens her body to face me. "She loved you, right?" I nod. "Well, when she found out, she obviously didn't want to put you through the trauma that goes with what being in a relationship with someone who has a diagnosis of bipolar disorder. It's hard work. I understand what she was doing. It's normal for a person with that diagnosis to feel this way. They feel like a burden to those they love the most."

"She was never a burden." My eyebrows pull together.

Foxy's pink lips turn up in sympathy. "You understand it, but the chemical imbalance in her brain makes her think all kinds of irrational thoughts. Things like she isn't good enough for anyone, *especially you*, and no matter how many times you tell her otherwise, she won't believe it. It's the curse of the disease. It's terrible, Trax. Her brain is *literally* her own worst enemy."

I nod in recognition. I'd read about that online. The illness makes you think irrationally. It's shit she's going through this, it's not something I can take away for her. It's something she's going to have to live with for the rest of her life.

Torque slaps my back. "It'll all be okay, brother."

I weakly smile as Neala pipes up, her bright red lips greeting me warmly. "And hey, she has us. So who the hell wouldn't be happy with us around, right Trax?"

"Right," I reply.

Cindi steps over bringing me a beer. She leans over thrusting her tits in my face as she places my stein on the table, then walks off just as quickly as she came. I clear my throat as the rest of the table laugh.

Foxy chuckles. "Jesus, could she be more obvious?"

I huff. "I'm so not in the mood tonight," I groan as everyone jolts their head back in surprise.

"You... the master of pussy, is not... in the mood?" Torque questions.

Foxy scoffs slapping his chest playfully.

"No, with Mylee here it kinda changes the dynamics of everything. I don't think I can manwhore while she's here... it doesn't feel fucking right."

Scratch raises his brow. "I'm impressed, Trax. You must really like this pussy."

"You have no idea, Scratch... no idea."

"Well, I think it's great. Especially if she has the support of someone who truly cares for her. I'm proud of you, Trax," Foxy states her eyes lighting up highlighting her round cheeks.

"Cheers, Foxy." I pick up my beer, taking a giant gulp, the bitter liquid hitting my tongue, then sliding down my throat helping the tension ease slightly.

I see Crest chatting to Surge, and I know I need to talk to him. I realize there's a lot to say, I just don't know how to even start that conversation. But I suppose I'd better grow some fucking balls because so far today I seem to have lost mine.

I stand up from the table, everyone looking at me as I grab my beer, taking a deep breath.

I need to go talk to Mylee's dad.

CHAPTER 4

TRAX

Walking over to Crest, my heart's hammering in my chest. I don't know if I feel sick from nerves or sick from regret. Maybe a bit of both. But as I approach, Surge looks to me dipping his chin with a tense smile. "I think you two have a fair bit to talk about. I'm not going to hold that up. Play nice, boys," Surge advises in his best fatherly voice, his arm still in a sling from when he was shot by the Yakuza masking as the Andrettis.

I glance to Crest, his almost white hair swept up in a wave, his white beard with slight flecks of blond covering his deeply tanned face shouldn't look as broody as it does, but somehow he makes white look edgy. For a man pushing this side of fifty, his broad shoulders and arms, which are way bigger than mine, would intimidate many men but me not so much. I've had too many good times with this man. I even looked to him like a father figure when mine was gone. He's been a part of my life for a long time, and even though he might not like to admit it, I'm not afraid to. I owe this man, a lot. Things might be tense between us now, but I don't forget the past and everything we've shared, including the love of his daughter.

As he crosses his massive bulging arms across his chest, the veins protrude against his flesh making him seem even more intimidating. I take a sip of my beer as he watches, assessing me.

"Crest, Mylee's gonna stay here. And if you're gonna kick up a shit, you shouldn't have brought her here in the first place. You knew I'd step in. She's my responsibility now. I need to take care of her."

He stiffens, his nostrils flaring as he tilts his head like he's not liking what I have to say.

"I need to know Mylee's regime. I need to know exactly how she manages her illness, so if things go south, I can take control."

He raises a brow. "Right, I see where you're going with this. While the idea of you controlling Mylee's life fucking irks the shit outta me, I do need to know someone will step up if she starts to have issues..." he cracks his neck like he's admitting defeat, "... I have a cheat sheet with all her medications written out and when she has to take them... the doses, phone numbers you might need, her psychiatrist, the hospital she stayed in, her prescription refills. It's all there. Don't let her run out of her pills that's the fucking key. It's mega important she doesn't skip her fucking pills."

My head bobs up and down rapidly taking all this in. "What happens if she misses a pill?"

He winces. "She'll start to have issues. Her mood might decrease. She'll possibly go into a depressive state. We don't know the outcome, it's so unpredictable. So *don't* miss the fucking pills."

A lump catches in my throat remembering her depressive states.

They were terrible.

I wonder if they're worse now.

"Crest..." He looks to me raising his chin in answer. "Is she... okay? I mean besides what happened today after seeing me, generally... is she doing okay?"

Rubbing his chin, he shrugs. "Before you… she was doing great. No issues for months." His fist moves out quickly, and just as I think he's about to hit me, he grabs my bicep in a soothing gesture and squeezes. "She'll be fine. I think the fact she melted down in front of everyone will definitely get to her. But once she's over that, she'll be okay." He pats my back in support. "You two kids are like fucking magnets, no matter how hard you try to pull yourselves apart, the friction pulling you together always seems to win out."

Tension rolls over me as I rub the back of my neck. "We're not together like that this time."

He chuckles. "Give it time. You'll both cave under the force of the pull. I've seen it. Love like yours… it can't be denied no matter how hard you try to pull against it, kid."

I take a deep breath, tension rolling through me. "I'm not fucking right for her."

He laughs. "And she sure as hell isn't right for you. But when did something being not right ever make it wrong? Whoever would have thought fucking peanut butter and jelly would have worked together, but there you go, look at that fine-ass combination."

"You're saying Mylee and me are like peanut butter and jelly?" I ask raising my brow with a crooked smirk.

"Exactly. Two things that are perfectly fine on their own, and putting them together should be weird as hell, but bam, it's fucking amazing. A staple diet of kids everywhere."

"You're saying we're a fucking staple diet?"

"Trax, you're taking this too goddamn literally." He laughs. "All I'm saying is when two things that shouldn't work go together, they just… somehow work. Don't fight it. It makes everything so much harder on you, but especially on Mylee. No one wants that. Just think about it, kid."

My chest squeezes, my stomach's in knots as I wonder if I can really do this. If I can sit back and give Mylee and me a shot. If I can let Mylee back into my life, knowing she has the power at any second to walk out and destroy me again. But then I remember my dark soul and how that might affect Mylee. Seeing my demons could influence hers, and that could be a problem.

"I can see your brain working overtime… just know you have my full support, Trax. I know I might have come off a little half-cocked in the room before, but… I just want what's best for Mylee. If you're going to push yourself away from her, then I know it will only harm her. Especially when you really don't want that either."

"I love her, Crest. But there's shit in my life I don't want Mylee to be around."

He places his hand on my shoulder. "I know, kid. I know. But she loves you, too. So damn much." He shakes his head. "Don't waste it."

Tension swirls through me like a hurricane pulling me in two different directions—the heart wanting Mylee, the demon wanting blood. I take another long drink of my beer, not knowing what to do.

If I can push my shit aside, just be there for her, then maybe I can do this. Maybe, I can be here for her. Maybe I can be the man she needs while she's under the protection of the MC.

He slaps my back dipping his head toward Cindi ordering us another round of beer.

Torque moves over to us. "It's good to see you two on talking terms," Torque grunts.

I roll my eyes. "Fuck up. Crest and I know how to handle each other, right?"

"Sure do. Honest talk and booze," Crest replies making me chuckle.

"Glad you've got your shit straightened out, but I need to talk to you both. Crest, I think you know why. We need to do this as a club thing. I gotta call church with the patched members," Torque relays, and I tense up taking a steadying breath.

I knew this was coming.

To be honest, I've wanted to know since the moment Crest and Mylee got here. But now, the time's come. The club needs to know why they're here. Why we're looking after Mylee. *What the hell are we getting ourselves into?*

Crest takes a gulp of his beer then wipes his mouth with the back of his forearm. "Sure, I'm cool with that."

Torque dips his chin while I stand from my seat along with Crest. We walk with my blood brother toward the chapel, he swings around and whistles gaining everyone's attention. "Patched members... church. Now!"

Heading inside, our brothers follow then close the wooden door behind us. We each take a seat at the giant oval table while the ruckus of the clubroom fades out. Torque and I both look to Crest as he runs his hand through his thick white hair while swinging around a chair and taking a seat next to Torque at the head of the table.

Torque bangs his gavel once with a loud thud. "So talk to us, Crest. Why did you bring Mylee here?"

The door opens again and a sleepy looking Sensei walks in. We all dip our heads to him as he strides in taking his seat. The door closes behind him as Crest looks from me to Torque then back to me and starts speaking. "When Mylee was ill, she went into the hospital... the psych hospital. They did an excellent job caring for her. They helped her mentally. Got her back to where she needed to be. But while she was in there, she met this guy... Everett Scott. They seemed to hit it off as well as you can for two patients in a psych ward. They looked out for each other. Until Everett got fucking weird. Started spouting stuff about government cover-ups and shit. How he knew Mylee and he were destined to be fucking together.

"Anyway, he left the hospital before her. His father has power and persuasion in politics. Thing is, when Mylee got out, Everett was still showing signs of instability. His father pulled him out of the hospital because he was trying to save face. He didn't like the idea of the press getting wind of his son's indiscretions, and being in the psychiatric ward was a no-go for him, so he pulled Everett out before his time.

"Problem is, Everett is completely unstable, and he's latched onto Mylee. We thought about dealing with him, but with him being Senator Scott's son, it could bring a whole lot of spotlight on the club. Right now we have a heap of deals going on, and we don't need a fucking spotlight on them. Deals that can't have senators or political parties of any kind looking into if you know what I'm saying?"

I catch on straight away. The Notorious Knights are doing some under-the-table shit, probably guns or drugs, maybe both. They can't have anything bringing attention to them right now. *I get it.*

"You want Mylee out of the picture, so this Everett won't come after her. And he, or his father, won't come looking for her at the Knights. Is that right?" Torque asks.

"Correct. We've sent word to the Scott camp letting them know Mylee's out of town. So the heat's off us for now, but we didn't tell them where she was going. Hopefully, this gets eyes off us, gives Mylee a break from that damn freak, and we can get our shit running smoothly again while we try to figure out a way to best handle Everett and his relentless goddamn... *affections.*"

"Is he likely to trace her here?" Torque asks.

Crest curls his lip. "No. Our club in Grand Rapids as you know is four hours away. There's no way he'd believe I would let Mylee be *that* far from me. Normally, I wouldn't. It's only because I trust Trax and the Defiance, I'm letting her be this far from me and the safety of our club."

It feels good to know he trusts me with her this much. It's an honor, to be honest. "Well, don't worry, Crest, I'm not going to let anything happen to her on my watch. You have my word," I announce.

Crest turns his head to look directly at me, his eyes hard. "I know you won't because you'll be the first man I'll *kill* if something happens to my girl, Trax."

I raise my brow but dip my chin in understanding. "Noted."

"Will you be riding back to Grand Rapids tonight?" Torque queries.

Crest rubs his chin. "If it's cool with you, I'll stay till morning. But I have a lead I want you guys to look into if you're all good with this?"

"Brothers, we need to vote. Having Mylee here could cause issues for our club. We all know the Knights would do this for us, but it should be a unanimous decision. So what say you?"

One by one, a vote goes around the table as a resounding "aye" is said by everyone until it gets to me. I could end this all right here. A no vote could send Mylee home and my troubles with it. She wouldn't see my demons—I couldn't inflict them on her. But for some reason, I can't find it in me to say the word 'no.' Instead, a simple, "Yes," slips from my mouth making Crest smirk.

Torque bangs his gavel. "So it's passed. Mylee stays..." He glances over to me. "To the next issue, what's the lead you have, Crest?"

He clears his throat as I crack my neck to the side. I can practically smell the blood in the air before he even says the lead's name. "Miller Willbrook. He went to college with Everett, they're still good friends. Miller's stuck by Everett's side through his mental illness. He visited him in the hospital and sometimes had meals with him and Mylee there." My jaw ticks thinking of Mylee in such a place. "For all intents and purposes, the guy is decent."

I shake my head cracking my knuckles needing a little tension release. "So why the hell is he on your radar if he's that squeaky fucking clean?"

Crest chuckles. "He's more than likely got intel on Everett. If we were to do a simple 'retrieve and release' and I'm sure if we scare him enough... he'll crack. He'll tell us something about what Everett's plans are with Mylee."

I scoff. "Retrieve and release? You still do those at the Knights?"

Torque scowls as Crest chuckles. "You don't?"

Sensei exhales sitting forward in his chair. "Lately all the retrievals we've had, have not had the opportunity to be released. Their own fault.... mostly."

Crest glances to Torque with a wide smirk and grips his shoulder. "Why, Torque, I'm beginning to appreciate your methods even more. And here's me thinking you were the soft one and it's me all along. Go figure. I need to harden my ass up. But with this one... with Miller, I think we need to play this smart. A businessman in with the Scott's going missing the same time Mylee's heading out of town might draw some unwanted attention to the Knights. We have to play this one different."

My lip curls up as I rub the back of my neck. All I want is to get my hands dirty. I need to get some of this motherfucking frustration out. If I have to do that with clean hands, how the hell am I going to let my demons keep a cool head?

This is bullshit if ever I've heard it.

"Agreed," Torque replies making me want to punch him right in the throat.

But I don't. I keep my shit together.

Marginally.

"So where's Miller? In Grand Rapids?"

"He's actually in Chicago on business, it's why I chose tonight to head down here. I wanted to get the guy with your help while he's away from anyone who can help him out. We can get him tonight. Question and release him without any incident. Then I can be back on the road by morning."

"I'll have Sensei and Chains go and retrieve him—"

"Bullshit!" I yell making everyone snap their heads to look at me.

"The fuck you say?" Torque scrunches his brow.

I stand from my chair slamming my hands on the table. "Sensei and I do retrievals. Don't pull me from my job just because you think I'm too close to this, Torque."

Torque rolls his neck glancing to Crest, then to Sensei, then back to me. "You *are* too close to this, Trax."

"Exactly why I'm the best motherfucker for this job. Who the *hell* is gonna make sure this shit is done properly if not for me?"

Sensei clears his throat like I've offended him, but I don't give a shit right now.

Fucker can be offended all he wants.

"Crest, back me up here. You know you want me on this."

Crest glances to Torque and shrugs. "I don't care who fucking gets the shithead as long as he's back here in one damn piece, so we can talk to the motherfucker. If Miller's dead, then it's all for fucking nothing, and Mylee's instantly put in danger."

"I got this, Torque!" I look at him sternly. "I got this," I reiterate.

He exhales with a shrug. "Fine! Sensei and Trax will fetch Miller while we set up in the Chamber."

Elation rolls through me. Knowing I'll be able to relieve some of my bloodthirst tonight, it's the only thing keeping me going right now. With the intensity I've felt today, I need this to make it through tonight.

I'm seriously damn twisted.

"Everyone in the Chamber should wear balaclavas. Nothing identifying is to be worn. Since this is a release, there should be nothing visible to tie to you or the two clubs. So all black, no jewelry, tats covered, no cuts. You know the drill... same goes for you, Sensei and Trax, when you retrieve. Cover up. *Wear* nothing obvious, *say* nothing obvious," Torque relays.

"Thank you captain *obvious!*" I mock.

His lip turns up at me as I plonk down on my seat. "You're a prick when you're ovulating, you know that, Trax?" Torque grunts.

"Fuck you!" I murmur under my breath.

"Enough! Fuck, you're just like the damn boys at home..." Crest rolls his eyes. "Sensei, Miller will be at his hotel by now. You'll have to grab him from there."

I let out a stifled laugh. "Hotel grabs, this should be interesting."

"If anyone can be creative, Trax, you can," Crest mocks.

"Oh, you don't even know the half of it. You should've seen this one time when I was with Sensei, and a Yakuza underling, who couldn't keep his cock in his pants—"

The room laughs excluding Crest who cuts in. "Somehow I know that would have been a sight to see, but I'm warning you, Trax, keep your shit together with Miller. We need information not bloodshed."

Rolling my neck, I groan. "I got it! Can we go now?"

"You're like an errant child, kid. Who's the techie here?" Crest asks.

Ace stands from his station as if it wasn't noticeable. "Yep. What do you need?"

"I've got Miller's cell number. Can you put a trace on it for Captain Impossible, so they know where he's located in the hotel?"

Ace smiles flicking his bobblehead of Iron Man. "There's a reason I'm the tech guy here, Crest, 'cause I have technology as good as Stark Industries."

We all raise our brows as Crest grunts. "Am I supposed to know what that fucking means?"

Ace slumps back into his seat defeated. "Yeah, I can track the cell. Gimmie his number."

Scratch chuckles giving Ace two thumbs up in support as Crest stands up and moves to Ace's computers. Crest hands over his cell information as they fuck about.

Torque leans in beside me gaining my attention. "Bring the suit in, in one piece. You hear me?"

I scoff. "I fucking got it."

"None of this hothead bullshit, Trax."

I turn my back to him effectively ending the conversation as an alert pings on my cell. I look down to see the tracker app with a red dot appearing in the heart of Chicago. I smile standing up as I glance to Sensei.

"Let's go."

Sensei glances to Torque, an unspoken conversation passing between them, but I don't care what it is they aren't saying out loud. I have a guy I need to get to, who knows information on the dick who's out to harm Mylee. My bloodlust is pulsing through my veins. The need to cause bodily harm growing by the second.

Will I be able to reign in my demons?

Fucked if I know.

All I do know is Miller better not say anything to piss me off because right now I've had a shit of a day and just looking for an excuse to tear off some limbs.

Please give me an excuse, Miller.

Just one tiny excuse…

CHAPTER 5

TRAX

Sensei and I pull up in the underground parking garage of the hotel in our van. He parks right at a back corner near the elevator. I smirk at his forward thinking. We hop out of the van all dressed in black, our balaclavas in our pockets as I look around to see a light illuminating our van a little too much. So, I glance around to find something as Sensei fucks about in the back of the van getting it ready for the retrieval. I find a small rock, glance around to make sure no one's watching then I hurtle it at the light.

A smashing sound rings through the parking garage as our van descends into darkness. Sensei's head pops around the back to look at me, his eyes go wide.

"What the fuck, Trax?" he murmurs.

"There's too much light," I reply.

Sensei shuts the back of the van and quickly checks around the parking garage to see there's no one around. But I already knew that.

"Lucky no one heard that, fucker. Now where is he in the hotel?"

Pulling out my cell, I look to the flashing red dot on the screen. "Follow me," I instruct as we make our way to the elevator. We enter turning our backs to the door. We know there could be a camera in here, so we keep our backs to the front the entire ride. The door pings, and we back out. We probably look like fucking idiots, but no one's here watching, so who cares.

We enter the hall and duck behind a partition while listening to the crappy music playing in the hotel bar. Licking my lips, I glace to Sensei as I check my cell. "I think he's in the bar."

Sensei groans. "This complicates things. If he was in his room, it would be much easier. Now there's other people around."

I grunt out frustrated as I rub the back of my neck. I need to get some of this anger out and soon. It's only increasing, doubling in its ferocity. My thoughts shift to Mylee asleep in that bed, zoned out because of a panic attack. My nostrils flare as my palm comes up and slams into the wall hard making a loud thump as the wall shudders.

Sensei glares at me while I breathe harshly out of my nose trying to cool myself down. "You need to calm your inner thoughts, Trax. If you let something as simple as having to wait to catch your prey get to you, you are further gone than I thought."

My eyes harden as I drop my hand from the wall crossing my arms over my chest. "What the fuck is that supposed to mean?"

He stands taller, taking me on. "It means you've been falling apart for a long time, even before Mylee came back. Now she's here, I see this as going one of two ways."

I cock my chin higher. "Yeah? How's that?"

"You can either let her save you or let her be your complete demise. Way I see you heading right now, you are letting your anger and your inner turmoil control you. Take the control back, Trax."

I scoff. "What the fuck would you know about control?"

He raises his brow. "A lot more than you think, and I will teach you. You just have to be willing to let go of that monster crawling around within."

My face scrunches, my stomach churning as the demon claws at my soul to be set free. "I don't have a fucking monster within, Sensei."

He lets out a heavy sigh. "The thing is, Trax, if you want what's best for Mylee, you'll—"

I lunge forward grabbing him by his black hoody and press him against the wall glaring in his stoic eyes. He remains calm and unmoving as my face contorts in anger. "Don't fucking talk about her." Tension rolls off me as I press him harder against the wall wanting more than anything to rip him to shreds, but the way he isn't fighting back makes it harder for me to do any-damn-thing. My lip turns up while I pant for breath as my cell lets off a small ping. Sensei drops his cool eyes from mine glancing to my pocket as I finally drop my hold on him and pull my cell out to see the dot moving and coming our way.

"Fuck! He's heading this way," I tell him as I reach into my pocket to pull out my balaclava. Sensei does the same placing his over his head, it barely covers the dreadlocks that fall down the one side of his face. I yank mine over my head quickly. Now we're really pulling off the criminal vibe as we stand back in the hallway leading to the suites.

Miller rounds the corner as we conceal ourselves behind a partition out of view. He stumbles ahead of us as Sensei stalks up behind him, and I slide out in front of him. His eyes widen as he takes in the sight of me. He attempts to say something, but I don't hesitate, the demon inside of me roaring to life as I clench my fist and slam it straight into his nose. My knuckles twinge but don't hurt as much as normal—they're covered in black leather gloves—while blood spills down his face, his entire body collapsing back into the arms of Sensei. It all happens without a hassle or a single word.

Sensei hoists him up over his shoulder, and we run like hell toward the elevator. I press the button as Sensei looks me over. "You good?"

"I'm good," I reply.

The elevator dings and luckily no one's inside, so we stride in taking it straight to the parking garage. The doors open, I step out scoping for anyone, but it's vacant. "Clear," I call out as Sensei steps out carrying Miller while I open the back of the van.

Sensei throws him inside then I step in and grab the cable ties. We've done this countless times, and we're pros at this snatch and grab shit. I tie up his hands while Sensei tapes his mouth. Then we prop him sitting up, so the blood from his nose doesn't clog his airways and he suffocates on the ride over.

Yeah, we learned that the hard way.

Once Miller's ready to go, we slide into the van. We don't take off our balaclavas, not until we're at least ten minutes into the drive. That's the rules. Plus, the windows are tinted enough so people can't see in to notice us wearing them.

Sensei pulls out of the garage, and we're off to the clubhouse—a successful retrieval. He looks to me then his eyes slip back to the road. "You lost your head back there."

I grunt. "You were talking about *her*. I tend to lose my shit when it comes to... her."

He exhales. "You need to calm that storm, it's going to end up with you losing yourself."

I scoff. "I'm well aware of the path I'm taking."

He glances to me again. "Do you? 'Cause from where I'm sitting, this shit's not pretty."

"I'm fine."

He exhales. "When you realize you're *not*... I'll be here."

Rolling my shoulders, I turn my head to the window and watch the city streets of Chicago pass me by. I'm fine. Sure, I might have a temper. Sure, I might fly off the handle sometimes, but doesn't everyone?

Yeah, fuck Sensei and his bullshit.

There's nothing wrong with me.

I can handle my own shit.

My bloodlust is my own.
I have it capped.
I have it locked down.
It's under control.

As Sensei straps Miller to the silver chair, I pace the chamber, the dank room reminding me how much I love it in here. The dull hue from the lights. The tepid temperature. The faint sounds of dripping coming from the doorway. Every inch of this room was made for me even though I'm not the man of the hour down here most of the time. This is generally Sensei's domain, but today I want to take the lead.

Torque and Crest walk in closing the door behind them. Their club cuts gone replaced with black hoodies and their faces covered with balaclavas like us. Four men clad in black and one business- looking suit tied to the silver chair, still out cold, with blood oozing from his nose. I can't wait to see his face when he wakes up.

"You got here in record time, boys," Torque relays as I walk over grabbing a length of metal tubing just in case I need it.

"It's easy when you have the tracker." I step forward toward Torque and Crest placing the hard tube against the wall near the silver chair. "Let me take the lead on this. I have more to gain, I think I'll be more convincing."

Torque scoffs. "Scare the guy to death more like it—"

"I think we should give the kid a chance. If he falls out of line, then let option two take over," Crest pipes in.

My inner demon roars to life slapping Crest on the bicep as I smile at him. He nods to me as Torque and Sensei both exhale but nod.

"Fine, but the moment you get too heavy-handed with him… you're out. Remember this is a retrieve and release. He gets out of this alive."

Turning my back to my blood brother, I roll my eyes. "I fucking know, let me get on with it. It's getting late, I need my beauty sleep."

"Don't we know it," Crest mocks. Rolling my eyes, Sensei walks up to me with a bucket of iced water.

He looks at me, and I nod with a giant smirk. "Let's get this party started."

Sensei hurtles the iced water onto Miller. His body jolts as his head flings up. Miller starts to shake as his eyes widen in fear. His nostrils flare in and out with his frantic breaths. He looks to the four of us all covered up as he shakes his head trying to obviously figure out what the hell is going on.

I step up to him, my gloved fingers grabbing at the tape as I rip it from his mouth in one fell swoop. He yelps out in pain as he gasps for air.

"Fuck! What the hell's going on?" he blurts out as he looks right at me, the fear evident in his eyes.

I bend down so my eyes are in line with his as I narrow them. His Adam's apple bobs up and down as I watch his body visibly shake. "You know Everett Scott, correct?" I ask.

He inhales and looks around at my brothers trying to ascertain why there's so many of us here. He's in shock, obviously, as he keeps quiet still glancing around the room taking all this in. So, I reach out grabbing his chin forcefully making him look only at me. He yelps out as I see a slow trickle of wetness appear at his crotch and run down his pants.

Fucker pissed himself.

"Don't look around, talk to me. You can get out of this if you cooperate, Miller."

His breathing is coming in fast and frantic as he rapidly bobs his head up and down.

Fucker's a pussy if ever I've seen one.

"Yeah," his voice is barely audible.

"What? I can't hear you," I spit at him.

"Yes! I know Everett, dammit."

I let go of his chin and stand back up folding my arms over my chest. "How often do you talk to him?"

He glances around the room, so I snap my fingers pointing my middle and pointer finger at him and then to my eyes. "Look at me, Miller. How often do you talk to Everett?"

His breath stutters as he sniffs shaking his head. "I... I don't think I should be talking to you."

I lunge forward without hesitation, my fist clenching and landing a blow right in his stomach. He hunches over, but he can't hold onto where the pain is radiating out from because his hands are tied to the chair. He puffs out heaving breaths. "I don't think you have any other option, Miller. You talk to us, you tell us what we want to know, or I get a little trigger happy."

His eyes dart open as he looks around the room again at my brothers.

"Don't look to us, we won't help you," Crest relays making Miller frown as he coughs a little.

He sits up taller looking back at me. "What do you want to know?"

I grin stepping closer. "Everett has a plan in action, we want to know what it is?"

He raises a brow and scoffs. "You're going to have to be a little more specific there, cowboy."

My lip curls as I grunt. Guy's grown some balls. I can fix that. Stepping forward, I raise my foot and stomp as hard as I can onto his expensive looking black shoe with my combat boot. He screams out in agony as he writhes on the chair.

"Stop being an asshole, Miller, and you'll stop getting hurt," I reply. "Though, I do like hurting people, so keep it up. It doesn't really faze me."

He grunts shuffling up on the seat. "What plan?" he reiterates.

"Has he talked to you about anything to do with Mylee Bannerman?"

His eyes widen as he tilts his head. "Mylee? A plan to do with Mylee?"

"That's what I said, fucker."

He clears his throat. "I think you've been misinformed. Everett and Mylee are a couple."

I scoff as Crest stands taller. "What makes you say that?" Crest asks.

"Everett talks about her all the time."

"Have you ever seen them together, Miller?" I ask, and he lets out a laugh.

"Why would I? Mylee's working abroad, Everett says he only gets to see her occasionally, but when he does, fuck is it wild... if you know what I mean?"

I tense up, the demon within me swarming as I rush forward without hesitation, my knuckles clenched as I thrust them into his face so hard and fast I can't think about what I'm doing. Anger swarms around me, a rage burning so hot as I punch and punch and fucking punch. I feel the bones crunching, I hear his cries of agony. The adrenaline races over me as I let the demon within me ravage my soul.

He talked about Mylee like she was a piece of meat.

She's anything but.

My demon ignites my bloodlust, and as I feel arms pulling at me to stop, I can't. Someone tries to grab at me, so I turn, swinging for them. I connect, but I don't wait to see who it is before I turn back to my victim. The insatiable need to feel the blood oozing through my fingertips is seeping through my pores. I rip off my gloves as I punch him again. The red liquid smothering my hand while the feeling of it soothes my very soul. Seeing it, feeling it, melding with it. It's intoxicating. The fire inside of me burns hot. So hot I can't stand it. Sweat pours off every inch of me as I grab at my balaclava and yank it off my head throwing it to the floor.

I reach out for the metal tube and swing it with all my might, the thwack and resistance of the tube doesn't dissuade me at all. In fact, it only ignites me further. I hit him again, the crack resounding through the room as blood splatters on my clothing making me feel more alive than I have in ages.

Suddenly, two hands grab me on either side and yank me back, effectively pulling me off Miller. I struggle to get free, the demon within raging to be out of control and finish the job. I'm a man possessed, and I need to feel it, his life slipping at my hands. The rush I get from it. The energy pulsing from his life into mine. I need it, I crave it.

"Stop!" Sensei yells as his hazy outline comes into view.

It's only now I realize his balaclava is off as he rubs at his jaw, a bruise forming. It must have been him I hit. My body goes limp in Torque and Crest's hands as they hold me tight to stop my tirade.

Sensei stares at me. His hands up to halt me from rushing forward as I pant heavily.

"Trax, stop!" he murmurs again.

He's said my name.

His balaclava is off.

I think mine's off, too.

Shit! Our identities are out there for Miller to see. This is not good.

I drop the tube as I pant. "I'm okay," I murmur, slightly out of breath as Sensei nods to Crest and Torque who slowly let me go. "What happened?" I ask.

Sensei steps aside to let me see Miller. I inhale sharply as I take in the sight in front of me. His face is a bloody mess, but it's his jaw that shocks me. His jaw is off at a right angle and to the side clearly broken beyond repair. The side of his skull is caved in. And the blood, there's so much fucking blood.

Defiance

I sink in on myself as I look down at my hands, they're covered in it. Some of his hair, a little bit of flesh. I love the thrill of causing pain—normally. But this, this has me shocked.

"You lost control," Sensei simply states as I let out a deep exhale.

I glance to Crest, my eyes heavy with an unspoken apology. "I..." I don't know what to say, so I don't say anything else.

Crest steps in front of me, shoving my body forcefully. I take a step back trying to stop myself from falling while he glares at me. "What the fuck! This is *exactly* what I told you *not* to do. I gave you strict instructions and a chance to prove yourself, and you shot that shit to hell. I should gut you right here, but Mylee would never forgive me." He runs his hands through his hair and turns his back to me.

Crap! My body feels numb as I drop to the floor.

I've failed Crest.

I've failed my brothers.

But most of all, I've failed Mylee.

I've never let the demon within me take hold completely before.

Everyone looks down at me but continues talking.

"What's the ramifications for you, Crest?" Torque asks.

"No fucking idea. Hopefully, this can't be tied back to the club, and he will be just another missing person. So you better make sure disposal is handled appropriately unlike this shit show."

"I will take care of this myself, you have my word, Crest," Sensei states.

"Was he the only lead you had?" Torque asks.

Crest rubs the back of his neck. "Yeah, he was all I had."

Sensei squats in front of me placing his hand on my knee, the sudden movement making me look up. "I think this proves you need to think about control, don't you?"

I glance over to Miller's mangled face. I curl up my lip as I glance to Crest. He pulls off his balaclava and lifts his chin. So, I look back to Sensei and sigh with a nod. "I'll train with you. I had no fucking idea I could lose control like that."

He weakly smiles. "The bloodlust, when it takes over, Trax, you have to know how to fight it, or..." he looks to Miller, "... this happens. I thought it might happen with you one day. You need to be taught just like I was. I see me in you, Trax. This is why I kept on you about it. I knew we would get to this point. It's also how I know we *can* fix it."

A calm silence filters through the room as I take in what's being said. I need to change. Something in me that's broken needs to be fixed. Now. How I do that, I'm not sure. But I know Sensei is the one to help me.

"Right, now I know we have no leads here, I need to go home in the morning. Trax, you gonna be okay to watch over Mylee? After this shit, I need to know you're in the right frame of mind," Crest asks.

I gather my bearings and stand up. "I only acted out because he talked about Mylee that way. I would never hurt Mylee. You *have* to know that, Crest."

He nods. "I know it. But fuck if you haven't pissed me the hell off." He throws the balaclava on the floor, hard. "Fuck! All right, I'll leave in the morning. I just want to make sure Mylee wakes up with a clear head. Plus, I don't wanna leave without saying goodbye to her."

I nod my head as does Torque, it makes perfect sense. Plus, Mylee would hate it if her dad left without a goodbye. "I'm going to go talk to Ace after I clean up. I want to dig up as much shit on this Everett jackass as I can before morning," I mention trying to gain some favor.

Crest lets out a small laugh. "Trust you to go all protector on her, guess it's damn obvious from this shit show."

"If some guy's out to hurt Mylee, you can rest assured I'm going to find a way to bring that bastard down."

Crest leans inward crossing his arms over his chest. "I'm not entirely convinced he's out to hurt her, it's more about wanting to be with her in his own twisted fucked-up way. I think we can see that by the way he's telling his friends he's in a relationship with her, when clearly he isn't."

"Wanting to be with her is even worse. And *not* gonna happen."

Crest chuckles, his chest puffing out as his arms drop to his sides. "Thought you might have something to say about that, too."

"Mylee belongs to me, not some fucking insane senator's asshole son."

Torque raises his brow as does Crest, they both swivel toward me.

"Careful boy, that's sounding awfully close to claiming talk," Crest grunts.

While letting out a small huff, I take a calming breath. Torque looks at me sternly. "All I'm saying is while she's here, she's mine. I'm going to take care of her, no one else is gonna come near her. Fair enough?"

Crest relaxes, a direct gaze set firmly on me. "Right! But don't you dare think about putting a claim on my little girl without discussing it with me. Get your damn head on straight first, then talk to me if you're gonna do it..." his face turns red, "... or I swear to God, I *will* end you."

"I hear you. Don't worry. I've tried to claim her once already, and it failed. Not gonna go there again anytime soon."

Silence filters through the Chamber. He looks at me like he knows how much of a hard time it was for me. Crest reaches out grabbing my hand, lifts me from the floor, then squeezes my shoulder. "It's shit how things went down when she left, Trax. She was ill. She wasn't thinking straight. I had to get her into the hospital. You were the collateral damage in all the mess. Yeah, that's fucked, but it is what it is. Just know... she never stopped loving you."

Taking a deep breath, I lower my head. "I'm glad she got the help she needed. I wish I were a part of it... I wanted to be."

"I know. At the time it was too damn hard, but now you can be here for her."

My head bobs as Torque looks at me. His mouth twitches, his lips tilting. "I think we can all agree this is the best place for Mylee right now. Trax'll watch out for her. We have no immediate threats to our club. The Yakuza are gone, the Andretti's are on our side. Everything's quiet on our end... I can't foresee any problems, Crest. She should be safe here, for now."

Crest exhales like he's relieved. "Good. I trust you both with her, that's why I brought her to you."

"We won't fail you, or her," I express.

"I know you won't..." Crest pauses. "Enough of this. Let's get this fucking mess cleaned up, have some more booze, forget about what happened in here, and have a good night. Yeah?"

Torque gestures to lead us out of the chamber to a night of frosty beverages. I hope I'm the right person for this job, if not, Crest is going to maim me.

Just like I maimed Miller.

CHAPTER 6

MYLEE

The Next Day

My head feels kind of groggy. I know this feeling well, but I haven't experienced it for some time. My eyelids are heavy as I open and close them a few times trying to gather my bearings. My mouth feels like cotton wool, it's so dry. I need a drink as I slowly sit up taking in the strange surroundings. I vaguely remember coming in here last night, but it's all such a blur.

I had a panic attack.

Because of that, I had the pills, and now my memory of it all is slightly foggy.

Bits and pieces filter through my brain. *Trax was a part of it.*

As I look around the room, I realize I'm in a clubhouse, but it's not Dad's.

I'm at Defiance.

I'm at Trax's club.

I came here with Dad to get away from Everett. It's all coming back to me now. It's clearer as the pictures start to replay in my mind.

Damn, I hate having these blackouts when I wake from an episode.

Why does everything have to be in such a fucking fog?

Squinting, I rub my eyes trying to wake myself up a little more. I have no idea on the time other than it's daylight outside. Glancing to the side table, I see a glass of water. My eyes open wide in delight as I reach for the glass downing the entire contents without hesitation. The cotton balls in my mouth only marginally dissipate—I'm always thirsty these days.

Damn meds.

Standing from the bed, the blanket falls away from me. I stumble a little but quickly right myself as I take a steadying breath.

I'm okay.

I can do this.

I'm a strong woman.

I've been through far, far worse than one panic attack.

On the floor, I notice my ballet flats, so I slide them on before I walk to the door. Taking a deep breath with my hand on the handle, I mentally tell myself, *I can do this.*

Opening the door, the sounds from the clubroom waft down the hall along with the smell of bacon. My lips slowly incline as I walk down the hall toward the clubroom. I have no idea what I'll be walking into, but I know I can't hide out in my room forever. That's not the girl I am anymore. So I hold my head high stepping into the clubroom.

There's a general buzz in the room—bikers eating breakfast, club girls serving food—an alive atmosphere of energy pulsing through the air. These guys all look happy like everything's fallen into place for them. Which is the complete opposite for me, of course. My life seems to be slowly falling out of sync again. Which is alarming me.

As I step into the room, one biker notices me, so I take a breath and flash him my pearly whites. He grins back, then another notices me. He too grins. Then another. Then another, until almost everyone in the room turns to look my way. They're all beaming so wide, I begin to wonder why they're all smiling at me.

It's making me a little uncomfortable as my hands link together, my thumbs tapping against each other nervously as I try to figure out what they're all staring at. Glancing up, I see Trax striding toward me. He really has gotten better looking these past two years. He was already muscular, but now he seems even more built with those bulging biceps smattered in tattoos. The way his waist tapers down into his jeans is pure perfection. I know he'd have one of those V's women go gaga over. Thinking about it is almost making me drool on the spot. His handsome face covered in a beard, that's not too long but enough to be sexy, his nose ring, and his eyes are the most intense blue I've ever known. There's something about his eyes. The way they hold so much emotion, the way they can tell you a thousand stories without saying a single word. His eyes are truly the window to his soul, and looking in them is a dangerous thing for me. I've been lost in them many a time. Right now, the way he's looking at me with that slight gleam in them, I know he's in a better mood than yesterday.

Seeing him in all his sexy glory should soothe me, but I'm still wondering why everyone's observing me as I stand here while he looks me up and down. His bright smile calms me as he walks right up to me, a soft chuckle echoing from his lips. "Morning, Mylee, sleep well?" he asks. His hands reaching up either side of my head, and I follow his movements.

I gulp as he struggles with my mess of hair. "I, ahh…" My eyes dart upward to him patting my hair down. "Was my hair everywhere?" I whisper making him chuckle.

"Yeah, you kinda had a nest going on there. But you're good, I got you," he consoles leaning in, planting a chaste kiss on my forehead, then wraps his arm around my shoulders pulling me to him.

"Thank you. I was wondering why everyone was smirking at me." This is a totally different Trax to the one in his room yesterday.

"They couldn't understand how a beauty like you could have a nest like that," he teases as I let out a small laugh. As his hands fall, I notice his knuckles are bruised and swollen. I find it odd, I'm sure they weren't like that yesterday when I arrived, but I ignore it as he leads me over toward the bar. I let out a relieved exhale as the other bikers in the clubroom all smile, some even winking their approval.

I glance to Trax raising my brow. "I don't want to jinx anything, but you seem to have changed your tune since yesterday?"

He weakly smiles with a nod. "Yeah, I reacted shit when you arrived. Shock can be a bitch... I also had a chat with your dad. Just know you're going to be in good hands here, Mylee. I'm not going to let you down."

Sighing, I tilt my head. "That must have been some epic chat?"

He chuckles. "You have no idea what went on. Crest is highly motivational, but you helped the cause, too." He winks at me as we approach the bar, and we stand there where the club girls are busy doing their morning thing.

"Cindi... Hayley... ladies, can you get us some breakfast?" Trax asks while I assess the two club girls.

"Sure thing, Trax. Full breakfast?" the brunette who I'm sure was in Trax's room when I arrived asks.

"You want a cooked breakfast?" Trax turns to me.

"If it means bacon, then God, *yes*." I groan making them both laugh.

"Coming right up."

"Thanks, Cindi..." Trax starts to turn to walk away but then stops. "Oh, any news on Ruby?"

I raise my brow.

"She's doing much better. Should be home today sometime," Cindi replies, and everyone within earshot lets out a cheer.

"That's fucking great news. Okay, gotta get Mylee settled," Trax calls out pulling me with him as we walk off to the table.

I turn to look at him. "What's wrong with Ruby? She's a club girl, right?" I ask vaguely remembering the name.

He exhales as we slide in taking a seat next to Dad, Torque, Sensei, Chains, Ace, and Surge. "She was drugged by the Yakuza. The assholes overdosed her, and she was pretty sick, but Kline and Foxy have been helping her recover in the hospital."

"Foxy?"

We all chuckle. "You have so much to catch up on," Trax murmurs.

I glance across to Dad, his kind eyes warm my soul. "I'm glad you didn't leave, Dad," I call out, and he smiles.

"Leave without saying goodbye to my baby girl? I wouldn't do that to you, Mylee."

Happiness ignites inside of me. "Thanks, Dad, I appreciate it."

"But I am leaving this morning. I have to get back to the club, they need me. But, if at any time *you* need me, just call. If at any time Trax thinks you need extra help, he's going to call me. Okay?" he states.

I glance to Trax who's watching me closely. "I should be fine. I have Trax, and I have Neala. If all else fails, I have my pills. If all *that* fails, they'll call you. But Dad, I've been fine for six months—"

"Fine until yesterday. Mylee—"

"Yes, but yesterday I saw Trax for the first time in two years. It was…" I hesitate as I glance at him, he exhales then I look back to Dad. "Trax and I know how to handle this. We spent a lot of time together, and now we have the bonus of having medication to help with anything that comes our way. We can do this… right?" I look at Trax on the last word.

He grins that lopsided smirk and tightens his grip around my shoulders. "Right."

Dad bows his head with a sigh. "I know you can. Otherwise, I wouldn't have brought you here. But you know no matter what, I will always worry about you, Mylee."

"I know, Dad… I know."

He shakes his head, standing from the table. "I should go. I've got a four-hour ride back to the club. I have to get back in time for a shipment. Trax, if you need anything…"

"I'll call," Trax replies.

I stand from the table, Trax's arm dropping from my shoulders as I walk around to my dad. He wastes no time taking me into a giant embrace, the tightest I've felt from him in a long time as he holds me to him.

I don't know how long I'm going to be staying at Defiance, but I know it's going to be a while—until they can figure out a way to deal with Everett. With him being a senator's son, they need something that's going to work without simply taking him out. So for now, Chicago Defiance is my home. But that doesn't scare me. If anything, it brings with it new excitement, a new chapter in my life. Something challenging to look forward to and maybe something old to rekindle.

I'm not sure.

Only time will tell.

After Dad left, we all ate breakfast sitting around and chatting like old times. It's amazing how easily I fit back into the groove of this club. When I was here last time, I sank into the background. Sure, I knew everyone, and they all knew me, but I didn't take the time to get to know everyone properly. I was way too wrapped up in Trax and needed to be away from people. This time, though, I want to make sure I get to know everyone, after all, I have no idea how long I'm going to be here. So I may as well make some friends along the way. If Trax and I are going to just be friends, then there's no point being all about him while I'm here. I need to broaden my horizon, get to know everyone. But for right now, I'm going to spend a little time with him to catch up and see how things are going in his life.

As we walk around the outside of the giant clubhouse, the stale smell of the South Branch Chicago River hits my senses, and I chuckle remembering this was always the one thing that reminded me I was here. We head down the back to where there are a set of swings for the children that sometimes come to the compound for family days. My lips twist up a little as I take a seat. Trax sits on the other one as I glance at the big burly biker seated on a child's swing beside me. I let out a small giggle as he rolls his eyes.

"Shut up, I'm a child at heart, you know this," he grunts making me burst out laughing as my lips break from a small twist into a full glowing smile.

"I do know this…" I look at him as I push off with my legs to swing slowly, but only a little as he stays stationary. "You still have the face of a kid to—"

"Shut up, woman!"

I let out a laugh as I rock back and forth. Gnawing on my bottom lip, I glance at him. "Do you think… I mean, if I had stayed—"

"Mylee!" he warns.

My muscles are tense as a lump gets caught in my throat. "So we're not going to talk about it, at all? We're just going to say we're better off as friends, and that's it?"

He looks to the ground letting out a huff. "I think while you're here and we're trying to figure out a way to get this Everett guy off your case, the best thing for us is to keep ourselves grounded. If we get lost in each other…" His eyes narrow as his forehead creases. "I just think, you're better off without me."

I scoff. "Why would you *ever* think that?"

He looks up at me with tension in his brows. "Mylee, honestly, when you came back to the club was it to be with me?"

I stop swinging and look at him slowly, a knot forming in my stomach. "No."

"Exactly. You didn't come here looking to start things up with me again. Just because when you saw me, it made you think we should, doesn't mean that... we should. It's just falling into old patterns. I don't want to get hurt, and I don't want to hurt you. It's too dangerous."

"You think you'll hurt me?"

"No, but—"

"You think *I'll* hurt *you*."

He exhales looking into my eyes as I chew on my bottom lip.

"I get it. I know I hurt you. I can never apologize enough for that. I suppose all I can do now is be your friend. If something more comes of it, then that's amazing. If not, then I will love being your friend. Because having you in my life, Trax..." I shake my head letting out a long breath, "... means more to me than anything else."

He smiles, finally kicking on the ground, so his swing moves through the air. Not a lot, just a little, so he's swinging back and forth making the mood a little lighter.

I move to swing too as we rock back and forth on the children's play set.

"Did you think two years ago we would be here today?" I ask.

He lets out a snort. "No. I didn't think I'd ever see you again."

I glance at him. "Well, I'm glad I'm here."

His eyes soften. "Me, too, Mylee. Me, too."

I sigh. "I'm glad we're able to talk, though, open and honestly. It would suck if you ignored me."

He chuckles. "I'm not a fifteen-year-old schoolgirl. I'm not going to fucking ignore you. We can work at this. I may not think we should pursue this romantically, but friends... friends we can definitely do."

Disappointment flows through me like a Mack truck, but I try to play it off. "So muscles, what are we gonna do today?"

He chuckles rolling his eyes. "Muscles?"

I waggle my brows looking at his biceps. They're practically bulging out of his shirt as he grips onto the chains of the swing. "Yeah, I see you're still working out."

He shrugs. "Guns get the girls," he mocks, but I inwardly cringe. Thinking of him with other women makes my skin crawl. His cocky smirk falls. "Sorry, bad joke... do you think... I mean, I think I'm ready to hear what happened the two years you were gone."

I glance at him, my eyes softening as my lips turn slightly in surprise. "Are you sure. I don't want you to think I'm forcing my story on you. I don't want you to get angry at me."

He shakes his head. "I should have let you tell me what happened. I was angry. Hurt you didn't come back for me. I don't handle anger well, Mylee."

Knowing he has anger issues because of me breaks my heart, but maybe if I tell him my truth, it might ease it for him. So I stop the swing and look right at him. "I feel like saying sorry won't cut it... leaving you was the hardest thing I've ever had to do. But after I left, I went straight into the hospital. My medication regime was started immediately, and it took a long time to get the dosages right."

His head jolts back, his tired eyes gazing over my features. "What do you mean?" he asks. The anger that's been weighing him down seems to shift, and a calmer tone settles in.

Swallowing hard at the memory, I gnaw on my bottom lip watching him take in my every word. "I started on a couple of medications. It worked... for a while. It stabilized my moods, but it had serious side effects."

He tenses. "What the hell? What kind of side effects?"

His chest raises and falls like he's panting for breath as my body begins to remember the feelings. The emotions. The never ending cycle of uncertainty that went with trying to find the right dosages and medication. It was a nightmare. Sometimes it felt like the remedy is worse than the disease. "The first tablets made me into a zombie. While it stabilized me, I was completely zoned out most of the time, but they wanted to keep me on the tablets to see if my moods would level out over a prolonged period. So, I kept trying. Then..." my eyes narrow, "... worse side effects came."

He shifts on the swing turning to face me even more, like he wants to move closer but is afraid to. "Go on."

My lips gingerly turn up, and I can't help but notice him focus in on my mouth.

I wonder what he's thinking.

Fuck, he's gorgeous.

I continue to tell him my story. "Well, I'm sure you've noticed my extra love handles." I grab hold of my belly. His lips match the motion of mine turning up at me clutching my small love handles. Compared to the skeletal frame I was before, I've definitely put on weight. "I put on eighty pounds in the first six months. Obviously, I've managed to lose most of it, but some of it has remained, and I think it will probably be part of me now."

His eyes widen. "Holy shit," he blurts out.

I grimace with a sad look on my face. "It's not even the half of it. My hair started to fall out... big lumps of it, too. Then the doctors decided the side effects were too bad, and it was time to pull me off that medication. Thank God."

He shakes his head looking me up and down suggestively. "Thank fuck for that. I mean I wouldn't care if you were the size of a house and you had no hair, but surely that couldn't have been good for your self-esteem?"

My smile is weaker, the sadness glimmering in my eyes as my thumbs rub over links in the chains of the swing. "Yeah, well... then they had to admit me to the hospital to wean me off the medication, so I could start a new regime of pills. The next lot still made me into a zombie, but over time the side effects diminished, and I cope a lot better now..." I pause with a sigh. "I still have days, but I'm hardly manic at all. Depression only sets in when something really bad happens, and the episodes don't last anywhere near as long, which is good."

He shakes his head looking impressed. "Mylee, you're brave. I know you watched your mother go through this, and when you found out you had it, too, I know it scared the shit out of you. But honestly, you can do this. You can live with it. Loads of people do."

My eyes glisten as they look up at him. "When Mom took her own life because of her bipolar disorder, I never thought my life would be the same. Finding her on the bathroom floor…" I close my eyes, a tear sliding down my face gently, my chest aching at the memory, "… it triggered my condition. My world went into meltdown. I… I don't know how you can be so tolerant, so understanding."

Trax steps off the swing, walks over, and kneels in front of me. He brings his hand up, cupping my face, my blonde hair threading through his fingers as he caresses my cheek and looks into my eyes. "Mylee, from the moment I met you, I knew you were special. Not different, special. To me, you're perfect as you are. I wouldn't change you. Not a thing. You hear me?"

My eyes glisten, my bottom lip trembles as I take a deep breath. "I want to be normal for you, Konnor."

He visibly shudders. "You're the right kind of normal I need, Mylee."

Elation rolls through me as I gnaw down on my bottom lip. He looks into my eyes. Something passes between us. I told him. Everything. Why I was gone for so long, and he didn't get angry. In fact, he's been great about it. "So what now?"

Trax exhales, dropping his hand from my face, stands up and walks to his swing taking another seat. My heart sinks a little. I thought we were making a little progress, but he's backed away.

"Thank you for telling me all of that. It can't have been easy."

I shrug. "It's been my life for two years. I've lived it. It's a part of me, so I'm okay telling the story."

He looks to the ground. "I'm sorry I wasn't there to help."

I shake my head. "There was no way you could have been, Trax, but you're here now," I offer hoping it will lift his spirits.

He nods. "Yeah... so you made it through, your medication is on track... so tell me, what else have you been doing with yourself?"

I smile a genuine smile.

He's not running away.

He's not giving up.

He's still engaging in conversation.

He's still in this with me.

"Mainly just working for myself. It's easiest when you don't know how your moods are going to be. Plus, I can work my own hours and when I want, basically."

"Still doing the websites?"

"Yeah, designing and testing. It pays the bills. It's easy to do on the road. I take my laptop loaded with all my software, and I can do it anywhere. Which is good for when the club's traveling around."

He raises his brow. "So you were still living at the Knights' clubhouse?"

"Yeah, Dad wanted to keep an eye on me. I came out of the psych ward then went straight into the clubhouse. I felt safe there. I know everyone, they all know me. It worked... until it didn't with the whole Everett thing."

He winces. "I'm sure they'll miss you."

Pursing my lips, I sigh. "Yeah, I miss them already, but the club can't have the Scott's digging around right now. You know how it is. If Everett and his senator father, Malcolm, come looking for me, the club *can't* come under fire. They don't need any kind of heat on them right now. Especially from the government. Dad has way too many important deals going through."

"I get it. Senators can be assholes. Having a mentally unstable son doesn't help his aspirations... I'm sorry I didn't fight more to come and see you when you were in the hospital. I should have pushed harder… past your father."

I snort out a laugh. "No, you shouldn't. Risking a war with Dad wasn't worth it, Trax. You did the exact right thing. I needed the time to get my head right because I certainly wasn't thinking clearly at the time."

Bringing his swing to a stop with a heavy sigh, he stands abruptly like he's having trouble being here with me. So I stand as well. The mood in the air changes dramatically. Tension fills the atmosphere, and my brows scrunch as I reach out grabbing his arm. He turns back to look at me, his eyes are distant. He looks hurt. Lost. I'm not sure what to do, so I do the only thing I can think of, I inch closer to him running my hands up his chest. His chest's heaving as he looks into my eyes, both our breaths coming in short and shallow. His hands come up quickly gripping hold of my wrists on his chest halting my movement upward.

Now we're locked together in an embrace, staring at each other, breathing heavily, neither of us saying anything as electric tension fills the air around us. It's like energy pulsing through my atoms, filling everything in an intense surge, pulsing, vibrating through every element within me and around us.

I stare at him, his eyes never leave mine. It's like I'm seeing him for the first time or for the thousandth. I have no idea, but right now, everything's changing. The idea of us just being friends sounds ridiculous as we stare at each other, breathless.

I inch closer needing to touch him, to feel his lips on mine, just wanting to remember what he tastes like. I know he wants this too. His tongue darts out subtly licking his bottom lip as his chest heaves, and I inch up on my toes leaning in. Tilting my head, my lips press closer to his, only a hair's breadth away from his. His breath wisps against my lips making them tingle. A shudder runs down my spine at the thought of us actually kissing again after so long apart. The excitement inside of me is at a toxic level as I inch closer. My lips graze his, the prickle of his beard teases my skin. I close my eyes ready to lean in fully, to feel him completely.

His hands tighten around my wrists on his chest, and he pulls back dramatically putting some distance between us, effectively breaking the kiss before it even had a chance to begin, before I had a chance to truly connect with him.

CHAPTER 7

MYLEE

My heart plummets while my eyes shoot wide open as he steps back dropping my hands from his. His drooping eyes tell me he's conflicted, but I break eye contact with him as I look to the ground feeling rejected. He doesn't want me. I made myself available, I told him my truths, and he's clearly pulled away. My breathing is fast as I try to control my rapid cycling emotions. I need to not let the storm swell right now. I know he's turning me down, but this doesn't need to send me over the edge.

I'm a big girl, I can handle him not wanting me.

Right?

"Mylee…" he murmurs.

I risk glancing up at him as I sniff. His eyes look pained. I don't know if that makes it hurt even more—the fact he looks so cut up about this too.

"It's fine, we're friends, yeah?" I try to break the clear tension between us.

His eyes clench like he's in pain. "We shouldn't—"

"Trax, we have chemistry, we always did. But it's fine. I know you don't want anything from me, so I'll try to reign myself in. I just..." I clear my throat, a lump getting caught as I try to think of what I'm trying to say. "I miss us."

His eyes open, they look forlorn, his face falling as he takes another step away from me putting even more distance between us.

Another nail in the coffin.

Another hit to my fractured heart.

I will myself not to cry in front of him as I wrap my arms around myself for comfort. I look back toward the clubhouse feeling like I need the support of the people in there more than the man I used to seek comfort from in front of me right now. I have no idea how this is going to work. Our attraction to each other is there, but he wants to fight it, and right now I'm going to let him. So, I turn, swallowing the lump in my throat, and start to walk toward the clubrooms.

"Mylee," he calls out, but I don't turn back to look at him. I can't, it hurts. I want to be with him, he's fighting it at every angle, but I get it. I left him when shit got hard, that hurt him. I know this isn't his way of payback, that's not his style, but I can't help but feel this is my penalty for leaving him. I have to suffer for the sins of my past. While I can't say this is entirely fair, and I don't like it, but I understand.

"It's fine, Trax," I blurt out. I'm hurting. I hate we have to be like this. Especially when I can tell he's fighting against everything in himself to be this way.

My heart's pummeling in my chest, and I feel like there's so much left unsaid. So much that needs to be straightened out right now, but just as I'm freely walking away, he's letting me go. So I guess that's all there is, right? I don't know how long I'm going to be here for, but Trax and I need to find some kind of balance. And nearly kissing can't be our thing. Right now, I need to find someone to take my mind off the love of my life, and the ever-present storm threatening to invade my senses.

But I won't let those fucking thunder clouds invade my mind.

Not today.

I've worked too damn hard to get to where I am, and just because I have an illness, it doesn't define me. It doesn't manipulate me in every emotional situation. I can push through this little problem and still see a clear sky at the end of the day.

I am strong.

I'm okay.

I *am* okay!

Taking a deep breath, I walk inside the clubhouse and finally away from the deep glare of Trax's eyes on my back as I traipse the hall looking for someone to take my mind off things. Walking into the open expanse of the main room, I see Neala sitting at the bar. I think she's the girl I need right now. Quickly stepping over to her, I slide on the stool beside her. She glances up. There's something about the way her face lights up when she smiles, it's like all your cares wash away, and she makes you feel that little bit more human again.

"Mylee, hey girl! You coming to play with me?"

I let out a half-snort, half-laugh sort of thing. "Not sure about play, but I'll sit with you and chat? How about that?"

She chuckles, slapping the bar signaling to Cindi to pour us some drinks. "Whatcha drinking?"

"I'm not a drinker these days, so I might have a soda or juice or anything really?"

Neala snorts again with a shrug. "Suit yourself, I'll have a double," she calls as Cindi rolls her eyes pouring Neala a double whiskey. All thoughts of Trax seem to vanish as I look her over noticing she might have actually been here drinking for a while, but it's practically the middle of the day. Something about her is off. Maybe she needs *me* more than I need *her* right now.

So I take a breath turning to look at her. "Lala, what's happening with you?"

She screws up her face as she lets out a loud huff, throwing her arm onto the bar followed by her forehead dramatically dropping onto her arm. I look around the clubroom wondering what I should do, but no one else is really paying attention, so I simply rub her back as Cindi hands me a glass of orange juice. I raise my chin in thanks as Cindi walks off leaving me with Lala.

"It's such a mess," her muffled voice murmurs from under her fanned-out hair surrounding her face. I try to hold back my laugh as I look at her. She really does look a right mess. She's certainly taking my mind off my own personal dramas.

"Oh, Lala, talk to me. What's going on?"

She bursts up, sitting up so dramatically she sways on the seat as she steadies herself. Not from being drunk just from the quickness of the movement. "So, listen... he said he doesn't want to play games anymore."

"Well, games are never good—"

"But I haven't been playing games with him, Mylee. He knows where I stand, but he's the one making all these damned rules all the time. The club comes first. Your brothers will kill me if something happened with us. Blah fucking blah, I'm a pussy, chicken shit, little man... *asshole,*" she murmurs the last word. I raise my brow as I scratch my forehead wondering how I can help her as I have no idea what the hell she's even talking about.

"So who are you talking about here?" I ask wanting to make sure I'm on the same page as her.

"Tremor, of course. God, keep up, Mylee. I think having the pres and vice pres as your brothers can really be a buzzkill, you know? I mean, sure people think it makes you the princess of the club, but when it comes to getting laid, *all* bets are off!"

Pulling my lips in to try to hide my smile, I glance around the room making sure no one can hear her. If Torque or Trax heard her speaking like this, she'd be in deep shit. But I have to admit, it's pretty amusing. Whatever Tremor's doing to her, he needs to fix his shit because it's obviously hurting her. Sounds to me like he's keeping her on the back burner. Sounds familiar if you ask me.

Sighing, I reach out grabbing her hands looking into her eyes. She looks back at me as I try to calm her down. "Lala, these men... these bikers... fuck! They have a mind of their own. Especially when it comes to the club. You have to know *it* will always come first. You should know that after growing up here, right?"

She slumps her body, her eyes drooping. Her head bows looking deflated. "I do know. But brothers *can* be happy. I've seen it. Men have old ladies all the time. Why does *me* being a biker princess have to change anything?"

I sigh. "It just does. You're royalty to these guys, Lala, just like I am to the Knights. We're daughters of honored members. That means something to these guys, and when brothers start showing an interest in us, it starts a whole new world of drama. You have to think about Tremor in this, Lala. He obviously cares about you, or he never would have acted in the first place. He's got to be so torn... the woman he adores or the club he lives for. This is just as tough for him, too. Don't forget that."

She sniffs as Ace strolls past casually making Neala's expression change as she sits taller. "Ace!" she suddenly calls out making him stop to turn and look at us.

A curious smirk lights his face as he steps up, his broad shoulders filling up the space as he raises his brow in curiosity.

"So, ah... you were out with Tremor on a ride today, right?" Lala asks.

"Yeees?" he drawls like he's sussing her out.

"So, umm... how did he seem to you? Was he sad, or mopey, or did he seem like he needed cheering up?"

Ace chuckles glancing at me. I jolt my head with wide eyes trying to gesture for him to give her something to work with. Some little hint to make her feel better. He seems to click, standing taller as his face falls. "Actually, now that you mention it, I think he could use a pep talk. He seemed off. He kept talking about you all day, wouldn't shut up about you basically. Was kind of annoying."

Neala's eyes light up as she glances at me like this is the best news in the world.

I beam at her and lean forward. "See, there you go."

She gnaws on her bottom lip like she's debating what the hell to do.

"Why don't you two just figure it all out? Go. I can keep Mylee company," Ace adds, and I raise my brow in surprise.

Lala looks to me like she's worried about leaving me, but she's also one foot out the door as it were. I came in here looking to talk to her about my problems with her brother, but hers far outweigh mine. Seeing her eyes light up at the thought of talking to Tremor right now is all the convincing I need. "Hey, go. You need to talk to Tremor way more than I need you right now. Plus, I can hang out with Ace and his man bun."

Ace and Neala both burst out laughing.

Lala stands from her seat leaning over giving me a tight hug. "Thank you for listening and dealing with me. I know when you came in, something was happening with you... I kind of stole the limelight. I'm sorry we didn't get a chance to talk about you." She grimaces, but I wave my hand through the air. "Stop! You made me forget all about it. Go talk through your problems with that prospect of yours."

She bounces on her toes, spinning, and she rushes off. I turn back to Ace who's watching my every move. He spins to face me then leans in bumping his shoulder into mine playfully. "So, coming back to our club must've been hard."

I snort as we both look out into the near-empty clubroom. "Yeah, it is. Trax's so complicated I don't even know where to begin, but you, you're their tech guy, right?"

Tilting his head, a slight smile touches his lips. "Tech guy, nerd, it's all relative."

"Well, I have a soft spot for nerds... just saying."

He chuckles with a shrug. "I'm glad. But I'm not your typical nerd. I'm more a badass hacker who can kick ass and spin tires like no other."

I can't hold in my laughter as I look at him. He's really quite the looker with his chiseled jaw, a five o'clock shadow, his medium build, and you can tell he works out from the definition in his biceps. Then his hair. I'm not usually a fan of long hair on men, but Ace's brown with flecks of gold hair is actually almost pretty. It's certainly not tatty or unkempt. For a man bun, it's just the right size too as it's pulled up high on his head. I can only imagine women would love to run their fingers through his silky locks when it's down. He is, by all accounts, a really good-looking man, and in another life maybe I would have found myself fawning over him. But my heart firmly belongs to another, and as much as I would love to think about moving on with someone else, Trax is never far from my mind.

Shaking my head, I roll my eyes. "Yeah, you're all brute and brawn with a head of hair like that."

He shakes his head from side to side like some scene from *Baywatch* making me burst out laughing. "Don't bag the bangs," he mocks continuing his hair flick even though his hair is tied up. He looks so effeminate right now I can hardly contain myself with fits of laughter as his pearly whites shine through a gorgeous smile. I can't help a wide smile crossing my face in return. "It's good to see you smiling. It lights up your entire face. Don't let Trax dampen your time here," he mentions out of the blue. I stop my fits of giggles, look at him while clearing my throat as I sit up straight all humor leaving me.

"He's having a tough time with me being here, I think." I take the conversation back to seriousness.

Ace grunts while rolling his eyes. "Trax is a big boy, he will deal. You need to make sure you're protected while you're here. That's the main issue, Mylee. With Trax having a crisis of conscience right now, you need all of us to step up to protect you, too."

I tilt my head. "What do you mean?"

"Trax is so focused on trying to be your friend, he's fighting hard to stay away from you. He's going to be concentrating on that rather than on keeping you safe. It's not his fault, he's got blinders on right now. But it's okay, that's why I'm here."

I raise my brow with a sigh. "Okay, I see your point. Trax is distracted. We have no idea if Everett is going to make a move on me, so where does it leave the situation?"

That beaming smile's back on his face. "With me."

I raise my brow, the idea only just now clicking in my brain. "You could do some digging for me? 'Cause you're the nerd guy, right?"

He laughs. "Yeah, exactly. So who is this Everett guy you want me to look into? Trax and Crest told me some basics but didn't really give me anything to go on. They were in a rush."

I tense. "Everett Scott and his father, Malcolm."

Ace looks at me sternly. "Malcolm Scott as in Senator Malcolm Scott?"

"Yeah, as in the Governor of Michigan. The guy who's aiming for the White House."

Ace's body tenses, his hand rubbing the back of his neck to ease the tautness in his muscles as he lets out a heavy exhale. "Um… okay. Yeah, right. I'm not sure what you want me to find, but I can look."

I figure if Ace is going to put his time and effort into this, he needs to know what he's dealing with. He needs to know what kind of people he's looking into. So I steady myself, my palms coating in a fine mist of sweat as I rest my arms on the bar, taking a deep breath looking off into space. "I met Everett in the psych ward when I was admitted after my diagnosis."

Ace swivels on his stool to face me. Resting his elbow on the bar, he props himself up to listen.

"He was so full of life when I met him. I was in such a depressive state, I guess I was looking for someone to make me feel…

something. I'd just left Trax, I was diagnosed with bipolar disorder. My life was spinning completely out of control. I didn't know what the hell was going on half the time. I was in such a deep, depressive episode, I couldn't think logically, and Everett was just... there. He was the only shining light in the dark.

"Not romantically, he was never anything like that, but he was a friend. Someone to help me smile. He kept saying I reminded him of someone, and that the reminder made him happy. So, I thought we were good for each other, you know what I mean?"

Ace grimaces as I turn to look at him, he's taking all this in, then I stare to the back of the bar gazing at nothing in particular, feeling almost numb as I continue, "Everett and I got along so well until another girl was admitted to the hospital. I started to talk to her, you know, just being friendly and all. But Everett didn't like it. He only wanted us to be friends only. That's when things started to get weird. He would corner me in the halls talking about government conspiracies. How they were trying to stop us from being together. How the government was all in on it and behind it from day one. I had no idea what he was talking about, so of course, I started to steer clear of him which only made him worse."

Ace rolls his shoulders with a heavy grunt. "Sounds like the guy's got any number of screws loose."

My head bobs rapidly. "You don't even know the half of it. It got so bad one day, he came into my room, tried to tell me we had to attempt an escape from the prison we were in. By prison, he meant life. He brought in a knife he somehow found and wanted us to slash our wrists because we were meant to be together. It was all so confusing. I don't know why he'd singled me out, out of everyone in the hospital. He just took to me, and he's been obsessed with me ever since."

Ace shakes his head. "So what changed? You were diagnosed two years ago. You've been out of the hospital for how long and living fine? Why's he coming after you now?"

I exhale. "I was released from the hospital when my meds kicked in. Luckily, he was pulled out before me. Unfortunately, in the hospital we exchanged phone numbers, so he kept in contact once I got out, but he was being kept under strict control with medication. But for the last... maybe six months, he must have gone off his meds because he's been getting worse and worse, his threats becoming weird again, until Dad took action to get me out of Grand Rapids and away from him. He's so unstable, so unpredictable. With Malcolm not really putting a leash on his son right now, we have no idea what Everett's going to do. If anything. He might be harmless, but he also might not. He showed me in my room at the hospital with that knife and wanting us to kill ourselves just how untrustworthy he really is."

Ace purses his lips. "I'm guessing that fucker, Malcolm, is trying to keep everything under wraps. Nothing like having a chaotic son as leverage for your opposition."

"Exactly, Malcolm wants it to be like Everett never existed. So he's trying to keep everything to do with him under lock and key. If we can dig up any information on either of them, to keep them both out of our lives, that might be the key?"

Ace lifts his brow in agreement. "Yeah, hopefully I can find something on one of them, so it'll keep them both out of your life. I started digging once your father told us a little about this in church, but now I know more." He dips his head. "I'll find something for you, Mylee. Leave it with me."

Looking to him, my eyes well... with happiness? I'm not sure. "That would be amazing. I'm so grateful. If you could help me bring down the Scotts and stop them from harassing me, I could have Everett out of my life once and for all. That would be utterly amazing. I wouldn't know how to repay you, though."

He waves his hand through the air, shaking his head. "Just being your friend is payment enough, Mylee."

I lean forward taking Ace into a tight embrace. He feels warm as he hugs me back. It's nice to feel a sense of comfort in my new home. I might actually be okay here after all with Lala and Ace.

Everything might actually be okay.

CHAPTER 8

TRAX

A shudder ripples through me as I watch Mylee lean in hugging Ace. Her arms wrap around him as his arms encase her body. Tension builds up making me want to hurtle something across the room. Or, at the very least, punch the motherfucking wall. But watching Ace and Mylee with each other has made something in me click, it's made me realize I'm jealous, and I don't fucking like that shit one little bit.

Though it was good to see her smiling before their talk got serious, it's taking everything in me right now not to march over and smash the ever-loving shit out of Ace for talking to my woman.

But she isn't my woman.

She can't be.

Movement grabs my attention, and I turn to see Torque step to my side raising his brow.

"What the fuck are you doing?" he asks curtly.

I tilt my head toward Ace and Mylee making Torque groan.

"If seeing her with other men is gonna be an issue, I suggest you don't creep around watching her. This is a club full of men, so she's gonna be talking to..." he shrugs his shoulders with a smirk, "... fuckin' men."

I groan shoving him as I turn to walk outside with him hot on my tail. "I know that, cockhead. Doesn't mean I have to like watching it, though."

Torque slaps my back. "I get it. You have to let her go and jump back on the horse yourself. Go spend the night with a club girl getting lost in some damn pussy." He tilts his head. "Or just swallow your fuckin' shit and *be* with her. Don't do this half in, half out shit."

Shaking my head, I exhale. "No, we've decided to be friends. It's better this way."

Torque snorts. "For who? Certainly not for you... you damn idiot. You proved that last night."

I groan as a car pulls up in the compound. Those of us who are outside turn to see the passenger door open and Ruby sliding out. All of us erupt in a round of applause while Mom gets out of the driver's side. We all crowd around Ruby to welcome her home. She looks pale but happy to see us as we all swarm around her. Her lips are parted, her teeth beaming bright white at the sight of all the fuss. Her face is glowing, showing her tanned skin for the beauty she is. But with that look on her face, she appears more beautiful. Even if not at full energy.

"Now c'mon boys, you didn't miss me *that* much, did you?" she calls out making me laugh.

Chains grabs her around the waist, picking her up causing her to giggle.

"You have to know we all love you, Ruby," Sensei calls out.

Freckles waves her hands in the air. "All right, enough. Let the poor girlie breathe, lads. She's just come home from being drugged by the Yakuza. Let her have some downtime, will ya?" Mom calls out in her Irish accent while pushing past all the burly bikers as we all make our way inside the clubhouse. "Chains, take her to her room, then leave. Don't ya dare try to get any. She's out of bounds tonight, ya hear me?" Mom demands.

We all chuckle. I don't think anyone had intentions of seeking solace in Ruby tonight, but it's good Mom made it clear.

"Thanks for everything, Freckles," Ruby calls out as she's whisked away while we all walk inside the clubhouse. My smile falls when I see Ace and Mylee still sitting together at the end of the bar. My eyebrows pull together tightly wondering if she's affected by me walking in here like I am just by seeing her. She glances up casually but quickly looks away again. I can't handle the damn strain. Walking to the opposite end of the bar, which is far enough away from them, I give it a tap needing a goddamn beer. As I sit down, I'm flanked either side as the seat next to me is quickly taken by Mom which effectively blocks my view of Mylee and Ace. She turns to look at me, raising her brow. The seat on the other side is taken by Torque while Cindi places beers in front of Torque and me, then walks off, leaving me with what looks like a family intervention. Well, that's certainly what it feels like.

"Surge tells me you have a new house guest. How are you goin' with that, boyo?" Mom asks.

I raise my brow to her with a sigh. "Honestly, Mom... you wanna talk about my love life?"

She exhales, turning to grab my face in her hands, looking me dead in the eyes which takes me by surprise. "I think ya need to get ya head out of ya ass. You look like a sour fuckin' fish." She pulls back lightly tapping the side of my face.

Torque bursts out laughing.

I huff. "Thanks for the pep talk, Mom."

She groans. "Trax. I love ya. You're my middle child, and God knows you're the hardest—"

"This talk isn't getting any better, Mom—"

"Shut up! What I'm tryin' to say is... this woman came back. Sure, she didn't necessarily come back for you, but fuck it, boyo, if she's here and she's willin'… 'cause God knows not a lot of women would be…" Torque chuckles making me glare at him, "… then stop bein' a dick. I don't know what's holdin' ya back. But I know something is, right?"

I let out a long exhale. "Mom, I can't. She deserves someone better than me."

"Bullshite! And ya know it. You're making excuses 'cause you're damn scared."

I scoff. "Scared? Scared of what?"

She sighs. "Bein' hurt again if she leaves. Trax, I know she hurt ya last time, but for God's sake, boyo, give yourselves the chance to make amends."

Torque grips my shoulder. I look back to him, tension swirling in my stomach as I gulp down a mouthful of beer. I have no idea what the right thing is to do. Do I follow my heart, or do I follow my head? I want Mylee. With every damn thing in me, I want her. But am I just being fucking chicken shit and using the fact that maybe I'm not good enough as an excuse?

I don't fucking know.

Not knowing what to say, I reach out for my beer, picking it up taking another long, deep swallow. The amber nectar hitting the back of my throat and sliding down effortlessly. It soothes my nerves. Makes me feel a little more at ease with this fucking 'family' conversation.

"Look, I don't wanna harp, so I'm not gonna. I'm certainly not gonna tell ya what to do, but Mylee and you are a good fit. Ya have history. The one thing I can tell from a mile away is ya love each other. Even after two years apart, the love's still there, boyo. Don't ya give up on it!"

I rub my brow as I lean against the bar while Torque does the brotherly pat on my shoulder again. "Okay, look, we're just saying we're with you, that's all. We wanna see you happy. But we also realize you two need to work at this on your own. So Mom and I are fuckin' gonna keep out of it... aren't we, Mom?" Torque urges making the corner of my lips turn up as Mom huffs in annoyance.

"Yeah, I suppose. I just—"

"Aren't we, Mom?" Torque affirms.

I smirk as Mom pouts. "Yes, boyo. I'll stay out of it as long as ya don't fuck it up even more."

I snort out a laugh. "I'll try my best."

She leans in planting a soft kiss on my cheek. "I only nag 'cause I care."

Torque and I both laugh. "I know, Ma. I know."

"Right, we got work needs attending to. You want in, or you wanna sit this one out?" Torque asks.

I raise my brow in confusion. "Why the hell would I want to sit this one out?"

Torque raises his hands in surrender. "Just making sure you don't wanna stay behind... keep an eye on Mylee and because of the shitstorm that was last night."

I scoff. "She's fine, Torque, she doesn't need a babysitter twenty-four-seven. As for protection from Everett, it's not likely he's going to visit anytime soon, and will you stop talking about last night. I'm fucking *fine*."

Torque shrugs. "Okay then... we ride."

I can't help but wonder what Mylee was thinking when she saw us walking out of the clubhouse—to know we were off on some mission, and I never told her where I was going. She's not my Old Lady, I don't have to tell her shit. Even though a part of me wants to confide every-fucking-thing to her, that's not my place, especially when right now I'm not sure we're even on speaking terms.

I'm such a damn idiot. I don't know whether I should have just fucking kissed her, so then at least I would have had the pleasure of tasting her lips again. I could have dwelled on that rather than regretting not kissing her. My head's a goddamn mess, but right now I need it to be in the game, not on Mylee, as the vibration of my engine rattles between my legs. Normally, going for a ride frees my mind, but not today. I have too much going on, too much to think about. I need to focus because we're heading into Triad territory, and even though these guys are on our side, you can never tell what shit might come flying at you at these exchanges.

We know that all too well.

Scratch rides first into the warehouse, shadowed by Torque, then me. The rest of the guys follow with Vibe in the truck covering our rear. I dodge the potholes filled with water as the roar of the engines echo through the large expanse. I see Harry Linn's telltale glowing Nissan Skylines parked three in a row waiting for us at the other end. Scratch is the first to pull up making the line. I draw to a stop kicking out my stand as I slide off my bike yanking off my helmet.

The car doors open, Harry and his goons step out patting down their tailored suits. I instantly smirk at the tiny man who grins widely throwing his arms open looking like it's his birthday, and he's the happiest he's been in ages.

"Fuckers... it good to see you! Torque, my main man," Linn calls out rushing over to Torque who's barely made it off his bike before Linn grabs my blood brother yanking him into a questionable back-slapping exercise.

Torque audibly groans grabbing Linn and pushing him back. "What have I told you about this shit, Harry?" Torque grunts.

Linn laughs with a shrug, a contagious gleam plastered all over his chubby face. "You know me... I like to push boundary with you. Little hug here, extra gun there... we be friend a long time you and me. We keep it that way, yes?" Linn chirps.

While shaking my head, I smirk in understanding. Harry Linn is one twisted motherfucker. He plays on the friendship for extra gain—his. *Typical.*

"We'll always be friends, Harry," Torque appeases.

Harry's smile falls as he stands up straight with a huff, folding his arms over his chest in what looks like anger. He signals to his men who suddenly pull up their weapons aiming them right at us.

My heart leaps into my throat as I reach for my Glock which is tucked in the back of my pants. Yanking it out at the same time as everyone else, I point it directly at Linn, my finger on the trigger lightly waiting to see what the hell is going on.

Torque's eyes frantically swing around the warehouse trying to figure out what sort of game Linn's playing at. "Linn, what the fuck?"

Harry stands in front of Torque, the only man in the warehouse without a gun in his hand.

Tension ripples through the air while his men continue their aim at us. We all set our sights on Linn, but no one's making the first move. My skin prickles with the turmoil that's happening in my brain. Linn's one of our longest allies. If he's turning on us, something's very wrong.

"You tell me something. Why you side with Andretti scum? I not sure I can continue our friendship if you friend with them. After all, they the ones who came in here and shot up all my men... you remember that, Torque. Yes? The day my men *die*, bullets riddle their body... for *you*?"

I swallow hard remembering that day well because we were, by all accounts, fucked. Locked in the warehouse with Linn's men surrounded by what we thought were Andretti Alpha Romeos shooting up the joint. It looked like we had no fucking way out. But we did, we made it out, all was not as it seemed.

Torque takes a step closer shaking his head. Linn's men aim their guns at Torque, but he doesn't flinch. "Thing is Harry, we've since found out those men, in the Romeos, weren't the Andrettis. They were wearing balaclavas, remember?"

"Yeees…" he draws out.

"They were the Yakuza driving Romeos which looked exactly like the fuckin' Andrettis and set them up to pit us against one another. It was all a big set-up. The Yakuza were screwing with us. But Enzo Andretti helped us rid the Yakuza from Chicago… actually, out of America. They're gone, Linn. We don't have to worry about the damn Yakuza anymore."

I glance to Sensei who's smirking as Linn takes in all this information. "Well…" he takes a breath, cracking his neck to the side, "… I can see now this been handled." He waves his hand through the air in response, and his men lower their guns making me release the breath I was holding.

Torque waves his hand through the air, and we all stow our weapons as I shake my head slightly in disbelief.

Fucking hell, talk about tension.

Linn suddenly bursts out laughing. He reaches out and places his hand on Torque's shoulder. "Oh, man, I sure had you going, Torque. I never shoot you guys. I think you too pretty to ruin your face, Torque," Linn jests reaching up and pinching Torque's cheek.

Torque pulls away from him dramatically. "Fuckin' hell, Linn, cut that shit out. Do it again, and I'll fuckin' pull the trigger on you myself," Torque murmurs.

I laugh as I glance over to Vibe, and with a raise of my chin, I let him know to start the transfer. He moves to the back of the truck.

"You too uptight, Torque. My gun ready? Yes?" Linn asks.

I gesture to the back of the truck beginning to walk off. Linn steps off but quickly catches up. "You're the brother… yes?"

I clear my throat. "Yeah, the better looking one."

Linn bursts out laughing, slapping my back playfully. "Oh, you pretty for sure. But Torque always be favorite."

I laugh while I glance back to Torque who's rolling his eyes as we walk to the back of the truck where there are three crates of

AK47s waiting. Linn jumps up into the back of the truck like a stealthy little ninja. He's fit as fuck! I hoist myself up with a little less flair. He gleams as he looks down onto the crates. "Real thing of beauty."

"They're ready to go. Serial numbers are scrubbed, same as every time."

Linn sighs running his hand over the guns like they're his long-lost fucking children. I have no idea what he does with so many guns, but he keeps us in business, so fuck if we care.

"Welcome home, babies," he murmurs under his breath, then he yells out something in high pitched Chinese. Immediately, a couple of his men spring into action and rush into the truck grabbing at the crates.

Ace jumps up in the back of the truck, his tablet at the ready. "Linn, we need to complete the transaction?"

"Sure, sure," Harry taps some shit or other into Ace's tablet. A bing sounds. Then just like that—Harry has his guns, we have our money. Another successful transfer.

"Thank you for your business, Mr. Linn," Ace says all business-like, and Harry winks and jumps down from the truck leaving me inside with Ace.

Inwardly, tensions rise inside me while I remember him with Mylee, he was the last one I saw with her before we left the clubhouse. The man who made me feel actual jealousy, the one to make me question everything. It's not his fault, he doesn't even know, but being in this close proximity with him is making my anger boil to the surface. I don't want to deal with my demon right now, so I go to walk past him and out of the truck when he steps up to me.

"Brother, thought maybe we could have a brew later? Talk to you about—" Ace starts.

Before he finishes, I turn walking off without uttering a word, bumping into his shoulder as I walk away and jump down from the truck hearing Ace mumble some shit. My head is all kinds of fucked up. I'm normally an action first kind of guy, but I don't want to be that guy right now. If I do that, I'll end up punching Ace for something he isn't even doing. So, I'm best to just walk away and say nothing right now. I hate Ace has the power to make Mylee smile, so for now Ace can cop my damn frustration. He's a big man, he can handle it. Maybe Sensei's Yoda mind tricks are working already, without even having a session with him, because for the first time, I was able to walk away before laying a blow. Maybe losing my shit the other night and realizing I went overboard was step one to caging my demon.

The thing is, though, he's not caged, not yet, so I gotta go.

Not waiting for the others, I walk over to my ride, kicking back the stand as I jump on. Torque looks to me, but I shake my head letting him know I'm not dealing. He seems to read something's up because he simply dips his head giving me the all clear to leave. I turn my bike over, swing out my back tire and high-tail it the fuck out of here. I need to get back to the club and away from this bullshit. I don't even care what my brothers think.

CHAPTER 9

TRAX

Walking into the clubhouse feels odd with so many of my brothers behind me on the ride back from our meet with Linn. But as I walk in, the smell of food hits me and my stomach rumbles as I walk up to the bar where Cindi and Hayley are starting to serve ready for our return.

"Hey! You guys back already? I didn't hear the usual loud roar of bikes?" Cindi hums placing a bowl of nachos on the bar in front of me. I scoop up a chip placing it in my mouth, the hint of chili burning my tongue mixed with the cheese and salsa. Chomping down on the Mexican feast, I swallow the delicious treat with a groan.

"Nah, rode in early, but the boys will be back soon."

"Good, 'cause the food's almost ready. We don't want all our hard work to go to waste, right Hayley?" Cindi prattles on, but Hayley rolls her eyes.

Dipping another chip into the hot salsa, I glance to Hayley who looks at me with a bashful gleam. She's always the quieter club girl—sweet, beautiful to boot, but reserved. Almost a little too timid for this place. But she'll find her feet, club girls generally do.

I reach out to grab another chip, but Cindi slaps at my hand with a chuckle. "Save some, you're gonna eat it all before your brothers arrive," she chides making me chuckle.

"Then they should hurry up because I'm damn hungry!"

She lets out a small giggle as she walks out the back to the kitchen swaying her hips. Hayley sets about pouring me a drink. I grab another tortilla chip, not caring about waiting as the roar of the unmistakable Harleys echoes out the back.

Now the dinner feast can begin.

It's Mexican night.

It tends to get messy.

Not sure why, but someone always ends up making a fool of themselves. Generally, a prospect who's had too many tequila shots. But it's fun, and we all have a good time.

Hayley places a beer in front of me, and I wink at her in reply. "Cheers, love."

She smiles as I hear delicate laughing coming from the hall. I turn to see Lala and Mylee walking into the clubrooms. My damn chest squeezes instantly.

Seeing Mylee looking cheerful makes me happy. She's wearing a pair of denim shorts and a simple white tank top. Fuck if she isn't the most delectable thing I've ever seen. Her blonde hair falls down around her round face perfectly. Her curvy hips swaying as she walks. She's fucking perfect.

Mylee looks up, her eyes lock onto mine. She stills for a brief moment, and I feel like I need to say something. Avoiding her is only hurting us both. Wracking my jaw from side to side, strength builds inside of me, and I find the energy within to make a move.

As I go to stand, Ace runs inside, jogging up to her and gaining her attention. Our eye contact is gone, so I slump on the stool as she beams at Ace. He hands her something then they turn walking off together. I don't miss his hand on her lower back as he leads her away. My hands ball into fists as I turn my back to them facing the bar feeling my gut churn at the thought of Ace having any-fucking-thing to do with Mylee.

Hayley casually walks up to me from behind the bar, placing a small whiskey tumbler in front of me with a weak smile. "Looks like you could use this," she murmurs.

"Thanks, beer won't cut it right now." The thought of having Hayley in my bed tonight is fucking tempting, the thought of scratching an itch that's been aching since Mylee showed up is tearing at my seams. But I can't find it in me to do that to Mylee. Even though I know we're nothing, not even friends, I can't fuck another woman while she's here. I know how fucking pathetic that makes me, especially if she's off screwing with Ace. *I swear to God I will gut him if they are.* My stomach knots, turning and churning just thinking about that shit.

I grab my whiskey, throw it back unrelenting, the three fingers in one fell swoop. The hit burning and leaving a woody spice flavor behind as the liquid slides down my throat. I need to eat, drink, and not think about my woman, who isn't my damn woman, with one of my best friends because this shit's going to mess me up even more than I already am.

Hayley walks over with another drink in her hand. Right now, I feel like I could kiss her. She tilts her head as she hands me the whiskey tumbler. I take it from her as she slides a bowl of nachos over to me too. "I'll keep the drinks coming if you promise to eat."

"Deal," I murmur.

I throw the contents back as my brothers all walk inside like the rowdy bunch of fuckers they are.

The clubroom erupts in noise as everything around me blurs in motion as I sit at the bar with my bowl of nachos and never-ending tumbler of whiskey. Just how I fucking like it.

Everyone's in full Mexican party swing. Foxy has the night off, so Torque's distracted. Sensei is too loved up with Sass. They're all too caught up in themselves to worry about what I'm doing, so I sit and drink.

One after the other, after the other.

My eyes begin to blur. I stop eating the nachos when my stomach begins to hate on me. My mind's churning. I haven't seen Mylee and Ace all night. I have no idea where they are, or what they're doing. But my mind can only think of one thing, and it's making me feel fucking sick. The thought Mylee is with one of my brothers makes me want to punch something, but right now I don't even know if I can walk let alone throw a decent punch.

I glance up to look at Hayley, her beautiful face nothing but a blur. I can barely make out the concern in her features as she slides a glass of water my way. I groan pushing it aside making the glass fall over, water pooling over the bar as she quickly dabs at it with a towel.

"Shit," she murmurs.

"I'm going to bed," I grunt.

She lets out a small exhale like she's actually relieved. "Do you need a hand?"

I chuckle as I stand from the stool, then proceed to slump over as the room spins. Hayley reaches out for me from behind the bar, but I right myself before I look like too much of a fucking idiot.

"I'm cool. All good. Just gonna head off to bed like nothing happened. Like she didn't rip my fucking heart out. It's all fine."

Hayley winces as I spin heading for the hall. Everything's blurry. There are people everywhere, all laughing, drinking, and having fun. The party's in full swing while I'm trying to make my way through everyone to get to my room. I know I'm stumbling as I bump into Tremor, who grabs my shoulders and straightens me up.

"Whoa there, VP. You good?" he asks.

"Nope. But I'm going to bed anyway," I slur.

Tremor chuckles slapping my back. "Good idea, brother, your eyes are going in different directions."

I snort out some kind of laugh as I push off him then continue down the hall. There are so many rooms. The doors all look the same.

Fuck.

Which fucking door is mine? I don't fucking know, I think it's this one.

After turning the knob, I walk in closing the door behind me. The room is dark as I stumble around, but suddenly a light flickers on. I jolt back slightly as I glance at the bed, and Ruby's face gradually clears in my vision. She looks sleepy. I look around the room in shock, scratching the back of my head in confusion. "This isn't my room?"

Ruby lets out a small laugh. She sits up in her bed pulling her covers back then stands, walking over to me. She still looks tired, but she's the Ruby we've all come to love and adore. She shakes her head with a giggle as she steps up to me, moving in to slide my cut from my shoulders. I raise my brow wondering what she's doing when she places it on her bedside table then begins to push me toward the bed.

I shrug, walking with her as she pushes me to sit down. So I do, just going along with whatever she's doing as she bends down, starting to take off my boots. I flop back on her bed, letting out a long groan as she laughs grabbing my hands, yanking me, so I move into the right position on top of her bed.

"Move over, you big lug," she scolds.

I chuckle shifting, so I'm on one side of her bed. She slides into the other beside me.

"There, that's better. Now close your eyes," she demands.

I shrug doing as she asks, my head hitting the pillow.

Oh, fuck! Shit! Everything spins, but after a while it's starting to feel like heaven as I sink into her soft bed relaxing.

Ruby leans over me turning off the light sending her room into darkness as she rolls onto the other side of the bed with a sigh. "Goodnight, Trax," she whispers.

Warmth floods over me, and I close my eyes.

Mylee's face is all I see, and contentment fills my drunken body. "Goodnight, Mylee," I whisper before I take a deep breath and darkness overcomes me.

The soft movement of fingers stroking my hair sends a soothing sensation through my body, even though the rest of me feels like I either want to throw up, or I'm spinning out of control. But that one simple touch makes everything calm down a notch. It's the only thing making me keep my eyes shut and stay exactly where I am. Everything in me hopes it's Mylee's gentle touch, her fingers stroking my hair as I lay on a bed that I know isn't mine. Memories of the night before wiped from my mind, and I have no idea what I'm about to wake up to. I don't know what I did last night, or who. But all I know is when I open my eyes, shit's about to get real, and if this isn't Mylee, I could be in for a world of fucking hurt that I thoroughly deserve.

Sighing, I man up opening my eyes to see Ruby smiling down at me. I weakly return her smile.

She giggles. "Morning, sunshine. How's the head?"

I groan raising my brow as I subtly look her over to see if she's clothed. She's wearing a pair of very unsexy pajamas. Then I look to see I'm in my shirt and jeans lying on her comforter on top of Ruby's bed. Inwardly, I take a deep breath relaxing knowing there's no way we had sex. "I feel like shit… how are you?"

"I'm actually feeling okay, but I'm guessing by the smell of whiskey radiating from every pore of your body, your head is pounding like a motherfucker. You were pretty wasted when you stumbled in here last night."

I glance up letting out a groan. "Shit! Did I make a dick of myself?"

"No, actually you pretty much passed out mumbling all night about Mylee."

Groaning again, I throw my head back in annoyance at myself. "Great. The picture of fucking masculinity."

Ruby snorts as she continues to play with my tousled hair. It's actually kind of soothing me. "Way I see it, you and her are going through something. You needed a moment. A night to gather yourself. Take some time out, Trax. Stay in here as long as you need. You know I'm good to talk to."

"I do, but I need a shower and some fucking grease to soak up this alcohol. Thank you for being there. Sorry, I crashed your first night home, I know you need rest."

"Actually, it was nice not to be alone. I wanted not to be by myself, then you walked in, well... stumbled. But in any case, I think we were here for each other last night."

I snort. "I don't think I did anything but fall asleep on your bed."

Her head bobs up and down a couple of times. "Exactly. It was just what I needed. Someone to be here with me. Just knowing you were here was all I needed. I didn't have the strength to help you back to your room, so I let you crash even if you did think it was your own room." She giggles.

Leaning up, I plant a chaste kiss on her cheek. Getting up from the bed, I move to grab my cut from the side table then pull on my boots. "Thanks, Rubes. And if you ever need me again, you know where I am."

Her face lights up in a genuine look of gratitude. "Same, Trax. Always here for you." She stands up walking with me to her door. As I open it, she leans in pressing her lips to my cheek. I turn just in time to watch Mylee walking past. She looks at us, her face falling as she takes in the sight—me leaving Ruby's room, and her kissing me on the cheek.

I want to tell Mylee it's not what it looks like. I want to tell her I didn't sleep with Ruby. But we're not a couple, so it's none of her business, and it's better this way. She should move on. I can't help the slight pang of pain rippling through me at the look on Mylee's face. I know how this looks. With how I was feeling last night at the thought of her being with Ace, she must now be feeling the same. Her bottom lip trembles as she looks at me. I stand stock still watching her watching me. Her eyes harden as she turns, scurrying away from Ruby and me. I let out a breath I didn't know I was holding.

Ruby sighs. "You gonna go after her?"

"Nah, I need a shower and maybe some more sleep."

Ruby winces but says nothing. She leans in giving me a supportive side hug then I turn walking out of her bedroom. Feeling like complete shit, I head toward my room to have a shower and wash away the alcohol from last night's bender.

I know exactly how Mylee would be feeling right now.

I know exactly how me walking out of Ruby's room would have looked.

But if Mylee is moving on, then so be it. It's harsh, but I'm not a nice man, I've never claimed to be. Mylee hanging out with other men, it's not something I'm okay with, especially when it's one of my fucking brothers. Perhaps she'll ease up on the friendship with Ace.

Or maybe I've just made everything ten times worse?

CHAPTER 10

MYLEE

Wrapping my arms around myself, I feel like a fool for ever thinking things could be different between Trax and me. I love him, there's no doubt, but I guess a biker doesn't change their spots. They love to get laid, and if I'm not the one giving it to him, then he's going to be getting it from somewhere.

Trax came out of a club girl's bedroom.

She was kissing his cheek.

There was no mistaking what I saw. He looked all kinds of disheveled, and I can only draw one conclusion—Trax had one hell of a wild night with her.

Trying not to let that fact get to me, I walk into the clubroom to see it brimming with activity. I notice Foxy sitting with some of the other girls, so I decide to sit with them. Time to make an effort. I walk over, they all look up at me smiling wide.

"Mylee! Sit! You have to help us plot the demise of our men," Foxy calls out.

"Umm... is that wise talk from the queen of the old ladies?" I ask as I take a seat with a giggle.

She nods while Sass and Neala's heads bob along with hers.

"Yes. We need to do something that's going to make them all cringe," Sass jests with excitement.

"Yes! I'm loving this. Making my brothers get all antsy is what I live for," Neala calls out, and I chuckle.

"You girls are mad. The Knights would slaughter their old ladies for pulling pranks on their men," I advise to which they all laugh.

"Oh yeah, we'll get in trouble, but it will be more than worth the punishment if you know what I mean." Sass beams a crooked smile then winks, which lets me know the punishment won't be with words, more with foreplay or some sort of bedroom kink. Foxy nods seeming to approve. Neala scrunches up her face appearing not to like the idea of her brother getting kinky with Foxy. I love the chemistry between these women.

"So what do you have in mind?" I ask.

Neala's eyes light up. "Something to do with eggs? Leave them out in the sun so they turn, then we can throw them at them when they least expect it," Lala coos.

What the fuck! We all shake our heads dramatically.

"No way. Can you imagine rotten eggs on their cuts? There's *no way* I want a part of *that* drama, like ever." Foxy giggles.

Sass laughs. "Yeah, too far... too far. I'm all for shits and giggles, but even I know that's pushing the boundaries."

Neala groans with a pout as I sit back watching the dynamics. "Fine, spoilsports. What about water balloons then?" Neala asks.

We all burst out laughing as I feel a tap on my shoulder. I turn to see Ace smiling down at me. All the girls quickly stop laughing as he looks at us suspiciously.

"You ladies causing trouble?" he asks.

"Of course, it's what biker women do, right?" I tease.

Ace tilts his head like it's the most truth ever spoken while the girls laugh behind me. As I look over his gorgeous face, he has his man bun pulled back but messily. He really is a sight to behold as he stands there looking down at me, all tall, muscles, and brawn.

After seeing Trax coming out of Ruby's room, I feel like I can allow myself a little extra time to appreciate looking at Ace. If Trax is going to play up, maybe I should too?

"What are your plans for the day?" he asks out of nowhere.

I shrug. "Not much. There's hardly anything to do around here other than work."

He purses his lips tilting his head. "What do you do?"

"I'm a website designer and tester. That's why I have a bunch of computer gear in my room."

His smile beams wide like a child on Christmas morning. It's like I've said something amazing to him. "I always wanted to look into website design. You think you can teach me some new techniques?"

Excitement grows inside of me, so I stand from my seat only now noticing the girls have completely stopped their conversation and are watching the interaction between us. "Yeah for sure," I reply as I look back to the girls who all raise their brows at me suggestively. In turn, I roll my eyes before I swivel and walk off with Ace with his hand on my back as he leads me toward the chapel. In all the times I've been here, I've never once stepped foot inside the Defiance chapel. I know it kind of goes against everything they stand for. It's not like women aren't allowed, it's just only certain people are supposed to be in there. I have no real idea why Ace is leading me toward it right now, but I'm just going with the flow. I trust him, so I'll take his lead.

My footsteps are light as I approach, and he opens the door leading me in. I feel like I'm breaking some cardinal rule by stepping foot on their sacred ground. He closes the door behind us. Suddenly, I feel like a giddy school girl. I can't contain my smile as I look around the room. The giant wooden table taking center stage in the middle of the chapel takes my breath away as he edges me further inside.

"I feel like I shouldn't be in here," I murmur making him chuckle.

"You really shouldn't, but my desk is in here. You kinda can't get to it otherwise," he tells me as he leads me to the back where I see his computer workstation all set up. We walk past some black filing cabinets, past his desk to see his elaborate computer equipment. *He really is a nerd.*

"Ohhh... you're showing me your man cave," I tease with a little sarcasm.

He lets out a loud laugh as he sits in the computer chair. I stand by him as he clicks on some keys to bring up something on one of his many screens. It's pretty much dark web shit from what I can make out, but he clicks out of it before I can see too much. I'm more about webpage design than the programming side anyway. Plus, I'm pretty sure what he does and what I do are two entirely different things.

"So, tell me. Do you use script when building a page? I just want to know what's the best way to go about it. We need some pages for our legitimate businesses. Torque wants me to build them, so I'm using those online web builders, but if I can do them properly, then I want to be able to. Think you can give me some pointers?"

"Well, yeah, but those online page builders can only do so much. You need to use HTML and CSS. Once you master it, you can really get around building a page much cleaner, which results in quicker upload and download times."

He smirks like I've said something funny. "I know a little about HTML. Okay, pull up a seat. We're gonna play around making a mock-up."

The tone in his voice makes me think he actually knows quite a lot about coding a website, and maybe this all might be a ploy to get me to spend some time with him. But I'll take it, it's nice to have a friend here.

Bumping into his side again with my shoulder, I let out a loud laugh. "No, stop. You're wasting time," I blurt out as he makes the GIF of a duck waddle across the screen.

He chuckles hitting the copy and paste key making another duck appear on the page.

I groan shaking my head. "Oh my God!" I laugh as I reach over him hitting the delete key frantically. He grabs at my hands to make me stop, pulling me to the side as we both laugh uncontrollably almost making our chairs topple over in the playful movements. I have to grab at my stomach I'm laughing so hard as he reaches out patting my back. I look up at him, our eyes connecting for a brief moment. His expression is glowing as our laughter dies down while we continue to look at each other. He sighs, finally looking away from me, back to the computer deleting the one remaining duck from the screen.

I let out another small giggle. "Fucking ducks!"

Ace reaches out pushing my shoulder playfully. He moves in grabbing the mouse absentmindedly about to save the file, but he's clicking on the wrong thing. He's about to upload the entire mess to the actual server. Our fake website has nonsense about ducks and biker terminology that's completely incorrect, and it's about to go live!

"No! Not that," I yell reaching out, my hand placing over his on the mouse to stop him. Then I lean him over to the right area to save the file instead of uploading the damn thing to the server. But in doing so, I'm leaning in really close, right by his side, so close I can smell his woodsy aftershave, and the stubble of his beard is tickling my cheek. I press my fingers against his on the mouse as closeness moves between us. He shifts his head slightly, so we're a little too close while I redirect him.

"There," I murmur, his face right against mine. Right at that moment the door swings open. Torque and Trax walk in, in the midst of a discussion about something.

I stand up abruptly even though I wasn't doing anything wrong, but it makes it look like I was doing something *completely* wrong.

Trax and Torque stare at me.

My stomach sinks as I watch Trax's face scrunch while he looks from me to Ace, shaking his head.

"Mylee what are you doing in here?" Trax booms.

Ace throws his hands in the air in surrender. "I brought her in here to show me some website tricks."

"You should've run that past me, brother," Torque grunts out.

Trax looks increasingly angry, the intensity of his stare grows by the second. My hands move in front of me, my thumbs rubbing together in nervousness as my body riddles in an uncomfortable tension. The air in the room frosts over as an arctic breeze shifts through the air.

Ace shakes his head. "This is on me, Pres. I brought Mylee in here. Don't lay her out for this. This is all me. We were doing tech shit, so I needed my computers."

Torque puffs his chest, but I can't keep my eyes off the reddening face of Trax. His eyes are what's scaring me, the darkness in them. He looks hurt. I don't know whether it's because I'm in here with Ace, or simply because I'm in here, in their sacred room, it's what's scaring me. I need to leave. I should never have been in here. A shudder runs over my spine as I look to the floor with a long exhale, starting to walk for the door. "Sorry for being in here. I don't want to cause any trouble."

Trax grunts moving forward stopping my movements. "Well, you should have thought about that before you fucked around with Ace."

"Trax," Torque warns as Ace stands from his desk rounding it to come and stand next to me, but it only makes Trax more agitated.

"What? Am I wrong?" Trax asks.

I find some inner strength, and looking up at Trax, I feel my confidence climbing. "What if you're not? What if Ace and I are fucking around? What does it matter to you, Trax? We're..." I point between him and me, "... only friends anyway. You've made that *perfectly* clear," I blurt out.

Everyone looks at me.

I'm normally the quiet and reserved one, but I'm sick of not standing up for myself.

Trax's lips flatten, his fists ball as he lurches forward.

Torque holds him back from getting to Ace.

"I swear to God, Ace, if you've made a move on her, I don't care if you're my brother or not, I *will* hurt you. I will *fucking* hurt you."

As Torque holds Trax back, I rush in front of Ace folding my arms over my chest in defiance. "You will *not* hurt Ace. He has been nothing but my friend since I got here, which is *far* more than I can say for *you*." I point to him. "The man I thought I could lean on, the man I thought I could fucking trust!"

Trax's body slumps, his face looks shocked. "You can trust me, you know that. Why would you say that?"

Anger boils inside of me as my mind wanders back to Trax coming out of Ruby's room. I move, pushing past him, trying to get out of the room. But Trax grabs hold of my elbow stopping me. I spin to look at him, my eyes hard and firm, his looking hurt and confused. Ace and Torque stand by watching silently.

"You slept with *her* while I was here. Then I had to watch you coming out of *her* room. I know you don't want to be with me, Konnor, but I don't need it rubbed in my *fucking* face how utterly *worthless* I am to you." I pull my arm free, racing for the door as Trax lets out a small grunting noise.

Thunderous footsteps stomp behind me as I run out the door and into the clubroom. I bump into Surge who steadies me looking down into my angry eyes as a booming voice calls out my name.

"Mylee, we're not done talking," Trax yells out.

My whole body's shaking with adrenaline as I spin around to see Trax standing in the doorway looking angry as hell. I notice everyone around the room has turned to look at us. Suddenly, everyone's looking at me, and I'm sure they're wondering when she's going to break. I can't stand it. I'm not that fucking weak, but I am that fucking angry, and I just need to get out of here. I need to get away from Trax as I breathe heavily.

Turning, I rush toward the exit so quickly I feel like I'm running faster than is humanly possible, but the booming sound of his footsteps behind me is unmistakable.

Somehow, I make it outside. The cool hit of air smacks me in the face, but before I have a second to think about where I'm going to go, two giant arms wrap around me from behind taking me in a giant bear hug. I try to fight him off in my temper, but I freeze feeling the warmth of his embrace as I fall back into his hold. I bring my hands up to rest against his forearms as he moves us back to lean against the side of the clubhouse. He says nothing, just holds me tightly, while I breathe in and out attempting to calm down.

He emotionally hurt me.

But somehow he knows how to make me feel better.

I don't know how, but he did exactly what I needed—he stopped the flow of my thoughts—my inner demons. The ones that take away all my self-confidence, the ones that remind me that even though right now I don't belong to him, he's still the one holding me. The simple effort of putting his arms around me, calming me, holding me, makes me feel like I have someone to lean on. Like I have the support I need right at this moment.

I breathe heavily as he leans into my ear and kisses behind it shushing me. "I'm here, Mylee. You're okay. Just breathe." I lean back against him closing my eyes and reveling in his warmth. Him holding me is calming the rage that built so quickly inside me. As I breathe slowly in and out at the same time as Trax, I can feel myself warming to him.

I sigh, finally leaning my head against his, and he plants a tender kiss against my ear. I melt into him. He's breathing heavily as he holds my back to his front. I can feel every muscle. He was always sexy, but I can't help but wonder if he's gotten even sexier in the past two years. Toned up even more. His arms have definitely gotten more bulk in them as they hold me to him.

I slowly release my grip on his arms. He reluctantly lets me go. I take a step away from him as he drops his arms, and I turn to face him. My eyes are heavy, my head is pounding.

His eyes appear concerned as I take in his worried expression. "Are you gonna hit me?" His voice is barely above a whisper.

My head shakes once as I let out a small breath. "Thanks for calming my anger, but it's you who put it there in the first place. You know that, right?"

He grimaces with a nod. "I know... I shouldn't have let you get to that point where you're so raging you have to walk away from me."

Looking away from him, I clench my eyes shut. "You just..." I clench my fists tight and open my eyes again. "You boil my blood with the shit you do to prove a damn point. And I know I wasn't supposed to be in the chapel, I know that's a thing, but Ace's computers were in there and—"

"Stop, Mylee! You think I give a shit about you being in the chapel?"

I raise my brow as he steps forward taking my hand in his. A tingle shoots through my very soul like always when he touches me. "Then what *do* you care about?"

He tilts his head like he's shocked I don't understand. "You... I don't want you latching onto Ace."

I jolt my head back in shock. "What the hell do you mean, *latching onto Ace?*"

He sighs running his hand through his hair. "I mean, I don't want you to form an attachment to him."

"But what about if he forms one for me?" I spit out.

He grits his teeth. "That can't happen, Mylee."

I scoff. "Oh, why the hell not? Who made you the king of who can and can't like me?"

He turns away from me, the vein in his neck looking like it's about to explode at any second from the tension. "I don't want you hanging out with Ace as much!"

I scoff throwing my hands in the air. "Oh, really? You're going to pull that crap on me? I don't think so, not after you had sex with Ruby last night just to rub this 'friends' shit in my fucking face, Trax!"

He bursts out laughing, storming up to me, grabbing my shoulders which forces me to look at him. My knees feel weak by the intense stare he's sending me as I look into his eyes. I melt slightly under his gaze.

"I did *not* fuck Ruby, Mylee. I stumbled into her room by mistake when I was so drunk trying to get *you* out of my damn mind. She let me sleep it off... *In. Her. Room.* You saw two friends this morning, nothing more. You made it into something that wasn't there."

I gasp my body almost going numb at the realization.

Trax didn't sleep with Ruby last night.

He's fighting the chemistry between us. We're not friends. We'll never be *just* friends.

My eyes water, my heart's racing as I look right at him, my bottom lip trembling. "Trax, I can't be your friend... I can't be here spending every day watching you talk to other women, wondering if you're with them. It will drive me..." I don't say the word, but he knows what I mean.

He leans his forehead against mine, both our breaths rapid and heavy. "I know. Seeing you with Ace fucking gutted me. I can't do this, though, Mylee. I'm no good for you. But you can't be here and not be with me. I'm not fucking strong enough."

I sniffle as his hand comes up cupping my face as we stare at each other, so close, our bodies are pressed completely against each other. "What are you saying?"

"I need you," is all he says before his lips crash to mine. Hard. Unrelenting.

I don't hesitate to let his tongue slide into my mouth. The moment we connect it's like everything clicks back into place. The stars align, my mind brightens, fucking fireworks explode as I wrap my arms around his neck needing him as close as humanly possible. I kiss him back, all tongues and teeth. The kiss is frantic, hot, heavy, full of need as he pushes me back against the side of the clubhouse with an oomph. I don't even care as he pushes his body against mine. In fact, I welcome this more aggressive side of him.

My hands thread through his hair as one hand of his caresses between my hair and my cheek while the other moves to my leg, lifting it up to hook around his waist. I can't help the small moan escaping my mouth as his obviously hard cock pushes into the seam of my shorts, which then presses against my clit. I'm so hot for him right now as emotions swirl through me.

I was so angry. At him.

Hurt too.

But it's all flowing away because of the amount of love I have for him. Right now, all I want is to fuck him. I honestly wouldn't even care if he took me up against the side of the clubhouse, I'm that needy as he rocks his hips into me making us both moan.

Suddenly a wolf whistle from beside us followed by cackling laughter makes Trax pull back breaking our hot kiss as I pant for breath, remembering we are actually in public. We both turn to see Chains and Lift grinning widely. Trax pulls me from the wall into his arms as he starts to lead us toward the door.

I clear my throat, a blush spreading across my face as I look to Chains and Lift who can't stop smiling while we walk past them inside. Trax chuckles while shaking his head as he bends down hoisting me over his shoulder. I let out a small scream as Lift and Chains start cheering. I laugh slapping Trax's toned ass as he rushes us inside then down the hall toward his room.

"You're a caveman," I call out as he thrusts open the door leading us inside, shutting the door behind him with his foot. He then slides me down his body, my feet hitting the floor as I let out a little giggle.

"Yeah, but you love it."

I bring my hand up to his cheek caressing his bearded face. I look into his sparkling eyes and sigh. "Remind me why I shouldn't have left," I murmur.

He moves in without hesitation, his hands shifting to the bottom of my tank top. He hoists it up and off me then he chucks it to the floor without a care in the world. His lips move in pressing to my collarbone as his hands snake around my back to unhook my bra, it too falls to the floor, freeing my breasts.

His lips travel down my skin, nipping and sucking as he goes, his fingers sliding down my arms as his mouth circles around my nipple. His teeth sliding against the taut bud, with just enough pressure to make me throw my head back in a moan while I press my chest further into his face.

My hands move in to roam through his mid-length hair. I tug on it slightly, pulling him back up in line with me. The lopsided grin I love greets me, and I lean in pressing my lips to his. I run my hands from his hair down his neck to his shoulders running my fingers under his cut. He lets me as our mouths collide harshly.

He backs me up against his desk, the backs of my thighs hit which makes me sit as he shrugs out of his cut. He grabs it before it falls to the floor, placing it beside us on the desk as my fingers make quick work of grabbing at his black shirt, pulling it over his head. Our mouths disconnect briefly only enough time for the shirt to come off.

I look down to see his chiseled stomach I've missed so much, his abs have gotten more defined in the last two years, he's definitely been working out. He looks fucking amazing as I notice that V leading into his jeans making me want to reach into his pants as soon as possible.

His hands move to the buttons on my shorts. He pops them open, gripping onto the hem, yanking them without a second thought along with my panties as I lift my ass off the desk to aid in his plight. I smile up at him as he drags them down my legs leaving me completely naked in front of him.

He suddenly drops to his knees in front of me as he grabs my thighs, pulling me forward. I let out a small shriek as I slide on the desk right to the edge, my legs dangling off, but he wastes no time as he throws my legs over his shoulders moving his head into position. I run my hands through his hair as he plants a chaste kiss on my thigh.

"Fuck! All I've thought about is tasting you again, Mylee," he admits.

Excitement bubbles up. I have to admit, I've spent many restless nights thinking about what this very moment reuniting with Konnor would be like. Right now I can't wait for this to get started.

His tongue flicks out over my clit. I throw my head back in delight with him finally touching me again. My teeth bite down on my bottom lip as he swirls his masterful tongue on my sensitive spot in just the right way—his tongue a precision instrument. He flicks and swirls as my hands slide down into his mess of hair gripping at it, holding him to me.

Soft whimpers echo from my throat as I ride the waves rolling through me. Moments ago I was over the top with rage and uncertainty, but now he's bringing me to a new kind of storm, a storm where the tornado is whirling inside of me threatening to explode at any second as I pant for heavy breaths. He flicks his tongue again, the warmth running through me as I gasp for much-needed air.

"Oh, Konnor," I murmur as my hips begin to rock against his mouth. A shudder runs down my spine as my back arches. I clench my eyes shut while flashes of light begin to strobe behind them letting me know my orgasm's on its way. Sweat beads along my skin as a wave of heat rolls over my body from the tips of my toes to the top of my head. I let out a raspy moan as my body shudders, my muscles contract while he continues to flick his tongue at just the right speed, and I explode.

"God, yes," I whimper as my body folds down on itself almost smothering his head.

He chuckles as he pulls me off him. I flop back as he stands up stepping in, sliding his hands under my ass lifting me from the desk in my very relaxed state. I slump my body as he hoists me from the desk pulling me around him. Instantly, I wrap my legs tightly against him as he carries me over to the bed. I can't help but feel his straining hard cock beneath his jeans. He's still far too dressed.

With my head flopped on his shoulder as he turns us toward his bed, I somehow find the strength to look up at him. He's grinning from ear to ear, and it fills my stomach with giddy butterflies as I look into his eyes.

"You better find some pep, baby, because I'm only just starting with you," he warns then throws me down onto the mattress.

I let out a squeal as I bounce on the soft cushioning while he moves his hands to his jeans undoing them, making quick work of pulling them down then off along with his boots and briefs. He stands up, his erection, long, hard, and fucking perfect. All for me. I gnaw on my bottom lip as I take in his gorgeous body. He truly is a work of art. His tattooed arms make me swoon as I shake my head in disbelief that I ever walked away from this man.

What the hell was I thinking?

I wasn't, that's the problem.

"You taste so fucking good, Mylee. I'm going to need a hell of a lot more." He licks his lips as he grabs his cock stroking it once, making my chest heave in appreciation.

He looks so enticing, I want a taste now, so I find the strength to sit up, rushing forward to take him into my mouth, but he puts his hand out stopping me.

He grabs my chin. "As much as I want your mouth on my cock, I need to fuck you. I've waited so long to be back inside you. I can't wait any longer. Get on your back. Pull your knees as far back as they will go," he commands.

I remember Trax's demanding side in the bedroom. I remember how much I loved it. I still do. So I scoot back onto the bed laying down, pulling my knees apart then back toward my head gripping onto them with my hands. He kneels on the bed. I'm panting with the anticipation of us being joined again. He moves in between my legs, grabbing my feet, placing them on his chest. His lopsided smile greets me as he tilts his head.

"Hold on," he instructs as I feel the tip of his cock sliding against my pussy, but before I have a second to prepare myself, he thrusts up inside of me. I gasp letting out a deep moan as my back arches off the bed in half-delight, half-shock.

His muscles clench as he grips onto my thighs, his nostrils flaring as he stills for a second, letting us both revel in the moment. A tingle shoots through me almost instantly. Being with Trax is all I've ever wanted, and as he starts to rock into me, energy ignites inside my body. Fucking Trax is so different than any other man I've been with. The chemistry is heightened, the emotions are charged, the pleasure undeniable as he pulls back thrusting up inside me again. He moves hard, deep. Both our breaths are quick and uneven as I move my hand from my knee to my breast needing a little more. I tweak my nipple making me moan as I roll it between my fingers. The pleasurable pain stinging through me as he pummels into me.

"Fuck, you're hot when you touch yourself," he groans, and I notice his face tighten like he's getting close.

He pushes deeper, a little faster, both our bodies building up a sheen of sweat as we rock together. His breathing becoming faster and faster. I can tell he's close, but suddenly he pushes my legs to the side, they fall as he slides down on top of me, moving into a more missionary position.

This is not the usual Trax. From what I remember, he likes to keep sex more dominant than sweet. But he moves over me, his eyes coming up to look down at me. He leans in pressing his lips to mine, his hands reaching out grabbing my wrists, pinning them beside my head.

There's my dominant man.

I wrap my legs around his ass as he thrusts up inside me. We rock together, his hands tightening on my wrists so tight it hurts, but in a really good way. His kiss is deep, passionate. He's letting me know how much he's missed me. How much he needs me. And I'm letting him know right back in the same way.

Through the kiss, I start to moan, the pressure building inside me. He's making me feel so damn good. I don't know if I've ever felt this fucking good during sex before. He's hitting every possible pleasure spot there is. Right now it feels like every atom in my body is tingling with adrenaline. I have to breathe. I need to let my moans out. I can't keep them in, so I break the kiss letting out a deep throaty moan. I know I'm being loud, but honestly, I don't give a shit. I've never felt like this before.

"Fuck, Konnor, don't stop," I almost yell as he rocks back and forth, his moans as loud as mine as we both strive for our climaxes.

His mouth connects to my neck. He nips and sucks as he fucks me until I'm completely breathless. I gasp for air, my eyes clenching tight while a light show performs behind my lids. A wave of warmth floods over me. I clench my hands, my nails digging into my palms as my muscles tighten, then explode in a storm of epic proportions.

"Konnor!" I call out as my muscles all contract around him causing him to groan out. He jolts a few times as his face falls into the crook of my shoulder and neck. His teeth clamp down onto my neck as he bites my skin hard enough that it will leave a mark. He thrusts up inside of me so deeply, I gasp as I feel his hot cum explode inside of me.

His body sags against mine as we both fall together panting and gasping for air. He's careful not to put all his weight on me, but he lets my wrists go. My hands immediately shift to his back needing to touch him. I rub his back, my fingers sliding up the silkiness of his skin while he lays on top of me as we both continue to ride out our high.

He takes a couple of deep breaths finally pulling his head up from my neck to look me in the eyes. His are brimming with delight, mine beam with happiness that I haven't felt in the longest time.

He brings his hand up as he slides a stray hair from my face, leaning in pressing a chaste kiss on my lips. "I love you... I've never stopped."

My heart fills with excitement. "I never stopped loving you either."

He leans in kissing me, then suddenly pulls back looking into my eyes. "I forgot to put a condom on."

I swallow hard. "We'll need to go to the pharmacy tomorrow morning."

A satisfied look crosses his face. "I should've known better."

I chuckle. "I should've, too. But we kinda needed each other."

"Yeah, but we have to use condoms from now on."

I smile like this is the most normal conversation to have while he's still inside of me.

"Yes. So, ah... I'm hoping like hell you have a stash of condoms in here, right?" I ask raising my brow.

That famous lopsided smirk is back on his face. "Why? You wanna go again?" he coaxes, his cock twitches inside of me.

I run my fingers up and down his back. "Oh, yes. We have two years to make up for, Konnor. Time we get started."

CHAPTER 11

TRAX

After spending all afternoon inside Mylee fucking her every which way possible, we eventually fell asleep. Having her in my arms again is the best fucking way to wake up. Sure falling asleep was never really the plan, but we wore ourselves out. I had nothing to do today anyway, so spending the time locked in my room with the woman of my dreams, well, what could be better than this right here?

The anger which had seeped into my bones seems to be ebbing since Mylee's here with me. Us, together, is having a profound effect on me. She's the calm I need within myself. She's the switch that turns off the raging fury in my mind. Maybe, even though she was the trigger to my self-destruction, is it possible she's now the remedy? Can one person be the cause and the solution? Can she be the single calming force in my life? The one thing I need to push me along on the right track.

My fingers gently stroke up and down Mylee's arm as I zone in and out of my semi-wakened state. I'm so relaxed I don't want to move a muscle as her slow, steady breaths let me know she's either asleep or extremely relaxed like I am as she cuddles into my chest. The sheets in disarray around us only make me feel whole again as I lay here staring down at her wondering how I got so fucking lucky to have met this bright spark of a woman. Sure, she has a complicated issue in her life, there's no doubt about that. Bipolar disorder is not something to take lightly. It's not something to sweep under the rug or be blasé about. But now she's on her medication, she seems to be doing better, much better than two years ago.

I saw the signs when she left the chapel. I could see the anger on her face. I knew she was having a moment, and I knew how quickly it could turn from anger to depression. So, instead of being a dick about her being in there with Ace, I knew I had to stop her from having a full-on episode. I had to calm her down using the only way I know. I had to stop the storm from even starting. I'm glad I managed to catch it in time before the downpour began. Once her brain kicked out of gear, and she fell over the edge, there would be no coming back for her.

I got to her in time.

That's the main thing.

I can't spend my time worrying about what might have happened had I not. What state she might be in right now if I didn't calm her down. Sighing, I gently press my lips to her temple as she murmurs slightly as if my movements woke her.

She slowly looks up at me, her sleepy eyes blinking a few times to gather her bearings. "Well, aren't you a sight for sore eyes?" she whispers.

I let out a small chuckle. "I should be the one saying that."

She shakes her head, leaning up gently placing a kiss on my lips before cuddling into my chest. She wraps her arm around my torso tighter in a locked embrace. "I wonder what the time is?" she murmurs.

I was wondering that myself. It's still daylight, but it's fading, so it must be getting late in the day. It might even be getting close to sunset. "I don't know, we've been in here for a good few hours."

She giggles. "Sooo worth it."

My fingers still trailing delicate lines up and down her arm as I take in a deep breath. But a rumble roars through the room. I peer down as she stiffens, then looks up to me placing her hand on her stomach. "Shit."

I chuckle smiling at her. "Was that your stomach?" I ask as she purses her lips. "You're hungry?" I have to admit we've been in here through lunch, and I'm pretty sure it's now dinner time. I'm fucking starving.

She turns up her nose, running her hand up my chest. "I'm so comfortable, I don't wanna go anywhere."

I snort out a laugh. "Woman, I'm not letting you go hungry. We've spent all day in here. We need to fuel ourselves so we can continue fucking into the night."

She lets out a loud giggle, slapping my chest playfully as I sit up from the bed. As I jump from the edge, I pull her up with me. She groans but moves as I walk to my clothes to put them on. "C'mon, get dressed 'cause you're sure as hell not going out there like that."

She pouts, rolling her eyes moving to her clothes, starting to pull them on. "For the record, I would rather stay in here and cuddle."

I snort. "For the record... I don't cuddle. I'm a badass biker. I fuck, I comfort, but I don't fucking cuddle."

She bursts out laughing, shaking her head. "Think what you want, badass... we were just cuddling! But your image is safe with me. I won't tell."

I smirk, giving her a wink. I know I was cuddling and honestly, I don't care. I'm just messing with you. I wouldn't be caught dead cuddling with any woman on earth, but with Mylee, I'll make an exception. She makes the inner protector in me want to come out. Everything in me makes me want to hold her at every chance I have. If I could permanently have her in my arms, I fucking would. Sure, I sound like a pussy, but it is what it is. This woman has me by my balls. She has had for years. I don't think she even knows the power she holds over me. Now she's back, and we're reconnecting, it's like the animal inside of me has stepped back inside his cage. Like my demons are diminishing and the need, the thirst for blood, for war, doesn't sit on the threshold watching, waiting to burst through.

For the past two years I've been crazed, a man possessed. Going out of my fucking mind because a part of me was missing—that part of me was Mylee. Right now, the rage isn't consuming me as deeply. The thirst has been quenched, not by blood, but simply by her. She's my missing piece. I don't know what I'm going to have to do to keep her here. I've only just gotten her into my bed. I need to find a way to keep her in my life. I have no idea how long she's going to be staying at Defiance, but I'm going to make it permanent.

Somehow.

I finish pulling on my clothes, then turn to see she's dressed. So I grab her hand edging toward the door as we finally walk out of my room for the first time since this morning. We walk down the hall into the bustling clubroom. As we step in, everyone turns to look at us with bright smiles on their faces as they all begin to cheer. Mylee's hand tightens in mine as she leans into my side. I glance to her to see her face flush, but she's trying to hide her smile.

I turn back to my brothers. "Shut the hell up, fuckers!" I call out, letting go of Mylee's hand, wrapping my arm around her shoulder pulling her into me.

Glancing up to look at the television hanging from the ceiling, I see a picture of Miller Willbrook flash across the screen with 'missing' in big letters. The sound isn't on, but I exhale knowing it's official. The man I lost myself to is now a ghost in the wind. He'll never be found, and it was all for fucking nothing. I tighten my arm around Mylee's shoulder. I did it for her, but we still have no leads. The rage may not be consuming me, but in the chamber with Miller, it took hold, it devoured me. It's where I realized I needed to change.

For my brothers. For Mylee. For me.

A sense of regret washes over me as I tighten my grip around Mylee. "C'mon," I whisper as I lead her over to where Torque's sitting with Chains and Sensei already eating their dinner. I gesture for her to slide onto the seat. I move in next to her as Mylee is glancing around the room assessing everyone. Mylee looks up at Torque who's equally assessing her.

She takes a breath as she clears her throat. "Torque... I'm sorry for being in the chapel."

I grip onto her hand for support. Torque puts down his fork and knife to concentrate on this conversation, looking right at her. "Ace gave you permission. I trust him. I trust Trax. They trust you..." he smiles, "... so I'm okay with it. Just don't take anything you see in there out of there. If you need to help Ace, maybe have him bring his laptops out here so you can work with him on them. Chapel's kinda sacred... you understand."

"I totally get it... club brat, remember?"

Torque sits back in his chair. "So now you're telling off is done, and you and Trax seem to be mending fuckin' fences finally, can we get on to celebrating?"

I raise my brow. "Celebrating what?"

"Celebrating the idea of you returning to your old self now your woman's back, and you guys figuring your damn shit out."

Mylee looks to me lovingly, and for all intents and purposes, we have figured our shit out. I finally feel like we might be in a good place.

CHAPTER 12

TRAX

Six Weeks Later

The last month has been fucking perfect. Mylee and I have been in a good place, and everything seems to be running smoothly as I sit with her in the clubrooms eating our lunch peacefully.

Sensei's been working with me using the art of Zen to help stream my thoughts and let them pass without becoming physical. He told me suppressing my anger is as bad as letting it out, but that somehow I need to tone it down. Using Mylee as my muse, he's been able to find a way for me to think differently. Think about her when my demon decides to show it's ugly fucking face.

Sensei said that my anger is a cover for the explosive feelings I had toward Mylee leaving, and as such, it manifested as a physical reaction. So, when the demon begins to take hold, Sensei came up with the idea of not allowing the anger to surface. Instead, I envision Mylee's face and some deep breathing techniques to calm me the fuck down—so far it seems to be working. Hopefully, now things will even out. He's been supportive and helpful and shit appears to be back on track. It's funny how the thing that made me angry in the first place is also the one thing that can bring me to true Zen.

Talk about irony.

Along with my visualization and breathing techniques, I'm also using boxing to help with the physical side of my demons. It helps get my physical stress relief out, so I'm not bottling up my emotions. I'm dealing with it. Even talking about when Mylee left with Sensei seems to help. A kind of therapy, I suppose. He should think about becoming our wise one if Surge ever wants to give up the role in the club. Sensei'd be good at it.

Suddenly, I'm broken from my thoughts when Torque strides over with a stern look on his face. He reaches out grabbing me by my shirt and hoists me up.

"What the fuck?" I blurt out as my sandwich drops from my mouth.

"Come with me," he instructs as Mylee chuckles seemingly unfazed by my brother's obnoxiousness.

I walk with him toward the chapel and note that Sensei, Surge, and Chains are already in here, and I let out a long huff knowing something's up. My thoughts immediately go to Mylee, and this Everett douche as Torque shuts the door behind me.

"Has he found her?" I blurt out, all breathing techniques and Zen out the fucking window. They all look at me furrowing their brows.

"No, this isn't about that," Torque replies cracking his neck. "The Andretti's are coming in for a meeting."

Opening my eyes wide, a breath catches in my throat. "They're what?"

"Not to discuss business, but about returning the damn favor we owe them. They've helped us a couple of times. Apparently, Enzo has something he needs help with... urgently."

Tension rolls through me as I glance at Sensei and Chains. "And you guys are okay with this?"

Chains shrugs as Sensei exhales. "They helped a great deal with my family, Trax. I feel we owe them... whatever the cost," Sensei replies.

I wince. "What if it's women? We know they deal in trafficking, that's not our scene, brothers. Honestly, I want nothing to do with that shit."

Torque nods. "That's why it's a meeting, and I haven't agreed flat out, but they'll be here any minute. I just wanted you to know before they arrived that they're gonna be asking for our help with something, and we *should* be prepared to give it."

Groaning, I nod once as a knock on the door thuds, and Chains opens it to Zane. "Italians are in the clubhouse," he murmurs.

Torque exhales. "Best behavior, boys."

Chains opens the doors to the chapel, and we all walk out to see the Andrettis filing into our clubrooms. I'll never get used to seeing them here in their immaculate pinstriped suits and shiny fucking shoes. Those gold chains, though, those things are just crazy. They look like a mixture of corporate business associates and a gangster music video. *Fuckers.*

I've also noticed that everyone who doesn't need to be here has vacated. It's only the patched members and the Andrettis as if it were a church meeting in the chapel, only the Andrettis aren't allowed in the chapel. We need to keep some things sacred.

"Torque, thank you for meeting with us at short notice." Enzo steps up to Torque and shakes his hand, but there's no humor in his tone or playful banter like normal.

Something has him rattled.

"A pleasure as always, Enzo. Let's have a seat, and we can discuss what's going on." Torque gestures for the wooden benches that Foxy always calls the summer camp seats. We sit down like normal, brothers on one side, Mafiosos on the other, and I take a deep breath looking over Enzo's features. He appears tired. Worn. Defeated.

This isn't the Enzo we know.

Someone's getting to him.

"Tell us everything," I demand.

Torque looks to me raising his brow in a look of surprise, but seeing Enzo like this has me rattled. I want to know what has this man, who's normally so full of vigor, so full of vengeance and venom, alarmed.

He's shaken.

Agitated.

Exposed.

Enzo exhales placing his hands on the table linking his fingers together in a tight ball. "The thing is, Torque, I know *you* know about our... darker endeavors."

I sit up a little taller as Torque sits forward. "Go on..."

"Women trafficking isn't the most..." he pauses but looks straight at Torque like he's unashamed, "... honorable of transactions. I know this, Torque. I know where you stand on it, too. But you have to understand, and I know you do, that family tradition is of the utmost importance in our kinds of *associations.*"

Torque shifts uncomfortably as he glances at me, and I take a deep breath knowing exactly what he's saying. We followed in our father's footsteps for most of Defiance's endeavors, including our war with the Andrettis. He's saying he's just doing what his father did, and that includes trafficking women.

"So you're saying you don't want to traffic women, but you do it because of your legacy?" I ask, and Enzo looks to me with a mild smile.

"You honor Guiness's name every day in the things you do, Trax. I try to do the same for my father."

Torque lets out a long exhale. "We ended our war, that wasn't in your father's legacy. You can stop this too, Enzo."

He sits back nodding his head, a forlorn look on his face as he rubs his brow.

He looks defeated.

I've never seen him this way.

"Enzo?" Torque softly states his name, and Enzo sits back up looking Torque in the eyes.

"They have Zia." His voice comes out like a breathy murmur.

Furrowing my brows, I glance to Torque who sinks down like he understands what he's saying. "Who has your daughter, Enzo?"

In shock, I jolt back a little. I didn't even know Enzo had a daughter. I knew he was married, but as far as I knew, he didn't even like his wife let alone have a child with her.

"The Scarsi Dettagli. They're another division of Mafiosos running the underground in Illinois. They were the ones helping us get the women down to Miami, then onto a speed boat to Cuba, to be... distributed."

I shake my head. "Why would they take your daughter?"

He sighs. "That's why I need your help. I thought with the changes we've been making like joining forces with you, changing the way our fathers have been doing business over the years, that we could attempt to get out of the trafficking market. The Scarsi Dettagli didn't want the Andrettis leaving the business, and so I had to pay a debt." His lip curls up as his fists clench together, his knuckles turning white. "They didn't tell me what that debt would be."

Torque groans. "It was Zia?"

Enzo cracks his neck. "And now my eleven-year-old daughter is somewhere in transition, and I have no idea what those fuckers..." he takes a breath, "... *are doing to her.*" The last four words are almost a whisper.

My hands ball into fists, and I stand up suddenly, my knees hitting the table with force. "We'll get her back, Enzo. She can't leave the country."

Enzo glances to me as Torque raises his brow in a look of surprise. I've never been an Enzo fan, but fuck if I'm going to let an innocent eleven-year-old girl suffer for the sins of her fucking father.

"We have time, they groom the girls before they take them to Miami for the boat. But I was thinking if we go in all fire and brimstone and take her, they will just come after her again. Then us. Then you."

I sit down rubbing the back of my neck. "What if we played them at their own game?"

Torque and Enzo look to me like I've lost my damn mind. "What the hell does that mean?" Torque asks.

"What if we trade them a girl... for Zia? They get a girl, we get yours back?"

Torque scoffs as Enzo raises his brow. "We're not finding some poor girl to trade, Trax."

I smile. "Not some poor girl, a willing girl. Someone who will go with them to get Zia back, and knows we'll buy her when she's up for sale. Someone who knows we will do everything to make sure she's safe. Well, as safe as she can be. It has to be someone who's got something they need, and will happily exchange."

"Do you have a girl who's gorgeous and can cage fight?" Enzo questions.

Everyone opens their eyes wide as if they're contemplating this idea.

"Yeah, that could work. Probably not Hayley, she can fight, but she's too timid to pull it off successfully. But Cindi could definitely get the job done. She not only has the acting skills, but she's one hell of a fighter," I advise.

"Yes, girl can move. I've watched her train," Sensei states.

Enzo winces. "They'll probably demand sex from her."

We all grimace as Torque nods. "I'll talk to her. I won't *tell* her to do this, though, Enzo. She has to *agree* to of her own accord. I can't make her, you have to understand that?"

Enzo nods. "I understand, and if she can't?"

Torque looks to me, and I smile. "Then we go in with hellfire and fucking brimstone."

Enzo rolls his shoulders. "I want that as our last resort. If we do that, they'll just keep coming."

"I hear you. We'll play this right. We got your back, Enzo." Torque leans out shaking Enzo's hand.

"Siamo una famiglia, Torque. It's taken us a long time to get here, but your family is my family."

Torque nods. "We are family," Torque replies, and I take a deep breath as we all stand.

"I'll get back to you as soon as I've discussed this with Cindi. If she says yes, I'll have your guys prep her for everything the Scarsi's will put her through. Then we need to find a buyer. Someone who isn't linked to the Andrettis in any way. Leave that part with us."

Enzo straightens out his suit and sighs. "I'll wait to hear from you." He turns signaling to his men, and they all walk out of the clubhouse as I turn to Torque along with Sensei, and we collectively let out a long exhale.

"Holy shit."

Torque looks to me and nods. "Holy shit is right. I have no idea how the hell I'm gonna sell this to Cindi, but she loves this club and will do anything for us. Though this... this might be one step too far."

I roll my shoulders. "She might actually be able to pull this off without it affecting her."

Sensei nods. "I agree. Cindi is strong, and one thing I learned from my times with her is that sex means nothing to her. Her skills as a fighter are second to none. She's the best match in this case. I don't think this will be an issue. Just a role to play."

Torque shrugs. "Well, I guess I'm gonna find out. In the meantime, keep the club running normally, go about your daily routine. I don't want shit to fall apart. We need everything here to run smooth, especially for Mylee and the other women. No one should know about this, other than the patched members."

I nod. "I appreciate that. Mylee doesn't need any damn drama, especially with the threat of Everett already lingering."

"Take Mylee out today, she deserves it. She's been cooped up here for too long. Take her somewhere nice before things get hectic," Torque adds.

"Right, will do."

"Do you wanna prospect on your tail?" he asks.

"Shit no. I got this, bro. I want some alone time with my woman."

He smiles slapping my back as I turn. "Now Sensei, I want to talk to you about your father, Hiro," I hear him saying as I walk off heading for my room where I know Mylee will be.

Opening the door, I can hear Mylee's on her cell. I step inside trying my best not to listen in to her conversation with who I assume is her dad, Crest, but it's hard when we're in the same room. Not that I'm complaining. This is where she belongs. Hell, if I had my way, all her stuff would be in here, but she's kept her room down the hall in case she needs it for work or whatever. I get that. But nights she spends with me as it should be and as much of her time as possible during the day.

Having Mylee at the club has made me feel calmer, less on edge. Even Torque's said he's seen a noticeable change in me. It fucks me off that one woman can have *that* much power over me. I knew when Mylee left, it broke something, but having her back makes my world complete. The two years without her was hell. I honestly don't know how the fuck I survived. Having her here now is a whole new kind of pleasure. I'm a man on cloud motherfucking nine, and I don't care who knows it. Plus, Mylee's fitting in here at the club so damned well. Already, it's like she knows and is close with everyone. She just fits.

Mylee's still talking to Crest, and I can't help but overhear. "Yeah, the tech guy, Ace, he's been looking into the Scotts while you're dealing with your shit, but so far he's not come up with anything substantial, there's nothing out of the ordinary. They're pretty much aboveboard from what he can tell," Mylee relays to her father which grabs my attention as I lean on the edge of my desk. I watch her as she sits on the bed staring out the window. I sigh, standing up and walking over to the bed taking a seat next to her. She turns to look at me. "Yeah. He'll keep looking. Don't worry, Dad. We've gotta find something, somewhere, to get Everett off my tail."

While I need this Everett guy to take a long fucking leap off the closest cliff, so Mylee's safe, what I don't want is for her to go back home to Grand Rapids once the coast is clear. My chest fucking aches just thinking about it. The thought of losing her again once this mess is sorted makes me tense, so for now, I need to make the most of the time I have with her. I need to let her know how much she means to me. And after hearing Enzo's daughter is missing, it only brings home how quickly things can change.

"Okay, thanks, Dad. I'll keep you posted. Talk soon." She hangs up her cell, looking at me as I reach out for her hand.

She laces her fingers with mine and sighs. "Dad's worried I'm spending too much time away, that you'll get sick of me being here."

I snort out a shocked laugh. "Are you kidding? If I had my way, you'd never leave."

Her beautiful face lights up like a fucking summer's day while she leans in pressing her lips to mine, then she kisses me briefly before pulling away. She purses her lips like she's deep in thought. It's fucking cute.

"What's going through that mind of yours, Mylee?" I ask.

She relaxes her shoulders. "Why were we all made to leave the clubroom when those suits came in?"

"Club business, nothing for you be concerned about. We need to help them with a little problem they're having. Okay, time to get out of those pajamas. I wanna take you somewhere," I tell her. "Get dressed... jeans, a leather jacket. We're going for a ride."

She bounces slightly on the bed and smiles. "Oh my God, Trax, I haven't been on the back of your bike in so freaking long. I always loved the feel of being behind you." All her thoughts of the Andrettis vanish as she bounces in excitement.

"Then stop talking and more getting ready." I slap her thigh while standing from the bed as she giggles excitedly, rushing up to run from my room at the fastest pace I've seen her move. She heads down the hall to her room to get dressed as I chuckle and gather my shit. I know exactly where I'm going to take her.

I gather my things together, grab my cell, and head to her room. I look through the door to see her jumping around yanking up her jeans. Warmth floods through me as I lean against the doorframe, just watching her. She's so fucking cute completely oblivious to my voyeurism. Then she rushes to the closet grabbing her leather jacket, flinging it on. I can't stop grinning as Mylee races about like she's in some fucking marathon. She runs back into the closet reaching out for a pair of ankle boots then flops on the bed lifting her foot up in the air. I let out a small chuckle which makes her head jump flip around in shock, and she gasps.

"Shit! You scared me." She giggles while continuing to pull on her boot but at a slightly slower, more normal pace.

I fold my arms over my chest. "You're fun to watch when you're excited."

She snorts, grabbing for her second boot and pulls it on. "Well, I haven't gone out anywhere since I got here, and getting on your bike as well... so yeah, I'm a little freaking excited, so sue me." Once she's done, she throws her arms out to the sides beaming wide. "Ready!"

I stand up straight. "Then c'mon, woman, let's get the fuck outta here."

She bobs up on her toes then races past me out of her room into the hall, taking off in front as I walk behind her, looking down at her round ass in those tight-as-fuck jeans she's wearing. Christ.

My cock jolts in approval as I look up before I change my mind and take her back to my room instead.

We walk into the clubrooms, and I see Torque off to the side. I grab Mylee's hand leading her toward him. She understands, following my lead as we step over to my blood brother.

He looks up nodding as we approach. "You heading out now?" Torque asks looking us over.

Mylee sways from side to side.

"Yeah, for a bit. We'll be back later."

Torque rolls his neck. "Keep an eye on your six. Any problems, call."

Tension rolls through me with the Andrettis in strife and Everett looking for Mylee. This may not be the best of ideas, but Mylee's been cooped up, and it was Torque's idea to take her out. If he didn't think it was okay, he wouldn't let us go without a tail.

"Got it. I'll let you know when we're on our way back."

Torque gives me a two finger salute. I smirk as he turns, walking off leaving me with Mylee. Mylee looks to me gnawing on her bottom lip like she's worried.

I slump my shoulders with a heavy sigh. "What's wrong?"

She winces. "Should we not be doing this?"

"Probably not, but I want to take you out. You deserve some freedom, Mylee, and where I'm taking you is safe. Nothing's going to happen to you. I won't let it."

She grips onto my hand. "I know."

"Good, let's go."

Having Mylee holding onto me while riding is exactly as I remember.

Fucking perfect.

She holds on with just the right amount of grip, moving with the bike at the exact right times. She's made to be an Old Lady, and I swear she's heading that way. We just need to figure out what the hell is going to happen when shit's over and done with—with this fucking Everett character—and where Mylee's going to be based. If I claim her, she'll have no choice but to stay in Chicago. But I need to talk to Crest about that first. She, by all rights, is Notorious Knights' property. She belongs to their club, not Defiance, so me claiming her is a big fucking deal.

She can't swap clubs without permission.

I know that.

There's a process.

It needs to be done right.

And if I'm going to do this, I need to make sure I do it the right way. But I have time, time to think this through, time to make a plan. Time to grow a set of balls and talk to Crest because taking his daughter from him is fucking massive.

I pull into the parking lot of Garfield Park Conservatory. Basically, it's a massive greenhouse filled with exotic plants and shit. Not a normal place for a biker to hang out, but I know Mylee will love looking at all the unique crap. Plus, it's a place full of people, usually school kids on excursions. So in my mind you can't get much fucking safer than this, right?

Bringing my bike to a halt, I kick out the stand, the loud rumble vibrating to a stop as I switch off the engine. The buzz from the ride waning as Mylee slowly releases her grip and slides off the back of the bike. I grab my helmet, yanking it off as she stands up tall pulling hers off. Her hair is swaying from side to side like something from a Hollywood movie as she places the helmet on the back of my seat as I stand up. We attach the helmets to the bike securely as she looks over to the large building letting out a small huff. I can't tell whether it's a shocked huff or a disappointed huff. So I turn to face her to see a smile broaden on her face, and I'm instantly relieved as her eyes twinkle.

"Never thought I'd see the day you'd come to a place like this, Trax."

I raise my brow. "Well, I'm just shit full of surprises, baby."

I reach out pulling her to me making her let out a small squeal, and then she giggles. We start to walk toward the entrance. I can't help but notice the teacher from the school tour that pulled up at the same time as us staring us down like we're some thug lowlifes threatening to tear their world apart.

Who the fuck cares what they think. So we walk straight past them, the kids staring at my club cut in awe as I wink to them, the teacher gasping while we continue to step up to the entrance. I waste no time heading inside. There's no admission fee, but you can make a donation, so I walk up handing over a fifty.

Mylee's eyes light up as I grab her hand and we walk through the lobby. It smells fresh, like a rain forest, and we haven't even gotten inside yet.

"Trax," Mylee murmurs.

"Yeah," I ask stopping at the door.

"Thanks for this."

We step over to the door, and I push on it, the temperature difference in the room hits me first as we step inside to see a giant room decked out like a palm paradise. The massive room has a glass roof, the heated temperature mixed with the mass of palm trees makes it look like something from Jurassic Park. I glance to Mylee, the sheer look of awe on her face makes coming here worthwhile. Her bright green eyes sparkle with such luminous intensity as her mouth drops open taking in the magical sight in front of us. Watching her is far more impressive to me than looking at the scenery.

Her eyes dart all over the place taking everything in as her lips turn upward, making her dimples sink in further. Her perfect teeth glisten making her glow like a ray of fucking sunshine.

"Oh. My. God... Trax, this place is amazing."

She turns to look at me like a giddy little teenage girl. I knew she needed something to make her smile. She needed something to get her out of the clubhouse, so coming here seemed like the right thing to do. I reach down grabbing her hand threading our fingers together as I start to walk us along further into the palm jungle. Her free hand stretches out wafting over the palm fronds jutting out from the path as she shakes her head in disbelief.

I love seeing her like this.

So happy.

So carefree.

It eases the tension about what's happening in our lives. Sure, right now everything's going okay, but eventually, something's going to shift, something will happen. News of Everett will change the mood, and his efforts to find her will increase. Or something will be done about him, and Crest will want her to go back home. Eventually, this happy bubble we're living in will come to a screeching halt.

Then what?

She leaves, and I go back to being *that* guy? That broken shell ready to take my vengeance out on the world and anyone in my fucking way. Hell, that guy even fucked me off. I like this Trax version better. I'm calmer around Mylee. I don't know how, but she soothes me as much as I soothe her.

We make our way through to the Fern Room. Mylee's eyes light up again as the sound of a waterfall trickles in the distance, and she tightens her hand in mine as her eyes widen in awe. "Trax, you've outdone yourself, bringing me here... this gives you *big* bonus points."

I let out a small chuckle. "That's the plan, to woo you with my suaveness, so then you'll suck me off later," I tease making her laugh.

Mylee slaps my chest with a roll of her eyes. "Trax, remember there's kids," she chides.

I smirk turning back to Mylee pulling her to me, leaning in I kiss her temple. "I still want a blow job when we get back, though."

She bursts out laughing. "I think I can schedule you in." She winks as we walk together through the room toward the waterfall. I look around at all the kids in the room while holding Mylee in my grip, and I can't help but wonder what it would be like to have a family one day. I want nothing more than to put my kids in Mylee's belly. But there's this thing about Mylee. Before she left last time, she told me in no uncertain terms she never wants kids.

Mylee's mother passed her bipolar disorder onto Mylee. It's genetic in her family. Her children will possibly develop the illness in their lifetime. She never wanted to be responsible for putting the burden on another human being. So she confided in me she'd never have children. Being with her means never having a family for us. But, that's the price you pay for being with the woman you love. I'm sure if we stayed together, and we wanted kids, there's other ways we haven't discussed.

But again, I'm getting way ahead of myself. Just seeing all these kids in here is making me wonder, making me think, what if? My life always planned for Mylee to be in it. When she left, I went off the rails, we all know this. Now she's back, and I want to make plans.

With my mind wandering all over the place, we finally make it to the waterfall. I look up at it, the water trickling down the rocks, crashing, making a soothing sound that's calming my raging thoughts. I move in behind Mylee wrapping my arms around her from behind as she looks over the waterfall in awe. She leans back against me, and I take a moment to just be here with her. I let all my thoughts disappear, and when she sighs, I press my lips in behind her ear as she turns her head to look at me.

"You know, I had no idea today could be so freaking perfect."

I hold her a little tighter. "Perfect, hey?"

"Yeah. I'm so fucking lucky to have you. The perfect blend of badass and teddy bear."

I chuckle, gripping her a little tighter again making her let out a little squeal. "Teddy bear? You ever say that shit again, and I'll spank some sense into you, woman."

She giggles turning in my grip, her fingers running up around my neck and into my hair. "Fine, more like an untamable lion... that any better?"

I tilt my head curling up my lip. "Marginally. But don't say this shit in front of my brothers."

She snorts throwing her head back with laughter. "God no, they'd slaughter you."

I poke her in the ribs making her jolt as she continues to laugh at my expense. "I should slaughter you. I let you get away with far too much."

She looks back to me, her eyes meeting mine. "You can teach me a lesson when we get back. I've been very, very, naughty and need some punishment."

My cock strains against my jeans as I let out a small groan. Leaning in, I grab her bottom lip with my teeth biting it. She giggles kissing me.

Eventually, I pull back remembering we're in public, there's children about, so I break away opting to take her hand once more. "Stop taunting me. Think of the children, Mylee."

She bursts out laughing again as she turns to face the waterfall. "Sorry, I'll just admire the pretty flower..." she pauses. "Weird how there's only one. It's like it's a rare occurrence or something for a flower to sprout up right there."

Without hesitation, I bend down picking the little white flower from behind the railing. Mylee gasps as I bring it up handing it to her. She purses her lips like she's scared we'll be busted as she looks around.

"Trax, what if they've been trying to grow that for like fifty years or something, and you just killed it?" She twirls it in her fingers looking happy as shit that I did it for her even though her words say something different.

"You said I was half-badass. I needed to prove I was full-badass by breaking the rules and destroying shit."

She lets out a small giggle as she brings the flower to her nose giving it a sniff. "You do realize... yes, it was badass, but Trax, you picked me a flower that was sweet and by definition *not* badass at all. So your effort to go full-badass was actually only half-badass because the act itself was half..." she smiles "... teddy bear."

I groan as I throw my hands in the air watching her eyes light up as she giggles. "Goddammit, I can't fucking win. That's it, I'm gonna have to do something real fucking manly tonight to make up for this shit! I need to go shoot something or punch someone. Maybe I need to wrestle a fucking bear. Will *that* give me my goddamned balls back?"

She plants a kiss on my cheek. "I can think of something I can do with your balls to make you feel like a man if you like?"

I groan again as I feel a gentle tap on my shoulder. I turn to see an elderly woman looking at me sternly, her eyes hard, wrinkles framing her face making her seem older than I think she is. I look down to see she's wearing a uniform with the Conservatory's name embroidered on it. Not only that, she's flanked by two security guards. I raise my brow smiling my cocky lopsided grin, but she doesn't budge, not even a bit. Normally ladies melt, no matter what age. *Shit.*

"Excuse me, sir, I don't want to make a scene, but we've had a couple of complaints about you and your *friend*..." she accentuates the last word, "... being a little too overly affectionate, talking inappropriately..." she looks to the flower in Mylee's hand, "... and I see we can add destruction of property to the long list. We would appreciate it if you would respectfully leave the premises."

My chest swells in anger. I brought Mylee here to show her a good time. I wanted today to be special, and this upstart old bag's going to kick us out? No fucking way!

"I think what you mean to say is... this your first and final warning, and you can continue on. Have a good day," I comment.

Mylee reaches out grabbing my hand, shaking her head as the old woman looks a little rattled. "Trax, it's fine. I've had the best time." She looks up at the old bag. "Your place is really lovely. I'm so sorry we caused a scene. We didn't mean to. We'll leave right away."

"Mylee!" I warn.

She looks to me with pleading eyes. "I've had the best time. We're pretty much done anyway. Let's not ruin it." Her big doe eyes look up at me, and while I want to make a fuss—I want to fight this shit for her, I want to be able to stay so she can see the rest of the place—but if she's ready to leave, then I guess I'll let it go.

The two security guys sneer, and I raise my head in defiance. "You will *not* be escorting us out. You don't need *that* scene on your hands, boys. We'll leave."

The woman signals to the guards, and they turn walking off as the woman looks to me with a sigh. "For the record, I have nothing against bikers, but if the visitors complain, I can't look to be playing favorites."

I raise my brow tilting my head.

She looks around then rolls up the sleeve of her uniform to reveal a property patch tattoo.

Mylee giggles as I smirk. "Bullshit!" I let out a laugh finding newfound respect for the old woman.

She quickly rolls down her sleeve. "Going on forty years. Married into it. Wouldn't change it for the world. My old man had to give up riding only a few years back when the arthritis kicked in. His hands are too far gone now. That's when I started working here to get some extra cash flow." She looks to Mylee. "Bikers take care of their women, girl. If you're in, hold on tight, it's a bumpy ride, but hell if it isn't worth it."

"Oh, I know... club brat."

"Mmm, the best kind. Sorry for the formal talk, had to do it in front of security."

I wave my hand through the air like it doesn't matter. "Forgiven. I hope the flower wasn't an issue."

She chuckles. "The flowers are rare, but it's going to a good cause, so I can let it go this once. But you best be off before security comes back to drag your asses out."

"Cheers!" I grab Mylee's hand and head toward the exit. Mylee looks to me, and I smile. "What are the chances?"

She shrugs. "I really liked her. She has lady balls."

I laugh. "Yeah, guess she would. Most old ladies do."

Mylee's eyes narrow looking like something's running through her mind. I don't want to ask her what considering we were just talking about old ladies, so I let it go leading her out, back out to the parking lot toward my ride.

"Sorry shit got cut short, I wanted you to see it all."

She twirls the flower in her fingers. "Trax, stop! I had the best time. Even at the end when I thought it was turning to shit, it turned around and surprised me. Today's perfect. Utterly perfect. I haven't had this much fun in a really long time. To be with you is all I've ever wanted."

My chest swells with pride, so I grab her, pulling her to me, and smash my lips to hers kissing her strongly. Her arms wrap around me. Our tongues collide in a flurry of passion. She lets out a small whimper as a fit of giggles echo from beside us, making me pull back from Mylee to see a tour group of kids. Fuck! Their faces alight with glee at the frantically kissing couple while their teacher ushers them away.

Mylee smirks as she grabs my shirt, pulling me to my bike. "We really need to stop kissing in front of children. We're going to scar them for life."

Grabbing our helmets, I restrain myself from kissing her once more. I slide onto my ride, and she moves in behind me, the motion feeling like she's done it a million times as she glides into place perfectly while I start the engine. The roar of the Harley erupts to life making the school kids all turn to look at us. I know my baby demands attention when she purrs, I don't blame them for looking.

I hammer down, pulling out of the parking lot leaving the kids behind as I make my way out onto the road to start the fifteen-minute trek back to the clubhouse. The wind flicks past me, my woman gripping my stomach. The summer sun reflecting off the asphalt is making for a warm, leisurely ride. I'm taking my time. Having Mylee holding onto me again while I ride is an all-new high, so I'm going to milk it for all it's worth. Even if it makes me look like a fucking Sunday driver. I'm going to enjoy this casual ride, nice, easy and clear, with the wind blowing and the relatively free-flowing traffic on the highway.

I'm just about to pass under the Ogden Avenue overpass when suddenly, a sedan flies past the bike at crazy speed. The shift in air making the bike waver as the car darts in front of us, then turns into the right hand off ramp forcing me to have to drop my gears to avoid a collision with the fucking idiot. My heart leaps into my chest as I rush down trying to bring the bike to a stop before we hit the motherfucker, but before I have a chance to work fast enough, another car comes up behind us, racing at full speed as if to try and catch up with the first car. It too turns for the off-ramp, but in doing so, the edge of the car catches the back wheel of my bike.

My ride slides out to the side, out of control. Mylee's grip on me tightens, but we're both flung from the bike as it hurtles over. I can't catch myself as Mylee's grip on me is forced away. We both fly from the bike, barreling toward the ground. I smack the asphalt with a thud. The moment of impact, my body aches and shudders as I roll in on myself with the force. I hear the unmistakable sound of crunching metal from my bike slamming into the ground which grates on my ears. I let out a loud groan as I roll, letting my body go limp remembering, the more you tense the worse it will be. So

I try to remain as loose as possible while my body takes the full impact of the hard asphalt. My jeans rip and tear, my leather jacket holds together, but my arm jars as I groan out in pain finally come to a tumbling stop on the road.

My body is throbbing all over. I hurt in every possible place I can think of, but I push it all aside when my mind instantly flicks to Mylee. I hear screeching tires, people are stopping to help, but I don't care as I somehow find strength, climbing to my feet as I glance around to find Mylee. I yank off my helmet, throw it to the ground, my ears ringing as I look near the bike. It's a fucking mess, the back tire almost completely gone, but then I see Mylee in a crumpled ball next to it. My feet don't fail me as I grab my arm. It hurts like a bitch, but I drag my feet, one foot in front of the other trying to get to her.

She's not fucking moving.

"Mylee!" I call out as fear fills every inch of me so hard, so fast, it's almost crippling me. But I rush as quickly as I can to get to her.

She's facing away from me, but I drop to my knees as I reach her. Moving in, I yank off her helmet—I know it's probably the wrong thing to do, but I need to check if she's fucking breathing. A slight moan echoes from her beautiful mouth as she clutches her stomach.

I pull her into my lap, looking her over to see if I can see anything. "Shit, baby, where are you hurting?"

She finally opens her eyes, they're glassy as she stares at me vacantly. It scares the shit out of me. "My stomach hurts, but so does my leg," she murmurs, rolling on her side a little more making her leg turn. Then I see a giant gash with blood pooling from her thigh.

It's only now I register the sirens and the massive amount of people surrounding us. Traffic has ground to a halt on the highway, and somehow the police are already here as I look up to see two officers running toward us. One squats down beside me, while the other is on her radio calling for an ambulance.

"We have help coming," the officer relays looking directly at Mylee. I slump feeling like I have no idea what the fuck to do.

"It's fine, I'm fine," Mylee murmurs.

I let out a scoff. "Bullshit! We need to get you checked out. You're not going anywhere but the hospital, Mylee."

The cop's head bobs up and down. "I agree. Your leg's probably going to need stitches at the very least."

She slowly sits up in my grip, shaking her head as she moves to stand. "I'm fine, I promise. No need to fuss."

I scoff. "You're going to the hospital. Don't argue this with me, woman."

She huffs as she stumbles on the asphalt looking a little woozy as the cop looks to me. "I think you should probably get checked out while you're there, too. You came off hard," he advises. "Can you tell me what happened?"

I look back to the scene where my bike's fucking totaled, and the two cars that caused the accident are nowhere to be seen. "There were two cars, one sped past us cutting in front making me slow down, thank fuck. Then the other came in behind him, bailed me up as he was trailing the other car. They were moving fast to get somewhere, I don't know what the fuck they were doing."

The cop winces. "Running from us. We got a call about a burglary. We were in pursuit in a high-speed chase. Unfortunately, I think you're the collateral damage. They're from a street gang and are known to us. When we saw they'd taken you out, we stopped to help. They got away, but we know them. Don't worry, they'll be charged with fleeing the scene of an accident. Amongst other things."

I glance to Mylee as she stumbles again, but this time she starts to fall. I reach out grabbing her, pulling her to me as panic floods through me. "What's wrong?" I ask as she looks at me, her eyes unfocused and glassy.

She waves her hand through the air. "No, I'm fine, I promise. I just feel a little queasy. My tummy's all tight."

The cop looks to me with a concerned gaze then stands up walking over to his partner radioing something into his coms equipment. Concern floods through me, too. I can't help but wonder if Mylee's hurt more than just her leg. She said her tummy felt weird. I'm starting to wonder if she has some internal shit going on. I'm starting to think the cop thinks this, too. "You're gonna be fine, babe, just relax," I tell her easing her into my lap as I sit and pull out my cell to send a message to Torque.

Me: *911, ride totaled, taking Mylee to hospital. Meet me there.*

I hit send as the ambulance pulls up, and they rush over. My body aches like a bitch, but I don't care about me right now. I only care about my woman and getting her to the fucking hospital where she needs to be right now. The paramedic bends down to look at Mylee, smiling at her.

"I'm Michelle. I can see your leg's injured, but are you feeling pain anywhere else?" she asks Mylee.

"Not really pain other than aching everywhere from the fall, but I feel nauseous, and my stomach's tight."

Michelle looks at me as if to assess if I'm in need of medical assistance.

"Don't even worry about me, just take care of Mylee for now. We need to take her to Northwestern Memorial. No exceptions," I demand.

Michelle raises her brow, looking at my club cut. "Okay. Let's get you in the ambulance, okay?" She gestures to Mylee as my cell begins to ring.

Michelle grabs Mylee from my lap and starts to walk with her toward the ambulance. She's unsteady on her feet as she hobbles, but I take the moment to grab my cell. It's Torque. I figure I better answer while Mylee's getting in the back of the waiting ambulance. "Hey," I murmur.

He lets out a heavy sigh. "What the hell, man? You can't send a text like that. What the fuck's going on?"

"We got tangled up in some fucking high-speed chase. Not us. We were the collateral damage. My bike's toast… Mylee's hurt. She's getting in the back of an ambulance now. I gotta focus on Mylee. Can you send a crew to get my bike? I gotta go with her."

"Yeah, of course, brother. Shit! Are you both okay?"

I run my good hand through my hair. "I don't know, man. Mylee's going to Northwestern. Can you call ahead, tell Kline we're coming in. I don't want anyone but Bex on Mylee."

"You got it! I'll send Vibe and Chains to get your ride. Sensei and I will be at the hospital… Trax, you okay?"

I rub the back of my neck. "Yeah, brother. Let me get back to my woman."

Torque mumbles, "See you at the hospital."

I end the call and walk over to the back of the ambulance where Mylee's now on the gurney. Michelle looks down at me. I raise my brow in an unspoken question. She dips her head in understanding. "You'll have to sit in the front with Havier. We'll be leaving in a minute, so I suggest you get in."

I glance up to Mylee. Her eyes are closed, and I wonder if she's deteriorating or if she's just resting. I really hope it's the later. Pain fills in my chest, but I turn walking around to the front of the ambulance and hobble in. Havier's sitting in the driver's seat punching some shit or other into some machine. I close my door, turning back to look at Mylee as Michelle takes her blood pressure, working on her silently.

"Hey man, can we get there quick? She was complaining about her stomach. I'm not a doctor, I don't know anything about medical shit, but I'm worried about internal injuries," I ask Havier quietly.

He jumps out of the seat, rushing to the back of the van. He leans in whispering something to Michelle, probably so he doesn't startle Mylee. Michelle nods, then Havier closes the back of the ambulance racing back to the front, jumping in and starts the engine.

I take a deep breath as Michelle starts to talk to Mylee asking her what the pain level is in her stomach. I crack my neck to the side hoping like hell I'm fucking wrong about this being worse than it looks.

CHAPTER 13

TRAX

The ride to Northwestern didn't take too long. Then the admittance seemed to take merely a flash. Kline was alerted to our arrival, so she must have arranged priority. *Thank you, Bex!*

So right now Mylee and I are in a bay in the emergency ward. Mylee's on the bed, her face pale as she lies quietly. I'm beside her holding her hand with my good arm, the other I'm favoring, trying not to let on that it's hurting like a bitch. But honestly, I think I've just pulled the muscles in my shoulder, nothing too bad. It's definitely not dislocated or anything.

The curtain slides back, and Kline rushes in. Her blonde hair pulled back in a high bun, her slim face with a thin layer of makeup making her already pretty features stand out even more. She smiles at me then she pulls the curtain closed behind her letting out a heavy sigh.

"You totaled your ride, Trax? How will you live without your baby?"

I chuckle as she walks over placing her hand on my bad shoulder making me wince slightly. She notices straight away frowning. I look straight at Mylee. "I can get another bike, Bex.

What I can't get is another Mylee. So make sure to fix her real good, yeah?"

She smiles as Mylee sighs. "I'm fine, honestly, so much fuss over nothing."

Kline instantly looks at Mylee's leg. "Well, that's a lot of blood pooling on the bandage, Mylee. I'm going to have to have a closer look. But when I'm done with Mylee, I'm going to check you out, Trax. No arguments."

I groan knowing I won't win with Kline, she's one of the most stubborn women I've ever met. "Fine."

She shoves me out of the way without a second thought. She's never been one to care about bossing bikers around. "Okay, so I'm going to check your leg for starters then I'm going to run a few tests, check for concussion, then examine your stomach, okay?" Kline asks.

I step back right out of the way. I don't want to interfere with anything as Mylee simply nods. The pain in her eyes evident.

I promised her nothing would happen today. I promised her the perfect damn day, now here she is in a hospital bed being poked and prodded. I just hope it's nothing more than a simple gash on her leg and we'll be home in a couple hours.

Kline goes about taking her temperature, her blood pressure, pressing on her tummy, then tending to the wound on her leg, and ending it all with a blood test. I say nothing, just sit back wincing when Mylee jolts in obvious pain, but I don't do anything to stop Kline from her work.

She's the best.

I know it.

I glance up as the curtain slides slightly to see Torque and Sensei standing in the entrance. I tip my chin to them as Kline continues to work with Mylee, so I look to Mylee. She glances at the curtain and smiles with a nod, letting me know it's okay for me to fill them in.

Standing up, I walk, more like drag my feet to them. They nod in unison as I slump past the curtain out into the main area with them away from Mylee.

Torque rolls his neck. "Jesus Christ, Trax. Way to scare me half to fuckin' death."

I smirk, slapping his shoulder. "Fuck, brother, anyone would think you cared about me saying shit like that."

"I'm not even going to joke around, Trax. You and Mylee... coulda died. By the look of you, you hit the deck damn hard. I'm not gonna fuck about and pretend this isn't a big fuckin' deal."

We've had some tough times over the last two years, but through it all, we're still blood. Even though I've been a dick, somehow he still cares. I don't know why.

"Yeah... it was damn scary. All I can say is luckily it was low speed. After the first car pulled in front of me, I was able to slow the bike enough not to make this turn out a whole shitload differently. I'm still not sure something isn't up with Mylee, though, but Bex is on it. Me, I'm fine, big bro, just a sore shoulder. I remembered to go limp."

"Stop, drop, and roll is not just wise for fire... as it were," Sensei adds, and I chuckle.

"Yeah man, exactly. Just let my body go floppy and hang on for the damn ride."

"Glad you both came out relatively unscathed as it seems for the most part anyway. We will wait to see how Mylee is doing, but for now... I'm fucking pleased you are both breathing at least," Sensei offers.

"Hmm, yeah, I think if the car had hit us any harder, we would have been toast. I'm just glad he clipped the tire and didn't ram us completely. If he'd gone straight into the back of Mylee..." A shudder runs through me as I swallow a lump in my throat not able to finish my sentence.

"She'll be fine. You both will be. At least it was just an accident... nothing malicious... not Everett related is what I'm saying," Torque adds.

"I have to admit, at the time, it's all I was thinking. But once the cops explained, I knew it was simply wrong place, wrong time."

"Chains and Vibe are bringing your ride back to the graveyard. We'll look into getting you another bike tomorrow. But for tonight, you be here with Mylee," Torque tells me, and I nod—like there was any other option. Torque looks me up and down shaking his head. "Sure you're fuckin' okay? You look like shit."

I roll my shoulder, cracking my neck to the side. "I'm fine. Just hurt my shoulder. Nothing too serious. A few cuts and scrapes, nothing like Mylee. I'm concerned about her stomach. I know Kline was prodding and poking around. She's running bloods, but I have no idea what she's thinking. She's not giving any-fucking-thing away."

Torque exhales reaching out grabbing my good shoulder. "I'm here for you. Whatever you need."

"Thanks, brother. Right now I need to get back to my woman."

Sensei and Torque both nod as I turn, moving back toward Mylee's bay. I slide back the curtain to see Kline finishing up with Mylee as she grabs the blood tests. "I'm just going to take these to the lab, but then I'm coming back to look you over."

I chuckle. "Yeah, yeah."

She walks out as I make my way over to the edge of Mylee's bed. I look down at her then take a seat, running my fingers gently over her arm.

Her lips turn up but only slightly, looking at me sleepily.

"You doing okay?" I ask.

"Yeah, Dr. Kline gave me something for the nausea and pain. I'm feeling quite lovely right now actually."

I chuckle leaning in kissing her forehead as I rub her tummy. "You good in here?"

She shrugs. "Not sure. She's doing some blood work to make sure everything's okay. When she pressed on it, she seemed to think nothing was ruptured or that there's anything too nasty going on, so that's got to be a good thing. Probably just winded."

"That's great. Now you lay back and rest, I'm not moving from here."

She looks up to me gently stroking my arm. "How's your shoulder? You were favoring it. I know it's hurting."

"Nothing gets past you, does it?"

She shrugs. "Nope, nothing. Now stop avoiding it and tell me you're okay."

I lean in kissing her head as she melts into me. "I'm fine. I'm pretty sure it's just a strain and some scratches, you're the one who really got hurt in this." My mind's racing through how I'm going to tell Crest what happened. "Your dad's gonna annihilate me."

Mylee chuckles with a grimace. "Guess he's not going to be happy, but I'll make the phone call once we know everything. It'll be better coming from me, and he knows how much you love me, so I'm sure he'll be fine."

I tense up. As much as I want to be a man and tell Crest myself, Mylee knows her father better than me, even though I feel like I know him well enough. If she feels it's better coming from her, then I need to respect her wishes. I don't want to be on Crest's bad side, but I also don't want to get on my woman's bad side either. Especially not when I want to convince Crest to let Mylee stay with me.

Now with her being injured, I've made everything a shit ton harder.

Kline came back in and looked me over like she said she would. She fucked about with my shoulder making it even worse, but told me it was a sprain after I had an X-ray taken, and that it will heal on its own. She patched up my cuts and scratches even though I complained the entire time, much to Mylee's amusement.

As Kline puts the last butterfly stitch on my arm, she leans in gently slapping my chest. "Good boy, see wasn't so hard, was it?" she mocks.

I let out a loud huff. "I thought the guys said your bedside manner was excellent. I think you're quite rough actually," I tease. She leans out flicking my recently bandaged wound. "Oww, woman!"

Mylee giggles behind us as Bex stifles her own laugh, standing up from her rolling stool as she pulls off her rubber gloves with a swift snap. "It's not too late to fake your death Mylee and run. I can help you with that," Kline mocks making Mylee burst out laughing.

"You're lucky you're club family, Kline, or I swear…" I look at her with my lopsided smile as she grins.

"Yeah, I know, I push my luck with you guys. Chains grills me for it all the time, the big lug."

She starts to walk out, but I grab her hand halting her exit making her turn back to look at me. "How are Mylee's tests coming along?"

"I'll put a rush on them, I should know in a couple more hours. I'll make it as quick as I can, okay?"

I let her go as she walks out of the room.

Torque and Sensei step in.

"We're gonna head out. I need to talk more to Cindi about…" He tilts his head, but I know what he means. "But if you need us, let me know."

"Thanks, I'm grateful you came."

"Anytime, but there's some other people here to see you, too."

I raise my brow wondering who the fuck's here. "Who?"

"Brodie and Grier," Sensei replies.

"As in Brodie and Grier the cops that helped us out with the Yakuza?" I ask.

"Yeah, fucking small world. They're the cops assigned to take your statement. We've just had a catch-up. Told 'em what you told us, but they need it from you... obviously."

"Yeah," I glance back to Mylee to see her sleeping soundly. "I'll head out to talk to them. Let her rest. Might see if they have any ideas about what we can do about this Everett problem we seem to have while I'm at it."

MYLEE

Trax and I are sitting in the emergency room, my bay seems to be one of the larger ones, and I can't help but feel lucky in this situation. The club knows Rebecca Kline, one of the head doctors here, so my treatment has been exceptional. I can't complain. Even though I hurt all over and I'm beyond tired, I still feel a sense of love and warmth from the Defiance MC. Knowing Torque and Sensei came to check in not only on Trax but me too, makes me feel like I'm a part of their family, even if I've only been here for six weeks. I love this club, I love the people, and I have to admit the idea of staying here is kind of the only thing on my mind right now.

Trax sits on the edge of my bed looking down at me as he gently strokes my arm. The adoration in his eyes is insurmountable as I stare back knowing exactly how he's feeling. We could have lost it all today, in the blink of a damn eye. One or both of us could have died, or been severely injured. I guess we need to be thankful we came out with nothing more than a few deep scratches.

Trax opens his mouth to say something as the curtain slides back, and Kline walks in making him stop as a pensive look crosses her face.

"Mylee, your blood work showed some results. So I've run some further testing just to confirm." She looks to Trax, then back to me making my tensions raise a little higher. "Mylee, are you okay for Trax to be in here when I tell you what's going on?"

Trax suddenly stands from the edge of the bed, obviously feeling the tension like I am as he looks to Kline shaking his head. He turns reaching out for my hand as I sit up a little taller.

Suddenly I feel like something's really wrong. I grab Trax's hand tight, mine shaking in his feeling scared. "Yes, I don't want him anywhere, but here."

Kline takes a step forward with a kind smile. "Mylee, the issues in your stomach, the tightness, the nausea, I ran a range of tests. The results turned back an above normal marker for the HCG hormone in your blood."

"English, Bex," Trax blurts out.

Kline takes a deep breath looking to Trax, then back to me, placing her folder to her side. "Mylee... you're pregnant."

Trax sharply inhales.

Instantly, I feel like my mind's starting to fog over, thunderous storm clouds are rolling over my head as I clutch my hand to my chest finding it harder to breathe. The world's caving in on me, and the room feels like the walls are seeping blackness. I shake my head back and forth in denial.

I never wanted this.

I never wanted kids.

I know bipolar disorder's genetic even if the professionals don't all agree that it is.

My mother passed it on to me. I vowed never to have children, so I wouldn't pass it on to them. And now, I'm... pregnant?

This can't be happening!

I burst into a torrent of tears as my body reacts before I can. The thunder clouds have swarmed in, and I'm not in control as my brain is swamped with a myriad of emotions. I throw my legs over the edge of the bed, trying to stand up.

I need to go.

I need to run.

But I'm so nauseous.

I stumble feeling dizzy.

I can't breathe. Oh God, I can't breathe.

"Mylee," Trax murmurs, but I can hardly hear him through the ringing in my ears. The thought there's a baby inside of my stomach right now, and I've doomed it to a life of living with this torment seeps into my veins. Guilt overwhelms me as panic sets in. I can't do this. I can't let another person go through this. Feel how I'm feeling right now—the pain, the anguish, the storm.

Oh God, the storm.

The feeling of arms wrapping around me does nothing to soothe me as I scream, attempting to thrust my hands out to the side.

"Babe, stop! Take a breath," Trax calls out, but I can't see, my eyes too clouded from the tears.

The force makes Trax break away as I thrash about, and I groan so loud my throat hurts. The storm is invading fiercely, so fast it's all I can see, everything's black. I want to turn back to find Trax, he's my light, my home, but my head's so muddled I can't think straight. Everything's a blur—my eyes, my thoughts. I spin, trying to search, trying to find my way through the fog. My hands rushing to my hair, pulling, sobbing, stumbling. But I can't find my way, I've lost myself once more.

Arms wrap around me again, this time they hold me tight, locking me in a death grip as I try to fight against them.

I feel a sharp prick in my arm.

I let out a sob knowing exactly what it means—they're knocking me out. It's come to this, I'm *that* far gone. I'm back to *that* girl.

My muscles give way to the pain, not only in my body but also in my heart and mind.

I can't cope—not with this.

I've been doing so well, handling my disorder, it's been under control, but right now I'm slipping, deeper and deeper as my mind can't cope. Trax's hands move around my legs, lifting me into his lap. I fall, my body limp with no energy left to spare.

I simply let him move me as I slowly feel the storm winning.

Darkness is taking hold of me yet again.

CHAPTER 14

TRAX

She wasn't coming out of it like normal, no matter what I did I couldn't seem to bring her out of it. I turned to Kline while Mylee pulled on her hair, sobbing, stumbling around the room in a daze.

"Kline will you fucking do something?"

She turned to me bringing a needle up into my line of vision. "I plan to. You just have to hold her for me."

My chest started heaving. "You're gonna sedate her? What about the fucking baby?"

Kline marched up to me, a sad look in her eyes. "Trax, right now, Mylee and the baby are under a hell of a lot of strain, the best thing for them is to be sleeping."

I groaned looking back to Mylee hunched over. "Fuck!" I rushed over to Mylee, grabbing her from behind, my arms wrapped around her. She thrashed in my grip, my heart leaped into my throat as I death gripped her.

I shook my head. It didn't feel right. Everything in me didn't want to do it. Knocking her out seemed severe, but Mylee was so out of it she was a harm to herself and our baby.

"Fuuuck!" I groaned as Kline moved in with the needle, her kind eyes looked to me sympathetically as she placed the injection into Mylee's arm.

Mylee's sobs sent a cold shiver through me, clenching my eyes tight feeling like at any second I might fucking break myself. Mylee's body loosened, and she collapsed in my arms.

"Are you okay?" Kline asked.

"No," I simply replied as Mylee's limp body let me know she was fading off to sleep.

My heart's racing a million miles a second. It feels like the wind has been knocked from me. Watching her fall apart was gut-wrenching.

Shattering.

Life altering.

Mylee's pregnant.

I know what that means to her.

But, what does it mean to me?

I know her view on kids. I know she never wanted to inflict this life on them. I know this is going to shatter her.

I don't really know how this happened? Sure, the first time we had sex we didn't use a condom, but after that, we've been super careful. Mylee was going to get the morning after pill, so what happened? Whatever happened, it doesn't matter, it has, and now we need to figure out what the fuck we're going to do.

As I look back up to Kline, she exhales running her hand over the back of her neck. "Sorry, I wasn't sure how she'd take the news."

Shaking my head, I stroke Mylee's cheek softly as I look down on her. "I have no idea how she's going to handle this. It could set her off into a downward spiral, Bex."

She sighs in understanding. "I'll have her psych informed of the situation if you think it's best. Maybe have him come down and evaluate her? She has some decisions to make. Having a baby is hard. Having a baby when you have bipolar disorder brings a whole set of new challenges... her medications are something she will need to take into consideration as well."

Running my fingers through my hair in frustration, I tip my head. "I know, and if I know Mylee, I'll have a fight on my hands."

Kline exhales. "There are no right or wrong answers in this, only what's best for Mylee and your baby. But she has to feel supported in whatever decisions you choose, whatever they are..." Her deeper tone on those last few words brings me to a thought I hadn't dare think.

What if she will want to terminate?

This life we created.

What if she wants to end it before it's begun?

Shit! I might even have a bigger battle on my hands than the medications.

Kline squeezes my shoulder in support with a sigh. "For the record, when she wakes up, we'll need to talk more about your options, but you need to be prepared for *all* the options, Trax. Not just the ones *you* want."

All I can do right now is grunt.

"Can I get you anything? Pain relief? Valium?" she jokes on the last one.

Letting out a small laugh, I raise my brow. "Maybe a fifth of Jack?"

"Sounds about right. I think you should call Torque. Sometimes a brother is really handy in times like these."

"How long will she be out?"

She sighs. "Couple of hours, at least, then we'll need to see how she feels when she wakes up. She will be groggy but should be calmer. Hopefully, she'll be feeling more like talking things through."

"Cheers."

"We should get her onto the bed," she suggests.

I take a deep breath as I somehow stand up with Mylee in my arms. She's a complete dead weight, but I don't care, even though my shoulder's screaming at me every which way.

I place her on the bed as Kline pulls a warmed blanket over her. "Okay, I'll give you some time. Call Torque!" She turns walking out leaving me to call my brother and tell him what the hell's going on. I walk over to the seat, grabbing and yanking it over, the metal legs screech across the floor, as I drag it to sit by the edge of her bed. I need to be as close to Mylee as fucking possible right now. I sit down, just taking a breath.

Reaching up, I grab Mylee's hand.

My eyes drift to her stomach.

Mine twists slightly at the thought of what's growing in there.

A part of me.

A part of her.

Ours.

Sniffing, I let out a staggered breath as I blink away the fucking tears.

I could be a dad.

I take a second to let that sink in. Heaviness wafts over me, and I glance up to Mylee, her face calmer now. The idea of us being parents together makes me... *happy.* I know it shouldn't. I should be scared out of my brain. But the fact there's a little peanut inside of Mylee right now, honestly, I don't want to give that up. I know it will be hard, I know a life with Mylee is what I want, but to throw in a kid. Fuck!

Taking another deep breath, I pull out my cell and dial Torque's number. I don't even really know what the hell to say. Telling him over the phone seems like a shitty thing to do, but I need him here.

He answers quickly. "Trax, everything okay?"

Sighing, I have to find my fucking balls trying to hold myself together. "Ahh... can you come back to the hospital? I know you just left but the results are in for Mylee's bloodwork." I stop and take a breath then continue, "I'm a little rattled. I need to talk to you—"

"On my way," he interrupts and doesn't hesitate or barrage me with questions. He simply hangs up the cell, and I know he'll be here soon.

Grabbing the back of my neck, I try to relieve the damn tension building. I place my cell in my jeans pocket then look back to Mylee. She's sleeping so calmly. I'm not a fan of sedating her, but sometimes you have to do what's necessary in order to bring her back.

What the hell am I going to do if she wants to terminate this pregnancy?

Being with Mylee meant never having our own children, but now faced with the option, I can't imagine it any other way. I love her. She's it for me, and I plan to tell her as soon as she wakes up.

I will stake my claim on her. I just hope this won't be the straw that breaks her, and she pushes away from me for good.

Her moods can be so volatile, so unpredictable, but that's no fault of her own. I don't hold it against her. I also know her medications will probably be an issue. This will definitely be a problem, and the idea of Mylee coming off her meds is scary as fuck. She's been doing so well, but being completely off meds while pregnant, and her hormones, could be epically dangerous. But if this is what has to be done, I'll be there for her, every motherfucking step of the way.

Because that's what love is.

And fuck, do I love this woman.

I sit staring at her for what seems like hours, but I know it's only minutes. I have no idea of time right now, the world is moving, life's going on around me, but I have no idea what to think, how to feel. I'm in limbo, not knowing how this is going to play out when she wakes up, and it's damn near killing me.

The curtain pushes back, and Torque rushes into the room. He looks at Mylee who's still zonked out, and he raises his brow as he puffs out air through his mouth. I glance at my brother, I'm barely holding it together. Torque scrunches up his forehead as he moves over to the bed pulling me into a hug, not a man hug but a real hug, a brotherly hug, surrounding me in a warmth I didn't know I was so desperately craving until now.

Torque pulls back holding my shoulders looking me in the eyes. "Tell me."

I gesture to the seats. "Bex did some blood work, and ... umm... Mylee's... fuck! She's pregnant."

Torque's eyes open wide. "Holy shit! Trax, you're gonna be a dad?" Concern's etched on his face like he's unsure of why I'm so frazzled by this announcement.

I shrug then look over at her, he follows my line of sight. "I don't know. Mylee's never wanted kids. Mylee has a genetic predisposition to bipolar disorder. Her mother gave it to her, and there's a possibility it could be passed onto her children. She's always said she would never do that to another human being. She's *always* said that."

Torque licks his bottom lip.

"You should have seen the reaction when Bex told her, brother. I've never seen her this bad. She fell apart. It took Bex and me to bring her down. I..." my voice gets caught in my throat as he reaches out, grabbing my shoulder in support. "Seeing her that way, knowing how much this will tear her up... part of me wants to take the easy route, but this baby is a part of her and me. I don't know how I could live with myself knowing we could have had it all, and..." I close my eyes feeling it all getting too much.

Torque lets out a long breath. "Fuck... this is heavy. I'm guessing Kline gave Mylee something to knock her out?"

I tilt my head once opening my eyes to look over at her. "Yeah, she'll be out for another hour or two."

"Right... there's a bar across the street. I think we need to get a beer, regroup, then come back when she wakes. You need a level head for this."

"I can't leave her."

"Brother, you're on the fuckin' edge. You're of no use to her the way you are. Bex's here, she'll call if Mylee miraculously wakes up early."

My stomach knots at the thought of leaving her, but I know he's right. She isn't waking up anytime soon, and to be honest, I could do with a stiff drink. So we stand. He pats my back as I walk over to her and lean down gently kissing her forehead. "I'll be right back." I know she can't hear me, but it makes me feel better. So I walk out of her room with my brother in search of something hard to keep me going.

We step out into the emergency ward to find Kline.

"I'm taking Trax across to the bar for a drink," Torque tells her.

"Excellent idea. Mylee will be asleep for a while, and if anything happens, I'll call immediately."

I crack my neck to the side feeling tension rolling through me. "Can you hold off calling her psych and stuff until I've talked to Mylee more about what *she* wants to do? I don't want to step in or take over until absolutely necessary. I want to give her the chance to come through this, to make some of her own decisions. So can we wait for now?"

"Probably a good idea. We'll assess her when she wakes up, but for now, you guys go. Have a drink, unwind. I'll look after everything here."

"Thanks, Bex," I murmur. She winks at me as Torque and I head off.

We exit crossing the street, the bar almost dead for a Wednesday afternoon.

Torque's quiet. Almost too quiet as we walk in and head straight for the bar. We take a seat on the stools, and I lean against the bar as the barman steps up.

"Couple of beers, thanks," Torque asks.

"Actually, make mine a Jack. Neat and a double," I correct.

Torque dips his head in understanding as the barman goes about pouring our drinks. After a few minutes, he places the beer in front of Torque and a small tumbler in front of me. I pick it up, throwing back the contents as Torque quietly sips on his beer.

Silence engulfs us, and I can't help but wonder what my brother's thinking.

Is he concerned for me?

Does he think I'll make a good father?

Does he think Mylee should terminate?

The silence is deafening as I turn to Torque and I tap the bar. "C'mon, out with it. What are you thinking?"

Torque chuckles taking another sip of his beer then wipes the back of his mouth turning to face me. "Honestly? This could be so fuckin' good for you. I've been watching you go down this path of self-destruction, you've been out for blood. Carnage. Chaos. But the minute Mylee and you got back together, it's like something in you flicked, something changed. The Trax I knew, the brother that was kind and funny, was back. This past six weeks while she's been with us you've been a different man. I know throwing a baby in the mix is gonna be fuckin' tough, not to mention the pregnancy, and I realize her disorder will play up throughout. But brother, you being a father... I can't think of anything you're more suited to right now with Mylee by your side. She makes you... better."

Taking a deep breath, my chest fills with warmth at his words. "She *does* make me better, and I know this could be good. I just don't know if it will get that far. She doesn't want kids. I honestly can't see this happening, Torque, and I don't know if I can support what I think she'll want to do."

He exhales. "I get it. Her fears are warranted. Her mother had it, now she has it, it's fairly likely her children will get it, but... at least you can be prepared for that shitty outcome if it happens. You can watch for the signs. Medical shit changes all the time. You can get a handle on it before it takes over. If Mylee chooses to terminate, then it could ruin what you two have right now, which is working so well."

I exhale. "I would stand by her no matter what, but knowing I have a fight on my hands is hard." I wince at the thought.

"What about her medication? Will that affect the baby?"

"Yeah, probably. I know this is something we have to talk about with Bex. Mylee coming off her meds is something I can't even imagine right now. Shit! Her dad's gonna fucking kill me."

Torque lets out a small chuckle in agreement. "Oh yeah, Crest's gonna certifiably ream you a new asshole."

Tapping the bar to order another drink, I moan, the barman understanding my signal immediately as he begins to pour.

"Look, I know this is gonna be a rough few hours coming up... I can stay, I can do whatever you need me to do, brother."

Sighing, I crack my tense neck. "Not sure what Mylee will be like when she wakes up. All I know is I'll probably have a goddamn fight on my hands. Then I have to talk to Crest which, of course, is gonna be a shitstorm resulting in my balls being pulled out through my goddamn mouth. It's going to be a hell of a fucking night."

"Well, I'm here."

"Thanks, man. Means a lot. Is Foxy coming to the hospital after school?"

"Yeah, she's working tonight. Why?"

"Mylee likes her, might be nice to have someone around to lend an ear if Mylee needs a woman's perspective other than Kline."

Torque pulls out his cell. "On it. I'll fill her in, tell her to keep her eye on Mylee, talk to her if she thinks she can help. Maybe not as a medical professional but as a friend."

"Perfect."

"Did you get a chance to talk to Cindi about Andretti and the Scarsi Dettagli?"

He shakes his head. "Not yet, you're more important right now. But as soon as I'm done here, I'll be spending some quality time with a club girl."

I snort. "Don't let Foxy hear you say that."

He chuckles. "Yeah, never thought I'd say those words again. Lucky they don't hold the same meaning anymore, or Foxy would seriously castrate me."

I sigh. "This shit couldn't have come at a worse time."

He shakes his head. "We'll get it done and look after Mylee. Don't worry. We're Defiance. We can handle anything. We're family."

The door to the bar swings open, both of us turn, and to our fucking surprise, Cindi's walking in. I raise my brow as she saunters over carrying a small gift wrapped box.

"Speak of the fucking devil," Torque murmurs as I exhale not really understanding why she's here.

She strides over to us with a weak smile. "Trax, I'm here on behalf of the club girls. We bought something for Mylee, it's just chocolates to make her feel better, but when I went to the hospital Kline said she was... resting. She also told me I'd find you two lugs over here."

Warmth flows over me, this is why I love this club. Not just the brotherhood, but the family. Everyone looks out for everyone. The club girls may not have had a lot to do with Mylee, but they know she means something to me. She's part of this club even if technically, she belongs to another club. Mylee's family, and Cindi just affirmed that everyone believes exactly that.

"Thanks, Cindi. Appreciate you coming all the way down here... means a lot."

She tilts her head, her empathetic eyes softening. "Trax, you know if there's anything... *anything* I can do to help you or the club, I will always drop everything to do it. You guys have given me so much. I'd bleed for this club."

I glance to Torque as he lets out an exhale reaching out for her hand. "Actually Cindi, there is something you can do for us."

She smiles wide, nodding her head. "Anything, pres, you got it."

He rubs the back of his neck and signals to the barman. "I think you'll need a drink for this." Her beaming smile falters as she looks from Torque to me, a concerned gaze crossing her features. "A beer for the lady, thanks," Torque requests. The barman nods and goes about pouring as Cindi gnaws on her bottom lip.

"It can't be that bad, can it? I mean, you're not kicking me out of the club or anything, are you?" she asks, her tone cautious like she's scared that might actually be the case.

Torque grips her hand a little tighter. "Fuck, no, nothing like that. You're an asset at the club, Cindi. The thing is, it's Enzo—"

She snorts out a laugh. "What's he gone and done now? Are you guys fighting again?"

I chuckle loving her way of thinking. "It's fucking strange we haven't had an argument with Enzo in so long, I see where you're coming from."

"Shut up, Trax, this is serious." I purse my lips raising my hands in surrender. "Enzo's gotten himself in some shit with another Mafioso... he needs our help."

Cindi tilts her head taking a deep breath. "I'm a little confused... I'm a club girl. Why am I suddenly privy to this kind of information? I mean, I know Ruby is sometimes let in on some shit, but me? I'm a nobody."

I exhale taking her other hand. "You're not a nobody, Cindi. You're gorgeous, you're talented, and you're one of the smartest and most cunning women I know."

She grins wide. "Okay, so what's going on? Why am I being let in on this?"

Torque cracks his neck to the side. "The Scarsi Dettagli Mafiosos... they have Enzo's daughter, Zia. They're known women traffickers."

Her eyes widen as she gasps. "Shit."

"Yeah... for Enzo to get her back, we need to make a trade, his eleven-year-old daughter for another female."

Her eyes narrow. "Me?"

My muscles tense as Cindi looks Torque straight in the eyes.

"You'd go into their system. Be placed up for bid. Be sold to the highest bidder. Whoever bought you would get you..." he pauses running his hand through his hair. "You know we'll sell fucking heaven and earth to make sure that final bid is us to get you back."

She swallows hard reaching out for the beer on the bar, throwing it back.

Torque glances to me but continues, "The thing is, Cindi, they want a fighter. So I'm sure you'd be placed in matches to check your capabilities. They'd want to test your body, to see what your strengths and weaknesses are up against your profile. They would keep you weak so you couldn't escape. They wouldn't be kind to you. We could probably track you, but once you're in their system, we wouldn't have a way to keep you safe. You'd be on your own until we can buy you back. You'd have to fight for yourself."

She takes another large sip of her beer as I shake my head, even I think this is too big of an ask.

"Now, there's no way in hell we're going to force you to do this. It has to be your choice, and yours alone. No one will be angry if you say no. We will understand fully, respect your decision, and find another way. We just know that with your fighting capabilities and your acting skills, if anyone could pull this off, it's you."

She lets out a heavy sigh, glancing to me. "Trax, you of all people have the hardest time with Enzo. In your opinion, does he love his daughter?"

I nod. "Yeah. I mean, I've always been one step removed from Enzo, but he's broken. I didn't even know he had a daughter, and that says it all. He wanted her kept out of the limelight, away from his 'endeavors,' so she wouldn't get caught in the crosshairs. That tells me everything."

She takes another sip from her beer, then nods. "Okay. I'm in."

Torque and I both sit up a little taller. "Do you fully understand what this means Cin—"

"Fighting, starvation, probably sexual shit, too. Yeah, I get it. This is the acting gig of a lifetime, Torque. Not only that, I get to do my two favorite things in the world, fighting and fucking. What's not to love about this role?"

I stifle a laugh as she looks to me. "Trust you to find a positive in this fucked-up shit."

She shrugs. "It's for an eleven-year-old girl. She's the innocent in this. She can't go through hell like that. Me? I'm built for that shit. Her, not so much. I need to get the kid out."

Torque grabs Cindi's hand making her look at him. His eyes are hard, focused as she steadies her breath. "We *will* get you out."

She smiles. "I know. I trust you. That's why I'm doing this... small-time role for big-time gain." She narrows her eyes. "We got this."

I pick up my tumbler throwing back the contents, and I can't help but wonder if maybe right now we're biting off more than we can chew, not just with Cindi and the Scarsis, but with me having to inevitably talk to Crest about Mylee.

Yeah, shit's getting real, very fast.

How the hell are we going to hang on for this motherfucking ride?

CHAPTER 15

MYLEE

I can't move.

I feel like my body is glued to the spot. Like my mind is a vast array of nothingness, and all I can do is hear what's going on. The sound of the heart monitor beeps in a normal rhythm making me aware I'm in a hospital.

I can't remember anything.

I can't feel anything.

All I know is that I'm numb.

My eyes slowly open, everything's a haze, it's like a whitewash. Heaviness floods my senses. I'm so tired. I can barely focus. The only thing I can see, in the short distance my eyes are focusing in on, is the curtain in front of my bay. I can see shadows walking past. I hear the nurses talking to each other, but I can't make out what they're saying, though.

Someone walks into my bay, wearing a lab coat.

I don't know who.

I can't move.

I can't function.

I blink a couple of times, but my head can't move, only my eyes.

I can't speak.

Nothing.

But when I see him—the doctor—my muscles tense as fear ripples through me.

His red hair.

His stocky build.

Everett is holding a clipboard as he looks down at me, a broad smile lighting his face.

"Hello, Mylee. Go to sleep... sweet dreams, my love," his voice is calm, unlike how I'm feeling as he fiddles with my drip. My breathing is harsh, frantic, but I can't move. The sedative too strong as my eyes blink, once, twice, and then fear swallows me whole as everything goes black.

My head's foggy.

I feel dopy.

Out of it.

Like I've definitely been drugged. But there's that other sense too. That cloud, the one that hangs over my head when I know I'm in trouble when the storm has hit, and now I'm in limbo.

That in between.

The aftermath.

My eyes are heavy, my mouth dry like it's full of cotton wool. I blink a few times trying to put the pieces back together but can't really recall much. I shift slightly, pain in my leg bringing back memories of the crash. My chest aches as I remember coming into the hospital emergency department, but as I glance around the room, I note this is an actual hospital room not the emergency area anymore.

I've been admitted.

As I glance at the edge of my bed, I see Trax sitting there facing away from me, staring aimlessly out the window. But there's a sensation across my hand of him stroking my skin lovingly, and it doesn't go unnoticed. As I look down, I see he's running his thumb up and down the back of my hand.

It fills me with warmth.

I instantly feel safe.

Calm.

But suddenly my stomach rolls making me feel nauseous, then it hits me, the memory flooding back as I glance at my stomach. I let out a small whimper as my hand flies to my tummy making Trax turn to face me. His eyes lock onto mine, his glassy as I look to him, and I can't help but let out another whimper. He leans forward bringing his free hand to my face caressing my cheek trying to soothe me.

"Hey shhh, I'm here. I'm not going anywhere. You're okay. You're in a safe place. Just breathe, Mylee," he instructs, so I take a few deep breaths continuing to look into his eyes as mine well up at the memory that I'm pregnant.

A lump forms in my throat as I move my hands to hold his. "Trax, I'm..." I pause, and he slowly bobs his head up and down.

"Yeah, baby, you are. *We* are. We're in this together."

I shift to sit up in the bed, and he helps me move. Trax slides in next to my side as we sit on the bed. He looks at me, but I can't seem to get a grip on what I'm feeling. I know this can't happen, but something deep down inside is making it all seem a little exciting. I never wanted this. I never wanted kids. It's too fucking hard. Plus, damning a child to the life I've lived is just plain evil. I couldn't possibly do that, could I?

Trax grabs my hand, forcing me to look at him. "You're thinking. You're overthinking. Mylee, I know you didn't want this. A baby was never in our cards. I know what your first instinct is, but you need to think about this."

I'm tormented at the thought of having to go through an abortion. The idea of aborting an innocent child is abhorrent to me, but the thought of condemning a child to my fate is equally as bad, isn't it? I'm so fucking torn. I cuddle into Trax's side needing his comfort as he wraps himself around me.

"You want to keep the baby?" I murmur asking Trax.

He nods against my head. "I do. That child is a part of you and me, and Mylee…" he exhales, "… that's incredible. I know there'll be challenges, but I know you. I've been through a lot with you. I've seen you off your meds, I've seen you manic, I've seen you depressed, and I've also seen you strong and can handle anything. I think we can handle *this* if you're willing."

"What about when our child has an event that might trigger their bipolar disorder. How will we handle that? Having two people with bipolar disorder will be hard on you?" I look up to Trax, he simply smiles swiping hair away from my face leaning in and planting a tender kiss on my forehead. "Then we deal with it. We're in this together. We're not the first family to go through this, Mylee, and we won't be the last. Plus, we have an entire brotherhood watching our backs, helping us through. We have far more support than most families because our family is massive."

My heart skips a beat. "True. I guess we have two families, the Defiance and the Knights. They'll both look after us."

"Exactly… that is if your father doesn't fucking exterminate me first."

Raising my brow, I let out a sigh. "Yeah… does he know?"

"No. Wanted to wait till you were awake, till we knew what we were doing before I got Crest involved."

"Good call. I'm so tired, I don't really know if I'm thinking straight, Trax."

"That's fine. Just talk to me. Tell *me* what you're feeling."

"Scared… if we do this. It means so much. Medication changes, body changes, our relationship could change. What if… what if you fall out of love with me?"

He glares at me like I've said the most stupid thing in the world. I know I'm not thinking straight, but the way he's looking at me right now, I know it wasn't the right thing to say. "How could you ever think that? I'm in this with you. I was in it with you two years ago. I've been with you ever since then just waiting for you to come back to me. The moment you stepped back into my life you've been mine, and I swear to God I'm not going fucking anywhere no matter what. Baby or not. Medication or not. You're mine, Mylee, all the way. I'll fucking tell the entire world I've claimed you if need be. I don't fucking care. I'll post a billboard in the heart of Italy if you want me to. 'Mylee's claimed' in big fucking flashing neon lights. You're mine, in the good and in the bad. I know we have some shit heading our way, but I don't care if you try to gouge my eyes out in a fit of anger, I'll still be there for you and our baby… always."

Tears fill my eyes as I rush forward embracing him tightly. *He claimed me.* Even with my head in a fog, I can still feel the joy while he embraces me tightly. "I love you," I whisper.

He pulls back looking into my eyes. "I love you, too. So we gonna do this? Are we gonna have a baby?"

I exhale looking deep into his gorgeous blue sparkling eyes. There's so much hope in them, the love oozing from him, the adoration, the desire. I can't deny him this even though I feel like a part of me will always feel tortured for doing this, like a part of me will always feel blame for what will happen to our son or daughter. I know if I terminate our child, I'd always feel guilt for ending an innocent life. Catch twenty-two. There's guilt in both scenarios, it's just which guilt is bigger, and right now I can't find myself being able to squash the growing excitement slowly winning out inside of me as I nod to him slowly.

His eyes light up as he takes in my approval. He smooths his hands over my face. "Are you fucking saying what I think you're saying?"

I exhale. "I need to talk to the doctors. I need to know more details. But I'm saying I will consider keeping our child. The idea of you looking after us is… kinda heartwarming."

He grins the widest I've seen in so long as he leans in planting a giant kiss against my lips. I smile, kissing him back. The kiss isn't heated or lustful, it's warm and loving.

I hear a throat clearing, and we pull apart to see Kline walking in. "Sorry to interrupt, but I'm glad to see you're awake and doing okay."

I glance down at my lap. "I'm still a little concerned about it all. But I am sorry I went all crazy on you—"

"You had a reaction, and it was perfectly normal in your condition. Though it doesn't change the result of the blood test, so I need to know if you want me to follow up. Would you like me to run some further tests to see how the baby's doing, or make... other arrangements, if you've had this discussion yet?" she asks.

Trax tenses slightly beside me, but I take a deep breath steadying myself even though my heart's racing. "Can you book in some further tests, please? I would like to see how our baby's doing."

Trax beams so wide, pulling me closer to him, kissing the top of my head as he relaxes beside me.

"Of course... now, in this case, would you also like for me to call for your physician or psychiatrist. You might need to have some discussions."

"Yes, please. I think this is something I need to have all the facts about. Umm... Dr. Kline, as for the meds I'm on now, do I need to stop them right away?"

"I think we wait for your treating psych to get here. He can fill you in on the best practices regarding weaning you off the meds *if* you need to, but for now, keep taking them. I'd like to point out how lucky you both are that the baby survived your accident. I'd call that a little miracle."

Unease washes over me. It's only now just dawning on me that we could have lost this baby before we even knew about it. The idea of staying on my meds doesn't sit right considering we have this little miracle inside me. I wish I could stop immediately. I don't want any harm to come to our baby, but I know there's a process. And before I see my specialist, I need to make sure I do this right. All I want is to get through this without any hassles. But with the threat of Everett still out there, and now the idea I have to tell Dad what's going on, things are only going to get harder for us both not easier.

"Thank you, Dr. Kline, for everything."

"You're welcome, Mylee, it's my pleasure. Any Old Lady of the club is a friend of mine."

Trax has obviously told her he was going to claim me while I was asleep. Either that or she figured, but either way, being claimed by Trax brings a new set of drama to deal with my dad. The idea that his little girl will be permanently staying in Chicago is going to grate on his very last nerve, not only that but the fact Trax has knocked me up, I know he's going to blow a gasket.

Kline walks out as I look to Trax raising my brow. I sigh. "I guess we should call Dad?"

Trax rolls his shoulders. "I should do it. I need to man up—"

"I don't think that's the best idea. He might lose his shit at you."

Trax raises his brow and gives me his lopsided smirk. "Oh yeah, that shit's inevitable. I need to take responsibility for this. I'm not really asking at this point, I'm calling him. End of discussion."

I like his determined tone, so I weakly smile. If he's brave enough to take on the typhoon that my father's going to rain down on him, then have at it.

The *Hunger Games* catchphrase seems appropriate here...

May the odds be ever in your favor!

TRAX

She hands her cell over to me as I sit on the edge of her bed. Tension barrels over my shoulders making them the tightest they have ever fucking felt. Knowing this will probably be the hardest call I will ever make is making it difficult to press the green button against his name, but I do so making sure *not* to put it on speaker. I don't want Mylee overhearing if he says shitty stuff because she's right next to me hanging on with bated breath.

He answers, his voice chirpy which makes me grin. "Mylee, my sweet girl, I miss you. How are you?"

Clearing my throat, I ready myself. "Crest, this is Trax."

"You're calling from Mylee's number, I thought it was her. Fuck! What's going on?"

I rub the back of my neck swallowing down the nerves. "She's fine, but there are some things I need to discuss with you."

He's quiet for a pass but then continues, "Okay, is she having an episode?"

"No... we were, ah.... out on a ride and got into an accident—"

"Jesus—"

"She's okay. Just some cuts to her leg. I brought her straight to the hospital. We're here now."

He exhales sounding annoyed. "Thanks for taking care of her, can I talk to her?"

"Sure but there's a little more you need to know."

He exhales. "Trax, I'm not fucking liking the tone in your voice. What the fuck's going on? Was it Everett?"

I'd almost forgotten why Mylee was even here. This Everett guy hasn't even been a damn problem. I need to look more into that, but one problem at a time. "No, we got caught up in a high-speed chase, collateral damage, but Crest, when they ran some bloodwork on Mylee, they found something."

"What the hell do you mean? Spit it the fuck out! Now!"

Mylee takes my hand for support. I look at her as she bobs her head giving me the go-ahead to tell her father he's going to be a grandfather. "Mylee's... pregnant, Crest."

I scrunch up my face waiting for the imminent yelling match, but there's nothing.

Just deafening silence.

It sends a chill through my entire soul as I look to Mylee, my breathing increasing in intensity. "Crest?"

"Is she keeping it?" His voice is quiet, and it's not the Crest I know.

"We're looking into that option, yes."

He lets out a heavy sigh. "She never wanted this. She must be going through hell right now. Jesus Christ, my poor girl..." He sounds broken, sad. Not the anger I was expecting, more like grief is taking over, and it's shocking me. I glance to Mylee noticing she's watching me intensely.

"Crest, I know Mylee didn't want to have children. We both know it. We didn't plan this. Fuck knows we didn't. But the idea we created a life together, something that's part of the both of us... that's gotta be some kind of fucking miracle. I know the fears that come with this baby and pregnancy, but I'm with Mylee in this. You know me. You know my love for her. We've created a life, and that life is your grandchild, Crest."

A tear rolls down Mylee's face. I move in wiping it away from her cheek with my thumb. She nuzzles into my hand as I smile at her. I hope she knows how honest my words are. Crest sniffs like he's having a hard time keeping himself together. "Fuck. I need to come down there. Be with you two, help sort all this shit out. Now is really crap timing for the club, but my girl comes first. How is she really, Trax?"

I look to her seeing a sparkle in her eyes, the fear, the anguish I'm sure it's still there, but there's also a spark that wasn't there when she first found out. That spark is what's making me sure we're doing the right thing. Keeping this baby is the best option for the both of us.

"She's scared, but she's doing fine. Do you want to talk to her?" Mylee looks a little apprehensive. "She wants to talk to you," I add.

Crest exhales. "Okay, but don't take this non-reaction as a non-reaction, Trax. I'm in pain for my girl's broken dreams. Dreams you've damn well shattered. I won't forget you did this to her. I might sound calm, but once I've dealt with Mylee, we're going to be having some serious fuckin' words you and me."

I let out a long breath. This is more like what I was expecting, and I know it's going to be a hard slog when Crest gets here, but I'll put up with whatever he throws my way because Mylee's worth it. Our baby is worth it, and I would put up with anything for them.

"I hear you, Crest, and I'm all for a chat, but right now, I think Mylee needs to talk to her father. She needs support, do you hear what I'm saying?" I warn, but he lets out a small laugh.

"You think I'm going to talk her out of this baby? Trax, all I've ever wanted is to see her happy, to see her with a brood of kids, and to make me a grandfather. I want that for *her*. I want that for *me*. I want that for *you*, but sometimes we don't always get what *we* want. If Mylee tells me she doesn't want this baby, I will support *her* in that, Trax. I'm on Mylee's side, whatever *she* chooses... remember that."

I exhale handing Mylee the cell. She takes it from me as I let out a heavy breath. The idea Mylee could still turn around and not want to keep our baby weighs heavily on me as she lifts the cell to her ear. I stand up from the bed moving over to the window looking out at the gray, overcast sky.

"D... Dad," her voice cracks making me shudder hearing her sound so vulnerable. "No, I'm okay. I promise. Trax's doing a great job looking after me. He's been amazing, Dad."

I turn back to look at her. She smiles as I take a breath walking over to the bed then sitting on top. I only needed a second, just a second to gather myself from Crest's words, but now I'm back, and I'm here for my girl. I bring my legs up on the bed beside her, sliding right next to her wrapping my arm behind her shoulders and pull her to me. She nuzzles into my side continuing to talk to her father while I try to tune out letting her have some time as I take a moment to just think about this life-changing event.

Mylee's pregnant.

With my child.

And from here on out everything's going to be different.

Crest is on his way. It's been a couple of hours since we called him, so he should be about halfway here by now. It takes four hours to ride from Grand Rapids to Chicago, but knowing him, he's probably breaking the land speed record to get here.

Mylee's psych, on the other hand, has been in and discussed all the options with us. He talked us through the risk factors weighing up the pros and cons of staying on her bipolar disorder tablet regime. Dr. Prescott advised that the medication she's on doesn't tend to have risk factors, but there's always some risk associated with taking any medication during pregnancy. So, basically his recommendation is for Mylee to stay on them. In the long term, the advantage of Mylee's moods being stable is of a far greater benefit to her and the baby than her being off her meds. If her moods are unbalanced, it could cause stress and possible dangers which come with bipolar episodes which could, in turn, be more harmful than the medication itself.

Standing to lean down, I plant a chaste kiss on Mylee's temple. "I'm going to talk to my brother about club business and see how far away Crest is. Won't be long," I tell her squeezing her hand.

Turning, I walk from her room glancing over to Foxy giving her a sly wink. She winks back, and I know she's going to look after my woman while I'm out trying to calm down my raging emotions.

CHAPTER 16

MYLEE

Smiling as Trax leaves, Foxy walks in taking a seat next to my bed, she sits back, the plastic on the chair squeaking with her movement. "Wow, this is so much to take in," Foxy says.

I snort out a laugh. "You should take it in from my end."

She chuckles leaning forward resting her arms on the bed as she looks up at me. "Mylee, I've been at the club long enough to know these men. Long enough to know how they work. Long enough to know that when they mark their territory, they fight tooth and nail to make the people they love happy."

"I get that. I've been around clubs long enough to see how it works."

She smiles. "Then you know Trax claiming you is a big deal. He's been so... broken, so... alone, until you came back. He was waiting for you."

"I think I always knew I'd find my way back to him."

"He needs you, and with this baby comes a new challenge, but I will be here, Kline will be helping you, too. You're always going to have access to the club, and everyone there's going to be helping as well. We're a family, family sticks together, no matter how hard it gets. We've got your back, Mylee, don't you worry."

"Thanks, Foxy, this means so much. I know I'm kinda new around here, but it's lovely the way you're all taking this on... taking *me* on."

"You're family, Mylee. You're a part of this club now. You're the VP's Old Lady. No matter what, we will take care of you. We're basically sisters you and me."

Foxy stands up leaning over taking me into a tight hug. I feel nothing but a sisterly embrace from her. I've never known what it's like to have a sibling, but right now, I feel about as close to Foxy as what it might be like.

"You're amazing, you know that?" I ask.

She pulls back from me with a small smile and giggles. "Thanks, and I mean everything I say. You're one of us now."

"I feel that, and I'm so glad."

Having this moment with Foxy is just what I needed. Not a doctor coming in telling me the ins and outs of how things are going to run. Not Trax and my father telling me I have their support because I know I have it no matter what. But having the other members of the club backing me, this is what truly makes me feel welcomed into the Chicago Defiance, and being welcomed by the club's first Old Lady, well, it can't be any better than that.

I glance at the doorway and notice the handsome older face of my father looking in. My breath catches, a sudden wave of anxiety flows through me at the sad look in his eyes. His broad frame steps inside the room as Foxy turns to see Dad, and she smiles.

"I'll let you two have some time. I'll be right outside if you need me, just call," Foxy beams.

"Thanks, Foxy, for everything."

She pats my shoulder as she lets Dad stride in to take the seat she was occupying. He reaches out grabbing my hand, his warm fingers feeling like leather as my eyes instantly well up with tears.

"Daddy," I murmur.

He weakly smiles, his white beard looking a little longer than it did just over a month ago when I last saw him. "Oh, baby girl, I had no idea bringing you here would result in this."

I look down to our joined hands, his weathered from age and too much sun. I shrug. "It wasn't planned—"

"No, of course not, Mylee. I'm worried about you, about what this means for you."

"I know, Dad. It's going to be hard, especially because you have to stay in Grand Rapids while I'm here. You need to be with the club, you can't leave them to look after me. You gotta let me do this with the help from Trax and his club, Dad."

He grits his teeth shaking his head. "I got you into this mess, Mylee, I should be the one looking after you. You have to come back home, so I can take care of you. I know how to handle it best."

I look at him trying to muster all my courage to tell him what I need. "Dad, I can't leave Defiance."

"You can, and you *will*, Mylee."

Slowly shaking my head, my heart pummels in my chest. "I can't, Dad. I'm a part of *their* club now."

His eyes shoot open, he flares his nostrils like he's getting angry with me. "The only way you would be a part of their club is if—"

"Trax claimed me," I blurt out.

His eyes bulge as the vein in his thick neck pulses. His jaw strains as he tilts his head like he's trying to reign in his anger. "Shit! Little fucker. I'm gonna goddamn kill that son of a—"

"Dad, this is what I want. Me, him... our baby."

Dad looks to me his eyes glistening like he's on edge.

"We're going to be a family. It's going to be fucking hard to get there, but I have so much support here, Dad. And I know you'll come to see that and support us, too."

He clears his throat. "I know you have support, Mylee, I saw it in the corridor out there. I saw it when I walked in here. I just... I hate the idea of you going through this and me not being by your side."

I tighten my hand in his. "I know, but you'll only be four hours away, and I'll call you every day if you want me to. I will probably do it anyway knowing me. So you won't be missing out, Dad, not at all."

"I don't think I'll be missing out, Mylee. I'm scared I won't be there when you need me."

"I will *always* need you, Dad, always... but Trax and Foxy, hell even Torque, and I'm sure Neala, will be watching out for me. Trust me, I'm going to have so many people watching me I'll probably be begging to come home."

He laughs. "Okay..." He tightens his hand in mine.

I look at him wondering why he looks so disheveled. "What's happening with the club? Is everything settling down?"

He snorts out a laugh. "Hardly. We have trades happening, but with the fucking senator breathing down our necks, everything's blocked at every angle. It's making running things damn hard for us. Those Scotts are a pain in my fucking ass. The minute we find something on them, to take them out, will be a good day in my book."

I weakly smile thinking about Everett and all the shit he's caused my family and me. "I have a guy at Defiance, Ace, who's doing some digging, but he can't seem to find anything so far that could do any damage to the Senator's career, or even in regard to Everett for that matter. They seem to be covering their tracks too well."

"Yeah, the Senator's doing a great job of hiding the fact his son is completely deranged. I mean I know he has an illness, but there has to be some kind of evil in him to say the kinds of things he was saying to you."

I shudder, remembering when he cornered me in the psych hospital and the conversation that took place.

My mind never truly felt clear there. Everything smelled stale. I was never sure if it was mold or more of an old shoe smell mixed with antiseptic. But either way, the smell was everywhere. In my bedroom, in the hall, in the dining area. It seeped into your pores and made you feel even crazier than when you arrived. Not that I was crazy, I was so deep into a bipolar episode that I couldn't crawl my way out. That's why I was there in the psych ward of the hospital. My depression so uncontrolled I couldn't keep myself from thinking horrible thoughts. From wanting to curl into a ball and think of ways of ending things. From thoughts so dark they scared not only my family, my friends, but me too.

Over the weeks, patients would come and go. Some nice, some kept to themselves, some talked to me, most didn't. But one always made an effort to spend time with me. In fact, his attention toward me seemed a little more like infatuation.

Everett Scott—he was the man walking toward me right now.

The hallway was dimly lit, the flickering of the one light that always seemed to be faulty made me cringe. It was so cliché. The psych ward having a flickering light, like something from a horror movie. I thought that shit was only shot in Hollywood, seemed I was wrong. My mood was down. I felt particularly low as I stood against the end of the hall while Everett stalked toward me. His eyes twitching like he was aggravated.

I knew when he got this way, it was best to avoid him. He could get restless. Sometimes say weird shit. So I made the move to walk off, but he rushed forward, blocking me into the corner of the hall. His arms coming up either side of me, his bulky frame trapping me against the peeling plasterboard. That damn flickering light enhanced my already racing heart rate as I looked to the floor. The walls feeling like they were closing in on me. Those ever-present storm clouds rolling in.

"Mylee, don't try to run from me. Is it the government? Did they tell you to run?" he asked.

I risked glancing up at him confused by his words. But the hard look in his eyes teamed with the red puffiness surrounding them, only made me more frightened. I shook my head. "Everett, I... d-don't know what you mean?" I stuttered.

"The damn government. They're the ones in on this, they have been all along. Can't you see? But we should fight it, Mylee. This conspiracy is bigger than them. We should fight it. My life is tied to yours... you should be able to see that by now?" He spoke with such passion, he truly believed every word he said as a shudder ran down my spine while his hand came up and caressed the side of my face.

I had nowhere to go. I was trapped. Tears pricked in my eyes as I looked at him. He had been my friend in this place, but he was slowly making less and less sense. His government theories and words about our lives being tied together were really starting to terrify me. But I wasn't sure if maybe I was going a little crazy— maybe this was all a hallucination.

"Mylee, you need to realize we're tied together. If you die, I die, right?" he murmured.

I opened my eyes wide wondering why he'd say something like that. Was it a threat?

"Why would you say that, Everett?" I blurted out as he brought both his hands to my face holding me tight. My body riddled with fear as I shook uncontrollably in the moment. I had no idea what to do. My mind a complete haze from not only the deep depression I was suffering but also the medication I had taken. I was almost drunk from the overwhelming anxiety. Everett was scaring me, his words so twisted, so confronting, so confusing. His face contorted in what looked like pain.

"We need to keep each other safe, we can do it this time. I can keep you safe," he whispered the last part as he leaned in, his eyes closing as I registered his actions. My body went rigid to the spot frozen in fear. He was so all over the place. He was angry one moment, and now, now he was leaning in about to kiss me. He inched closer, my body unable to move, his hands tightening on my face holding me into position. My eyes squinting, my muscles

contracting, retreating from the intrusion. I didn't want him to kiss me. I felt violated as he came closer, so close I could feel his breath against my skin. But I was so lost, my mind not functioning, my body not moving. I was paralyzed in the moment.

"Hey!" someone called out as stomping feet came rushing down the hall.

Everett quickly backed off before the kiss made contact as the male nurse rushed toward us. "No fraternization between patients, Everett. You know that!" he said looking to me raising his brow as if to question if I was all right.

My body shook—fear, adrenaline, anxiety swallowing me whole. I didn't hesitate. Everett was far enough away from me that I could make a run for it. So I did. My feet fled. I took off, one foot after the other as tears filled my eyes. My arms wrapping around myself as I raced down the hall toward my room. The comfort of my room, where I would lock myself in my bathroom and shower to wash away the feeling of Everett's hands on me. Where I would cry into the rivulets of the water until my tears ran dry.

Until tomorrow, when it would all happen again.

Dad looks at me, grabbing my hand. "Hey, where did you just go?"

Shaking my head, I try to fight off the memory. "Nowhere good. Everett slipped into my mind."

"I'm sorry I left you in that hospital with him for so long. If I knew he was playing tricks on your damn mind, Mylee... if I knew he was hurting you—"

"It's no one's fault. I wasn't strong enough to realize he was a threat at the time. I know now, and so we can fight against him. But as long as he doesn't know I'm here, we're good. I'm okay."

Dad exhales. "Last I heard he was going mad not knowing where you are. I think they're getting ready to commit him again. If they do that, the threat might resolve itself."

"Wouldn't that be nice? I mean I don't like that a man is so crazy within his own mind he can't function properly. Hospitals are the best place for him where they can keep him under watch and guard."

"Exactly. So you can get on with your life, your new family, and not have to worry about a thing."

I weakly smile. "Here's hoping."

"Trax will look out for you, I have no doubt. He knows if he doesn't, he'll have me to answer to."

"Not just you, but the entire Notorious Knights."

Dad laughs. "Exactly. Everyone back home misses you, Myls."

"I miss them, too, but eventually I was going to spread my wings."

"Yeah... just didn't think it would be four fuckin' hours away. Thought you'd end up with someone from our club... Aero maybe?" He stands up moving in pulling me into a tight embrace as I wince. "I'm so proud of you, Mylee. I thought I'd walk in here and you'd be a mess. But you're holding yourself together well. You've come so far from the girl who was diagnosed two years ago." He pulls back looking into my eyes.

"Me and Aero, we were never gonna work. It was always Trax, Dad." I smile. "I couldn't be this girl without you. You made me into this woman, this much stronger, capable woman. That's why I know I can do this with Trax and the club. We can do this... together."

He looks at me and smiles. "I believe you can, and you will. This baby will be good for you. I know you always had an opinion about having children, but, Mylee, when your mother and I had you, it was the best-damned thing we ever did. We knew the risks of passing on her illness to you, so we went through the same thing you're going through now, but to us, having you was more important. You're so worth all the uncertainty. We were scared, we felt guilty, and the moment I saw your symptoms coming on, I felt like shit because we knew you were going to more than likely end up there. But it was worth it… to have you in our lives, baby girl. Because you are the most precious gift to have ever graced mine and your mother's lives."

I sniff. "Thanks, Dad, it means everything. I… I just miss Mom so much sometimes it completely paralyzes me. The thought I'm going to be going through this without her advice about how to raise this child …" My eyes mist up as I try to rid the tears.

"I know, I know, baby. She would have loved nothing more than to see you become a mother, even though I know she'd feel all your torment right with you. It's a cross you must bear, but what's done is done, Mylee, and unfortunately there's nothing you can do to change anything now. If this baby has issues, there's nothing you can do to stop it. You just have to be prepared for when it's triggered."

"I know. I hate I've cursed this baby before it's even born."

"It is not a curse, Mylee. It's an adjustment. It's a test you're given to work with to guide you in life. You work with it, you move with it, you flow with it. It pushes you, and you push back. It's a part of you. You can't change it. You accept and embrace it. Bipolar disorder is not *what* you are, it doesn't define you, it's simply one piece of the complicated puzzle. We all know that puzzles have way more than one piece to them, right?"

"Right… when did you become so insightful?"

He chuckles. "I've been to a lot of psychiatrist appointments in my life between you and your mother. So I've picked up some of their wisdom."

I lean in gripping his hand tighter. "I'm glad they rubbed off on you because I really needed to hear that. You know exactly what to say and when to say it."

"I'm your dad, I'm meant to be perfect."

I snort rolling my eyes. "You're crazy."

He chuckles. "Yeah, a hell of a lot of the time, I am. But we all have a little crazy in us."

I raise my brow. "Ain't that the truth?"

Movement in the doorway makes me eyes swing to it. I see Trax beaming from ear to ear.

Dad looks to Trax letting out a deep throaty groan like he's annoyed. "Right, I have some business to attend to. I'm going to be here for a couple of days before I have to go back. So relax, let us all take care of you, okay?"

"Okay. And Dad?"

"Yeah, baby?"

"Don't be too hard on, Trax."

He grunts as Trax heads back out of the room obviously knowing Dad's coming for him.

"I make no promises," Dad sneers as he steps out of the room his footsteps pounding like lead weights.

Oh fuck.

CHAPTER 17

TRAX

Standing in the hall waiting for Crest has me anxious. I know he's coming, I'm just waiting for him. I saw him briefly when he arrived, but he was way too concerned about seeing Mylee to care about talking to me, but I know we're about to get into it now.

Crest rounds the door of Mylee's room, his finger coming out, pointing straight at me, then down the hall with a grunt. I sigh in understanding. He wants to take this argument away from Mylee's room so she can't hear us. She doesn't need the added stress of hearing her father ream me a new one.

We walk down the hall in awkward silence until we reach an outdoor area where it's completely void of people.

As soon as the door shuts, Crest lets out a grunt throwing his hands in the air, his booming voice echoing around the vast area. "You claimed her!"

I tense as I gauge his level of anger. "She's been mine for years, Crest. I know it. She knows it. Hell, *you* know it, too. We just needed for everything to fall into place."

"You fucking claimed her!" he reiterates stepping so close I can smell the tobacco on his breath.

I look him dead in his eyes with an exhale. "I did. And I'd do it again in a second. I mean it, Crest. I love her."

His eyes are cold with a stern glint in them as he steps even closer. His hands grab at my shirt, scrunching tightly as he bores into my eyes. "You. Claimed. Her. Trax."

I shrug not knowing what else to do. It only makes him worse as he shoves me hard. I stumble back a step almost falling, but it's like everything moves in slow motion as his fist clenches. My eyes widen as I follow his movement, his weathered tight knuckles flying straight at my jaw, but I'm too stunned to deflect before searing pain sweeps over me. A crunching sound reverbs through my ears as the firm knock to the side of my cheek pushes me to the side. I grip onto my jaw as I spit out a small line of blood.

The punch was hard.

It was deserved.

Suddenly, it sinks in—I claimed her without running it past him, without asking for his permission. It's like asking your father-in-law for permission to marry his daughter but in a different kind of way. She's a biker brat, she belongs to another club, and now I have taken over her ownership without seeking permission. When I had full intentions of talking to him about it. *Fuck!*

Slowly, I raise up clenching the side of my face. His eyes are hard as he stares while he shakes out his hand.

"I should've asked your permission. Agreed. I should've come to you, asked if you were good. Agreed. But you have to know if you said no, I would've done it anyway."

A slow grin crosses his face as he shoves me away from him again. "Yeah, I fucking know it. What I didn't know was this was going to happen so soon. One month, Trax! She's been here not even *two damn months,* and you're already taking her from me."

"I'll never take her from you, Crest, but she's my woman now. I'll do everything I can to look after her, to take care of her and our baby."

Slumping his body, he sighs. "Yeah, yeah. I trust my daughter and my grandchild in your hands. That's why I brought her to you in the first place. No one loves her the way you do. I've always known it. But if you *ever*... and I mean *ever* fucking undermine me again, so help me God, Trax, I'll do more than thrust my fist through your motherfucking teeth."

Chuckling, I rub my jaw again. "Okay, for the next big question that needs to be asked, I'll get your permission first."

He cockily smirks. "Let's just get through this pregnancy before we start thinking about *that* big fucking question."

"Right. We'll get settled, but I can promise you, Crest, I *will* come to you one day asking for your permission for Mylee's hand."

He groans. "Prove yourself during this pregnancy, then we'll fuckin' talk."

"Deal." I place out my hand for him to shake. He lets out a small laugh as he slaps my hand away making me flinch at his reaction. He steps up, wrapping his arms around me in a tight bear hug. Closing my eyes, I feel the warmth of a father figure, something I haven't had for six long years since my father's accident with Zoey. It's good to have a connection to Crest that isn't brute manliness. It's a deeper connection, and while living in the brotherhood is all about being a man and showing your tougher side all the time, sometimes when connected by someone who brings two men together, it's showing your softer side that truly connects you to each other, making your bond even stronger than you know. He is, and always will be, a part of my family. He's the grandfather of my child, a man I look up to, and he's the father of my woman, a man I respect above all else.

I'm normally a hard man, a broken man, but right now with Crest and Mylee down the hall carrying our unborn baby, I'm starting to feel like all the fractured pieces of me might be finally starting to meld back together.

One small piece at a time.

Crest pulls back slapping my back a few times for good measure. "You're going to be good for her, kid. I can feel it."

"I'm gonna do my best. I'm gonna do everything I can for her, for our baby. Make a life for us, protect us from everything coming our way... every-fucking-thing."

"I trust you. If there's one thing I know in all of this mess, it's the fact you'll lay down your life for Mylee. I've never once doubted that."

"I'll never give you a reason to doubt it, Crest. I promise you, my kid, my woman, I'm gonna make us the happiest fucking family you've ever seen."

"Yeah, you will. 'Cause if you don't, I'm going to ream you a new damn asshole."

I snort out a laugh. "Are we good?"

He chuckles. "Yeah, we're always good. You have the best interest of my baby girl at heart. Just don't leave me out, that's all I ask."

I sigh regretting my actions. I should have asked him, but my claim on Mylee came out before I had a chance. "You'll know about everything as it happens. You have my word."

"Good, now let's go sit with our girl and make her laugh. She needs to keep her spirits up because tomorrow's going to be a hard day for you both."

I take a deep breath knowing tomorrow's where the rest of our lives change dramatically. I feel good knowing we have a great support team around us—my family, her family, the club. Everyone's here for us. We just have to take this leap of faith together.

We can do this.

MYLEE

Leaving the hospital was a wake-up call. It brought home the fact that I have to step into the real world and actually do this pregnancy thing. Trax has been nothing but the doting partner, and while everyone's being so unbelievably supportive, it's a scary thought coming back to the clubhouse.

As Trax leads me through the door—my heart's racing so fast, my leg's aching from the accident—I take a breath remembering this is my home. These are my people. I *can* fucking do this.

I step inside, and the moment I do, a roaring cheer erupts through the clubhouse. A small laugh escapes my mouth as Trax pushes me inside. I hadn't realized I'd stopped walking as I glance back to him with a wide smile.

"See… everyone's happy for us," he murmurs.

Lala and Freckles bound over to us. Lala instantly rushes her hand to my stomach as Freckles swats her daughter's hand away while I giggle.

"Lala, you don't randomly go touchin' people's stomachs," Freckles calls out.

But Lala takes no notice and bends down in front of me, her face to my tummy. "Hello in there, my little niece. Your Auntie Lala is going to have so much fun with you."

Trax shakes his head as Freckles rolls her eyes, and Lala finally straightens herself upright after she's finished talking to the baby.

"He's going to be a boy," Trax corrects.

I turn to him raising my brow with a smirk.

Lala's mouth twists up. "Nope, it's a girl. I can feel it," she coos, then places her hand on my tummy once again. I look back at her with a chuckle while warmth floods through me.

This is actually happening.

It finally clicks.

I'm pregnant.

I knew, I mean in the hospital it registered, but not until right now with all this hype is it truly sinking in.

This is big.

This is kind of… amazing!

"Welcome to your party, Mylee. We're celebratin' this amazing news," Freckles cheers.

Again my brain registers as I look around noticing the balloons, streamers, and the giant inflatable baby—geez that shit's actually kind of creepy—it makes me laugh. I glance to Trax who's grinning wide. *I wonder if he knew about this.* He shrugs as warmth flows through me in delight.

"You guys... thanks so much."

Lala grabs my hand dragging me away as she leads me over to a group of people. Sass, Foxy, Ruby, everyone's here including all the brothers. I'm swarmed by people congratulating me, and I lap it up. This is going to be a good thing. So I get lost in the party, enjoying it as I glance over to Trax who's standing with his brother watching me with a giant lopsided smile on his face. He appears undeniably happy.

The party continues on with fun, laughter, drinking—orange juice for me, of course. I'm busy chatting with Lala when Ace makes his way over, his man bun in perfect order. I smirk when he throws his hands out to the side.

"Well, well... congratulations are in order," he praises leaning in giving me a brief hug.

"Honestly, I wasn't sure I would cope, but having you guys supporting me like this..." I trail off.

He bumps my shoulder. "Mylee, you know you always have my support. No matter what life throws at you. But this? This is fantastic news. Fuck! I couldn't be happier you and Trax are settling down. I couldn't imagine anyone better, you're perfect for him."

My heart leaps into my throat. I sigh as I reach out grabbing Ace and pulling him into another tight hug. Ace has always been good to me, been such a great friend.

A clearing throat makes me pull back to see Trax standing beside us. His eyes show he's perturbed, so I break free from Ace as I roll my eyes.

"Urgh, get over it," I mock.

Trax raises his brow feigning disapproval. "Get over it? I'll show *you* get over it," he grunts as he grabs me around the waist hoisting me into his arms.

I let out a scream as I throw my arms around his neck while everyone laughs. "Trax! Put me down. This is our party."

He chuckles. "Party's over, baby," he yells as he walks us through the crowd toward the hall.

I giggle as I wave to everyone while we disappear down the hall. We step up to Trax's room, he walks us in closing the door with his foot. He strolls over to the bed then proceeds to place me down onto the mattress. His broad frame, teamed with his lopsided smirk makes my clit throb instantly. His tongue darts out licking his bottom lip seductively which only makes me clamp down on my bottom lip.

He saunters toward me as he shrugs out of his cut. I raise my brow as he places it on the table beside the bed. "Don't throw me cheek like that in front of my brothers, Mylee." He steps up to the edge of the bed, his fingers linking with the hem of his shirt as he yanks it over his head, his abs almost glisten against the slight sheen on his body which makes the bruises seem darker. Slight tension fills the room.

"It's just so easy to tease you when it comes to Ace," I taunt him.

He groans, throwing his shirt to the floor bringing his knee to the edge of the bed beside my leg. His hands move either side of me, the bed dipping with his weight as he moves over the top of me. My hands slide up his strong biceps. That spark that we both always feel ignites between us as I pull my lips in tight together, and he glares down at me.

"You're being very disobedient, Sparx."

My brows pulls together. "Sparks?"

He inches closer. I feel it, the energy, the pulse, the spark. "I know you feel it. I fucking come alive near you, Mylee. You electrify me, even when you're being a brat. You never fail to ignite me. So, I'm calling you Sparx from now on… with an x at the end to match my name. Trax and Sparx."

Drawing my bottom lip in by my teeth, a shiver washes over my spine. Foxy and Sass both have Old Lady names. I'm so fucking honored that Trax is giving me one too. One to match his nonetheless.

"Sparx… I like it."

He rolls his hips into me making me whimper. "Great, now be a good girl and stop with the Ace bullshit."

I smirk. "But if I do that, you won't punish me." I wiggle my eyebrows.

His glare hardens as he groans. "I let you get away with way too much."

"Then, right now, do whatever you want. I've been bad, so teach me how to be good."

His eyes widen. "Fuck woman!" He sucks in a sharp breath as his hips roll into my pussy. His hard cock ever present. "Even when being a bad girl, you know how to be so, so good."

I tilt my hips grinding my pussy against the seam of his jeans causing sweet friction between us. We both let out a heavy breath as he shakes his head. He leans in giving me a quick peck on my lips, before pulling back to look at me. He exhales, then bends down sliding his hands down my thighs. The movement is slow, seductive, and it sends a tingle all the way down my spine. I smile as I watch him.

His hands move to my ankle boots pulling them off swiftly as he then makes his way up to the hem of my jeans. All the while, I lay back on the bed, just letting him dish out whatever he wants. He's running this show. I'm just holding on for the untamed ride. He undoes my jeans then pulls them down slowly along with my panties being cautious of my thigh wound.

He grins widely as he looks at my pussy. I roll my eyes as he stands back from the bed and starts to unbuckle his belt. Instinctively, I begin pulling off the rest of my clothes, throwing them off the bed as he steps out of his jeans. His rock-hard cock springs to attention as he stands before me. I flop back down to the bed.

"Oh no, baby. Up you get. Roll over. On all fours," he demands.

My stomach flutters with anticipation as I move on the bed. He kneels behind me, the mattress shifting as my knees dig into the soft fabric. My hands splay out as my hair falls down around my face. His hands slide in around my hips—warm, inviting, demanding—as he positions me as he wants me. Anticipation is building, adrenaline is pumping, the need to be with him is overwhelming as my clit throbs so much I feel like it might burst. I want to touch myself to ease the pressure as he moves in behind me, the head of his cock pressing against my pussy.

"Don't talk like that to me in front of a brother again. Do you hear me?"

I smile. "Yes."

A sudden slap on my ass sends a sting reverberating through my body as I wince but clench my eyes at the desire flowing through me while I shudder with need. With want.

He better fuck me soon, or I'm going to start begging for it.

"You better promise, Mylee. Or I'm *not* going to fuck you."

I audibly whimper as I push back slightly, so the tip of his cock edges inside of me ever so slightly. I relish in the feeling. "I fucking promise, Konnor. I need you."

With a loud groan, he thrusts forward and up, his thick cock pushing inside of me, so full, so hard, I clench my eyes tight unprepared for the intrusion. My fingers dig in grasping the soft fabric of the quilt. I let out a loud moan as his fingers grab my hips holding me in place.

I don't know if it's the fact I'm pregnant which makes everything feel more sensitive, more lustful than normal, but right now he's only just thrust inside of me, and I feel like I'm right on the edge.

"Shit, Konnor," I somehow blurt out.

He takes that as his cue to start moving.

Hard.

Fast.

Unrelenting.

I can hardly keep up with him. He's moving so untamed, wild, feral. He's fucking me. The sound of skin slapping echoes through the room, the force of his thrusts only makes for waves of deep pleasure to roll through me. I can hardly catch my breath as I try to keep up with him.

His form of punishment I'll take any day of the week. Fuck me! I *need* this every day of the week. If fucking feels this good, I want to do it all day long while I'm pregnant. I don't care how fucking big I get.

His hand slides down from my waist underneath me. I chew on my bottom lip as his finger finds its way to my clit pressing on it, making everything heighten even more. It's like the world shifts, and I gasp for much-needed air. My back arches as my skin riddles in sweat. I flame so hot I can barely contain myself. Lights flash behind my eyes as I scream out his name.

"Konnor," I yell as I explode in the most excruciatingly amazing orgasm of my life. My muscles contract so tight I feel myself squeezing around his cock as he groans, jolting still. I feel his cock throb then unload inside of me with untamed force.

"Fuck," he roars as his fingers grip onto my hips so tight I think it might bruise my already bruised body.

We both pant as I collapse to the bed. Both our bodies drop from the exhaustion. He falls to my side pulling out of me as he goes. I turn my head to the side to face him, then he smiles at me while reaching out swiping some hair from my face.

"Fuck! My desires got the better of me, and I treated you roughly. I'm a dickhead."

"I know you'd never hurt me. Besides, I like it when you punish me," I murmur.

He chuckles. "I can punish you whenever you want, Sparx."

I lean over planting a soft kiss on his lips, the moment now tender unlike the hard fucking from moments before. I like how we can go from hard to soft. We have variations in our relationship, and we know exactly how to deal with each other.

This is why we work.

We know each other so well.

This is why I *know* we *will* work.

Why we *have* to work.

Because together, we just... fit.

Laying in Trax's bed, his arms around me, I can't help but think being pregnant makes sex feel even better. Is that possible? I need to Google that shit. If it is the case, we're going to be having a lot of sex. Letting out a contented sigh, I glance around his room, taking in its size. It's big. Not huge, but much larger than my room. I know I need to make the move now. Being pregnant and claimed means I need to be in here with my man. I have to move my things in and be with him, but we also need to make this room baby friendly.

Rolling on my side, I rest on my elbow looking at Trax as he continues to lay on his back looking at the wall.

"We're going to have to move out my desk, maybe paint the walls. Make this a real little family area. I have a heap of closet space, so there's no worry about all your stuff fitting in here. But you *are* moving in here, Sparx. Don't even think about fighting me on this."

I run my finger up and down his bare chest. "Wouldn't dream of it. I'm your Old Lady. I belong in here with you. I was actually just thinking about moving all my stuff in here. I would like to keep my room as an office, though. I want us to just be a family in here, and work should be separated."

Trax grabs my arms, spinning me, so I fall back to the bed as he moves in on top of me. I giggle as he looks down then gently places a kiss on my nose. "As it should be." He continues to look down at me with nothing but love in his eyes.

I move my hand up to caress his cheek. "Tell me... do you want a girl or a boy?"

He rolls off me, laying back on the bed pulling me into his chest for a cuddle. "It has to be a boy. I don't know what the fuck I'd do if it were a girl."

I let out a laugh. "You'd spoil her like a fucking princess."

He lets out another contented sigh. "Yeah... yeah, I would. Maybe I do want a girl after all..." His face contorts. "Oh shit! Then she's going to want to go on dates when she's older. No. Fuck! No. It has to be a boy... boys are all I can handle." He turns toward me, his hand reaching out rubbing my bare tummy. His body bending over as he shuffles down the bed, his lips pressing on my stomach making my heart flutter. My fingers threading through his hair. "You hear me in there, you have to be a boy, so I can teach you how to ride a bike and shoot a gun... I can't teach a girl that shit."

"Why the hell can't you teach a girl that? I know how to ride and shoot a gun?"

He looks up at me, his brows creasing as he takes in this information. "Well, shit! Yeah, I suppose you do. Crap! I'm going to have a biker brat. Fuck... I'm going to be a dad," he gushes excitedly making me smile so wide, loving how enthusiastic he is right now.

Seeing him happy is making *me* happy. Knowing he's in this with me makes everything that little bit easier. This is by no means going to be easy, but maybe, just maybe, it might be the best thing to happen to both of us.

CHAPTER 18

Trax

One Week Later

The last week with Sparx has been great. Knowing we have an appointment in a week with the OB/GYN to see the baby for the first time is all I can think about. But Enzo has been on our case and, to be honest, I don't blame him. While I'm celebrating the surprise of bringing my child into the world, he's dealing with the departure of his, and we need to get our asses in gear and get this sorted for him before the Scarsis won't accept the trade.

Enzo has already told them we have a woman to trade in Zia's place. Torque was able to get Cindi prepped and prepared for the handover. Woman is crazy if you ask me, but if she's down for it, then more praise to Cindi, and the club will be indebted to her.

Ace has uploaded a file on Cindi making her seem like she has no past, no connections other than the club, and it's as if no one will miss her. The file is really convincing if you ask me. It contains everything including her fighting abilities.

So today, we're heading off into Scarsi territory to make the trade. Cindi for Zia, and hope like hell nothing goes wrong. We're all mingling in the clubhouse ready to ride out to the meet point.

Ruby is holding onto Cindi like she'll never see her again. I exhale hating that if this all goes south, we could lose Cindi—this is a huge fucking risk.

Sparx is standing back in the corner watching. She knows a little of what's going on but not the full extent. I didn't want to scare her.

Kline walks up to Cindi along with Ace. "Cindi, Ace has designed a tracker that's untraceable to outside sources. If you're scanned, no one will pick it up, but the club will be able to see where you are at all times." Kline holds up a syringe, and Cindi nods with a bright smile.

"Of course you did, Ace," Cindi beams. "I swear if *Cyberdyne Systems* ever exists, you're gonna be working there," she calls out, and we all chuckle at the Terminator reference as Kline injects the small bug into Cindi's underarm.

"Okay, we all know how this goes. We play by Enzo's rules, follow his lead. It's his family on the line here. Disperse," Torque calls out.

I stride over to Sparx grabbing her hands and looking her in the eyes. "Look after that baby of ours."

She smiles. "Look after you. I can't do this on my own, Daddy."

A beaming smile lights my face as I lean in and kiss her hard, the kiss is quick as Torque sends a sharp whistle through the room. I break away from her as I mouth 'love you,' and I turn walking over to Cindi and wrap my arm around her shoulders. "C'mon beautiful, you're riding with me."

She chuckles. "Well, I thought you'd never ask," she chimes with a wink.

Cindi's grip on me is tight as we ride the twenty-five-minute journey to the Illinois International Port District. It's further out from both the Andretti and Defiance turf, so we're heading into Scarsi territory. This is unknown terrain for us. We don't know exactly how the Scarsi's operate, Defiance has never dealt with them. We've never had to. Enzo bringing us into his war with them doesn't seem like a good idea to me, but it's too little too late to back out now.

When you owe a debt, it must be paid.

And we owe Enzo.

Plus, this is something I can't let pass, nor can my brothers. An innocent eleven-year-old girl being sold into a trafficking ring is *not* acceptable. We won't stand for it. I won't stand for it. So if swallowing my fucking pride when it comes to Enzo and helping the fucker out means I need to step it up, I'm going to.

The roar of our bikes soars down the street leading to the docks. If we wanted to be unannounced, we went about it the wrong way. But they knew we were coming, so what's the point in being stealthy? I notice the red Alpha Romeos are already here, and as we slowly pull up, one by one, the engines turning off and dulling the roar to a silence, only the calm, soothing sounds of Lake Michigan roll and rock against the side of the docks.

Enzo, Franky, and his men step out of the Romeos, and we slide off our rides as Cindi converts into her character immediately. She yanks off her helmet, throwing it to the ground, and then starts to bolt. Opening my eyes wide, I race after her, my strides twice the size of hers catching her almost instantly as I grab Cindi around the waist holding her to me. She lets out an almighty scream as she throws her legs in the air, thrashing about.

"No, let me go. You can't do this to me, you fucking assholes. I hate you, you motherfucking—"

I cover her mouth with my hand as I drag her back toward the group and struggle to keep hold of her. I lean against her ear. "You're doing perfect, keep it up."

She struggles even harder, kicking me in my shin. Pain sears through my leg as I let out a grunt. "Fuck!"

"Feisty. I like her. Maybe she *will* be better than Zia after all," a voice chimes from behind us as we all turn to see a bunch of men in well-tailored suits with a bright blue handkerchief hanging out their top pockets. The main guy stares at Cindi and me. She stops kicking for a moment as she glares at the guy. He's tall, well built, oily black hair slicked back with far too much grease. He has an air about him as his eye twitches in a menacing way. I'm sure women would find him attractive, but there's something about him, he sends off a vibe, something that screams don't come near me.

His lackeys flank him either side, none as tall as him as they stare us all down. The tension in the air rife with unspoken words.

Enzo steps forward, the hard edge in his stance lets me know he isn't fucking around. "If you've hurt Zia, I swear to God, Matteo..."

I raise my brow. Matteo Scarsi, the Don of the Scarsi Dettagli, in the flesh. Well damn!

"You'll what, Enzo? You're a small fish in a very big pond, stronzo. And I don't care much for seafood."

"Asshole? Is that the best you've got?" Enzo goes to lunge forward, but Torque and Franky both reach out grabbing him before he gets himself shot and his little girl shipped off to Cuba. Enzo curls up his lip. "You like what you see in Cindi? Take her and give me back my principessa."

Matteo curls up his lip with a shrug, then looks over to Cindi and me. "Bring me the feisty fighter."

Cindi screams under my hand, her hot tears run over my fingers and down her face as she kicks against me again. I'm almost having trouble remembering this is all for show. She's doing such a good job, it's making me want to light this place up instead of handing her over.

I struggle to walk with Cindi over toward the Scarsis. I feel every set of eyes on me as she kicks and screams against my hands. But I push through, dragging her in front of Matteo. His eyes linger up and down her body as a sly smile creeps up on his face.

"I like it when they fight." His hand comes out grabbing the hem of her top, and he yanks it down, ripping her top right open exposing her naked breast.

She stills looking down at her top as she tries to back away, but she's only backing into me as I shudder on the inside hating that she's going through this.

Matteo takes a deep breath as he licks his lips, his finger moving out, and he slides it over her neck. She stops thrashing, stilling, her body shaking as his finger slides down her neck and then onto her breast. I feel like a dick for not doing anything as I look away.

"Enough of the games, Matteo. You have your trade, now give me Zia!" Enzo calls out, and Scarsi snaps his head up dropping his hand from Cindi to look at Enzo.

"Fine. The girl is a good trade. You can have Zia back, and your effort to get out of trafficking is accepted. But this is it, Enzo. Our alliance is done. You can't come to me for anything ever again."

Enzo nods once, a slight look of relief flooding his features.

"Bring the principessa, take the fighter. I'm going to have fun with her." He waves his hand through the air as one of his men yanks Cindi from me. I hesitate to let her go as my hand drops from her mouth, and finally, she's able to scream to her heart's content as he pulls her into his arms, fucking guilt consuming me.

"You fucking traitors, Defiance. I'm going to kill you all for this. How could you do this to me, you fucking biker scum-ass bastards? I hate you, Trax," she screams making me glance up at her as he drags her inside, but she looks right at me as he pulls her through the door. "I hate you," she yells, but I catch the sly smile on her lips and the wink she throws my way.

Fuck, she's so damn good. She really does need to be an actress. I just hope whatever they do to her, she can handle because that performance really had me fooled.

Another man walks out with a small girl in tow, but she has a black sack over her head, and I sigh as I take in the sight. *Shit.*

"You put a bag over her head, you fiche fottute!" Enzo runs forward, but suddenly the Scarsis all draw their guns on us. My muscles tense as I grab for my Glock without hesitation, and draw it up aiming it right at Matteo's head as my brothers all do the same. I notice the Andrettis don't move.

Scarsi's men smile at us as I glance to Torque who holds firm. "I see your bikers aren't so smart, Enzo, pull on the leash, and if you call me a fucking cunt again, I will revoke our deal."

I furrow my brows as I aim it higher and click off the safety making Matteo look directly at me and take a deep breath. "I wouldn't do that if I were you, Trax. Things are going smoothly, and if Zia is going to go home tonight, you and your brothers should stow your weapons. Now."

"You drew yours first, we're just playing copycat," I mock.

He chuckles. "I like you." He looks to Torque and raises his brow. "I like him, president. Watch him, he has spirit... drop your guns, boys. Enzo, get the girl, let's get this all over with. I'm done with this boring shit."

The Scarsi's all stow their guns, so I click my safety back on and place my Glock down my pants as my brothers follow suit. Enzo races forward and pulls the sack off his daughter's head. She's really sweet with curly black hair. Her eyes blink rapidly as she looks up at her dad. Zia's eyes light up, and then she bursts into tears.

"Papa!" She throws her arms around her father, and he lifts her up cuddling her to him as the Scarsis turns one by one leaving only Matteo and two guards.

"You're done with us, Enzo. We won, remember that." He grunts then turns, walking inside the building as I step over with Torque to Enzo. Tears fill his eyes as he plants a kiss on his daughter's face.

"Zia, I will always fight for you, my principessa."

"I know, Papa. I knew you would come."

He clears his throat as he looks into her eyes. "Did the bad men hurt you?"

She shakes her head. "They gave me milkshakes and a whole load of candy. But I did watch a horror movie, they said you wouldn't be happy about that."

Enzo laughs shaking his head. "Principessa, you can have all the candy in the world. I don't even care about the movie. You go with Uncle Franky and get in the car. Papa will be with you soon."

She nods as he puts her down. Franky takes Zia's hand and walks her to the bright red car. Enzo turns to Torque and me and lets out a heavy sigh. "Thank you, boys. I mean it. Thank you."

I glance back to the building to see all the Scarsis have left. "It's not over. Plan B has to come into effect yet."

Enzo nods. "Yes, let's hope like hell it works. We need to do everything in our power to make sure it does."

CHAPTER 19

MYLEE

One Week Later

Things have been tense at the club over the last week. For Trax and me, it's getting used to this whole pregnancy thing, but for the club, it's them getting used to Cindi not being here. I know plans are in place to bring her home, I just hope whatever their plan is they can pull it off.

Today, though, is our first appointment with the OB/GYN. I'm nervous. Trax is doing everything right. He's making sure to keep me calm, and honestly, I'm so fucking lucky to have him.

I've begun feeling a little queasy, so I think unfortunately morning sickness has started to kick in, which I'm not looking forward to. My knee's bobbing up and down as we sit in the waiting room. I'm anxious. I want to know our baby's doing okay.

Trax chuckles placing his hand on my knee to stop it from bouncing. "Will you stop, you're getting yourself worked up. It's not healthy for you or little squirt."

Swallowing hard, I sigh. "I know, but I can't help it."

He leans in grabbing either side of my face, forcing me to look at him. "I know this is scary, but I'm here, I'm not going to let anything happen. Everything's gonna be fine."

I let out a staggered sigh as I hear someone call out my name. Trax lets me go, so I drop the magazine I was holding on the table as we both stand up and walk toward the room.

A bed sits in the middle as I stride in. Trax moves to the chair next to it.

A woman walks in wearing a bright smile and a white lab coat. "I'm Kaylah, your technician for today. I've read up on your case, and I'm glad to be working with you. How about we get started and have a look at your baby?"

I'm so nervous, I can't say anything in response, so I simply nod.

She gestures for me to lie down. "Okay, Mylee, unbutton your jeans and lift up your top," she instructs.

Trax reaches out grabbing my hand for support.

Kaylah picks up a bottle of gel giving it a shake. "This might be a little cold." She squeezes some onto my stomach. Instantly, I flinch from the harsh coldness even with the warning.

Kaylah grabs the probe positioning it on my tummy as my hand tightens on Trax's so firmly I worry I might break his fingers. But he doesn't say a word.

I glance at him, but he's watching the screen. It momentarily makes me smile that he's so happy about us being pregnant. His demeanor soothes me as I turn to look at the screen seeing nothing but black and white blobs.

"Umm, not to sound like an idiot, but can you point out squirt for me?" Trax asks.

Kaylah looks back to the screen focusing on the black parts, clicking on a few things. "Yes, sorry, of course, but first I just want to check something with the OB/GYN. I'll be right back." She places the probe down and abruptly walks out of the room.

"What the hell? Is something wrong?" I ask, my stomach churning.

Trax studies the screen intensely. "No. It's fine. She's just checking something. It's fine. It's fine... it has to be," he murmurs the last part.

"Trax..." I whimper.

He holds my hand tighter and stands, leaning down kissing me, but it doesn't help.

He's scared too.

Something's wrong.

There's something wrong with our baby.

I just know it.

The door opens, Kaylah and our OB/GYN walk in both sporting smiles in stark contrast to how I'm feeling right now.

"I'm Dr. Branson. You've been referred to me by Rebecca Kline. I'm happy to meet you finally. How are we today?" he asks in an upbeat manner.

What the fuck! I want to punch him in his fucking face. Maybe I have anger issues too. I cock my brow as I glance to Trax, the king of anger issues.

"Is something wrong?" I whisper.

He slides onto the stool looking over the machine picking up the probe and pressing it to my stomach. "Kaylah picked up something. She just wanted to confirm it with me before she said anything."

My heart leaps into my throat. "We can't make out anything on the screen, please tell me the baby is okay."

Dr. Branson's warm smile does nothing to soothe me as he presses onto my stomach a little firmer then points to the screen. "See how there are two black spots?" he asks, and I squint. He then points to a scan on the wall of an ultrasound picture. "When there's a baby in the womb, there's usually one black spot like in that picture up there... You, however, have two."

Trax gasps like he's understanding. I, however, still don't have a clue. "So what does that mean? Is the baby in trouble? What's going on?" I blurt out in quick succession as Trax's hand tightens in mine.

"You want to see? Here's one…" He points to the little pebble inside the first black dot.

My heart squeezes. "And it's okay?"

"I think you're missing what I'm saying, Mylee."

"What do you mean?" I grunt out in frustration.

He points to the second black spot, to another pebble. "And here's baby number two."

"Two babies? Twins?" I stutter out.

"Yes, two healthy, little babies. Measuring at eight weeks."

I gasp for air. "Whoa two? I don't—"

Trax tightens his grip on my hand making me turn to look at him. The soft look in his eyes eases my tension straight away. He looks into my eyes, bringing his hand up to my face gently stroking my cheek as he breathes in and out slowly, making me mirror his breaths. I didn't even realize he was doing it or that I was in a place where I needed it. He knows me better than I know my damn self.

"You're okay, baby, just breathe. In and out. Breathe with me."

I take in a deep breath and let it out slowly as he keeps his eyes focused on mine. "Sparx, this isn't a big deal. This is cool, having two means twice the fun."

I let out a stifled laugh, my shaking hand coming up to wipe a falling tear from my eye. "Trax, this is huge for us."

He smiles, his eyes glistening as they sparkle. "We will raise our twins tough, their mother is one of the strongest women I know, and look at their father. I mean… he's pretty fucking epic."

I can't help but laugh as he wipes the single tear away that's escaped my eye. "We got this. You, me, and the twins. This is going to be amazing, babe. Right now just enjoy the moment. Look at the screen… take it in because Sparx, we're having twins. That's fucking amazing. You need to remember this moment for how utterly fantastic it is." He beams looking into my eyes.

His encouraging words are making this all seem so emotional. I have to remember this is all new territory, but if I spend this entire pregnancy being nervous, I'm going to miss out on the journey and the exciting parts.

I need to enjoy it.

I need to remember it.

So, I turn back to the screen while Kaylah and Dr. Branson smile kindly as if they have seen this all before.

He clicks on some more buttons. "You want to hear their heartbeats?"

"Oh gosh, we can do that?"

He smiles as I look to Trax feeling suddenly overjoyed as a small excited giggle escapes me. "Yeah… yes, please."

A whooshing sound filters through the room, and after a short time, Dr. Branson starts taking some snapshots for us to take home.

I can't believe this. We came in here this morning thinking we had one baby, but we're going to be leaving here with two. How the hell did that happen? All I know is I'm so glad I have Trax here with me. I'd be lost without him.

"Okay, I think we have all we need. I'll book you in for another scan in a few weeks, but you can check in with me at any time if you need to."

"Thank you. Thank you so much. Sorry about the tears," I murmur.

"Don't be. Finding out about twins is daunting. Seeing one baby's a shock, add in another unexpected one, and most people are terrified. Your reaction was quite normal."

It's weird because I generally put my reactions down to bipolar disorder, but I know my psych has often said I have normal reactions and nothing to do with my illness. I guess this was a *normal* reaction.

All I know is this changes things. Lucky we hadn't started decorating the room, now we'll need to plan for two basinets instead of one. The room is big, but it's not massive. We're going to be crowded, but it will be worth it just to have my family all together.

TRAX

Sparx was a trooper at the appointment, and for the entire car ride home she's been trying to hide her smile. I know she's equal parts anxious as she is excited, but I know her excitement will win over.

I grab her hand as we walk inside the clubhouse. Surge and Mom are sitting at the bar as we walk in.

Mom glances up at us. "Boyo, how'd your appointment go?" she calls out, so I lead Sparx over to my mother, and the man who's like a father to my brother and me.

Sparx beams as I wrap my arm around her shoulders pulling her to my side and raise my brow with a cocky grin. "Seems I have super sperm," I mock.

Surge chuckles as Mom grimaces. "What on God's green earth does that mean?" Mom asks as Mylee pushes my shoulder.

I place my hand on Sparx's stomach. "It's twins!"

Mom lets out an ear-piercing scream as she stands from her stool throwing her hands in the air. Everyone turns to look at us.

"Geez, woman, calm it down," Surge berates.

Mom quickly slaps Surge on the chest. His arm now out of the damn sling as he winces from the sting as Mom races forward grabbing Sparx, hugging her in a swaying motion from side to side. I chuckle as Sparx hugs Mom back.

"Oh, lordy, lordy, Lord, we need a celebration. A lunch. Yes, we need a feast—"

"Mom, stop. We don't need a celebration every time we get news. We've had a big morning. Let's let Sparx have some rest," I state.

She lets Sparx go pulling back at an arm's distance and looking over her as Sparx smiles.

"Oh gosh, of course. You must be tired. Go, have a nap. Then later I'll make you some soothin' tea."

"Thanks. I'm exhausted."

"Of course, you go, girlie. Lay down and rest. We can celebrate later."

"C'mon," I tell her.

I glance to Surge, and he subtly nods as I wrap my arm around her, then we head off down the hall. We step into my room, and I walk her to my bed as she sits on the edge. I bend down pulling off her shoes and glance up at her. "I was proud of you today. You can handle any shit that's thrown at you."

She exhales flopping down on the bed. I stand up moving to the bed sitting next to her and look into her eyes. "Will it be a challenge? Fuck yes, but we can do it!"

Sparx looks at me. "Fuck yeah, we can!" She leans in giving me a swift kiss on my lips. The spark, the sizzle that ignites when she kisses me is there like it always is, but now is not the time to take this further. Right now I need to let her rest. "Trax, these babies... they're going to have the best chance at life. You know why?"

I raise my brow. "Why?"

"Because you're their dad."

I lean in kissing her again, a little longer this time. But eventually, I move back and place the covers over her. "Now you sleep. I'm going to go and work on some club stuff, but I have my cell if you need me."

Her eyes blink like she's already drifting off. "Don't let me sleep too long."

I chuckle. "Yes, ma'am." I turn, heading for the door leaving her to rest while I go in search of my blood brother. While Sparx's taking in the news of having twins, I am over the fucking moon about it, and I need to tell Torque before Mom gets to him.

CHAPTER 20

TRAX

Walking into the chapel, Torque and Ace are busy at Ace's desk. I can see they're looking at the detection on Cindi's tracker. From what I can see, she's somewhere in Miami. They both look up bobbing their heads in greeting as I approach.

"Fucker, you've been MIA this morning, where you been?" Torque asks.

I can't help the rush of adrenaline that courses through me. "At a doctor's appointment with Sparx. Got the first scan of the baby today," I reply. They both look at me seemingly now more interested.

Torque drops the folder he has in his hand to the desk, and he exhales with a shrug. "And? Is it a boy or a girl?" he asks.

I let out a laugh as I walk up to him and Ace. "Too early for that yet, but..." I pause for effect, they both frown as I beam with pride. "It's twins," I blurt out.

They both open their mouths wide as Torque punches me in my bicep. "No fuckin' way?" he asks as I chuckle.

"Yep, two mini-mes."

Ace shakes his head as he continues to type on his computer. "Jesus Christ, two more Trax's in the world... fuck me!"

I snort. "Shut up, asshole. What are you fuckers talking about anyway?"

Ace chuckles as he looks up. "We're tracking Cindi. She's stalled in Miami which is good. We've put in our bid on their site. Hopefully, it's accepted before she's shipped off to Cuba. If it is, we'll send in our buyer. If it's not, we're off to Cuba for extraction."

I smirk. "Have you convinced someone to play the part yet?"

Torque chuckles. "Working on it. I have the man, just getting him prepped."

"Should I ask who?"

"You wouldn't believe me if I told you."

Raising my brow, I smirk. "Hmmm... intriguing, I like it. What else is happening?"

"We're also working on the latest shipment to Linn, everything seems to be running smoothly. Which is nice for a damn change," Ace chimes.

Torque grunts. "Yeah, things are a little too calm around here. We go into meetings without a shootout or double cross. Fuck, I don't know," he mocks, and I raise my brow.

"Now why would you go saying shit like that for?"

Torque laughs throwing his hands in the air. "Maybe I need to go have an argument with Enzo. Keep things interesting?" he teases as my brows knit together.

"You sound like I used to. Have we traded places or something?"

Torque snorts. "Since Sparx came along and your sessions with Sensei, you've changed. I like it. Don't go back to that chaos and carnage shit," Torque adds slapping my back as he starts to walk out of the chapel. "You're gonna be a father now, stay on the straight and narrow, brother. The *straight and narrow*," he yells as he walks out leaving me with Ace.

I look to him tilting my head. "Was that his version of a pep talk?"

Ace chuckles. "I have no idea. I think you having kids has thrown him. He's in a good place with Foxy, but maybe it's making him think about where they should be going. They have their house down the road, they're settled, but maybe he's starting to think of more... I dunno?"

I raise my brow. I wonder if he wants to go the kids or marriage route with Foxy first? I guess only time will tell. But right now I'm alone in the chapel with Ace. The guy who I've treated like shit since Mylee showed up. Their 'friendship' has always been a sour point for me, and maybe now I have him alone, I can bury the hatchet. I figure a good way to do this is to talk to him about Mylee. So I round his desk. He looks up at me with a questioning brow.

"Did Mylee ever get you to look into anything? I was wondering if she ever asked you to do some digging."

"Yeah, brother. On the guy she's here hiding from... Everett Scott."

I take a breath. "Did you ever find anything?"

He slowly slides out the spare chair, so I take the seat next to him. He types something into his computer, and a file pops up. A picture of a guy with red hair and too many freckles to count shows up on the screen, but his build is large like maybe he used to play football.

"I couldn't find anything on him other than what we already know... psych patient, mentally unstable, son of Malcolm Scott, the senator. Nothing on Malcolm either. Absolutely crystal clean. It paints a picture that the Senator is actually a good guy... but what I can see is Everett's making waves back in Grand Rapids. He's doing everything in his power to try and find Sparx, but no one's budging or telling him where she is. The only problem is, it will only be a matter of time before he finds her. Maybe we need to take out the threat before the threat gets to us?" Ace asks.

I grimace. "That would normally be my go-to plan, but with him being the son of a senator, it makes it all a little harder."

Ace rubs his chin. "Maybe we can hire someone to take the hit for us?"

Shaking my head, I flare my nostrils. "No, we can't have anything linking back to us. If it gets out, that could bring not only us but the Notorious Knights down as well. We need to think wisely about this. I have no goddamn idea how to go about it. All I know is I need to protect my woman and our unborn babies from this psycho. She has enough to worry about than thinking about this asshole coming after her."

"Leave it with me. I'll keep digging to try and find something. I'll keep putting out false leads for Everett to track, to lead him away from here. So he thinks she's anywhere but at Defiance."

"That's a great idea, I like your thinking. I'm glad to have you on the team, Ace."

Ace sighs. "I really like Sparx, she's a great girl. I know she'll do well at this club, Trax. She's good for you. I know she's going to be a great asset for us to have here, so I want to be clear she's a friend and that's all."

I pat his back. "You're damn straight because if you make any moves on my woman, I will have your foot so far up your own ass you'll be spitting out your toenails."

Ace chuckles. "Noted. But it won't be a problem. You have my word."

I stand up moving to walk from the chapel feeling not only a sense of relief from talking it out with Ace but also a sense of dread from the unknown of Everett.

"Trax," Ace calls out. I turn back to look at him.

"Congratulations on the twins."

Smiling, I walk out of the chapel.

Two Weeks Later

It's been three weeks since the trade of Cindi for Enzo's daughter, Zia. We've been tracking Cindi's movements, but that's the only thing we can track. We can't check her vitals. We can't see if she's healthy, her mental state, nothing. So we're all on fucking edge. But finally Scarsi has approved the sale, and the money transfer has gone through.

Apparently, there was a bidding war for her online, and that was the hold-up in getting her back. Some Russian gangster wanted her too. So no matter the cost, we had to outbid. Torque had to put one of the gyms up for sale to top up the money, and Enzo equaled it, but we finally got the money together. Then, all we had to do was send in the buyer. He had to fly to Miami to collect the 'package' and then he will deliver her back here for us. If all things go smoothly, they should be arriving soon.

We all sit around the chapel table watching Cindi's tracker with bated breath, and it moves closer and closer to the clubhouse. Anxiety fills through me. I have no idea what state Cindi will be in when she arrives. All I know is that everyone is anxious to see her.

The tracker moves closer and closer, tension bubbling in the air as silence filters through the room, and a burning question echoes in my mind.

"Who was the buyer?" I blurt out, and Torque looks to me letting out a heavy breath.

"A friend of the club," he replies then subtly glances to Sensei who tilts his head as if to say 'why the hell are you looking at me' as the tracker moves inside the compound. We all stand and rush out of the chapel inside the clubrooms to see Zane and Tremor escorting Cindi inside.

She walks slowly like she's weak, but she smiles so wide as she sees us all. She looks skinnier like she's definitely lost weight. They haven't been feeding her, but she looks clean. There're bruises from obvious fights, but she appears to be taken care of besides her malnourishment. Relief floods through me as we all rush toward her, crowding around her as she wraps her arms around us all.

"Man, it's good to be home!"

We all cheer as a tear runs down her cheek, and I shudder thinking of what they must have done to her. "I'm sorry, Cindi," I plead, but she shakes her head.

"It honestly wasn't as bad as I thought. The Scarsis were polite to me, they never hurt me. That Matteo is hot, and he seemed to take a liking to me, so that part was fine. And these bruises? Trust me, the fighting was fun and the other girls came off second best. Honestly, the worst bit was one meal a day. Girl's gotta eat, so ahhh... can I have something to eat?"

"On it!" Vibe calls out as he rushes to the kitchen, Ruby and Hayley flanking him as they wipe tears from their faces.

We all move back to give her some room as a man walks into the clubhouse, and I recognize him instantly—Hiro Maki, Sensei's stepfather.

I raise my brow as he stands wearing a suit looking very... gangster.

"Father?" Sensei calls out like he's as confused as the rest of us as to why he's here.

"Hello, son, seems I'm in the business of buying women nowadays," he jokes, and I smile slapping his shoulder.

"Geez, don't let Shinobu hear you say that," I joke.

He chuckles shaking his head. "My wife knew what I was doing. I would not go into this without her blessing. But with the help your club gave my family, I was honored to be able to step in and help out in your time of need."

"And we thank you, Hiro." Torque dips his head. "Thanks for getting our girl back to us. And playing the part so well."

He bows his head as Sensei chuckles walking over to his father and dragging him away obviously to get the details.

We played the Scarsi Dettagli at their own game, and we kicked their asses without them even knowing. Enzo got his principessa back, we got Cindi, and Enzo's out of women trafficking for good.

Win, fucking win, fucking win.

You can't get any better than that.

Ace walks up to me, and I glance at him. "Good work on the tracker. You're kind of a smart ass."

He chuckles. "Yeah, I know. But this was a team effort, and you helped Cindi in this as well as me. I think we both deserve a beer. Want to join me?"

I raise my brow. "Sure, beer it is."

CHAPTER 21

TRAX

Two Weeks Later

Standing back as I lean against the bathroom door, tension ripples through me as I listen to Sparx heave into the toilet. I feel fucking terrible that I can't do anything to help her. To top it off, she doesn't want me in there with her, so I'm standing back listening behind the closed door feeling helpless as she vomits. She's three months pregnant, the books say the sickness should be starting to ease soon, but if anything, it's getting worse. I hate she's having such terrible morning sickness, but the problem is it's seven at night, and she's still sick.

Why the hell do they call it morning sickness when it lasts all day and fucking night?

"Babe, maybe we need to call the doctor again?" I call out. The sound of the toilet flushing eases my nerves slightly as I crack open the door to see her slumped on the bathroom floor next to the bowl, her pajamas a disheveled mess as she looks completely spent. I weakly smile as she frowns at me.

"What's the point, it's just morning sickness. They can't do anything. I swear these kids are trying to kill me from the inside out."

I let out a stifled laugh as I walk in taking a seat next to her on the floor, the air smelling stale, but I try not to think about it as I plonk down wrapping my arm around her, pulling her to me. Her body collapses against mine in defeat, and I hold her tightly stroking her hair. "Sparx you're doing so fucking well. I'm so proud of you." I turn to her looking her up and down. "Strip," I simply say. She wastes no time in standing up and pulling off her pajamas.

I also don't hesitate to stand up and pull off my jeans and shirt then reach in turning on the shower. I want to make her feel better. Make her feel loved. It's not about anything other than letting her know I'm here for her. Especially after everything she's going through. I'm just planning on washing and holding her. So, I lead her in, her hair instantly wetting under the hot water. Her lips slowly turn up, and I love seeing a little bit of a spark in her eyes. She grabs the toothbrush quickly brushing her teeth under the water. I watch her body move, the rivulets of water and suds sliding down as she rinses her mouth. I lick my lips taking in her naked form as I lean in planting a soft kiss against her lips. Wrapping my arms around her, I pull her to me, and of course, my cock stirs. I mean I am naked in a shower, so I can't fucking help it. But what really surprises me is that her hand is snaking down between us. Her fingers wrap around my cock, a hiss leaves my lips as they break apart from her and I look into her eyes. A small sparkle in hers makes me smirk. Her hand slowly moves up and down on my shaft, pleasure rippling through me, but this isn't what this was supposed to be about.

Taking a deep breath as the water flows between us, my hands grip onto her arms as I look into her eyes. "Baby, we don't have to—"

"I just want to lose myself, just for a little while, make me feel better," she murmurs as she strokes on my cock making it very hard to concentrate. So I grab her a little harder, pushing her back against the wall. She weakly smiles, and I lean in kissing her. Hard. My tongue assaulting hers as she pulls on me with such a flawless technique I'll be coming before I have a chance to even take another breath.

My hand slides from her arm, straight down between her legs. She parts them like a good girl, and I find her clit instantly. It's already swollen and throbbing for me as she arches her back off the wall in pleasure. We work together building each other up. She pulls on me in just the right way sending waves of pleasure through me as I rotate on her clit bringing her quickly to her peak.

Our kiss is frantic. It's chaotic, it's breathy as we work together. A shudder runs down my spine letting me know I'm so fucking close. My balls tighten, squeezing up as they prepare to let loose. I groan so loud into her mouth as my entire body stiffens while I jolt hard—my cock throbbing as I feel the pressure build and then release, my hot cum exploding straight onto her stomach. My knees buckle slightly with the relief, but I know she's close. I can't stop my movements on her as I continue to flick her clit. Her nails grip into my shoulders as she holds on, and our lips break free needing some air.

"Shit, Konnor," she almost yells as her nails dig into my skin. I'm sure they will have drawn blood as she explodes around my fingers.

I take a few breaths, then pull back and look at her stomach. I smirk as she glances down, and I pull her under the water to wash her clean. My hand moves over her silky skin, and I pause over her belly button—there's twins under the small bump. My palm splays out over her belly, and she seems to understand I need a minute to let that sink in. Leaning forward, she cuddles into me, her hand moving over mine as her head rests on my shoulder.

"I love you," she murmurs.

I look at her in awe. "I fucking love you," I reply, pulling her into a tight embrace, my lips colliding with hers. I brought her into the shower to make her feel better, but I guess I needed her to make me feel better too.

Once we're done in here, I'm going to take my girl out into the fresh air and spend some time outside.

MYLEE

The Next Day

I slowly wake but being in the arms of Trax makes a slow smile cross my face. He's been amazing the past few days that I need to show him how much I adore him, so I lean up pressing my lips to his mouth. His lips turn into a grin against mine as he slowly wakes up looking at me. He beams appearing completely happy. I feel like the morning sickness fog is lifting. I've been in such a state the last few days, this damn sickness really getting the better of me, but I feel better and more lucid.

He looks into my eyes and kisses me. "How are you this morning?" he asks.

"I think I'm hungry."

His eyes enlarge. "You think you might be able to stomach some breakfast this morning?"

I shrug. "I can try. I'm pretty hungry today, and for the first time in days, I don't feel like I want to, you know... hurl right now." I giggle.

He leans in kissing my nose, then jumps out of bed in a rush putting his clothes on. I smile as I sit up in bed slowly. I don't want to rush and risk upsetting my stomach, so I move in small, slow, measured movements as I get out of bed. I don't bother to get changed. I don't care if I go into the clubrooms in my pajamas.

They've seen me at my worst, so seeing me in my pajamas when I'm feeling better seems okay.

He grabs my hand, and we walk out of the room toward the clubrooms to the smell of bacon. It seems like every morning, without fail, Ruby and Cindi are cooking the guys bacon. How the hell aren't they all the size of a house?

It's good to see Cindi has come back with no issues at all. Her time with the Scarsis didn't harm her in the slightest—actually she seems even happier if that's possible. Torque followed through and has her enrolled in acting classes. It was a big gamble which paid off for her and the club.

We step into the clubroom and everyone turns to us. They're looking at Trax and me, smiling with genuine happiness on their faces. Happiness that I'm out here with them, joining them, back in the land of the living, back with the family, with the brotherhood. People wave tilting their heads to me in friendly greetings. A warmth floods through me. It's nice.

Trax tightens his hand in mine turning to look at me. "You doing okay?"

Genuine peace flows through me. "I'm doing just fine."

He exhales sounding relieved as he leads us over to a table where Sensei and Sass are sitting. Sass is getting ready to go to the garage, so we take a seat. "Morning, it's great you're up and about, Sparx," Sass calls out to me as she pops a bubble of gum. Sensei wraps his arm around her shoulders looking completely smitten.

"Morning, it's a great feeling," I reply as Trax grins wide. It's so much better than watching the worried frown he's been sporting the last few days.

"I need to see those pictures of your babies when you've got time. I have to head off to work soon, but maybe tonight?" Sass asks. I forgot Dr. Branson gave us some printouts of the scans. We haven't really shown anyone other than Torque and Freckles. I guess with my morning sickness, the celebrations were kind of put on hold. A sense of family and home floods through me.

"I'd love that. I'll show you when you get home tonight."

"Awesome. Better go, but you have a good day, yeah. Keep that smile on your dial," Sass chimes.

"Thanks, you have a good day, too."

She leans in kissing Sensei a little deeper than I want to see as I turn my head to look at Trax who smirks raising his brow. They eventually break free, and Sass rushes off leaving Sensei shaking his head as he takes a deep breath turning back to look at us. "I don't understand how the hell I keep up with her."

We both let out a laugh as he waves his hand in the air signaling for Ruby. She walks over making me smile at the club girl everyone loves so much. "Morning guys! So happy to see you all out and about. You up for some breakfast this morning, Sparx?"

"I think so."

Her eyes light up like this is the best news she's heard all day. "Okay, you want something big? Or wanna start off small?"

"Definitely small to start, maybe just some toast and chamomile tea?"

Trax places his hand on my knee. "I'll have the same, but coffee instead. Thanks, Rubes."

She bounces on her toes as she rushes off in the direction of the kitchen.

"What do you say about us getting out of here today? You, me, going and stretching our legs for a bit?" he asks.

"You wanna go somewhere?"

"Yeah, I want to go shopping."

I let out a laugh. "Shopping? A biker, shopping? Now I have heard it all," I scoff as Sensei chuckles along with me.

"I should be recording this for evidence," Sensei mocks as Trax groans.

"Not just any fucking shopping... I want to buy stuff for our room, stuff for you and the babies."

My heart leaps into my throat. Not sure I could fall any more in love with this man if I tried right now. I giggle and lean in kissing him quickly on the lips. "You're way too good to me."

He snorts. "This ain't no normal shopping. We'll only be buying the shit I think is safe for our kids. I don't want any second-grade crap. Only the best."

I chuckle. "You have final say on everything, I promise. I'm excited we're doing this together."

The look on his face tells me he's excited to be doing this together too.

He really is going to be a great dad.

CHAPTER 22

MYLEE

We ate breakfast. It felt good to actually get something into my stomach and keep it down. Those ginger and B6 pills of Kline's are magical. I think I love her a little bit. But right now, Trax and I are walking to his truck on our way to pick out baby stuff. To say I'm excited is an understatement as I walk up to the passenger side.

Neala hops out of her car beside us. "Hey, where are you two going? What are you doing? Who are you going with?" she blurts out in quick succession with a giggle as Trax looks around the back of the truck letting out a laugh.

"What the hell, Lala? Stop being nosey," Trax grunts as she curls up her cute button nose at her brother.

I, on the other hand, am too excited to not say something. "We're going baby shopping for your little nieces or nephews... or both. Shit! I have no idea what we're buying for."

Neala puts on a stern face grabbing my shoulders. "It's okay, we got this. I'm coming with you."

Trax scoffs. "What now?"

"Actually... I would like another woman's opinion. It might be helpful, Trax."

He groans, storming around to the driver's side. "Fine, get in," he demands then slams his door.

Lala and I both giggle jumping into the truck, and we head straight to the baby emporium. The drive there is fun. Lala talks about all the things we can buy while Trax groans the entire time like a man with heartburn.

It's quite entertaining.

We get to the shop and head inside. Lala is like a child in a toy store. I've never seen her so excited. It's like we're shopping for her baby, not ours. But Trax is dragging his feet watching Lala and me as we tease him.

"You know, oh brother of mine, if you have twin girls, you're going to be so out of your depth, I'm going to love watching you squirm on a daily basis," Lala gushes holding up a little frilly lace dress as I watch Trax's face fall.

"Holy fucking shit, I never thought of it being two girls. Two boys, yes, one girl, maybe, but two girls... fuck!" Trax groans.

While watching her running around, I decide to ask how she's doing. "Lala, what's happening in your love life? You're getting awfully clucky," I add causing Trax to stop walking. He turns glaring at me which makes me laugh as he shakes his head adamantly, a look of absolute fear etched into his features.

Neala laughs, but there's sadness behind her tone. "No, there's definitely no babies in my near future. Hell, I don't even think there's a man in my near future."

Trax goes about picking up random things as if he isn't listening, but I know he is as I step closer to her. "What do you mean?" I ask.

"Well, it's no secret Tremor and I have a *thing*."

Trax lets out a small grunt. I send him a sideways glare, but he continues to gather baby supplies while trying to remain stoic.

"But he's so on and off. He's worried about getting his cut, so I have cooled things with him for now. I just don't see how things will ever be okay with us. I really like him, but his focus is so intent on the club that I feel like I'm not important. So, for now, I have given up trying to be…" she shrugs, "… enough."

Trax turns to face us, the bib in his hand curled into a tight fist. "You want me to punch him? 'Cause I will. I'll punch him."

Neala laughs, but it's only half-hearted as she continues looking at baby clothes. "No, he'll fix his shit. Whether I'm a part of his future or not, I don't know, but for now, I'm not. I know he respects Torque, and my brother, the almighty president, not being completely on board with us, has really put Tremor off. I just have to deal with the fact I'm not good enough for him."

Trax groans, shaking his head. "Now I'm gonna have to punch him."

Lala laughs. "No, don't. I'm fine. Honestly. Leave it. You have better things to concentrate on… like little babies and naming them awesome things."

Trax grimaces as he looks to me. "Shit. We have to think of four names."

I laugh looking at him. "Why four?"

"Two boys… two girls," he replies.

I wince in understanding. "Shit, yeah, of course. Urgh, how the hell are we going to come up with four names?" I whine as Lala pulls out her cell.

"Leave it to me. I'll Google the best names ever… how about Bethzy!"

Trax and I both look at each other. "Bethzy? Is that even a name?" I ask.

"Yeah, or hey what about Genesis… oh, Lizeth," she calls out as Trax and I laugh walking off from her while shaking our heads.

"She is *not* naming our kids," I whisper to Trax as he bobs his head in agreement.

"I don't think she should name her own when she has them either." He chuckles.

I laugh as a shudder runs down my spine. Placing the items on the store counter, I turn to see someone wearing a baseball cap.

He's facing us, looking right at us, but I can't see him as his cap is too low. Tension rolls over me as he suddenly turns, ducking out of the store from behind us, but I couldn't make out who it was— but the stature was definitely of a man. Trax is distracted with Neala as she continues to rattle off baby names, but I can't help feeling a little rattled by cap guy's sudden departure. I didn't see him in the store, but the creepiness that spread up my spine has me on edge.

I haven't had any sort of episode for a while, but I have been a little out of it with my morning sickness, so my brain may not be functioning properly right now. My paranoia is probably misfiring. That's all this is, right? I don't want to ruin the fun we've been having with one of my paranoid delusions, so I'm just going to let this go. I don't want to make Trax think I'm going crazy by me being worried about some guy who did what? Run out of the store when I spotted him. I'm completely overanalyzing this situation anyway. That's what my brain does. And right now I need to take a moment, calm down and get back into the happy place with Trax and his sister. Because we're having a great time.

Trax makes the purchases buying up half the store, and we head back to the truck. We jump in, and Trax starts the engine and takes off as Lala carries on in the back seat. Trax reaches out taking my hand looking at me seeming to asses me. "You okay, baby? You've gone all quiet."

I shake it off. "I'm good, just tired."

"Okay, should we stop for some lunch?"

"Yes! I'm down. Let's get some food. You know I love to eat," Neala calls out making Trax chuckle.

"It's not about you, Lala. Are you up for it, Sparx? Or you wanna go back to the clubhouse to eat? Don't want to throw too much at you all at once."

I wince. "Would you mind if we went back to the clubhouse?"

Trax looks at me sideways. "Of course."

I smile at him. I'm glad I got out, though I'm feeling somewhat weird about my chance encounter with a random stranger. I'm just wondering what to do about it. I'm going to need to think about whether I need to bring it up or not. The last thing I want is to look stupid in front of these guys, but if it is something, I don't want to be caught out. I need to think. I can't do that in public. That's why I want to go back to the clubhouse. I need to be in my own surroundings with the people I trust around me.

I need to be home.

I need to be safe.

I just need to be calm.

And right now, I can feel myself getting worked up.

So I need to stay focused and not let the storm roll in.

Not when I've been doing so well.

TRAX

We pull up at the clubhouse, and I jump out starting to unload all the baby shit we bought as Lala and Sparx walk inside. I noticed Sparx has been quiet since we left the baby emporium. I'm wondering what the hell happened in the last few moments of our shopping trip to make her like this. I'm concerned. She was having a great time, then something seemed to spook her. I don't like it. I want to talk to her about it, but Lala is too busy walking off with her before I can get a word in. So, I grab as much shit as I can and walk inside dumping it by the bar then head straight over to Ace.

"Hey, how's shit?" he asks as I approach.

"Need a favor," I blurt out.

He chuckles. "I'm doing great, thanks for asking."

"Shut up! Come with me into the chapel. Now," I tell him. He raises his brow but doesn't hesitate as he stands up walking with me to his den. I shut the door behind us as I walk us over to his computers, and he takes a seat without me even having to tell him.

"What do you need?"

I exhale. "Okay, I don't know what I'm looking for, but I need you to hack into the security footage from the baby emporium on Michigan Avenue from about half an hour ago and show me what happened. Can you do that?"

He snorts. "Have you met me?"

I push his shoulder. "Hurry up."

He taps into his computer as video footage comes up on the screen. I instantly see Neala, Sparx, and me in the shop. Ace slightly chuckles. "You been buying baby shit, brother? Naw!"

"Shut the fuck up! Can you get another angle? I think something in there spooked Sparx, I just don't know what."

He takes on a more serious tone as he clicks on something. A different angle comes up showing another camera, and I see a man standing in the corner of the shop. He's wearing a blue baseball cap, so I can't see his face. His back is to the camera, but he's watching the three of us, intently. My muscles clench, and I point to the screen. "You see that?"

"Yep," is all he says. He zooms in slightly as I see Sparx turn to the guy, then he runs, taking off as she notices him, like he was watching her then, and when he was busted, he bolted so that she couldn't catch him.

My skin prickles in goosebumps as I glance to Ace watching as Sparx tenses. She looks around like she's unsure if she's seeing things or not. *Damn.*

I bet she isn't sure on whether this is her mind playing with her. This is why she went quiet on me. "Fuck, is there any way we can figure out who the guy is?"

Ace huffs, typing a few more things into his keyboard making the screen flick to an outside camera. The man is running out the side of the shop, then he turns the corner and out of the view of the cameras.

"You see the cap he was wearing," I ask.

Ace nods. "Yeah?"

He exhales. "You think this could be Everett?"

"Can you zoom in on it as he ran out. It looked like it had something on it..."

Ace reverses the image and plays it back slowly, but the image is too grainy for us to make it out.

"Damn, thought it might have been a lead."

"The emporium doesn't seem to have a camera on the side of the shop where he ran. I'll check to see if there are any street cameras, but you might need to give me some time to look into it. To suss it out more."

I pat his shoulder. "Thanks man, do me a favor? If you find out anything, don't say a word to Sparx. Come to me first, okay?"

He exhales. "You think this could be Everett?"

Gritting my teeth, I purse my lips. "I think if it were Everett, himself, Sparx would have reacted differently. It wasn't him, but maybe he's sent someone to look for her. If his goon's found her, this shit's bad."

"I agree. I'll put my feelers out, see if Everett's moving. See if anything's happening where he's currently located. See what I can find out. If something is shifting, we want to know."

"Fucking straight we want to know. My woman's pregnant. I can't have some fucking psycho lunatic coming after her."

"Noted. Leave it with me. I'll keep my eyes on everything, don't worry."

"Thanks, brother, appreciate it." I slap Ace on the back and walk out of the room while he tries to dig up some info. Heading off to find Sparx, I want to let her know I saw the guy too. That she isn't imagining things, but I need to do this carefully. I don't want to scare her into thinking Everett's coming after her, but I also don't want her thinking she's going crazy either. I have to play this just right.

CHAPTER 23

TRAX

I walk into the bedroom. Neala and Sparx are sitting on the bed looking through the baby outfits and smiling, but Sparx's smile isn't as wide as it should be. As I walk in, they both look up as Lala holds an outfit to Sparx's tiny stomach.

"Just think, Trax, in a few months, they will be here wearing these. Won't it be adorable?" Lala asks. It makes my chest squeeze at the thought. I've never really pictured myself as the doting father, but with Sparx by my side, I know we will be great at it together.

"Lala, I love you, but get out," I gruff.

She snorts out a laugh shaking her head. "Bikers, you never change, always so damn bossy..." She turns to look at Sparx. "I had a great time today. If you need help with baby shopping again or help planning the baby shower, let me know. I'm your girl."

"Thanks, Lala, for everything."

Lala walks out of the room but not before punching me in my arm on the way out. I close the door behind her. Walking over to the bed and sitting down, I wrap my arm around Sparx's shoulder, kissing her hair.

She lets out a long exhale, cuddling into my side. "What a day."

"It's been a big one, you've done well..." I pause trying to choose my words wisely. "That guy in the store today was fucking weird, though, right?" I try to play it off.

She looks up to me like she's shocked by my words. "You saw him?"

I shrug. "Yeah, he rushed out of there like he was in a real hurry. Maybe he was freaked out by all of Lala's crazy baby names."

It looks like she visibly relaxes. "You think that's all it was?"

I bring my hand up to her face smoothing some hair back from her cheek. "Yeah, I mean she was freaking me out with those damn stupid names. Poor guy probably thought she was weird."

Sparx finally lets out a small laugh. "Yeah, true. They were terrible... I... I wasn't sure if I was being... you know... a bit paranoid."

I raise my brow. "Paranoid?"

Her eyes blink rapidly. "No, you're right. I don't even know why I thought that."

I grab her hand. "It's okay to have doubts. I know that probably seemed fucking weird to you, especially with the threat of Everett, but babe, you never have to hide your thoughts from me. I never want you to feel like you're carrying any issues alone. If you feel like something's wrong, you talk to me, no matter how crazy it might sound. I will never judge you for it. You know that."

"Yeah, I know, but for a minute I thought I wasn't thinking straight. It happened so quick, I didn't want to alarm anyone. I didn't want to seem... overcautious."

My brows knit together. "If you ever think there's a reason you feel unsafe, you need to tell me. Don't *ever* hide it from me. Don't think it has anything to do with you. He just left quickly... that's all." I downplay it even though I don't think this is the reason at all. I don't want her frightened, she doesn't need this right now. So I stretch the truth. It's what's best for her.

Seemingly satisfied with my twist, she exhales. "We bought baby stuff, Trax. It seems so real now."

A genuine smile crosses my face. "Yeah, we're actually going to be parents. Can you believe it?"

She snorts slapping my chest playfully. "You're going to be such a good dad."

I lean in kissing her as I push her back to the bed careful not to press on her tummy as I lay over her kissing her strongly.

The Next Day

It's another beautiful morning. Sparx's decided she's going to try to take some time to catch up on the website work she's fallen behind in. So I'm taking the opportunity to go and catch up with Ace to see if he has found out anything on the guy from yesterday. I make my way to the chapel to see he's busy on his computer as I walk in.

"Mornin'," I call out as I approach.

Ace bobs his head in a greeting but continues typing away. "So, I've tried to do some digging. I've been up most of the night looking into shit for you."

"Fuck! Thanks, man." I had no idea he was going to do that.

He looks to me. It's only now I see the redness in his eyes and the deep purple bags under his eyelids. I can see he's telling the truth.

He waves his hand through the air. "Nah, honestly, I want Sparx safe so I'm doing the best I can for her..." He pauses typing in something else then swivels his screen to face me more, so I take a look. What appears to be the guy from the baby emporium is lined up next to a picture of a guy who looks disheveled, and dare I say it, a few pennies short of a dollar. Scrunching my face up at Ace, I huff. "Who's this guy?"

He exhales. "Okay, so this guy here…" he points to penniless, "…he's this guy here." Then he points to the guy in the baseball cap who was in the baby store yesterday. "I was able to find cameras which showed him leaving the store then getting into a vehicle off Michigan Avenue. From there I was able to zone in on the plates of his car. I tracked who the car's registered to. It's this guy… Jason Ledermann. I couldn't really find any reason as to why he'd be in the baby store. He has no current marital or relationship status nor siblings who are expecting babies, so I started digging. It took some time to figure it all out, but it turns out he did a stint in a psych ward in Michigan at the same time as one, wait for it… Everett Scott."

I let out a long exhale rubbing the tension knot in the back of my neck. "Fuck! So was it a coincidence he was there the same time as us, or did he know Sparx was going to be there and was he looking for her?"

Ace types some more information into his computer bringing up some video footage from outside the baby emporium. It's of us pulling up, then his car pulls up a little behind us. I scrunch up my face while shaking my head. "So if it isn't a coincidence, how the hell did he know we were going to be there? Were we followed?"

Ace shrugs. "I don't know. Maybe it was just a coincidence? He didn't approach her, he didn't say anything, take any pictures, do anything. Maybe it was just by chance?"

"I doubt it, wishful thinking, but I can't help but think maybe somehow Everett has spies in bigger places. He has people working on his side. If he knows Sparx isn't in Grand Rapids anymore and is in Chicago with us, then it might not be long before he makes a move and tries to come after her himself."

Ace grimaces. "At least he skipped out before you, so he didn't see where you went. For now, Everett doesn't know Sparx is here."

"I was wearing my cut at the shop, might not be too hard to figure it out if they're smart."

"We need to tell Torque. Inform him we might have trouble coming our way," Ace states.

"Yeah, I hate to admit it, but I have no idea what's coming, if anything. We need to be prepared without getting Sparx involved."

Ace stands up from his desk, gripping my shoulder. "Don't worry, brother. We're all here to protect you and your family. Nothing will harm her or those babies. We'll all make sure of it."

"Right, I'll go find Torque. Maybe we should call church, let everyone in on what's happening."

Ace tilts his head. "I think that's best."

I turn to head for the door to go in search of my blood brother.

After finding Torque and telling him in layman's terms what I'd found with Ace, he called church. As everyone files in, I can't help but feel a little nervous. Defiance has been settled for ages other than our small dealing with getting Zia back for Enzo, but now I feel like we have something bigger coming our way. We're made for this, though, and I know they will protect what's mine.

Everyone takes their seats as I wrack my jaw from side to side, and Torque bangs his gavel. "Right, now all you fuckers are here, there's some important business we need to discuss."

I look around to my brothers. All of them ready and willing to lay down their lives for any one of us, but will they be willing to risk it all for Sparx?

"As you all know, Mylee was sent here because of a threat to her safety. The man threatening her is Everett Scott. It seems he has spies in Chicago scoping out her whereabouts." My brothers all look to me as they all shift uncomfortably. "For now, we don't know if Everett knows if she's here or not, but we have to assume his spy, Jason, who saw Sparx with Trax when he had his cut on, will at least now know of her connection with the club, and... something will be coming. So we all need to keep our ears to the ground but not be obvious about it in front of Sparx. As far as she's concerned, it's business as normal."

Everyone agrees as I lean forward. "I'm going to do everything to keep her in the compound. She's not going anywhere. I know it's going to be hard, without giving anything away, but I'm going to try, only letting her go to her appointments. Plus, I'll be with her for all of those, so nothing will fucking happen while I'm around."

"Should we be doing something about this Jason?" Chains asks, and my ears prick up. I hadn't thought of that, but maybe that's a good idea. I glance at Torque, and he tilts his head.

"Could be an option. Ace, do you think you can find him?"

Ace snorts rolling his eyes. "Already have. He's staying in a motel not too far from here. We can have brothers there in fifteen minutes."

"Torque, if we have the opportunity to get to this fucker, we need to take it!"

"Sensei, Chains, you take the lead on this," Torque instructs.

I sit up higher in my chair. Normally, this is where I would kick up a stink about not being with Sensei for the retrieval, but training with Sensei over the past couple of months has taught me to cool my head. With his breathing techniques, meditation, and the information he's given me about being responsible for my own actions, have somehow gotten through my fucking brain and instilled a way to control myself before I lash out. Let's just hope I can put it into practice. I don't have to be the front man in everything, I can sit this retrieval out, and I understand why Torque has called for Chains instead of me after what happened last time.

Torque rolls his shoulders. "We bring him in. Find out what Everett knows about Sparx and *try* to do it neatly. Trax, I need you to keep a level head in this."

I scoff. "I'll be fine."

I don't miss Sensei's hard eyes on me, along with my brothers. "Maybe you should..." he pauses, his eyebrow raised, "... sit this session out, Trax?" Sensei questions.

My brows crease together. "You're fucking kidding, right? You've trained me. I'm ready for this. I'm not sitting the fuck out? I'm the one wielding the weapons on this, Sensei."

The room shifts in uncomfortable silence, and Sensei exhales. "Only if I'm by your side."

My lopsided smile adorns my face. "Wouldn't have it any other way."

Torque looks to the room as everyone is quiet taking this all in. "Right, Chains and Sensei will bring Jason in for questioning, and the rest of the club will keep Sparx distracted. Does everyone understand?"

A resounding, "Aye," fills the room.

I relax further into my seat knowing everyone is onboard.

"Okay, remember, not a word of this to Sparx. Disperse," Torque calls out.

Everyone stands up as I take a breath tipping my chin to my blood brother. Right now, I want to go find Sparx, make sure she's doing okay, and that she isn't suspicious of anything. So I make my way out of the chapel and back to our room. I walk in to see her busy working on her laptop. My chest warms liking that she seems back to her old self, pre-morning sickness, as she sips on some ginger tea.

"Hey, Sparx, how you feeling?" I ask.

"Okay. Much better. So that's good."

Walking over to her, my hands move in to massage her shoulders. She sinks into my touch with a moan as a flicker of excitement rumbles in my stomach. But not from her delight. Soon Jason will be here, and soon he won't know what hit him.

Leaning down, I plant a kiss on her head as she leans back against me, and I inhale the fruity smell of her hair. I'm doing this for her. Everything is for her and our babies.

And Jason is going to pay the ultimate price.

As I pace back and forth in the chamber, another drip of water drops into the small puddle on the floor with a plop. The echo sounding through the dank room doing nothing to quench my excitement. Ideas run through my mind, different methods of pulling information from Jason, of watching him squirm. The thought he was watching us in that damn baby shop makes my skin crawl. The fact he's working for Everett only makes this easier.

The fucker's going down.

The cold, heavy door slowly creeks open, and my heart leaps into my throat. I spin around in anticipation, but Torque steps down the steps and inside closing the door behind him. I slump my body and turn back to my pacing.

He lets out an audible chuckle as he stomps over to me slapping me on the back, but I shrug him off. "Sheesh, you're so fuckin' tense, brother."

I face him with a stern glare. "Really? You're gonna say that shit to me right now?"

He jolts his hands up in surrender. "Okay. I get it... try to keep your cool in here. We need information from this guy. Remember that."

My face scrunches. I turn to pace for the third time. "I'm not a dickhead, Torque. I know what we need, but don't think I'm *not* going to make this fucker hurt."

He sighs. "Yeah, right. I know if this were someone who was fuckin' around with Foxy, I'd be as worked up as you are, but

Trax... information first, you got me? We don't wanna damn repeat of last time and get nothing."

I look at him exhaling. "I got you."

The door pulls back again, and I spin so fast I almost fall over. Torque grabs my shoulders steadying me as we look to see Sensei and Chains stepping in with Jason. My stomach flips as fucking butterflies flutter in my stomach like a fucking school girl. I'm that excited. Seeing him stumbling into the room, his bare feet tripping on the stone floor, his head covered in a sack, his hands bound. Fuck, I almost have a hard-on.

I'm sick.

I'm twisted

And I fucking love it.

Oh fuck! Instantly Sensei's teachings rip through my brain. The realization that my demon is rearing his ugly head is seeping into my pores. I need to rein myself in, I need to breathe, I need to pull myself together.

Sensei gazes at me, his eyes assessing me as he ushers Jason to the silver chair watching my breathing techniques. I've already pulled out the plastic wrap underneath. It's normally Sensei's job, but I thought I'd help a brother out. Chains slams Jason down onto the silver chair, and he whimpers, beginning to struggle as Chains holds him in the seat, and Sensei goes about strapping him in. Jason's murmurs are obviously muffled. I think he's gagged under his hood.

I stand back. Waiting my turn. Anxiety seeping through my pores. I need to get to him. I need the information. It's killing me. But finally, Sensei and Chains pull back from Jason. He's all settled in the silver chair, and I take a breath.

What a sight.

A slow grin appears on my face as I take a deep centering breath.

"Take off the sack," I demand.

CHAPTER 24

TRAX

Chains leans in pulling off Jason's head sack with force. So much so that his head flops forward forcefully making him whimper like a pussy. I smirk as his head slowly shifts upward, his eyes focusing in on the four burly bikers before him. His eyes shift from each one slowly finally landing on me, then they open wide like he realizes he's in deep shit.

"Oh, so you recognize me, do you, Jason?" I ask, and his eyes bug out of his head. The fear is oozing out of his pores so much so you can practically taste it in the air. It breathes life into me, it fuels me, it's driving me further. It's making me hungrier, feeding my appetite to hurt him, to bring him pain so unimaginable only the devil himself knows how to cause it.

But then I take a deep centering breath and remain calm. Sensei yanks down the gag making Jason lick his lips, jostling his tongue around his mouth to wet it from being silenced. He gnaws on his bottom lip, his eyes shifting from me to around the room taking it all in. His body slumps, and he exhales. "Wh-Where am I?"

I crack my knuckles. "Hell."

His head snaps back to me, his eyes alight with intense fear. "What do you want from me?"

I step forward, all eyes in the room on me, but it doesn't make me nervous, it doesn't make me tense, I thrive on it. I know this is my show tonight, and Jason's the one along for the unwilling ride.

"The truth."

He tilts his head. "About?"

"Why you were in that baby emporium."

He glances to Sensei who's standing right beside me, then back to me as if he's trying to think of his next words carefully. "I was buying baby clothes for my sister's baby shower."

I rest my hand on his knee, making him tense up completely. "Wrong... you don't have a sister. Want to try that again?"

His breathing comes in hard and heavy as he glances at Torque and Chains. I reach up grabbing his chin hard. My fingers digging into his skin making him whimper as I force him to look at me. "Don't look at them, they won't help you. Now tell me, why were you there? Was it because of Everett?"

His eyes widen. He shifts up the seat like he's backing away, but he's not getting very far. "Fuck. H-How did you find me?"

I forcibly let go of his chin making his head fly to the side. "We're the ones asking the damn questions. Now, I'll give you one last chance, tell me why you were in the baby emporium or things are gonna start to get messy in here."

He turns to Sensei, a pleading look in his eyes, and Sensei lets out a small chuckle. "Don't look at me with your pleading eyes. This is normally my job. Any other time, I would be the one punishing you, so don't think for a moment I'm going to help you out of this. Just tell him the information and maybe... he'll go easy on you."

I turn to Sensei with a gesture of thanks. He slaps my shoulder in return. Jason sits, eyes wide like he knows he's completely screwed but turns his nose up in defiance. I chuckle with a shrug while walking over to Sensei's cupboard in the corner of the room. It's full of Japanese torture weapons, but I want to go more old school. So, I search until I find something I like.

Pulling out a Louisville Slugger, one custom made with the Chicago Defiance logo on it, I chuckle throwing it over my shoulder as I saunter back to the middle of the room. Sensei raises his brow as I drop the tip of the bat to land on my boot. Jason stares at it in confusion.

"So, slugger... feel like talking yet?" I ask.

"I told you, I was there for my sister's—"

I pick the bat up without hesitation and swing as hard as I can, full force onto his kneecaps. The sound of his bones cracking and disintegrating beneath the bat's blow echoes through the room along with his almighty wail. My chest puffs out as I smile wide, his eyes roll into the back of his head in agony. His knees collapsing, his legs dangling like they're not really being held together by anything now but jelly.

It's a beautiful sight to behold.

Sensei's arm reaches out, his hand places on my shoulder, and I take a breath. I need to calm it down. Remember what he told me. If I enjoy this too much, enjoy the kill too much, it could take over.

I have a family now.

I need to rein myself in.

Turning to look at Sensei, his concerned eyes tell me everything I already know. I'm losing myself in this.

I clear my throat looking back at Jason. He's panting, still conscious, so I step up to him, grabbing his hair, forcing him to look at me. "Tell me why you were there, Jason. No fucking about."

He sniffs, I think I even see his eyes watering. "Everett sent me to find her. He thought Crest might have sent her to a brother club. I was scoping out all of the clubs. Yours was on the list. So I was following people in and out of the club to see where they were going to get a lead. Then I saw you guys going in the baby emporium. I noticed it was Mylee from the photographs Everett had supplied, so I had to get proof."

My stomach churns. "What do you mean proof?"

He takes a couple of steadying breaths. "Proof of where she is."

Standing up, I begin to pace as my stomach churns. The thought of Everett knowing Sparx's whereabouts frightens the shit out of me. I'm not scared to admit it because I have no idea what the guy's capable of. All I know is my woman is pregnant, and some nut job wants to come after her.

"*Where is he?*" I yell turning back to face Jason.

He shakes his head adamantly. "I don't think you understand, Malcolm has so much money he'll pay *way* more to keep me quiet than what you guys can dish out in torture to make me talk."

I jolt my head back wondering why he said Malcolm, Everett's father's name, instead of Everett. But I put it down to a simple mistake while the guy's shitting his pants.

"I do like a challenge," I reply as I walk back to the cupboard to look for the one thing I have in mind. I grab the small tool and stroll back over to him with purpose and poise.

Dropping to my knees, in line with his broken ones, I smirk at him. He glances down at me. Pain evident on his face as I raise my hand to show him a pair of pliers. His eyes widen, and I shrug.

"You don't look like you take very good care of your nails. You're a biter I see. Well, I guess you won't be needing them." I move in with the pliers to his pointer finger with one hand and with my other I hold his finger down as he struggles against me. I position the pliers under the tiny bit of nail I can get under, and I wriggle from side to side. It pulls and squelches as he screams out in pain, the screech echoing against the thick concrete walls. Blood pools at the site and drips from his finger as Sensei bends down beside me to obviously see how I'm coping. Seeing the blood, something inside of me, the animal, the demon is loving this. But I'm keeping Sparx and my babies in the forefront of my mind right now.

I need to keep focused.

I can't lose control.

"Fuck, how can you do this to people?" Jason screams out.

My head jolts up, and I scoff. "How can *I* do this to people? How can *you* stalk someone, giving away their whereabouts to a crazy motherfucker putting her life in danger? How can *you* do that, you son of a bitch?" I stand up dropping the pliers, anger burning red hot through me as my hand balls into a fist, and I thrust it forward right into his nose, the snap of his bone cracks through the air as his head smacks back into the silver chair, blood squirting all over my shirt. I land another punch in his face, then another, my breathing rapid, I'm losing myself as I land another punch but my arm is quickly restrained, and I'm pulled back hastily by my brother and Chains while my anger surges through me, and I fight them to get back to Jason.

Sensei appears in my line of sight. His eyes look at me while he takes a deep breath. "Don't let the anger rule you, brother. Take a breath, in... and out."

My frustration begins to wane looking at Sensei's calmed state, and I exhale long then inhale deep.

"Good, brother. Maybe I should take it from here?" Sensei asks, and I pull myself from Chains and Torque's hold.

"I'm good... I'm good." Cracking my neck to the side, we all turn to look at Jason. His head is to the side, blood pissing down his face from his nose and mouth. I look to the floor, several teeth lay on the plastic sheeting surrounded by his blood.

Sensei steps to the side letting me back to Jason. He looks like shit as his eyes focus in on me, though he appears like he's only half awake. He spits out a line of blood as his head moves up to look me in the eyes. "Feel better?" he murmurs.

I scoff out a laugh. "Yeah, actually... I do. So, you want to tell us where Everett is, or this is only gonna get worse for you?"

He rolls his eyes. The fucker has the nerve to actually roll his eyes, making my anger spike again. "You think, after all this, I don't know where I'll end up."

"You tell us what we want to know, and we'll let you go."

He snorts. "Oh, yeah, so I can run to the cops and tell them everything. I don't think so. I'm not going anywhere but the bottom of the South Branch Chicago River."

Pursing my lips, I shrug. "Not our style. We have somewhere much better to store our bodies than the river."

"In any case. I'm a dead man, so I'm not telling you shit. I just wish I took more time to admire that sweet pussy of yours. She sure has a fine ass, and I know from watching you two together she sure would be a damn firecracker in the sack. I want to shove my cock so hard in her ass she'll be screaming for a week!"

Heat rolls over me so insatiably hot, beads of sweat instantly pebble on my skin as I think of him getting anywhere near Sparx. Anger ripples through me at his words. The demon inside needs to be let out, and so I waste no time trying to lung for the blade placed down the back of Sensei's pants.

Sensei instantly twists my hand to stop me while Torque rushes forward grabbing hold of my arms.

"Breathe, Trax." Sensei looks firm into my eyes as I breathe out harsh breaths. It's enough to shock me back into reality. I lost myself for moment and realize maybe I'm too close to this to handle it the right way.

"I need you to take over, Sensei," I state firmly.

He nods like he already knew, stepping back from me and swiveling to face Jason. "One last time, where is Everett?" Sensei asks with more calmness in his voice than I could possibly feel.

"So your first tried his best, do you think you're going to be any better or will you be a pussy like him, too?"

Sensei turns to Torque. "We're not getting anywhere."

Torque nods once.

Sensei reaches for his blade pushing forward. Jason's eyes widen as he tries to back into the chair, but Sensei is too quick as he thrusts the blade into Jason's gut. The push and pull of the blade slices with ease into his torso, blood begins to ooze from his chest. Jason coughs and splutters as Sensei stabs over and over again, blood now spraying all over his clothes as he methodically ends his life.

The demon inside me rejoices, the man in me relieved Jason got his just desserts. Though, I'm disappointed I couldn't bring the final blow myself. Sensei was right to take over, no point in losing myself in this when the end result is the same. Jason's dead. We have no intel. Better to have me functioning than a complete mess.

It's good I've regained control, even if I did lose my way.

I think I've come a long way.

Sensei steps back from Jason's now lifeless body wiping his blade with care and precision as always. It almost feels like this is how he calms himself after a kill. Sensei turns to look at me, and I give him a curt nod as he walks over to us.

Looking to Torque, Sensei rolls his shoulders. "We still have no idea on Everett or his motives and whereabouts. We're back to square one. There was no way Jason was going to break."

"Yeah, I agree. Let's break for the night, get cleaned up," Torque suggests.

I finally relax. "Thanks, brother. Fucking hell, I lost it for a second."

"Just focus on your family, Trax. Don't let the rage consume you again," Sensei tells me, believing that this time, I think it will truly be the last.

It's strange being on the other side of this, not being the one landing the final blow but watching how Sensei controls the ending so meticulously, so calmly, without letting his inner demons take hold over him. I realize I have more work to do, but I know now that I can combat my demon with Sensei's help.

CHAPTER 25

MYLEE

Five Weeks Later

The past five weeks have been weird. Good, but weird. I've been keeping busy with my website work and website testing, but it's almost like Trax is trying to make sure I keep myself occupied and busy. Like he wants me to be here at the club all the time. Whenever I offer to go on the grocery run with the girls or to go out to buy baby stuff, he's constantly blocking me, telling me to stay here and relax, that the club girls have got it covered. I mean I don't mind being looked after, but there is such a thing as cabin fever. I'm starting to think I might get it if he doesn't let me out of here soon. The only thing he lets me go to is our doctor appointments, which he always comes to with me, and for that, I'm grateful.

The thing is, though, I'm starting to stew on it. Like, is there a reason he's keeping me indoors or is it all in my mind? Surely, if there was a threat—an Everett-size threat—he would let me in on it, right?

As I sit working on another website, I groan as hunger pangs rips through my stomach. My hand moves down to the small bump on my belly. The noticeable difference in size now makes me smile as I rub my hand over my tummy.

The light from the laptop blares while Trax is off doing something with the club. We have an appointment this afternoon with the OB/GYN for my four-month check-up, so luckily, I'll be getting out of the club for a little bit today and seeing the outside world. It's been weeks since I stepped foot outside the compound gates. I really can't wait to get a taste of fresh air. It might sound a little dramatic, but I just want to be able to walk around the city streets. Even if just for a little while.

I know Trax is protective of our babies and me, but if he's protecting us from something or someone, he should at least be telling me about it. But I know how it works, if he's keeping me under lock and key, there's not a damned thing I could do about it anyway. I'm his Old Lady, if he wants to keep me here to protect me, then I know all those brothers out there will do absolutely everything in their power to make sure I stay exactly where I am. No point in even trying to fight it. I know how a brotherhood works, I was raised in it, and I've lived it my entire life. This is why I fit into the Old Lady role so easily. I'm not a pushover. I will fight Trax when I need to, but I know when a war can't be won too. So if Trax wants me here, I'm not going anywhere.

My hand circles on my stomach again as the door to our room cracks open. I turn to see Trax pop his head through the opening. His eyes instantly drop to my hand on my stomach. He steps in closing the door behind him. "You and the babies okay?"

I lean back into the desk chair letting out a happy sigh. "We're perfectly content."

He beams wide squatting in front of me, placing his hands on my thighs as he looks up into my eyes. "You think we'll find out the sexes today?" he asks.

Reaching out, I swipe a flop of hair from his face. "Maybe, but today's about the screening tests, nothing serious, just to test for things we need to be on the lookout for."

His smile falters, and he sighs. "Down syndrome and shit?"

"Amongst other things. It's normal, nothing to worry about."

He takes a deep breath. "Well, I don't care. If our babies have any problems, we'll deal with it. I'll love them no matter what."

I lean down planting a kiss on his lips briefly before pulling back. "And that's why you'll be the best dad ever."

He stands up looking down at my computer, then to the wall randomly. "We really need to think about rearranging this desk and turning it into the kids' area."

"Yeah, well you bought the paint and stuff. We just need to move the desk into my old room so we can put the basinets up. Make it a real little baby zone."

"I'll put some time aside, and we can do it together. Create the two areas, one for your office, the other for our family."

My stomach flutters. "I'd love that."

He looks to his watch with an exhale. "Okay, want to get ready for your appointment, and I'll take you to get some lunch before we go?"

Excitement flitters through me as I jump on the seat slightly. "Really? We're going to go out for more than just the doctor's appointment?"

His smile is weak like he knows he's been holding out on me. "Yeah, you deserve to go out. You've been cooped up in here for far too long. Let me take you out. It can be like a date."

I snort out a laugh. "I think we're past dating, don't you?"

He chuckles. "Let me take you on one anyway."

Butterflies flutter in my tummy. "Okay... awesome."

He grabs my hand hoisting me up from the seat as he pulls me into his arms. I wrap my arms around his neck tightly while looking deep into his eyes. "You're my woman, Sparx. You know there's nothing I wouldn't do for you, right?"

"I know, trust me, I know. I get that everything you do is for us," I tell him.

He leans in pressing his lips to mine. I kiss him back feeling nothing but total devotion pouring back from him. The kiss deepens, that usual spark shooting through me, our tongues going rouge against each other's, and I can't help but wonder if we have time to take this further. Before I can make my move, he pulls back from me with the biggest of smirks, shaking his head. "You're trouble, you know that?"

"Who? Me?"

He laughs as he spins me, and I stumble slightly in my awkwardness, just as his hand comes out slapping me hard on my ass. I giggle as I rush over to the closet pulling out a flowing white dress. It's a nice day, and I'm pretty sure we'll be taking the truck. As much as Trax loves his new bike, he doesn't like me riding on the back of it at the moment. I know once the babies are born, I'll be able to go on the back of his ride again, but while I'm pregnant, he doesn't want to risk it. He's extra cautious with the precious cargo onboard.

Trax watches me undress and looks at me shaking his head, his eyes going straight to my pot belly, and he walks over as I reach for my bra. He slides in behind and wraps his arms around me from behind. His warmth encases me. I giggle as his giant hand spreads out on my stomach taking it up almost entirely. His chin rests on my shoulder as I stop my movements just taking in this moment with him.

"I love you like this. You're so fucking beautiful."

I bring my hand up threading it through his longer than normal hair. "You make me feel beautiful. I'm so much happier when you're around, Trax... I'll never leave you again."

He sighs leaning in planting a kiss on my cheek. "Let's not think about it. You came back, that's all that matters. I have you now, and I swear, baby, I'm never letting you go."

I spin in his arms, my naked breasts rubbing against the leather of his cut as I look up at him. "You couldn't even if you wanted to because I'll never let you."

I lean in, kissing him strongly again this time letting him know just how much I love and adore him. He's my everything. He means absolutely everything to me, and right now I couldn't love anyone or anything more in the world if I tried.

Eventually, we pull back, and he chuckles turning me around making me groan in contempt as I regrettably get dressed. As much as I want to fuck Trax right now, my need to get out of this compound is winning more.

"Right, let's do this!"

"It's a date. A hot date I might add." His eyes roam up and down my body in my flowing dress.

I scoff rolling my eyes. "Shut up. You have to say that, or I'll punch you."

He snorts out a laugh. "I only speak the truth. Now grab your shit and let's go."

Leaning around, I grab my cell then shove it down my bra, reaching out for his hand as we leave our room and walk down the hall to the clubroom. Freckles and Surge are sitting at the bar, they turn to look at us as we walk past.

"You going somewhere?" Surge calls out with a hint of deeper meaning in his voice that I'm unsure of.

I tilt my head wondering what this is about while Freckles beams at me as if nothing's going on, but Surge isn't as good at playing it cool as Trax's mother.

Trax grips my hand tighter. "Yeah, taking my woman out to lunch, then to the doctors for a four-month check-up."

Surge's face tightens into something harder. "Why don't you have lunch with us?" he asks as Freckles snorts. "Stop it, Surge, Sparx hasn't been out in weeks. Let the poor girl have one lunch date with her man. Trax has it covered... right?"

She looks to Trax tilting her head like she's asking him an unspoken question. I'm not liking how this conversation is going.

"Yeah, got it covered. Sparx deserves lunch. I'm not taking her far, just to The Heart of Italy, to that that special Italian restaurant."

Surge's eyes narrow like something clicked in his mind, although nothing has clicked in mine. I have no idea what's going on, but I don't care. As long as I get some nice pasta, I'm happy.

"Good work, boyo. Tell them Italians we say hi," Freckles relays. I raise my brow in curiosity. Maybe we're going to see that Enzo guy. I don't care as long as I get food. Pronto.

"Right, we're off. I'll see you when we get back."

Freckles winks at me. "If you get pictures of them babies, can you try to get one for me, too?"

"Of course, Grammy," I tease.

She beams so wide, it's contagious. "Grammy! I love it. Oh lordy, lordy, Lord, I'm gonna be a grandma. I'm so fuckin' happy for you two. But go on, go... have your lunch then bring me a photo of my grandbabies."

Trax smiles pulling me to him as we head out to the truck. He leans in kissing my temple as we round the truck, and I let out a heavy sigh. He looks to me raising a brow. "That's a big sigh, you okay?" He opens the door for me helping me up into the truck.

"Yeah, just wish people would stop pussy-footing about around me."

He walks around to the driver's side getting in closing the door to start the truck. "What do you mean?"

I look to him doing up my belt. "I mean, I know something's going on at the club to do with me. I know I'm obviously being kept here. That little show by Surge wasn't because he wanted to eat lunch with me. Something's happening, isn't it?"

He exhales pulling out then heads for the gate as it opens to let us through. "Babe, there's nothing for you to worry about. I promise."

"Would you tell me if there was?"

He peers sideways at me. "If it were necessary, yes. But sometimes what you don't know doesn't hurt you."

I let out a stifled laugh. "Ha! So there is something you're not telling me?"

He groans pulling onto the service road. "Sparx, trust me. You're safe if we keep doing what we're doing."

A chill runs over me at his words. So he is hiding me from the world, or more importantly from someone—Everett. "Has he found me?"

Trax looks to me. "Babe, please don't worry. He hasn't found you. If he had, there would have been trouble, yeah? And there hasn't been. We're just being extra cautious, especially with our twins on the way. I don't want to risk anything. He is, by all accounts, a crazy fucker, so I don't want to take any chances."

"Okay, I get that."

He reaches out grabbing my hand. "I will always look out for you, for the three of you. You're my life, Mylee."

I sink a little knowing Everett's out there, on the hunt. However, knowing Trax and the club are doing everything to safeguard me, it's bearable to deal with. So far, nothing has come of it. I've been at Defiance for months without Everett making contact, so they must be doing something right.

We continue into the Heart of Italy as Trax drives us to our destination telling me about how they have the best calzone. Pulling up the truck, he jumps out running around to open my door, before I have a moment to think. I giggle at his chivalrous side—this big burly biker going out of his way for his woman. You'd never think he could be like this to look at him with his stereotypical broad shoulders, arms, and neck covered in tattoos, his pierced nose and tatty hair, not to mention the scruffy beard and cut. He looks like a rough around the edges badass, but he's *my* badass, and I love how he falls over himself for me. I couldn't feel more honored if I tried.

We walk inside the restaurant, and it's bustling with lunchtime visitors. But Trax doesn't keep his hands far from me. I notice his eyes are everywhere taking in everything around us. He's on edge. Which has *me* a little on edge. As he leads us in, suddenly Enzo appears letting out a loud almost shriek as he rushes toward us, along with two men flanked by his sides. They're all wearing smart black pinstriped suits with gold chains hanging around their necks. They look completely ridiculous in this pizzeria, but the smiles they're sporting make me feel welcome as Enzo grabs Trax pulling him into a man hug, much to Trax's discomfort.

"Trax, my boy, so glad you wanted to come to my place for lunch with your woman. I have a table at the back set up for you two, all romantic like candles and everything. You have whatever you want on the menu, anything you need, it's yours. My house is your house."

Trax and I grin. "Thanks, Enzo. I know we've had our... differences, but I do appreciate you looking out for us like this," Trax states.

Enzo leads us to the table, the two guys in the matching suits following us, like they're our guards or some shit. I wonder briefly if this is why we're here. I think Trax brought me here for lunch because Andretti's men can watch over us while we eat. Trax can enjoy our lunch together while Enzo's men keep a lookout for Everett. I think he's a bigger threat than Trax is letting on. But I'm not going to let Trax know I'm in on what he's doing. At least he's making an effort to get me out of the clubhouse even if we are protected by Italian Mafiosos.

I don't mind.

Having the protection around me, though a little daunting, it's actually good. I don't have to worry about Everett, and I can relax and enjoy my lunch. I slide into the red booth smiling at the table adorned with a gingham cloth covering it, a set of candles, and even a single red rose in the middle. It's super sweet as Trax slides in the other side facing out so he can see everything. I sink into the booth seat taking a breath. It's not normal, not in the least. I can see the suited guys standing off to the right watching us like I suspected. I know they will stay there for the entirety of our lunch. Nothing about my life is normal, but for me having a lunch date with my biker man, it couldn't be more perfect right now.

Enzo steps up placing some menus in front of us. "Your menu, madam. Please, eat as much as you can, you're eating for three, so I expect you to have one of everything on the menu. Your boy here did me a solid, so anything you want, you can have."

I laugh. "Well, it smells amazing in here."

He puffs out his chest wide. "I like her, Trax. You're welcome here any time, lovely lady. I'll get you some water? Juice? Soda?"

"Juice would be nice, thanks."

"Coming right up. Trax you can have a soda," he states walking off not giving Trax the choice.

I laugh as Trax rolls his eyes. "Fucking Enzo," he murmurs as I reach out across the table grabbing his hand. "Thanks, for this. I know you and the Andretti's don't have the best track record, but thanks for bringing me here. Plus, Italian food… yum!"

"Only the best for my girl."

CHAPTER 26

MYLEE

Our lunch date continues, and I eat far too much food feeling a little too full, almost to the point of nausea. I notice the Mafiosos haven't left our side the entire meal, but I actually feel grateful not annoyed about it at all.

After thanking Enzo, we left and are making our way into the city to see Dr. Branson the OB/GYN. But as we round the corner, the traffic is piled up. I can see flashing lights way ahead in the distance. "Shit, I think there's an accident or something?"

Trax groans looking to the clock on the dash. "Hopefully, the delay isn't too bad, or we'll be late. Lunch ran a little too long," Trax stresses.

The traffic moves slowly. My anxiety creeping higher and higher. I hate being late and knowing there's nothing we can do to get through this traffic any quicker is annoying me. "It's okay. When we get there, I'll pull up out the front, and you can run in, then I'll park and follow you."

I relax a little as we slowly edge up closer and closer to the accident. Eventually, we're able to pass the graphic scene.

Trax grips onto my knee. "Don't look, babe," he warns.

I quickly look to Trax while he watches the road as we finally pass the pedestrian versus car accident, and he makes his way to the building pulling in right next to the door. "Go straight in, do *not* stop for anything. I will wait right here until I see you go inside, then I'll be there as soon as I can," he instructs. I lean over giving him a brief kiss then turn quickly jumping out of the truck before someone honks at him. I run to the door, turn back giving him a brief wave before I walk inside and up to the counter. Turning back and looking out the glass door, I see him driving off like a lunatic as I take a breath and swing around to the redheaded receptionist.

"I'm sorry I'm late. I'm Mylee Bannerman. I'm here to see Dr. Branson."

The assistant hardly looks to me. "It's fine, that accident out there is causing chaos here today anyway. Come with me, I'll take you straight through, the doctor's waiting."

Nerves run through me. I want to wait for Trax, but I don't want to keep Dr. Branson waiting any more than we already have. "My partner, Konnor, is just finding a parking space, so can you let him come through when he arrives?"

"Of course."

We reach the door, but the redhead doesn't look in, just merely opens it absentmindedly gesturing for me to walk in. I step inside as she closes the door behind me. Looking in, I see Dr. Branson standing by the giant window wearing a lab coat, he's gazing out onto the street obviously checking out the accident. But as I take a closer look, I feel like his height is different, maybe even his stature. Shit! Something about him looks off. Has his hair color changed?

When he turns around, all the air is knocked from my lungs once I take in the man before me.

He's definitely not Dr. Branson.

It's Everett *fucking* Scott.

I gasp.

I want to make a run for it, but my body won't move.

I'm stunned to the spot as fear creeps over every inch of my body, my skin prickling in goosebumps as a cold sweat runs over me. "Everett?"

"Found you!" his voice is deep, menacing, and it sends a chill through me. Then it hits me—a memory, a flashback. Me, in the hospital, him over me in a lab coat at my drip. He was there. He knew where I was the entire time. I just didn't remember until this very moment seeing him in the same outfit.

"You! You were at the hospital when I found out I was pregnant, weren't you?"

He tilts his head smirking at me—it's menacing and evil. "If I knew where you were all this time, don't you think I would have come sooner?"

I jolt my head back. "So, you weren't there?"

He laughs. "I think you might have been dreaming of me, beautiful."

My body shudders as I glance around the room. "Where's Dr. Branson?"

He looks to the floor behind the desk. I can barely make out a hand sprawled on the floor, so I move slightly to see the doctor knocked out with blood pooling from his head. I let out a loud gasp as I spin without hesitation to run, but his fast pace catches me quickly. He spins me, his body pressing me up against the door blocking me in. His warm breath breathing against my face as his onyx eyes stare deep into mine—his are cold, dark, haunted.

"You were never meant to leave *me*, Mylee," he murmurs as his hand comes up caressing my face, a cold shudder running down my spine in fear.

"Leave you? I was never y-yours."

He snorts out a laugh. "We're destined, you and me."

I raise my brow, curling my lip. "How can you think that?"

He takes a deep breath. "We were at the hospital at the same time, fate brought us together. Destiny intervened showing me the way. For the world to be right, for the world to be on the right path, *we* have to be on the right path. Do you hear what I'm saying?"

Tears well in my eyes, thoughts of my babies cross my mind. I don't want him to hurt them. I don't care about me, just don't hurt my babies. I have no idea what he's planning, all I know is I need Trax to get here and soon. But right now I need to delay Everett. "Why don't we take a seat, and we can talk this out?"

He lets out a sinister laugh. "You think I'm stupid? You think I'm crazy? I planned all this meticulously." I raise my brow, trying not to answer honestly. "Mylee, I know your biker will be here any minute, so we have to leave... now."

My brows pull together. "No!"

"Yes!" He grabs my hand yanking me. I move to pull away, but he drags out a syringe with an attached needle from his lab coat pocket. I tense up halting my movements. "You walk out of here with me calmly, like nothing's wrong, or I will stab this into your stomach."

I tense up, but notice there's nothing in the syringe. I wonder what the hell game he's playing at here. "There's nothing in the syringe, Everett?"

He cocks his brow at me. "There's air, Mylee. Do you know what happens when you inject air into the body?" My body trembles not really wanting to know the answer. "When an air bubble enters through a vein, it's called a venous air embolism. Or if it enters through an artery, it's called an arterial air embolism. The air then travels to your brain, heart, or lungs and causes a heart attack, stroke, or respiratory failure... wouldn't want that now... would we?" His words send shock right through me. I gasp as my palms coat in a fine mist of sweat. I can't believe it, why is he doing this?

"What do you want?" I whimper.

"I told you. Come with me quietly. We have work to do." He spins me, wrapping his arm around me while the other carefully positions the needle at my side making me whimper out a stifled moan as he reaches for the door. "Not a peep, you got it?"

I shudder as he slowly opens the door. We step out into the small hall. Unfortunately, there's a wall blocking our view into the main waiting room so no one can see us from here. Tears flood my eyes as he pulls me in the opposite direction making us head out the back way, away from the reception desk. Away from where I know Trax will be coming in any second now.

TRAX

Finding a parking space was a fucking nightmare. I know I'm probably missing out on important shit right now. All I want is to fucking get in there with my woman to see what the hell's going on. Once I finally found a space, I raced inside, and I'm now walking up to the front door in a mad rush. Yanking open the door, I stride in to see Mylee isn't in the waiting room. She must have gone in already.

Fuck.

I don't want to miss anything, so I walk over to the reception desk. The redhead looks up at me through her glasses and smiles a little wider than your typical smile. I inwardly chuckle knowing why.

"Afternoon. I think my woman, Mylee, has gone in with the doc, can I head in there?"

She bats her eyelashes at me. "Sure thing. She went in about five minutes ago, just head straight on through."

I turn heading past the wall to the door of the doctor's room, but the door is slightly ajar. I furrow my brows thinking it's a little odd as I approach. Pushing the door to see no one's inside, I take a breath thinking they must have gone to have the ultrasound area already when I hear a slight groan from the floor. I turn back, then I see it. Someone's laying on the floor behind the desk.

I burst through the door, my heart leaping into my chest as I race around the desk to see Dr. Branson in a pool of his own blood, oozing from his head. My chest tightens, and I immediately begin to panic.

Where the fuck is Sparx?

I roll the doctor over, his eyes flutter open as he looks to me. I wave my hand over his face as he comes to. "Are you with me?"

He groans a little more. "Someone got me good."

I tense. "Someone hit you?" I ask as he moans against his movements. "Do you know who?"

He shakes his head. "Some guy dressed in a doctor's robe, he kept saying he was coming for her, that he was going to take her. They were destined to be together, then he knocked me out when I tried to get him to leave."

Panic washes over me, and I stand abruptly. "Fuck! It's shit you got hurt, but I have to go," I tell him bolting out of the room, my feet feeling like fucking lead, they're so heavy. I can't seem to move fast enough, nothing I do is making me move quicker than I need to.

I burst out of the room, running out into the reception area. "Did you see where a doctor took my woman?" I burst out, the redhead shakes her head looking confused.

"No, she's been in with Dr. Branson ever since she arrived."

Running my fingers through my hair, I groan. "Dr. Branson's hurt, you might want to see to that. Is there a back exit?" I ask.

"Yeah, but it's only for staff."

"This is an emergency, I think someone's kidnapped my woman. Show me the exit. Now!"

She stands up rushing from behind her desk. We run down the back of the hall toward a door that's ajar and swinging freely in the breeze. Dread fills me as I get to the top of the stairs and look out to see fresh tire marks. I grip my hair as I look to the redhead, her head swings from side to side like she's confused.

"This door shouldn't be open," she murmurs. I let out a loud groan as I rush down the metal stairs looking around trying to see anything, but all I can notice is an empty parking lot with fresh tire marks. My chest aches with overwhelming pain.

Everett has Mylee, and I have absolutely no idea where to begin looking.

What the hell to do.

Holy shit.

I breathe in and out so fast I realize I need to keep myself together.

I need to think.

I've got to keep my shit together for my woman and my babies.

Yanking my cell from my jeans pocket, I hit the number I need right now. The only man I can think of to help me.

It rings, and for a moment I think he isn't going to answer, then I hear a giggling girl sounding an awful lot like Cindi down the line and muffled kissing noises. "This better be fucking good, Trax."

"I need you right now... Everett has Sparx."

Ace grunts, the cell muffles slightly like he's arranging himself, then he clears his throat. "Fuck. Where are you?"

"At the doctor, he took her, Ace. I wasn't there to stop him. I just... oh *fuck!*" I yell out so loud it echoes through the parking lot.

"Okay. I'm on it, you coming back to the clubhouse?"

My stomach sinks. I don't know what the fuck to do. My instinct is to go, search the streets, just fucking look. But what the fuck am I looking for? My time is better spent back at the clubhouse trying to narrow the search area down, with my brothers by my side. And I have a call to make, a fucking call I never ever wanted to make to her father—to Crest, the man I look up to, the man I respect, the man I have now let down.

Fuck.

CHAPTER 27

MYLEE

My hands are covered in sweat as I stare out the window of the car wondering what the hell I'm going to do. I'm caught here questioning just what Trax is thinking, what he's doing, what hell he's going through while I'm stuck here in a car with a crazy guy I met while in a psych hospital. I take a deep breath turning to look at Everett trying to think of how I should play this. "You look like you're doing well, Everett," I murmur.

He looks to me letting out a small laugh. "I've never been better, Mylee. You, me, we never belonged in that place. My father, he put me there for no good reason. It only made me edgy, made my skin crawl. I'm better off out of there."

I raise my brow wondering why the hell he hasn't been recommitted a long time ago—I suspect he's completely off his meds right now. He never wanted to take his medication, and that fact always sent him spiraling. His thoughts on government conspiracies, the way the world was working against him, always made me question his logic. I tried to stay away from him in the hospital, but he gravitated toward me, never leaving me alone. It got so bad they had to put him in solitary for a while because they thought he might do something to harm either one of us. Or another patient. His attachment to me for some reason seems like it's something to do with a childhood friend of his who died when she was young.

He said in the hospital I reminded him of her. My golden locks, my innocent features. Through me, he was connected to her. When she died, that's when he became unstable from what I've been able to understand. They were playing in his father's barn with his rifles. They were only about six or seven when the gun went off accidentally killing the girl instantly right in front of Everett. He was never the same and has been in and out of psych wards ever since. His father, the senator, trying his hardest to hide his son's secret past—the past where Everett shot his best friend, then lost his mind in the process—is something that doesn't sit well on record for a man running for president. Malcolm Scott has done a good job keeping his private life under wraps. The world knows he has a son, but they know nothing about said son. It's all been hidden really well, and I know if news broke of the Senator's son being mentally unstable, then the Senator's chances for the race to the white house would probably be tarnished.

A lump forms in my throat, and I clear it shifting in my seat to face Everett more, trying to seem like I'm engaging his conversation. I want to appear friendly. I want to gain his trust. "Everett, I know our time in the hospital was brief, but I feel like I got to know you… about your past, about where your mind goes. But what I don't understand is where we're going right now?"

He smiles. It's not a comforting gesture. It has a hard edge to it, and it unsettles me. "I'm taking you somewhere I should have taken you long ago. It's just, I've had a hard time tracking you down. But I've had people on my side, Mylee. People who understand me."

I bob my head as if I'm following.

I'm not.

"People, like who?"

"I have a few people that were in hospitals with me. They understand. They think like us. They know the system is flawed, that the government is stopping the right people from being together."

"People like you and me?"

He lets out a small laugh. "See. You get it! This is why I knew this would work, Mylee. You're perfect, even if..." he glances down at my stomach, "... you're tainted."

A shudder runs through me as my hand inadvertently runs to my tummy to protect my two unborn babies. I don't want to question him or bring any added attention to my children. They need to be protected and kept as safe as possible. I have no idea what his intentions are, but I will do absolutely everything in my power to protect my babies.

No matter the cost.

My eyes begin to well in fear as I glance out the window, I don't want him to see me wavering. "Are we heading back to Michigan?" I ask trying to sound blasé.

He chuckles. "Yeah, gotta get you back home. You've had your fun with those Defiance bikers. They kept you away from me for long enough. It took a hell of a lot of effort to get you away from them. My dad set up the plan to run a pedestrian over near your doctor's office to cause a delay in traffic so you'd be running late. That diversion allowed me to get into the doctor's suite unseen. It worked like a charm, too. Shame the pedestrian died, a casualty of love and war, but it's worth it to have you by my side, my love. I'm pissed off your biker bastard didn't make it in, I had a plan for him, but that doesn't matter now."

I let out a gasp as I realize what he's saying. His dad's in on this? He had someone killed so Everett could get to me. Holy shit, this is bigger than I could have possibly imagined! Not only that, but Dr. Branson could be dead for all I know.

Fuck! If Malcolm's in on this, then is Trax safe?

Is he even looking for me?

What the hell is Everett up to?

What the hell is he planning?

I knew he was crazy, but now I'm beginning to understand—he's fucking lethal.

TRAX

Rushing into the clubhouse, Torque is by my side instantly as his face falls. "Is it true, did Everett get Sparx?"

I grunt. "Do you fucking see her with me right now, brother?" I blurt out in anger more at myself.

He grits his teeth as we walk straight toward the chapel without hesitation. "What the fuck happened? You had Andretti's men with you for lunch? Did they not keep up their end?" Torque asks.

I roll my shoulders. "No, this is on me. We were running late, fucking traffic accident right outside the place. So, I let her go in without me while I was getting a parking space. I should have known. *I should have fucking known.* I watched her walk in through the doors. I thought once she was inside, she'd be safe... I mean she was fine, there were people everywhere. I wasn't going to be long. I thought she'd be okay. Fuck, Torque, *I did this.* I let her get taken."

He grabs my cut pulling me to face him. "Stop! You can't play the blame game right now. It's done. We have to figure out how the hell to get your woman back."

"Amen," Ace calls out from behind his desk as I look over while he continues to type away on his computer.

"Do you have anything?"

He exhales. "I hacked into the cameras as soon as we hung up. The doctor's office doesn't have anything, but the gas station across the road did, so I pulled that up. It showed Everett hauling Sparx out the back into a black Hyundai Sonata. I couldn't get the plate numbers from the footage, so I tried to follow the path they took. Trying to get cameras that lined up has been difficult, but I've managed to get a match eventually. He's driving fast, so I've lost which road they took, but I have the plates and have programmed it into the system so when it pops up as a match on any of the cameras it should ping letting us know where they're headed."

Taking a breath, I try to take all of that in. My heart's beating rapidly in my chest. "Okay, can we ride while you track it?"

"Yeah, I can put it on my cell and mount it to my bars, kinda like a GPS. It should tell us the exact route he's taking."

I look to Torque, his eyes hard in understanding. "We ride. I'll get the boys." He grips my shoulder looking at me, the eyes of my blood brother staring firm. "We'll get her back. We'll get *them* back. Don't worry, we got this." With a simple exhale, he walks out of the chapel as I hear a loud whistle echo through the clubroom, but I'm too caught up in my own thoughts to listen to him telling my brothers the deal right now.

I look to Ace with pleading eyes, my stomach sinking through to the bowels of hell. "Can we really do this... track him down?"

"I got this, you follow me, and we'll find her. We got the plate, it's programmed... as long as it keeps pinging the cameras, we'll be able to follow it." Ace grabs a few pieces of tech equipment then we walk out into the clubroom where my brothers are all lining up, their subtle nods don't go unnoticed. I risk a glance to Mom, her eyes watering as she holds onto Neala tightly. I can't acknowledge them right now as I turn walking toward the door, not waiting for anyone. I need to ride. I need to ride now. My woman and kids need me. I'll be damned if I'm waiting for anyone.

I walk outside, the sun hitting my face making the sweat already rolling down my temple feel even colder against my skin. Just needing to feel the vibration of the heavy metal between my legs, I make my way to my ride. I have to be on the road, going after her. I need her back in my arms. I want that fucker to pay for taking her. I swear to God if he's even touched a hair on her head, I will gut him quicker than he has a chance to take another breath—be damned Sensei's teachings.

My ride turns on effortlessly, the rumble vibrates up through me as I yank on my helmet roughly. I'm frustrated. I need to get going, but everyone seems to be fucking dawdling. Ace is beside me appearing to feel my agitation. He starts his ride as Torque slides on his bike while I signal to Ace to lead the way. Normally, it would be Scratch, but Ace is the only one who knows where the hell we're going, so Scratch will have to take a general position for this ride.

Ace pulls out, and I follow behind him, skidding my tires out on the turn. Torque pulls up beside me, giving me the strength I need as we ride beside each other. Scratch pulls in behind us, and everyone else follows. My brothers are with me in this. We have no idea what we're riding into, what the hell we're going to be facing, but none of us care because when one of us are in, we're all in, and right now this is my fight, and my family is at my back.

No matter what.

That's what brotherhood is all about.

We've been riding for a while, but I'm getting frustrated. I feel like we've been out now for at least an hour when Ace pulls off to the side of the road stopping quickly. We all follow as my fists clench against my bars in annoyance. We should be riding, not stopping. But I pull over while Ace is frantically working on his cell.

"Shit," he murmurs.

"What the fuck is going on? Why'd we stop?" I call out.

"I think they've switched cars."

My eyes open wide as my chest heaves. "What? Why do you think that?"

Ace zooms in on a picture of the Sonata stopped at a gas station, then there's a snapshot of Sparx and Everett getting out of the car then into another one, but the plates are too hazy to see what they read.

"Fuck! Without my other tech gear, I don't know how to trace this second car, I've only got limited shit with me," Ace states.

"So we're an hour and a half from the Defiance clubhouse with no fucking idea where the hell he's taking her?"

Ace huffs. "I think it's safe to say he's heading toward Grand Rapids. We're definitely headed in that direction, just don't know *where* in Grand Rapids."

I grunt. "Fuck! Fine! We need some way of tracing her. Is there another way, Ace? Think!"

He looks up at the sky as if to look for some kind of fucking divine intervention, then looks back to me. "Fuck! Why didn't I think of this first. Did she have her cell on her?"

"Yeah, she shoved it down her bra before we left."

Ace scrunches his face like he's frustrated but then quickly taps something into his cell. "Give me a few moments, I'm going to try and see if I can track her cell from here. If she still has it on her, it might be our best bet."

I turn toward Torque, and he lets out a sigh. "Trax, we're heading into Knights' territory. If they hear about Defiance riding in Michigan without us filling them in, you know we're gonna to be in for a world of hurt."

I groan. I've been dreading making this call, but I know I need to. Plus, maybe having the Notorious Knights on our side as we ride in to get Sparx would be helpful. The more to take down this cockhead, the better. I just hope Crest doesn't ream me a new asshole for being a fucking failure at protecting his princess. Spinning on my heels, I walk away from the guys dialing Crest's number. Taking a deep breath, it rings twice before he answers.

"Trax, you better have something good to tell me."

"Crest... I failed."

Silence filters down the line for a brief moment before he clears his throat and grunts. "Trax, what the fuck does that mean?"

Running my hand through my hair, I cringe. "Everett has her."

"You've got to be fucking kidding me. Jesus, Trax! I brought her to you to keep her safe. I trusted you. It's been one thing after the other since I brought her there for your damn protection..." he pauses. I let him gather himself as my stomach churns with anxiety. "Fuck! When? How long has she been gone?"

Sighing, I crack my neck to the side. "A couple of hours, give or take—"

"What! *Are you fucking insane?* Why the hell are you only calling me now?"

Swallowing hard, I knew that was coming. "We're on our way into Grand Rapids. Ace was able to track the car Everett took her in, but now they've switched cars, and we don't have the tech equipment we need with us to track the new car. From what we can make out, it's a Honda Civic, a midnight blue color, but that's all we know. We've been tracking them, following them. We know they're headed your way, but we've lost them. Though, Ace is now trying to get a trace on Mylee's cell signal to see if we can follow it."

Crest lets out a heavy sigh and is quiet for a pass. The heaviness of the situation obviously catching up with him. "Shit! Trax... she's my baby girl."

I rub my temple. "And she's my Old Lady... the mother of my unborn children, Crest. I know how you feel... we have to get her back."

"I'm getting the boys together, and we're gonna ride, right now. Where are you?"

"The Gerald R. Ford Freeway... we're about an hour or so out."

"Right. We're gonna go searching around town for blue Civics till you get here. We'll meet you at the turn-off. We'll get her back. We have to. Don't worry. If there's one thing about Everett, all he wants is for him and Mylee to be together, so as long as we find him, we'll find her."

For some reason, it doesn't soothe me. "See you soon. And Crest?"

"Yeah?"

"Sorry."

He exhales. "Your apology means nothing, just fucking get her back."

I end the call as I turn to see Torque watching me closely while Ace works frantically on his equipment.

Fuck, I hope he's come up with something.

CHAPTER 28

MYLEE

It's been hours since we left the doctor's office. I know Trax must be going crazy if he's still alive. My cell's tucked in my bra, but I don't want Everett to know it's there. I just hope like hell it doesn't make any sounds while we're together. I did manage to turn it to silent when Everett turned his back at the gas station. I momentarily thought about making a run for it too, but he didn't really give me much time to do anything. My plan was to say I needed to use the ladies room, which I actually do need—baby bladder and all—but he only had time for us to stop the car next to another one, get out, and steal the Civic. I was so shocked I didn't even realize what was happening until it was too late as I was shoved into the car, and he sped off.

I feel so out of my depth. I'm so scared, the darkness of thunderclouds threaten to roll in above my head, but I don't want my fears to settle in. I must keep my wits about me, but it's hard when my brain is fogging over. I need to keep control. I'm doing everything possible to keep my mind focused and active, not to let it drown in the fog or the storm that's brewing.

The day is shifting to night, and the further we drive, it becomes more obvious we're driving past Grand Rapids and out into farmland. I can't help but wonder where the hell he's taking me. The sun's setting, it's getting close to nine at night, and I'm stressing wondering if anyone's going to come.

I hope Trax will be doing everything in his power to search for me, to find me, but Everett's doing his best to keep us moving. Changing up the vehicles we're traveling in is only going to make it even more difficult for the club to find me. But being so close to Grand Rapids makes me think of Dad and the Knights, and what the hell they're going to do if they find out I'm here being held by Everett.

Everett won't only have Defiance coming after him, but the Knights too. He's in for one hell of a shitstorm. And I can't wait for it to rain down on him.

Pulling off into a farm, he looks at me raising his brow. "I'm so excited we will finally be able to be connected like we're supposed to," he utters breaking the deafening silence that's been riddling the car for the past few hours.

I tilt my head. "What do you mean?"

"After the cleansing ritual, to rid you of your demons, to rid you of your evil, you will be purified, and we can be together like we were truly meant to be all those years ago."

"All those years ago?" I question, we were only in the hospital two years ago, he's not making sense.

I'm confused.

"Yes. We were meant to grow old together, you and me, remember? We've said it ever since we were six."

I click remembering about the girl in the barn who died, the one he connects to me for some reason—I still don't really know why. "The girl in the barn, the one who died, Everett? She's not me. I'm Mylee."

"No." He shakes his head. "Something changed when you were shot. You forgot. You altered your name slightly... only slightly. You look so much like her." His eyes widen. "The government! The government is the ones trying to keep us apart, Rylee, don't you see?"

I open my eyes wide. "Rylee?"

"Yes. Now you remember, don't you? Is it coming back, Rylee? Are you coming back to me?"

I shudder in understanding. I completely get why he clung to me, not only is my name only one letter different to hers, but if I look like her too, then no wonder I've sent him over the edge. He must have really felt something for this Rylee, they must have been good friends for him to have such a bond to her all these years later. But then again, I guess, if they were best friends and he shot her, accidentally killing her, then your family covers it up for your entire life, and you're bound to have some mental issues.

Poor guy.

I actually feel for him now.

The amount of pity I have for him doesn't lessen my fear, though. The fact is, he has me confused for a dead six-year-old girl. A girl who isn't coming back. There's nothing I can say or do that's going to change his mind.

He pulls up to a barn, stops the car, and jumps out. I tense up as he rushes to my side yanking me out of the car forcefully. I grimace at the tightness of his clenched fist around my bicep as he pulls me inside the barn. The barn is paneled in wood and appears really old. Like it has been here for a century. It creeps me out.

"The barn's just like the one we grew up in. Isn't it, Rylee?" he calls out looking up into the rafters above us, his eyes alight in wonder as a cold shudder runs through my very soul. This is all a little too creepy. The fact Rylee died in a barn, and now I'm alone with him in the darkening night is scaring the shit out of me. My instinct is to run, but I'm petrified and don't want to put any risk on the babies, but staying *is* risking them too.

I'm so freaking torn.

I have no idea what to do.

Everett drags me to the middle of the barn to a lone wooden chair. I crease my brows leering at it as he looks me up and down with a beaming smile. "You're wearing a white dress, it's perfect for the purity ritual."

Tensing, I'm scared to ask, but my curiosity wins out. "What's this purification ritual?"

He shoves me down onto the seat, the wood creaks with the force as he pins me down. "I need to cleanse your body, get rid of the bad energy inside of you. You can't have demon spawn inside of you, Rylee. When Dad sent Jason to find you, Jason told us you were shopping in a baby emporium. I couldn't believe it. At first, I thought it was for the other girl. She seemed to be more into the baby stuff holding it up to her stomach and such, but then after Jason went missing, Dad got his people to dig deeper. It was then we knew you were staying with the Defiance. There were two reasons for this—one Jason followed you from their clubhouse, and two, that biker was wearing his cut. Then we found out you were with *him.*" His nose turns up in a snarl. "It's you that's knocked up. He was keeping you hidden from me. You weren't going anywhere but to your doctor, so with Dad's help, I had no choice but to take you from there. It was my only option, the only way I can cleanse you of the abomination, Rylee."

I snort, shaking my head. "Do you hear yourself?" I lash out instantly regretting it as he glares at me.

"*Do you hear yourself?* You were such a sweet, innocent young thing, then you lived with bikers all your life, and that's when the change happened. When the bullet took you, morphed you, then the government intervened... when my father and his politicians *took* you from me."

My stomach sinks in anguish. He's so confused. He thinks Rylee was taken after she was shot, put into the Notorious Knights biker club, and that girl is me, but she simply isn't.

Rylee died, and I'm just the unfortunate woman who's similar to her and lived in the same state. It's all a coincidence that somehow I ended up in the same psych ward as Everett. If we never crossed paths at the same time, he wouldn't even know about me.

"Rylee, I'm going to make everything better. Once you're clean, we will ascend to a better place. We can be free together."

The sincere look in his eyes petrifies me. That right there is crazy talk as he pulls some rope from the ground moving behind me and threading it around my wrists behind my back. My arms are almost locked to the back of the chair as I sit on it, my stomach churning while panic starts to set in.

I can't help but wonder what the hell this purification ritual is exactly. I have no idea how the hell I'm going to get myself out of this. I can't pull my hands free. I have no idea if Trax is coming for me. I hope he'll be looking, but is he looking in the right place? Will he be able to find me in time?

Everett walks off making my heart rate spike up a notch as I watch him. He grabs a hay bale starting to spread it around me in a large circle.

"Everett, what are you doing?"

He looks at me but says nothing. The sight sends a chill through me as I immediately begin to struggle in the seat to get my wrists free from their restraints, but they're tied really freaking tight. So tight the furry texture of the ropes grinds against my skin, tearing at the surface. I feel blood dripping from my wrists and down my hands as I try to maneuver it.

He makes a full circle with the hay rubbing his hands together like he's done a hard day's work, then walks off toward the door of the barn like he's going to fetch something. It makes me even more fearful considering what he might be coming back with as I'm left in here alone. Darkness filters in through the open doorway, and I can't help but question whether these might be my last moments on this earth. So I stop struggling as I look up to the moon that's shining in through the crack in the door. Tears pool in my eyes as I think of Trax.

The love of my life.

The man of my dreams.

The man who took me in, without hesitation, even with all my faults.

I never got to thank him.

Never got to truly tell him how honored I am to be the one he's having a family with.

That he chose me to be his Old Lady.

There's so much left unsaid. After everything we've been through to get to this point, for it all to possibly end now—I don't know how this is going to play out—but if I die tonight, I don't want things to be left unsaid. So, I figure, even though he's not here, I'll say them now. "Trax, I know you can't hear me..." I sniff, tears filling my eyes as I stare up at the moon, "... but coming back into your life is the best thing that's ever happened to me. I know it's been rocky, I know it's been unexpected, but these babies, though surprising..." I can't help but smile, "... I love them, Trax. I know I said I never wanted kids, but that was only to protect them. To protect them from what I've become, from what *they* might become. Not because I didn't want them, not because I wouldn't love them. Because I do. So much." I let out a small sob. "Just as I love you with all my heart. If I never see you again, just know my last thoughts are of you, always—"

A round of clapping disrupts my monologue as I look to the doorway to see Everett round the barn door as he steps in. "That was sweet. But it only proves you need to be cleansed, sooner rather than later. I was going to wait until midnight for the ritual, but I think I need to move it up to... right now!"

My stomach sinks through the floor making me feel sick. "No, Everett, I'm sorry. Please forgive me. I can wait until midnight. I promise I won't say anything again. Please, just wait!" I want to bide as much time as possible to give Trax enough time to find me, but Everett beams at me with a crooked smile.

"No. You need to be cleansed, now. It can't wait, you're far too tarnished." He grabs something from his jacket, the glimmer of something silver shimmering against the purple hue of the night as he brings it in line with his face. I notice it's a lighter as he flicks it on. The flame flickering in the slight breeze.

Tension ripples through me as I shudder with fear wondering what the hell he's planning on doing with that. "E-Everett," I stutter calmly. "How am I going to be cleansed?" I ask.

His eyes grow dark as he looks down at me with hooded eyes. His almost demonic face flickers in the light. "In flames. You will be purified by fire then we will be reborn together as one. As we should have done, my love."

Opening my eyes wide, my skin riddles in goosebumps, the hairs on my arms standing to attention. This is madness, he's completely insane. I have no idea how I'm going to get out of this. The thought of burning alive scares the shit out of me. Storm clouds are rolling overhead, but I also know I need to keep my mind clear, I can't get lost in my emotions. I need to fight my way out of this.

For my babies.

He moves to the outer rim of the hay circle and bends down, the flickering light of the flame igniting the hay, making me instantly break out into sweat. I'm shaking so hard as the circle lights up, flames flapping, swarming and engulfing me in a plume of smoke and fire. I can't hear anything but the intense crackle of the flames bursting and popping as I cough while adrenaline spikes through me. I look at my stomach, thinking of the two lives inside of me.

This can't be it.

They haven't had a chance.

I can't let this be it for them.

My fighter instincts kick in. The wall of flames is high, I can't get through them. I know Everett's on the other side, but I need to get off this damned chair and get low. Smoke rises and luckily Everett made the circle too wide so the flames are not intense right now. I tilt my body making the chair fall to the side. I turn slightly to protect my babies in the fall. I hit the ground with a thud, my shoulder taking the full impact as I groan out in pain. My eyes water as I try not to let the pain or emotion overtake me. I have to keep my head clear. I cough and splutter through the damn smoke and heat haze. The flames aren't hitting me, but they are close. I have no idea what else to do.

I think to Trax, I love him so much.

Today was such a great day.

If today is my last day, at least I got to have one last date with him.

I hope he'll be able to pull through this.

It will devastate him.

But I know me, and our babies will be with him, always.

As I lay on the ground, smoke invading my lungs, fire lapping all around me, my eyes close. An image of Trax fills my mind making a calm wash over me as everything finally turns black.

CHAPTER 29

TRAX

My heart hasn't stopped racing. Even though I'm on my ride which normally soothes me, the fact we've been able to ping Sparx's cell, and we're tracking where she's located, it's eating me up. I know where she is, I just need to get to her and fast. The fact I can also see the Notorious Knights pulled up on the side of the road ahead as we enter into Grand Rapids does nothing to ease the tension inside my body. All I know is I'm not fucking stopping to chat to Crest. I know it would be the decent thing to do, but we're already behind the eight ball and delayed. We just need to keep moving so we can catch up to that son-of-a-bitch.

As we ride up alongside Crest and his men, they pull out joining our group ride. Two clubs riding side by side. The noise of the hogs is loud through the darkened night.

I tip my chin to Crest, and he does the same in return, making me feel like maybe he might not kick my ass too hard when I finally get a chance to speak to him face to face. But who knows. After we get Sparx back, he might shoot me himself.

Ace continues to track Sparx's cell leading the way. My nerves are fucking shot. I know Everett has to stop at some point, and when he does, we'll be on him. I have no idea what our game plan is. We didn't discuss it. We're riding in blind, but I know we're all coming in fucking hot.

Eventually, Ace leads us down a long dirt road of what looks like a farm. I see an old barn in the distance, a set of gates leading up to the barn and at the gates a car is stationed. As we ride up, I notice three men stepping out of the car. I don't hesitate, reaching around my back to the Glock that's down my pants pulling it out.

I notice one of the guys has the same blue baseball cap Jason had on in the baby emporium which I now notice has Senator Scott's slogan printed on the front. The other two men reach into the car pulling out guns aiming them at us. Firing off rounds aiming at no one in particular. Bikes break off as the sounds of guns firing echo through the night. I don't hesitate to fire my weapon, the Glock instantly reflecting back in my hand as I aim for cap guy. The wind as I ride my bike making it hard to get in a good shot as he aims right at me. His rifle goes off, a bullet flies straight past me, nipping the side of my helmet making my ears ring a little as I blink a few times aiming for him again. Without hesitation as I ride right for him, I pull the trigger, the bullet hitting him right above his left eye. His body swings to the left, blood sprays all over the car. I grin beneath my helmet as I don't waste any more time. I watch as Torque and Chains make quick work of the other two idiots, and I hammer down along with Crest and Ace as we ride toward the barn. I can see and smell smoke coming from inside, and this instantly puts me on high alert. I hammer down even harder. I have no idea what the hell I'm going to be walking into, but all I know is my woman and unborn babies are in there, and I need to get inside.

Now!

I see the flicker of flames as I get so close I can smell the fire. My bike not even brought to a full stop as I slide it to the side. It falls to the ground as I jump off running, ripping off my helmet as Ace and Crest pull up jumping off and running inside along with me. My heart beats out of my chest when I see the ring of flames.

I squint shaking my head trying to figure out what I'm seeing, but as I look through the red blaze, I can vaguely make out the image of Sparx on the ground, passed out.

My stomach sinks as my eyes search around for Everett who's nowhere to be seen. Ace and Crest run off as Torque rushes to my side. I step up with him toward the flames in a mad panic. I look, trying to find a way in, but the heat is so intense I have no idea how to get through to her.

"Mylee!" I call out my stomach wanting to unload its contents all over the floor.

In grief.

In utter panic.

Suddenly, someone lands on my back like they just jumped from a height. The weight almost knocking me into the flames as a fist lands into the side of my head. The sting dazing me for a second as I stumble on the spot trying to grab the idiot off my back. Torque races forward to help me, but I stand up taller righting myself as I look to my blood brother. "Torque, help Sparx," I scream. He hesitates but then rushes off in the direction of Ace and Crest.

I grab the hem of Everett's shirt who's still on my back, and yank him over the top of my shoulders. He groans as he flies over and to the ground. I spin as I bend over him, kneeling either side, it startles me for a second as I get a good look at him. It flashes back. Even though I've seen his picture it didn't click until right now seeing him in the flesh. He's the asshole I saw with Mylee in the hospital, the one who she was laughing with. My stomach swirls with anger as I bring my fist back, landing a solid blow into his nose. It cracks under the hit, the audible break sounding through the barn as he groans, blood spilling from his nose, his face swells almost instantly.

I go to hit him again, but his hand comes up to the side with a stray rock smacking me in the side of my cheek. I flop to the side, disorientated, as he gets up to run away like the coward he is.

Shaking my head, I stagger while chasing after him. He reaches for a pitchfork as he shoves the pointy end toward me. I duck out of the way, bending down grabbing a fist full of dirt and throwing it at his face. He coughs and splutters, his eyes closing and opening a few times as he drops the pitchfork in shock. I step in, my hands grabbing him around his neck, squeezing tight.

This fucker tried to kill my woman.

Tried to burn her and my babies alive.

He's going to fucking pay.

His eyes bulge as his hands come up to mine squeezing around his neck. He claws at my hands trying to get me to loosen, but he fails.

Suddenly, his knee comes up between my legs hitting me right in the balls. Pain like I've never felt before ripples through me. I let go stumbling backward as he gasps for air but only takes a moment to gather himself before he's on me. His fist slamming into my face. The agony reverberates through my entire body as I swing around toward the fire, getting a little too close for comfort. He pushes me, making me stumble. He grabs my arm, thrusting it straight into the fire. I scream as my wrist burns in the flames. My skin bubbling with the heat. But through the pain, I bring my free hand up punching him in his ribs. He lets me go as I quickly pull my arm from the fire. Bending over in agony, he comes for me again.

No, this fucker has done enough.

Now, I'm fucking angry.

So as he comes toward me for another round, I reach behind me pulling out my Glock aiming it at him. He skids to a halt as his breathing becomes rapid and shallow. He looks from me, then all around like he's trying to find a way out.

There isn't one.

He's a dead man tonight.

"Trax, we can sort this out. I'm the son of a senator," his shrill voice begs.

I curl up my lip as I unclick the safety. "You tried to kill Mylee, you don't get an out."

"Then kill me like a man. No guns."

I snort. "Oh, right. How would you like to die, Everett?" I ask.

"I need to be reborn in the fire."

This guy's lost it. But if he doesn't want a gun. Fine. I can give him no gun. I lower my Glock taking a deep breath as a slow smile creeps up on his face.

"Fine. No gun. But you're not dying the way you want either," I declare bending down picking up the pitchfork. The weathered wood grates against my fingers as I race forward shoving it straight into his stomach. He lets out a gurgled grunt, his muscles fight and contract against the intrusion, so I push a little harder. Blood pools on his white shirt as his eyes open wide. He coughs out a long line of blood.

"You don't make the rules here, Everett... I do. Now go to hell, and stay there," I grunt as I thrust the fork up into him deeper. His eyes close as he slumps onto the fork, so I drop his lifeless body to the ground.

I don't have time to check if he is, in fact, dead but I know no one could survive that. I have to get to Sparx. I turn around to see Ace, Crest, and Torque with giant, thick blankets putting out the flames. Crest's already in the middle of the circle, untying Sparx's hands from behind her back as the rest of the bikers, Defiance and Knights, rush into the barn to see what's happening.

I move as fast as I can over to Sparx, dropping to my knees in front of her as Crest finally manages to get her hands untied, and I pull her to me. She's so limp as relief floods through me, but she's completely out of it.

"Mylee, baby, c'mon. C'mon, baby," I murmur stroking her hair away from her face as Crest strokes her torn wrists.

"Coma! Get your ass over here," Crest calls out to one of his men. I look up to see a young guy, well built, kind of ex-military looking. He steps in, looking down to Sparx.

"We need to get her out of here and away from this fucking smoke," Coma instructs. I fear the worst as I lean in picking her up, even though my wrist is killing me as I run outside placing her on the fresh grass with all the men following me. Coma runs to his bike pulling out a first-aid kit from his saddle bag.

I glance to Sparx, her breathing is shallow making me start to panic as Coma returns sitting down beside her placing a small oxygen cylinder over her mouth. I look up to see Crest is on his cell. I overhear him talking to an ambulance as I look to Sparx who still isn't waking up even with the oxygen. I stand up and begin to pace while running my hands through my hair.

Shit.

What if she doesn't wake up?

What if she is really gone?

What if I lose her and my babies?

I can't handle this. I can't fucking lose them all.

"*Fuuuck!*" I call out as I start to walk in circles. I'm freaking the fuck out as I look back to Sparx, her body unmoving as Coma works on her.

But there's nothing. She's breathing, but she's so lifeless.

Hands grab me pulling me to face them. Crest comes into view, his concerned face makes me feel even more broken. "Trax, brother, you need to calm down. She's okay, she's going to be fine. You need to keep it together for when she wakes up because we don't know how she's going to pull through this mentally. She will need you to be the strong one."

It's just the jolt I need. "Okay... yeah, okay."

Torque moves to my side, yanking on my arm, bringing it up to look at my burnt flesh. "You make sure they look at that when you're at the hospital."

I pull my arm away from him. "I don't care about me, I'll be fine."

Torque grunts. "I know you don't care, but Sparx does. She'll be pissed if you don't get yourself looked at. You know I'm right."

Groaning, I roll my eyes leaning down to stroke Sparx's hair then kiss her forehead while hearing the drawling blare of ambulance sirens in the distance. Relief washes over me that they're on their way, but I'm also worried about the repercussions of what might come from what's transpired here tonight.

I killed the son of a senator.

Shit like that doesn't tend to go down well.

I might get Sparx back just in time for me to get locked up. I have no idea how this is all going to go down. All I know is for right now, I want my woman and my kids looked after. I can deal with the fallout later.

The ambulance pulls down the dirt road. I don't miss the look on the faces of the driver as they take in all the bikers on the lawn.

Crest looks to me with a sigh. "I'll meet you at the hospital. You ride with her," he demands.

As if there was any other option.

The ambulance EMT rushes over to assess Sparx, and I let them do their thing. For once, I'm not going to interfere or try to get them to do things my way because all I care about is her safety right now. They know how best to do that, not me. I know when to bow out.

They stretcher her into the back of the ambulance, and I get in, but it doesn't go unnoticed that the Knights' VP, Aero, is closely monitoring the situation. *What's with that?*

I look to the officer tending to Sparx as the driver closes the door. "She's pregnant... twins," I murmur. "Will the babies be okay?"

"We'll do everything to keep her oxygen levels up and to keep her stable," is all she says not filling me with any kind of reassurance.

I sit back as dread slides over my entire body. What if we lose the babies? I think that would kill Sparx. I don't even know how I would deal with it.

The officer looks to me, glancing down at my arm. "That's a nasty burn you've got there."

I huff. "I'm fine."

She chuckles. "It's *not* fine, it needs attention. If you let it go it will get infected, and that won't be good for anyone. Trust me. Let me tend to it."

I groan but concede, letting her dress my wound. It hurts like a motherfucker. I hadn't really felt how bad it was until right now as everything's starting to sink in.

We arrive at the hospital a short time later. Sparx is admitted into an emergency bay, and just as we are, she starts to wake up. I shift to her side instantly as she looks up to me with tears in her eyes. Her hand moves straight to her stomach.

"It's okay. I'm here, I'm right here."

"The babies?" she asks as a doctor walks into the bay.

We both look up to him.

"We'll do a scan to check on them. You've inhaled smoke so we want to ensure your oxygen levels are okay before we move you around too much."

Sparx coughs a little, looking at the doctor, tears still glistening in her eyes. "Is there any risk to the babies?"

The doctor tilts his head. "With the risk of carbon monoxide poisoning, there's always a chance of the babies having some issues, but right now, it's best for you not to worry."

Sparx moves a little, trying to sit up, so I reach out helping her as she looks to the doctor. "Can you please do some testing, make sure our babies are okay?"

"Of course. I will get an OB/GYN to come in to do some testing straight away."

Even I relax slightly at hearing that. Sparx seems to sink into the bed seemingly calmer. Knowing our babies are okay will make us both feel better.

While we are waiting, a nurse came and tended to my arm. Sparx was really upset I'd gotten hurt. We had a talk about how she was feeling, but she's actually doing remarkably well. She said as long as the babies are safe, she'll be fine. Knowing I came to save them makes her feel so undeniably loved, she has no idea how to thank me. I told her there was no need. I love her, and I will always be there to protect my family.

Always.

Movement in the doorway gains my attention, so I look up and see Crest. I smile as he swallows hard peeking in to see Sparx awake. "How's my baby girl?"

Sparx's bottom lip trembles as she bursts into tears at seeing her father. He races in as I move aside letting him embrace his daughter. "Don't cry, baby girl. You're safe now. He's gone."

Her eyes widen as he pulls back. "Malcolm... Everett's father, he was in on this."

My head snaps to look at her as Crest tenses. "Why do you say that?"

Sparx sniffs. "Things Everett was saying. Trust me, will you look into it?"

I nod. "Yeah, babe, I'll have Ace go through everything, but for now you need to rest."

Crest looks at me. "Thanks for doing everything in your power to get our girl back."

I'm shocked. I thought out of all the emotions I'd get from Crest, it would be anger, but instead, he's thanking me. I smile as Crest simply turns walking out of the bay. Sparx lets out a little cough as I scrunch my eyebrows in shock.

I guess Crest is full of surprises. But the biggest surprise from this conversation wasn't Crest's non-reaction. It's that Malcolm might be involved. I just want to know how. But that can wait. Right now I need to make sure my woman and my kids are doing okay.

Them first, the Senator later.

CHAPTER 30

TRAX

A little while later, an OB/GYN walks in with a machine making my nerves spike up another level. The idea something's wrong with our twins has me on edge as I sit next to Sparx's bed.

"You ready to hear your babies?" she asks. I bow my head as Sparx just swallows hard. I grab her hand letting her know, no matter what, I'm with her in this.

She squirts the gel onto Sparx's tummy while Sparx flops her head back on the pillow almost like she's scared to look, but almost instantly, I hear the whooshing sound of two heartbeats. Joy fills my chest as I grip onto Sparx's hand so tight as her head flies up almost like she's shocked. Her face lights up in the brightest smile I've ever seen as her eyes well with a glistening sparkle. "They're okay?" she asks, her voice a breathy whisper.

"Their heartbeats are strong and healthy. From what I understand, you're staying in overnight to ensure there are no complications from the inhalation of the smoke."

"Yes, definitely," I agree as Sparx looks to me.

"I'm so happy they're okay."

I lean in planting a kiss on her lips as the doctor turns off her machine, subtly walking out of the bay leaving us alone to celebrate our good news. "I don't know what I would have done if I lost you today."

She brings her hand up caressing the side of my face. "You didn't. I'm okay. We're okay."

"I can't ever go through that again." I lean in kissing her strongly, knowing she's my world, my life, my everything.

Her and our twins.

The stay overnight in the hospital was cramped and awkward, but we're about to head home. Sparx is getting dressed as a knock sounds on the door. We both turn, my stomach sinks as I see none other than Malcolm fucking Scott standing in the doorway with two security goons on either side. His pristine politician suit tailored to perfection, his gray hair styled to within an inch of its life. He looks like the next fucking president.

A shudder runs over my body as I step in front of Sparx who looks as shaken as I feel.

Malcolm holds up his arms in a gesture of surrender as he steps inside the room closing the door behind him, leaving his goons outside. I tense as he takes a breath.

"Before you get trigger happy... I know what happened at the barn."

Dread fills me while I glance at Sparx.

I killed his son.

This could go one of two ways.

Either, I'm going away for a long time or I'm going to kill a senator, then go away for a long time.

Fuck! I had it all.

A woman I love. A family on the way. Now, I could be put behind bars, losing it all.

Or, I could find out he was behind this all, and Sparx is about to see my demon set fucking free right here in this damn hospital room.

"My son's dead, but in the grand scheme of things, it's better this way." I tilt my head wondering if I've heard him correctly. "He was ill. Nothing I did helped him. He was a tarnish on my career. If news of what happened to Mylee broke, it would ruin everything I've been planning."

I glance at Sparx as she slides in closer to me, so I wrap my bandaged arm around her. "Are you trying to tell me, Senator, that you're not... angered by your son's death?"

Pursing his lips, he shrugs. "Thing is, Trax... that's your name, isn't it?" I don't say anything in reply, but he smiles menacingly as he takes a step closer to Sparx's bed. My lip turns up in disapproval as he stops, placing his hands on the end of the bed and exhales. "My son lost himself the day he shot Rylee. I guess some boys can't cope with the adrenaline that comes with killing people... you know what I'm talking about, don't you, Trax? I mean, after all, I'm sure it would've been you who plunged that pitchfork into Everett's stomach... right?"

Again I say nothing as he chuckles while cracking his neck to the side. "Fear not, Trax, I'm not here to place blame. I'm not here to bring you down. I'm here to thank you."

My head jolts back as I scoff.

Sparx tightens her hand in mine as I keep my eyes firmly on Malcolm. He pushes off from the bed and starts to pace the room. "I'm going to confide something to you, Trax, because I know that with me knowing your secret, you'll be able to keep mine. Tit for tat and all that."

My lip twitches wanting to run over and smack the fucker in the face. His cockiness and arrogance far outweighs mine even on a good day.

"My squeaky clean image is only kept that way by an amazing tech team. I mean c'mon, what politician has a track record like mine? I mean, really?"

I scoff out a laugh. "I have to admit, we couldn't find a thing on you. You almost had us fooled into thinking you were actually a decent guy."

He shrugs. "Well, I am most of the time. I only have ties to one organization. You might have heard of them."

Huffing, I can't help but take the bait. "Okay, I'll bite, who?"

He grins wide. "The Scarsi Dettagli. Ring any bells?"

My jaw wracks from side to side as I breathe harshly in and out trying my hardest to keep my shit together. "You're going to run for President, and you have ties to women traffickers?"

Sparx opens her eyes wide as she lets out an audible gasp.

"Not so squeaky clean. In fact, the young girl, Rylee... she was sold. Everett didn't know. He also doesn't remember this part, but they were playing in the barn with the guns. I came in to take her, told Everett she was going and never coming back, but she tried to fight me off. Everett went to shoot me, but shot Rylee instead... but being the fucked-up idiot he was, his mind blocked out me even being there." He lets out a menacing laugh. "It was perfect really, played right into my hands. He only remembered them playing in the barn with the guns and him shooting her.... pathetic boy."

Sparx sits up taller in the bed. "It sounds like you wanted Everett dead!" she spits out her tone full of venom, and I tighten my hand in hers in an attempt to quiet her down.

Malcolm chuckles. "Now you're getting it. I should have known you'd outsmart him, Mylee. My plan was to let him find you, carry out his stupid plan with my help, so he would end his own life in the process. If he took you out... well, you were just collateral damage."

Anger seeps through me, my demon starting to rear his ugly head. I want nothing more than to tear Malcolm limb from limb, but Sparx tightens her grip in my hand as if to sense I'm starting to waver.

"You thought it would be okay for your son to take out as many people as he could, just so he would end his own life to make *your* life easier?"

He smiles. "If Everett took his own life, not only does it make *mine* easier, but I get sympathy from the voters. Plus, I don't have to clean up his mess anymore. I wasn't expecting it to turn out this way. This is a little more mess, but I can still spin it..." He grins widely, and honestly the look in his eyes right now is menacing. "I'm willing to make it like this never happened, if you're willing to keep it quiet on your end. No charges will be laid against the club for the men who were shot at the gates, *or* for the murder of Everett. Everything will be swept under the proverbial rug. It all just... disappears." He waves his hands around.

I swallow hard. This would solve everything, but politicians are known for their lies and deceit.

How the hell can I trust him?

How do I know he won't play me for a fool?

I want to rip his heart out. He orchestrated this entire bullshit to get rid of his son. He didn't care if Sparx got hurt in the process. This fucker's got to pay. Problem is, a senator going missing is a big fucking deal. But, having one on our side, yeah, that could come in handy. Especially one running for President, especially one who I know for certain isn't above breaking the law.

I need to push my demon down.

I need to take a breath.

I need to think logically here.

I step forward, taking a stand, toe to toe with him as he puffs out his chest while I look him square in the eyes. "You stay the fuck away from Defiance, from Mylee, from me, and from the Notorious Knights. If I let you walk out of here knowing you set all this in motion, then it's a two-way street, Senator. I have something on you, you have something on me. But the way I see it, your son tried to kill my woman and my two unborn kids... you owe me one. And one day... one day, I'll come knocking for that favor."

His face lights up in a bright smile as he chuckles slightly. "The Scarsi were right about you, Trax. When they told me they met with you at the deal for Andretti's daughter, I started looking into your club. That's how I found the link between Defiance and the Notorious Knights. From there, I found the link between you and Mylee. It wasn't hard once I started looking." He shrugs. "Then when I realized that Miller had gone missing in Chicago after a business trip, I figured it must have been Defiance who took him. It was you, wasn't it?"

I tense up feeling Sparx's eyes on my back but say nothing.

Malcolm laughs. "Of course, nothing to say. Don't want to incriminate yourselves. I bet you did Jason, too, right? He was a handy helper that one. I sent him, though, not Everett. Once I realized it was Defiance who had you, Mylee, I forced Jason to tail anyone who left the club. Jason was my guy, not Everett's. Everett loved to take credit for everything. He was such an attention whore, that kid. Fuck, you did me a favor, Trax."

I shake my head with an exhale. "You really are a fucking lunatic."

He lets out a loud laugh slapping my bicep. I curl up my lip wanting to punch the fucker again. "Oh, Trax, you have no idea! So, remember, this just goes away now if you keep your pretty little mouth shut. If you don't, your babies will be born with their father in prison."

I glance back to Sparx as she gnaws on her bottom lip. Every inch of me wants to fight him. Wants to let my anger take hold. He's caused so much pain. Sparx could have died, my twins could have died, but right now I don't have a choice. For Sparx, for the club, for the Knights and for me, for all of us to come out unscathed, I have to shake on this.

"How do I know I have your word?"

He grabs the hem of his cuff straightening it out. "I want to be the President of the United States of America. Having my son trying to burn a woman to death won't work for me. You knowing about my links with the Scarsis is also fodder. I have more to lose than you. I will have a non-disclosure agreement drawn up to make this all go away. If you breathe a word of it to anyone, there will be consequences."

I glance at Sparx, she raises her brow in agreement. "If you ever, and I mean ever, come near us again..." I leave that hanging in the air.

He nods like he understands.

"Okay then... you have yourself a deal."

EPILOGUE

TRAX

Six Months Later

I sigh as I look into the back seat of the truck. My twins settled in their car seats as Sparx pulls her head out from the inside of the truck to stand by my side. She looks tired given she just gave birth forty-eight hours ago, but fuck if I'm not proud of her. The twins came out a little small, nothing to be worried about, but other than that, they're healthy as fuck, not to mention a good set of lungs on them. I swear for their first night in this world, all they did was scream. But for the moment, at least, they seem to have settled. I hope the car ride back to the clubhouse has them keeping calm.

Sparx smiles up at me, her stunning green eyes alight with such a fierce happiness I haven't seen in her before. She looks so fucking gorgeous I can't even comprehend it. "Fuck you're amazing," I say out loud.

It was meant to have just been said in my head.

She chuckles leaning into my side wrapping her arm around my waist. "I don't think you realize what you've done for me, Trax."

I jolt my head back. "What I've done for you?"

She nods. "You made me realize I can do anything. I was being held back by a diagnosis. I was scared to live because of the effects of a disorder which could drown me. But with you by my side, pushing me to see that I am strong, I am capable, I can get through the storms that come my way, it's been empowering. I've come through the other side of this journey. Dealt with my demons. And I know that if our babies are dealt the same hand I've been... that we know the symptoms well enough, we know the signs... we can master this as a family."

I lean in planting a tender kiss on her forehead, feeling elated that she's happy knowing that no matter what shit might come our way in the future, we'll face it.

Together.

"We got this, babe... you, me, our twins. We're a perfect little unit. And sure, the three of you might have the same health issues, but hey, what family isn't a little crazy now and then?"

She gasps with a bright smile slapping my chest as I lean down kissing her strongly. She kisses me back as she chuckles against my lips. Pulling back, she shakes her head. "You're going to pay for that little comment later. But, in the meantime..." She reaches back into the truck pulling out a small purple bag. I furrow my brows as I look to her and chuckle.

"You buying them more shit already. Sparx they're not even two days old."

She chuckles shoving the bag into my chest. "Just open it."

Gripping the bag, I open it and inside is a very masculine bracelet. I raise my brow as I look at the black rope band with silver cuffs. It has a silver shield with a skull, the skull has a 'D' obviously for Defiance on the head matching the same as the one my brother wears around his neck. Then there's a black pebbling in the shield. It's badass and totally me. I pull her to me as I lean in planting a kiss on her forehead. "Babe, I fucking love it. But what's the special occasion?"

Defiance

She grabs it, opens it up then hands it to me showing me the back. Something catches my eyes—on the back of the shield it has yesterday's date engraved on it—the twins' birthday.

I look to her, not really having any words. She understands as she grabs the bracelet looping it over my scarred wrist. "I thought it might be nice to cover bad memories with good," she instructs as the shield with the skull is big enough to cover the scar from where the fire scorched my wrist.

She's goddamn perfect.

She leans in kissing my lips briefly before pulling back and slaps my arm. "C'mon, let's get these babies home before they start crying again."

I look down at my bracelet and smile as I walk to the driver's side sliding in as the twins start to cry in unison. I groan as I start up the truck while Sparx turns back cooing over them. She's taking to motherhood like a duck to water. She suits it perfectly as she deals with the twins all the way back to the clubhouse.

As we pull into the compound, everyone's waiting for us like a giant welcoming party. There's banners, balloons, and people are popping party poppers. It's crazy as I chuckle parking the truck. Their excitement actually relaxes me knowing we have the help of not just my immediate family, but of this brotherhood.

We will be fine.

The four of us, one big happy family.

And fuck if it doesn't feel utterly fantastic.

I look back now thinking of how it came to this—Sparx and me. They say that deviance is an absence of conformity to the normal. If you look at me, I was a deviant without Sparx. A vigilante, a man out for vengeance. Sparx, she too was seen as someone not of the 'norm,' someone outcast from the social acceptance of the world. So when we deviated toward each other, the things that made us which were frowned upon by others is what actually brought us together.

She's kind and gentle where I'm harsh and strong. We're opposites, yet we work so well together.

I need her to breathe like she needs me to stand.

We may be society's outcasts, but to each other, and now to two little babies, we mean the damn fucking world. I wouldn't have it any other way. Even if my babies won't stop damn crying.

I slide out of the truck to Torque slapping my back as he chuckles. "You look frazzled, brother."

"They haven't stopped crying."

I open the door to let Sparx out. She picks up my baby girl, and she stops crying as I grab my boy who stops crying instantly. Holding my son in my arms makes me feel complete. As I stand here with everyone looking at me holding my baby boy and Sparx holding our daughter, everyone cheers.

Crest walks up along with Mom.

"Let me get a look at my grandbabies," Crest demands.

"Me, too!" Mom almost yells making me laugh.

Neala squeals running over like a crazed woman as she moves in beside Mom. "So, tell us, have you finally picked their names?"

I glance to Sparx. She winks at me, then I look at Mom. "Patrick... after Guinness, we'll call him Rix for short." Mom's eyes well as her hand rushes to her mouth. She begins to cry moving in to kiss little Rix's cheek.

"Oh, Konnor... oh, bless you, boyo," she murmurs bringing her hand up to caress my cheek. I smile as I glance to Torque who's beaming while Neala's eyes well. Naming my first-born son after our father was always something I wanted to do.

Crest clears his throat looking to Sparx. "And the girl?"

Sparx's eyes glisten looking at her father. "Grace... after Mom."

Crest's eyes begin to glisten, too. He moves in pressing his lips to Grace's forehead. She wriggles against him making a slight gurgling noise which, in turn, forces the hard shell of a man to chuckle. "My little Gracie."

"To Rix and Grace," Torque calls out pulling Foxy to his side as she smiles at him lovingly. I can't help but see the sparkle in her eyes. She'll be the next to pop out a kid, I'm sure.

"Right, can we get these three inside and resting," I call out making Sparx laugh.

"God, you're so overprotective. We're fine. Let everyone have their fill of the babies, Trax. We can rest later."

Everyone laughs. "Good to see who's wearing the pants, big brother," Neala teases slapping me across the back of the head as she steps up wrinkling her nose at Rix.

"Shut up. When you love someone this much, see if you don't turn sappy for them, too," I berate.

I don't miss the sideways glance Lala sends Tremor. He exhales looking away from Lala toward his ride like he's thinking of taking off. It confuses me. I know shit between them is strained right now, but they were in a good place a year ago. What the hell has changed?

"Yeah, well, looks like I'm going to be serially single. So I can just be your babysitter forever, okay?"

I snort out a laugh. "You know I'm going to hold you to that."

Lala brings her finger up to caress the side of Rix's face, and she smiles so wide it's contagious. "I don't even care right now. Look. At. This. Face."

I chuckle as I glance to Sparx to see her smiling as Torque walks over with the biggest of fucking grins. Being an uncle suits him.

"Can't say I ever saw this day coming, but I have to admit, you holding that little kid looks damn good on you, brother," Torque marvels.

I snort. "Yeah, gotta admit, this is a feeling I'm liking. Me, my woman, my kids... doesn't get much better than this, right, babe?" I call out.

Sparx cuddles into Grace. "Absolutely... cloud fucking nine right now."

Neala continues her half attention on Rix, half on Tremor who's definitely getting on his ride. The unmistakable sound of his engine roaring to life making us all look up as he kicks his stand up and hammers down taking off, pulling out of the compound. His eyes watching Neala as he goes. Neala's body tenses as she watches him leave. I furrow my brows glancing to Torque wondering where the hell he's going—it's my kid's welcome home party.

Neala seems to be none too impressed as she huffs, her face scrunching up while she chews on her bottom lip.

"Where's Tremor going?" I call out to Torque.

He looks from me to Neala then back to me like he wishes I hadn't asked. "He's going to hang out with some... chick," Torque hesitates. A cold silence filters around us as I glance to Neala whose body tenses like she's just been stabbed by a damn knife. She turns up her lip, tears welling in her eyes which she blinks away.

"Right," Neala murmurs as she plasters on a fake smile then turns to storm away. The heaviness of her stomping could probably be heard in the Heart of Italy.

"Jesus Christ... Tremor's gone and made everything ten times fucking worse," I murmur as everyone agrees.

This is *not* going to be pretty!

in
Sufferance: The Chicago Defiance MC Series Book 4

Parallel Line – *Keith Urban*
Call Out My Name – *The Weeknd*
I Said Hi – *Amy Shark*
In My Blood – *Shawn Mendes*

CONNECT WITH ME ONLINE

Check these links for more books from Author K E OSBORN.

READER GROUP

Want access to fun, prizes and sneak peeks?
Join my Facebook Reader Group.

https://goo.gl/wu2trc

NEWSLETTER

Want to see what's next?
Sign up for my Newsletter.
http://eepurl.com/beIMc1

BOOKBUB

Connect with me on Bookbub.
https://www.goodreads.com/author/show/7203933.K_E_Osbo
rn

GOODREADS
Add my books to your TBR list on my Goodreads profile.
https://goo.gl/35tIWV

AMAZON
Click to buy my books from my Amazon profile.
https://goo.gl/ZNecEH

WEBSITE
www.keosbornauthor.com

TWITTER
http://twitter.com/KEOsbornAuthor

INSTAGRAM
@keosbornauthor

EMAIL
keosborn.author@hotmail.com

FACEBOOK
http://facebook.com/KEOsborn

ABOUT THE AUTHOR

K E OSBORN

Australian author **K E Osborn** was born and raised in Adelaide, South Australia. With a background in graphic design and a flair for all things creative, she felt compelled to write the story brewing in her mind.

Writing gives her life purpose. It makes her feel, laugh, cry and get completely enveloped in the characters and their story lines. She feels completely at home when writing and wouldn't consider doing anything else.

Made in the USA
Monee, IL
10 March 2021